'A fe

'C ...ne, charming by nature, this book is a
...oalm for the soul and the heart.'
The Sun

'A gorgeous journey told through charms.'
Heat

'Eccentric, charming and wise, this will illuminate
your heart.'
Nina George, author of *The Little Paris Bookshop*

'A charming, unforgettable story.'
Harper's Bazaar

'With many poignant as well as laugh-out-loud moments,
in the vein of *The Unlikely Pilgrimage of Harold Fry*, this is a
lovely feel-good read.'
Compass

'As charming and witty as the title suggests.'
My Weekly

'We love this sweet
Tak

© Sam Ralph

Phaedra Patrick studied art and marketing and has worked as a stained-glass artist, film-festival organiser and communications manager. She is a prize-winning short story writer and her debut novel was translated in twenty languages worldwide. She lives in Saddleworth with her husband and son, where she writes full-time.

Wishes Under the Willow Tree is her second novel. For more information, please visit www.phaedra-patrick.com and you can also follow Phaedra on Facebook, Twitter and Instagram.

Wishes Under the Willow Tree

Phaedra Patrick

ONE PLACE. MANY STORIES

HQ
An imprint of HarperCollinsPublishers Ltd.
1 London Bridge Street
London SE1 9GF

This paperback edition 2018

1

First published in Great Britain by
HQ, an imprint of HarperCollinsPublishers Ltd. 2018

ISBN: 978-1-84845-676-1

Printed and bound by
CPI Group, Croydon CRO 4YY

For Pat, Dave, Mark and Oliver

1. White Opal

hope, desire, fidelity

As Benedict Stone huffed his way to work, the sweet smell of the cherry scones in Bake My Day made him forget for a moment that his wife, Estelle, had packed her purple suitcase and moved out of their home.

His mouth watered and he stopped, sniffed and needed something weighty in his stomach, to help sugar-coat his sorrows. He curled his fingers into his palms and tried to resist, but it was like an ultra-strong magnet pulled him inside the baker's shop.

A fella like you needs more than just a slice of toast, a sausage roll, bought by a schoolboy, said. *You need something sweet too*, a chocolate cookie, on display in the glass counter, chipped in.

Benedict tried his best to ignore them, but the lure of a succulent bacon sandwich and an oozy jam doughnut was too strong. He bought both and devoured them before he reached the front door of his shop, Stone Jewellery, just a few metres away.

When he unlocked the door, his stomach dropped as he glanced at the *25% Off Sale* sticker he'd taped into his window three months ago.

He switched on the light and took off his jacket. Grey aluminium and glass cabinets lined the walls of the two-man deep and two-and-a-half-man wide space. The walls were all painted dolphin grey, and the floor was grey too. Benedict thought that the colour scheme was calm and elegant though his assistant, Cecil, claimed it needed more va-va-voom.

A black door behind the counter led through to Benedict's workshop. The small, square room housing his workbench was his sanctuary. When he shut himself away in there, he could block out the outside world and almost convince himself that all was still fine with his wife.

He went inside and straightened up a file on his bench. He liked his tweezers, pliers, snips and soldering iron laid out in lines like a surgeon's instruments. If Cecil moved his mallet by as little as a centimetre, Benedict could tell. Even with few entries in his appointment book, he felt driven to work. He crafted silver bangle after silver bangle, which he stacked like miniature tyres on the shelf.

Benedict slumped into his chair and placed his hands on his rounded stomach. He imagined the food dancing in there, laughing at him. *Ha ha. Benedict Stone is a big guy but he has no self-control.*

Shaking his head with remorse, he picked up a brooch he'd been working on. He switched on his gooseneck lamp and his face reflected in the shiny black metal.

2

Stone was a good name for him. His hair was short, swept back and graphite grey, the same colour as the stubble that peppered his upper lip and chin. Estelle said that he had a kind face, like when kids draw eyes and a smile into uncooked pastry. His hands were so large they looked as if they'd been inflated by a bicycle pump, but his fingers were surprisingly nimble when handling delicate silver findings.

Everything he wore was neutral, from his suit to his socks, except for his size fourteen burgundy loafers. He'd ordered them custom-made, online, but the company had sent the wrong shade.

'I'm sure you can live with a bit of colour in your life for once,' Estelle had said with a sigh. 'Dark red shoes won't kill you.'

But each time Benedict wore them, he felt conspicuous. His width and height attracted attention, and now he sported berry-hued loafers.

As usual, Cecil arrived at the shop ten minutes late. He had a tropical dress sense, wearing a powder-blue suit, with a peach shirt and an emerald-green tie. His white hair was waxed into a small triangle which reminded Benedict of a budgerigar's quiff. Cecil spent a lot of time with his two young nieces, so often spoke as if he was on social media.

Each day, he brought his cat, the fearsome Lord Puss, into work. A white Persian, who thought he was superior to humans, Lord Puss sat on a purple velvet cushion on the counter, where he greeted customers with narrow lemon eyes and a flex of his claws.

'Aloha,' Cecil called through into the workshop.

'Hello. The kettle's boiled,' Benedict shouted back, pleased to hear Cecil's voice. He'd spent the weekend alone, mooching around listlessly and wondering what Estelle was doing without him. He watched too many action films and wondered where the heroes got their energy from.

'Coolio.' Cecil set his cat basket down and Lord Puss swanked out. The cat blinked around with disdain and settled onto his cushion.

Cecil made two cups of tea – one black for him and one white with three sugars for Benedict. He placed coasters on the workbench and set the cups down. 'Ooh, what are you making?' he asked.

'A silver brooch.' Benedict held it up for Cecil to see.

'*Another* triangular one?'

'Yes.'

'It looks a bit *Star Trek-y.*'

'Great,' Benedict said.

'Yes, if you want to look like Captain Kirk…'

Now that Cecil said this, Benedict thought the piece did look a bit space age. He placed it at the back of his bench.

'We should make more effort to follow trends,' Cecil said. 'What about festival jewellery, or friendship bracelets? How about ear cuffs, or adding gems to your work?'

Benedict stared at him, as if he was speaking a foreign language. 'This is Noon Sun,' he said. 'The villagers like simple, classic things.'

Cecil opened the appointment book and flicked through it. 'Well, I can see that you're not going to be rushed off your feet, when I go into hospital for my hernia op. I've told Lord Puss that you're going to look after him.'

'I don't know how I'll cope without you,' Benedict admitted. He imagined Stone Jewellery being as still and quiet as his own home and the thought made his jaw ache. He wished that he could chit-chat with customers like Cecil did, but his own words queued up in his head like cars in a motorway traffic jam.

'I don't like to leave you on your own here, especially with Estelle moving out. How are things between the two of you?'

Benedict's smile slipped. He picked up the triangular silver brooch and gave it a polish on his trouser leg. He would only allow his friend to see his hurt. Even though Cecil was a gossip, cooing and flattering customers, Benedict knew his assistant had integrity and always looked out for him. 'All fine, I suppose,' he mumbled.

'Benedicto. You don't have to put a shine on things, for me. How are things *really*?'

Benedict's shoulders sloped. He wished that his life could be as shiny and simple as his jewellery. 'Not good. Estelle's still staying at her friend's apartment, whilst Veronica's working away in America. She's been gone for six weeks now…'

'Couldn't she just check on the apartment each day?' Cecil asked.

Benedict looked down at his big hands. 'She wants a proper break, to clear her head. But the longer she's gone, the more it feels that she won't come back. Anyway'— he lifted his voice, to try to sound more positive— 'I hope she'll be back for our tenth anniversary, in three weeks' time.'

'Fingers crossed. Have you got anything spesh planned?'

Benedict opened the drawer in his workbench and took out a long grey box, lined with white satin. The necklace inside wasn't yet long enough to reach a quarter of the way around Estelle's collarbone. It was made up of hundreds of interlinked jump rings, each the circumference of a ladybird, in platinum, rose gold, yellow gold and silver. If Benedict didn't think that a ring was good enough, he dropped it into an old teacup on his bench. It was almost full to the brim of the ones he'd rejected.

Cecil nodded. '*Très* elegant. But what else are you planning to do, to win her back?'

Benedict frowned. 'I've bought her flowers, I took her out for coffee... What else can I do, but wait for her to make up her mind?'

Cecil moved the lamp out of the way and sat on the workbench. 'You're going to have to make a proper effort to stop her slipping away. In the medieval days you'd get on a fine white charger and joust for her.'

'I can't ride,' Benedict said as he picked up a link. 'I'd squash the horse. I want her to come home, but the thing we want more than anything, is the one thing we can't have...' His throat suddenly felt like there was a pebble stuck in it and he couldn't swallow it away. 'We've really tried, but I don't think it will ever happen for us...'

'Children?' Cecil asked quietly.

Benedict nodded. 'We want a family so much.'

No matter how many times he thought about his and Estelle's unsuccessful attempts to have a baby, it always felt like he'd been shoved off a railway platform onto the track, in front of a speeding train. He was forty-four years old now and time was flying by. He longed to feel tiny fingers curled around his own and a small heart beating against his chest. The ache of wanting a child weighed him down like wet cement.

'Estelle says she's come to terms with being childless. But I haven't.' He swallowed. Not wanting Cecil to see that his eyes were growing watery, he shifted his seat closer to the bench and stared at the necklace. 'I'm happy to adopt, but Estelle doesn't want to. I hope that staying at Veronica's gives her time to realise that it's the best way forward...'

Cecil gave his shoulder a firm pat.

Benedict moved his lamp back into place. 'I'm sure everything will work out for us,' he said, sitting more upright in his chair. 'I just need to bring Estelle home.'

That night, finding it difficult to sleep on his own again, Benedict ambled downstairs in the dark. He wore his grey suit jacket over the top of his striped pyjamas, and his burgundy loafers with no socks. The only sounds he could hear were the creak of the hallway floorboards, the Noon Sun village clock striking twelve, and his own heavy breathing from taking the stairs.

He picked up a torch, a tartan picnic rug and a shopping bag full of food, and opened his front door. He took three gulps of the chilly October air and padded out to the weeping willow tree, in the middle of the lawn. Using his head and shoulders to part its leaves, Benedict clambered into the hollow space. It was once an easy thing to do when he and his brother, Charlie, used the tree as their childhood den. But now, squeezing under proved quite a challenge.

He sighed and shone the torch inside the bag. After pulling out a four-pack of chocolate brownies, he prised open the lid. They were perfect, chunky brown squares with a dusting of icing sugar on top. He fought the urge to eat them, but it was as if he was a robot – hand out, pick up a brownie, munch, repeat.

When he had finished, his shoulders sagged with shame and he leaned back against the tree trunk. His parents had planted it when Benedict was eleven years old and his brother Charlie was three.

Their dad, Joseph, travelled overseas to source and buy gemstones, which he sold on to museums, shops and auction houses. When they could, Benedict, Charlie and their mum, Jenny, joined him.

Benedict was attracted to the solidness and definiteness of the neutral gems; the greys, blacks and browns – Smoky Quartz, Brown Jasper and Onyx. Charlie's hand shot out for the biggest and brightest – the Red Aventurine, Tangerine Quartz and Golden Beryl.

Joseph drilled holes through each of the imperfect stones and Jenny snipped random lengths of silk thread. Benedict tied gems, a few inches apart, to form sparkling strands and Charlie stood on Benedict's knee to tie them into the weeping willow.

It was a family tradition that, one day, Benedict hoped to carry on with his own children. But now his future stretched before him, and there was no tinkle of children's laughter to be heard. The thought made his heart feel as heavy as a cannonball.

He looked up at the room that Estelle used as her art studio and thought how it would make a perfect nursery. But then his eyes moved across to their own bedroom. He wished she was in bed now, waiting for him, so they could rub their feet together under the covers.

Benedict climbed out from under the tree. He left the rug on the ground and crumpled up the bag. He took out his mobile phone from the pocket of his jacket and his big fingers flexed. They seemed to take on a life of their own and he knew that he shouldn't send a text under the influence of excess calories. But he couldn't stop. He scrolled to his wife's number and tapped out a message.

'I love you. Please come home x'

Inside the house, Benedict trudged upstairs. In Estelle's studio, he stared at her canvasses, stacked against the wall. She said that her paintings weren't good enough, but they looked wonderful to him. He cleared some clothes and paintbrushes off the bed, kicked off his loafers and lolled sideways until his cheek touched the pillow. Then he lay there, motionless, until his eyes began to flicker and close.

The loud banging noise startled him out of his sleep. Benedict sat up with a jolt and looked at his mobile phone to see the time – 1 a.m. Ugh. His tongue felt like it was covered in chocolatey fur. He paused, wondering whether to lie back down, or go to his own bed.

But there was the noise again. It was a knock on his front door.

A shot of adrenaline made him stand up. His heart pumped fast and he remembered his text to his wife. '*Estelle*,' he said aloud and his lips flickered into a small smile.

He finger-combed his hair and felt his way out of the room. Negotiating the stairs in his bare feet, he yelped as he trod on something sharp – a small stone. He brushed it off his foot with his hand.

The knock came again, louder and more persistent.

The rain hammering against the door sounded like zombies drumming their fingers, trying to get inside. He hoped that Estelle was wearing a coat, or had taken a taxi. She would be soaking wet.

He fumbled for his keys and clumsily unlocked the door. Outside, the security light pinged on, illuminating the raindrops so they looked like a shower of diamonds. It took a while for Benedict's eyes to adjust, and he rubbed them with his fists.

She stood with her back to him. Her dress was wet and clung to her legs. Droplets hung from the hem.

The skin on Benedict's forearms tingled with anticipation. 'Estelle…' he said.

She turned. 'I thought you were never going to answer.'

Benedict felt recognition glimmer inside him. He took in the shape of her chin, the jump of her nose, the raindrops glittering in her hair. He stared until he felt like he was in a trance.

He knew her face.

But it wasn't his wife.

2. Ruby

visualisation, dynamism, vibrancy

Benedict wondered who the girl was. He seemed to know her from somewhere. She barely reached his shoulder in height and her wet, dark dress clung to her knees, so they poked through the cotton like knobbles of tree bark. Her legs were bare and she wore battered tan leather cowboy boots. Her arms hung by her sides, in a denim jacket at least two sizes too big for her, and the sleeves covered her fingertips. With her ears poking out through her long, damp hair, her face had an impish quality. Eyebrows, bushy and set too high and angled on her forehead, gave her an air of surprise. Dangling from the end of one sleeve was a small white drawstring bag, the type you get when you buy jewellery in a posh shop.

The outside light clicked off and they both stood in darkness.

'I thought no one was home.' Her voice was deeper and slower than Benedict expected. She had an American accent. 'Where were you?'

'Um, I was in bed, asleep.'

'You're wearing a suit jacket.'

'I know.' He wondered why she was questioning him, as if she knew him.

'Benedict Stone?' she asked.

'Yes.'

'I'm Gemma.' She offered her hand in a karate-chop move.

It was slim and wet, and Benedict's brain ticked as he shook it. *Gemma*. Did he know a Gemma?

Estelle used to tell him that she'd bumped into so-and-so in the village, who went to school with such-a-person, who was married to thingamajig. He would smile and nod and not have a clue who she was talking about. *Gemma*? He couldn't place her.

'I'm Gemma Stone.'

Gemma? Gemma *Stone*? *Gemma…Stone*.

'Your niece,' she said sharply.

'You're Charlie's daughter?' He gasped. Now that he looked, she had the same nose and chin as his brother. 'Is he here?'

'No.'

'You're alone?'

'Yes.'

She stuck out a foot and shook it. 'And I'm *very* wet. Are you going to invite me in?'

Benedict took a few seconds to peel his hand away from the doorframe. He shook his head with confusion. 'Um… yes.'

Gemma bent down and picked up a small, saggy rucksack that lay at her feet and slung it over her shoulder. 'I'll follow you, Uncle Ben.'

'It's Benedict, actually.' He headed into the house and Gemma followed. Her boots squelched and left wet oval-shaped footprints on the floorboards. 'This is the kitchen.' Words swam in his head. 'Can I, er, get you anything?'

'I got a sandwich at the airport.' She stuck her head around the door. 'It smells musty in there. And it's dark.'

'I'll switch a light on.'

'Yeah.'

Benedict squinted as the kitchen light seemed twice as bright as usual. 'About Charlie...?' he tried again. How long was it since his brother walked out on him, to go and live in America? Eighteen years?

Benedict still pictured Charlie as a young boy. He'd brought his brother up, since their parents were killed in an accident when Charlie was ten and Benedict was eighteen. He sometimes reached up and touched the underside of his chin, positive that he could still feel the tickle of his brother's copper hair tucked there.

Gemma stretched out her arms and gave a noisy yawn. 'I'm *so* tired after travelling,' she said. 'I'll go to bed and we'll talk tomorrow, okay?'

'*Bed?*' Benedict repeated. 'You're staying the night?'

But she was already making her own way up the stairs.

Benedict stared up at the ceiling as the floorboards creaked in his bedroom, Charlie's old room and then Estelle's studio. What the hell should he do? Should he follow her up, or try to sleep on the sofa? Should he offer her a change of clothes?

He rubbed his neck and went upstairs anyway, trying to climb them as noisily as he could, so she could hear him approaching.

When he reached the landing, he heard clattering inside the bathroom. Something fell and skittered around in the sink. The toilet flushed, water gushed and the plughole gurgled. There was a bang and Gemma said, 'Crap.'

Benedict cleared his throat loudly. 'Ahem.'

Gemma opened the bathroom door by a few inches and pressed her forehead against the doorframe. 'Before you ask me anything else,' she said, sighing. 'I have mental and physical exhaustion.'

'I just want to know… Well, is your dad okay? Where is your mother?' Questions bolted around his head like piglets let loose on a farm.

Gemma switched off the bathroom light and pulled the door shut behind her. She carried her clothes in a clump and she wore a pair of Estelle's pyjamas. They were white with large pink roses and the sight made Benedict feel light-headed. The pyjamas should have his wife inside them, not a stranger.

'I'm going to take this room.' Gemma jerked her thumb towards Estelle's studio.

'Er, okay,' Benedict said, too taken aback to add anything else.

His niece dropped her pile of clothes on the floor and pushed her soggy rucksack and boots against the wall with one foot. Leaving the door open, she peeled back the covers and clambered into bed. 'Thanks, Uncle Ben,' she said. 'Goodnight.'

When Benedict woke the next day it was 7.30 a.m. and his mouth was as dry as a sand dune. He lay for a while and shielded his eyes with his hand against the mustardy light that sliced around the curtains. At first, the morning felt like every other lonely one since Estelle left, too still and silent. But then Gemma murmured in her sleep, and the strange noise made the roots of his hair stiffen.

Turning, he saw one of Estelle's empty perfume bottles sitting on top of her bedside table. He reached over, picked it up and held it under his nose. The musky rose scent transported him back to the heat and bustle of a Greek market where his wife laughed and haggled for the amber-coloured bottle. He could almost see the glint of sunlight on the sunglasses pushed back into her black bobbed hair.

When they were on holiday, Estelle liked to go out and explore. 'What's the point of sitting still when we're someplace new?' She'd smile as she set off to walk to the nearest town. She liked to find local craft shops and, when she returned, present to Benedict what she'd bought – a small ceramic butterfly, or a hand-painted dish for olive oil.

Benedict barely glanced at them. He liked to stay around the pool, listening to families splashing around and imagining that one day he might throw an inflatable Frisbee to his own kids. He tried not to look at the trim dads in their Speedos, when he himself sported an oversized T-shirt and baggy shorts. 'Isn't this hotel great for kids?' he said. 'It's got a children's club too.'

Sometimes, Estelle's moving out felt like he'd been rugby-tackled and knocked, breathless, off his feet. At other times, he told himself to be more optimistic. She was just helping out a friend and would be back soon. Things would return to normal and they'd pick up their conversation about adoption again. He would try to persuade her it was the best way forward.

Benedict picked up his mobile and saw that Estelle hadn't replied to his text from last night. For a moment, he wondered about sending another one, but Gemma groaned in her sleep and he slipped the phone under his pillow.

He slid out of bed, pulled on his dressing gown and put on his loafers. Stealing a glance in the studio, he saw his niece was curled up with her back to him. Her rucksack was on the floor and it didn't seem to contain much, for a trip to England from America.

He crouched and strained one arm into the room and pulled her discarded clothes towards him. They were still damp from the rain. Damn, did he even know how to operate the tumble dryer?

As he gathered them to his chest, something white landed on the floor with a thud. It was the bag that had dangled from the sleeve of Gemma's denim jacket last night. He froze, scarecrow-still, as she muttered in her sleep. When she started to snore, Benedict pushed the white bag back into the room with his foot.

Downstairs, Benedict read and reread the instructions

that Estelle had handwritten and taped next to the dial on the tumble dryer. Since she'd gone, he realised how much she did in the house. It was as if a fairy magically popped in and did all the cooking, cleaning, the grocery shopping and the washing-up. For the past six weeks, he hadn't done much. When his clothes needed a wash, he took them to his friend Ryan's launderette, Soap'n'Suds, in the village, and Bake My Day provided most of his meals.

Benedict turned a dial on the dryer and hoped for the best.

The dining room used to be tidy, but now there were piles of his clothes, newspapers and screwed-up plastic bags on most surfaces. Estelle liked fresh flowers on the table but instead there was a pile of cork placemats and a heap of junk mail.

He used to think that the house was friendly and well lived in, but now it just looked ancient. The pine kitchen units had darkened over the years to a burnt orange colour, and the lino was torn and needed replacing. Estelle had suggested many times that they spruce up the place, but Benedict wanted to save money, for when they had a family.

Could he really blame her for moving out, when his motivation had shipped out too? Cecil was right; she deserved a jousting knight on a white horse. But that wasn't him.

As Gemma's jacket and dress began to spin, he wondered about her impromptu arrival. Why had she arrived so late, and why was she on her own? Something wasn't right here and the familiar urge of wanting to eat crept up on him like a mutant blob in a fifties sci-fi movie.

It usually started with his stomach feeling as hollow as an empty beer barrel. Then a chirpy voice in his head announced that food would make him feel better. Benedict didn't experience hunger as such, rather the need to feel full, to take his mind away from the present.

His fingers twitched as he opened the fridge door. On the top shelf sat two chunky slices of lemon cheesecake. *Lemons are nice and healthy*, they said to him.

'Shut up,' Benedict growled and set to work making an omelette instead. He sniffed and wondered if it would cover the musty smell that Gemma had complained about.

He ate it standing up, in front of the sink. Then he succumbed and ate a slice of lemon cheesecake anyway.

When Gemma woke up, he would make her some breakfast and ask for Charlie's phone number. Benedict wondered what his brother had told Gemma about him. He rubbed his neck with shame and wondered if Charlie would reject him all over again.

When the tumble dryer rumbled to a stop, it had gone past nine. Benedict pulled out the clothes, folded them roughly and carried them upstairs. He was late for work and eating too much had made him feel cranky.

In the studio, Gemma was still in bed and he bent down to deposit her dried clothes on the floor.

'What the hell...?' The bed juddered and she sat up, clutching the blanket to her chin.

Benedict stood up so quickly that his back cricked. 'Ouch.' He flailed one hand behind him in a failed attempt to support it. 'I thought you were asleep.'

'I was, until you crept into my room, like a pudgy vampire or something.' She flopped back onto her pillow and specks of dust burst into the air. She reached up, trying to catch them. 'This house is dirty.'

'I know.'

'Are you married?'

'Um, yes.'

'You're not sure?'

Her question felt like a small punch in his gut. 'I *am* married. And I dried your clothes.' He stepped over them and opened the curtains.

Gemma squealed and covered her eyes with her hands.

When she lowered them, he'd forgotten what she looked like. Her hair was now dry, with strands stuck to her cheeks. It was a russet red, darker than Charlie's copper mop, and it reminded Benedict of autumn leaves. Her irises shone teal blue against the pink of her eyelids. Again, because of the high angle of her eyebrows, he wasn't sure if she was surprised or not.

'When you're dressed,' he said, 'I'll make you an omelette.'

She screwed up her nose. 'I hate eggs.'

'I have cheesecake too.'

'*That's* a dessert.'

Her answering back made his head throb. 'I'm not

running a café. After you've eaten, we'll phone your dad. You can tell him that you're safe and we can make arrangements.'

'What arrangements?'

'For whatever you plan to do.'

Gemma frowned. 'I planned to come here.'

'To Noon Sun?'

'Yeah. For an adventure.'

'Adventure?' Benedict's brow puckered as he thought about the sleepy village, with its row of lacklustre shops. 'You'll be lucky. And it's dangerous to turn up on a stranger's doorstep unannounced.'

'You're my uncle. And it's not unannounced.'

'It is, if I didn't know you were coming.'

'My dad said that you knew.'

'*What?*' Benedict said. 'I think I'd remember that. We haven't spoken for years.'

'Didn't he write or something?'

'No.'

Gemma puffed out her breath. 'I hate arguments.'

'It's not really an argument,' Benedict replied.

But he hated them too. He detested when he and Estelle had chats that turned to discussions which evolved into heated debates. When they couldn't find a way forward and she would hug her pillow to her chest and stomp into the studio to sleep there instead.

'When your father moved away, we lost contact,' he said vaguely. 'I'm not trying to get you into trouble, but there's been some miscommunication. So, as soon as you've eaten, we'll get in touch with Charlie, and your mother, to sort things out. Okay?'

Gemma sat up. She drew her knees up to her chin and hugged her shins. 'It's not so easy.'

'Why not?'

''Cause Dad lives on a farm in north Maine, but there's no phone line. He doesn't even have email.' She rolled her eyes. 'And he and my mom split, a few years ago.'

'Oh.' This threw Benedict. He had always imagined Charlie and his wife Amelia were still together. 'Sorry to hear that. Does he have a mobile number?'

'Sure. That's the only thing he does have.' She frowned, but her eyebrows remained high and pointed. 'It's 605, or is it 4? I think it's, um…no. Sorry.'

'Don't you have it stored in *your* phone?'

'Someone took my purse, from the airport restroom. My phone and passport were inside it.'

Benedict stared at her in disbelief. 'So you don't have a purse, phone or passport?'

'Well, I did have them, but not any longer.'

Benedict dug his hand into his hair. 'I'll call the airport and see if your purse has been handed in.'

'I reported it missing last night. They'll call me if they find it. I've thought of everything.'

'How can they call you, if they have your phone?'

'Oh.' Gemma scrunched her mouth into a small circle. 'I hadn't thought of that. Hey, you could write him a letter,' she said brightly.

Benedict's mind conjured up the last slice of cheesecake

in the fridge. He wanted it badly. 'You can't really stay here…' he began.

'You have a spare room.'

'Yes, but…I'm waiting for my wife to come back.'

'Where has she gone?'

'It doesn't matter.'

Benedict needed a sit down. He wanted to get into Stone Jewellery and shut himself away in his workshop. He could make another brooch, or links for the anniversary necklace. It would be nice and quiet. 'It's a long story,' he said.

'Well…' Gemma jumped off the bed and scooped up her rucksack from the floor. A large hairbrush and a small teddy bear with a purple ribbon around its neck fell out. She picked them up and stuffed them both back inside. Her mouth was set in a thin, determined line. 'If you don't want me here, I'll get my stuff and go.'

Benedict studied the back of her head. 'Where to?'

'What do you freakin' care?' she snarled. 'I'm almost seventeen years old and I can look after myself.'

Benedict gulped. He hadn't calculated in his head how old she might be. Panic began to churn in his stomach. 'You're only sixteen?' How could he turf her out, in a strange country? But he also thought about Estelle, arriving back at the house to find it in a mess and a teenager sleeping in her studio, and wearing her pyjamas. How was he going to deal with that? It was a shame he couldn't ring Cecil for advice. 'Look, have your breakfast first.'

'I don't want a crappy omelette, okay?'

'Have some bread then…'

'Jeez, you sound just like my dad.' Gemma's voice fired up a notch. 'He doesn't listen to me either.' She slumped back on the bed and kicked her heels against the base of the mattress. Thud, thud, thud.

'You must eat something...'

More quickly than Benedict's eyes could follow, she reached down to the floor and picked something up. She raised her hand to her shoulder as if performing a shot put. Then she thrust it forward. 'Just stop talking.'

Benedict felt something hit him on his left cheek. Thwump. The pain made him screw his eyes shut. '*What the*...?'

Gemma's eyes widened. She scrambled off the bed and held out her arms as if carrying a large dog. 'Oh God, I'm sorry, Uncle Ben. I didn't mean to hit you. I meant to hit the door.'

Benedict squinted. On the floor was the small white drawstring bag. 'Well, that's okay then. Is this what you threw at me?' He nudged it with his foot. 'You can't go round lobbing stuff at people. That bloody well hurt.'

'I *said* sorry.'

Benedict's cheek throbbed.

'You should open that white bag,' Gemma said. 'I brought it for you.'

'To throw at me?'

'I can't be responsible for *all* my actions. Open it up.'

Benedict bent down, picked up the bag and eased it open. He immediately recognised the jumble of gemstones inside – an egg-shaped green speckled stone, a chunk of Turquoise and a piece of Rose Quartz in the shape of a heart. His head felt floaty as he picked it out. 'What is this for?'

'I want to know what they mean.'

It had been many years since Benedict had seen the gemstones, since he pushed them into his brother's rucksack before he left for America. 'They used to belong to my parents.'

'There must be more to the story than that.'

Benedict felt a trickle of sweat run down his spine. He tied the drawstring tight and handed it back to her. Surely Charlie wouldn't have told her the reason why the two brothers had fallen out? When he spoke his throat was the thickness of a drinking straw. 'No, there isn't,' he said.

'Well' —Gemma snatched the bag of gemstones back off him and held them to her chest— 'I'm sorry for throwing these at you, Uncle Ben. I'll leave today and not come back. But not until you tell me more about these gems…'

3. Moonstone

release, empathy, intuition

Benedict went downstairs whilst Gemma showered and changed. He made cheese on toast, just as he used to for Charlie's breakfast, and when his niece joined him in the kitchen, they sat at opposite ends of the table. The atmosphere felt chilly.

She wore last night's clothes, the crumpled navy cotton dress and the enormous denim jacket. Her legs were bare in her cowboy boots. To Benedict, she looked too young to be travelling alone. If she were his child then he'd have packed a warm coat, jeans, gloves and woolly socks, and he'd heard you could put GPS tracking devices on mobile phones.

He tried to search out elements of Amelia in Gemma's face, but she hadn't inherited her mother's olive skin, dark eyes or walnut hair. He didn't know where her arched bushy eyebrows had come from.

As he studied her, a memory popped into his head.

When Charlie was eleven or twelve years old, the two

of them had watched a magic show on TV in which a man walked on a bed of nails. Afterwards Charlie said he was going to try it. 'All I need are some nails and a plank of wood,' he said.

'But it was just a trick,' Benedict argued.

But Charlie was convinced he could do it. In the shed, he found a jar of nails and a large piece of chipboard. He tugged the board under the gem tree and spent ages knocking the nails through. When he finished, he hoisted up his creation. 'Done it.'

Benedict wanted to warn his brother that this could hurt, and that he might need a tetanus injection if the nails were rusty. He always rushed to protect him.

'I'm going to do it.' Charlie let the board drop flat on the grass, the spikes pointing upwards.

'Okay then.' Benedict tried to sound calm as he stood at the back door.

'Watch me.'

'I'm watching.'

Charlie kicked off his flip-flops. He gave Benedict a big grin and his copper hair shone bright in the sun. He placed his bare right foot flat on the nails then stood for a moment, pressing and testing out the pressure. His head was bent in concentration. He put all his weight onto his right foot then raised his left one.

Benedict grasped a wad of tissues, ready to run and mop up any blood. He wondered where he'd put the antiseptic ointment. However, Charlie held out his arms and walked slowly and steadily across the plank. When he reached the end, he jumped off and ran around the garden, whooping and punching the air. 'Did it,' he shouted. 'I told you it wasn't camera trickery.'

Benedict gave a rictus grin of relief. 'Yes, you did. Well done.'

Charlie was never more alive than when he tried something new. Perhaps Benedict shouldn't feel surprised that his brother thought it was okay for Gemma to travel on her own. Perhaps his niece was as spontaneous and determined as her father.

He wondered if he should tell Gemma that she reminded him of Charlie but, instead, he bit into his toast.

'Kindergarten food.' Gemma nodded at her plate, but she picked up her toast anyway. She nibbled off the crust first, then turned the toast round and round, eating it in a spiral until a small square remained. She popped the last bit into her mouth with relish. 'I'm still hungry,' she said as she munched. 'Do you have any fruit?'

Benedict hadn't bought fruit since Estelle left. The produce at Veg Out greengrocers was rather lifeless. 'Fruit?' he repeated.

'Yeah. You know the stuff that grows on trees? Healthy, juicy, bright colours...'

A laugh escaped from Benedict's lips and it sounded strange to him, like it wasn't his own.

Gemma gave a small smile too. Her eyes crinkled at the sides, as Charlie's used to. Benedict had forgotten about that and he felt a flitter in his chest. 'I don't have any,' he said.

'You're not a healthy eater, are you?' Gemma looked him

over. 'It puts a strain on your heart being that chunky. You should cut out the candy.'

'Thanks for the advice, Gordon Ramsay.' Benedict carried the empty plates over to the sink. 'It's not fat, it's insulation against cold Yorkshire nights. Now, how are we going to get in touch with your dad?'

'Don't worry. He knows I'm fine.'

'Gemma.' Benedict held out his palms. 'You've travelled thousands of miles on your own, with hardly any luggage. You arrived on my doorstep in the middle of the night. Charlie is supposed to have arranged your visit, but I've not heard from him. And you've lost your purse and passport and phone.'

'Hmmm.' She threaded a piece of hair into her mouth. 'You make it sound worse than it is.'

'Really?' he said. 'I'm not sure how.'

She scraped her chair loudly away from the table and stood up. Her eyes seemed to grow darker. 'Do you know, I grew up seeing other kids' uncles come to their school plays, birthday parties and give them twenty dollars at Christmas? And all I had was you,' she accused. 'The invisible uncle in the UK, who asks too many questions.'

Benedict felt guilt gnaw inside him as he thought about her growing up in a different country, without him around. 'Did your dad tell you anything about me?'

Gemma shrugged. 'He said he used to sit with you, and your parents, under a tree in the garden and you all hung gemstones into it. He called it your family tree, or the gem tree. Is it still here? I wanna sit under it.'

'Yes, it's still here.'

Gemma shook the gemstones out of the white bag and onto the table. 'So, tell me about these gems,' she said.

Benedict's stomach churned. He couldn't tell her the truth, that was for sure. 'I told you. I gave them to your dad, before he and your mum left for America. That's it. What do *you* know about them?'

She stared at him for a while then seemed to accept his answer. She sat down and pointed at each of the gems in turn. 'This one is Tiger's Eye. This is Citrine and this is Aquamarine. This is, um, what's the pink heart-shaped stone called? Rose Quartz, that's it. Garnet, Poppy Jasper, Blue Lace Agate, Amethyst, Sunstone…um, Carnelian and Golden Topaz.' She picked up a blue stone, the colour of the Mediterranean Sea. 'I can never remember this one.'

Its name popped into Benedict's head. When he'd hung the gems into the gem tree, his father had told him the name of each. 'It's Lapis Lazuli.'

'Okay. Lapis.' She picked up a round stone, the size of a blueberry. As she turned it between her thumb and finger, it shone white, silver then puddle grey. 'Do you know the meaning of Moonstone?'

'The meaning…?' Benedict tried to recall his trips with his parents and what gemstones they'd come across, but all he saw was his mother, laughing and ruffling his hair. 'I know that most Moonstones come from India and Sri Lanka. They get their name because they look like the moon…'

'Duh, everyone knows that.' Gemma laughed. She set

the stone on her palm and lifted it up. 'Did you know that the Romans thought that Moonstone was made from frozen moonlight?'

Benedict said that he didn't.

'It's sometimes known as the dream stone and can bring you sweet and beautiful dreams. If you give your lover a Moonstone when the moon is full, you're supposed to always feel kinda passionate about each other.'

Benedict felt impressed by her knowledge; however a sixteen-year-old girl using the word *lover* made him feel uneasy.

'Dad only really told me about Moonstone and I wanna know about the others too.'

'Your grandfather, Joseph, kept a journal when he was younger. He used to make notes about gemstones.'

'Really?' Gemma's bushy eyebrows arched up.

'I think it's in a chest in the attic,' Benedict added. He hadn't been up into the dusty, dirty space for years.

'Can we look at it? Please, Uncle Ben. Before I go…' She jumped to her feet and did a strange shuffle, her feet dancing on the spot. 'Just one look. I'll sit under the gem tree, then I'll get my rucksack and leave. Your house will be empty again, for when your wife comes back. Please, Uncle Ben.'

Benedict was surprised to find that a lump had risen in his throat and he cast his eyes over this teenager who reminded him so much of his long-lost brother. He'd planned, one day, to show the journal to his own children but that was unlikely to ever happen.

And everyone seemed to leave this house. Benedict's parents died. Charlie moved to America, and Estelle was staying at Veronica's. He was tired of being the one who watched everyone go. Gemma was the only one who'd actually arrived.

Even though he hardly knew his niece, the thought of her too moving on made his gut twist. Also, familiar feelings of responsibility, which he'd once had for Charlie, were beginning to edge back, like ivy creeping around a gatepost.

He couldn't allow her to leave without her purse, phone and passport, and with so few belongings. Whether he liked it or not, he was responsible for her. He mused on the word she had used. *Empty*. He hated it.

'Okay,' he said eventually. 'We can go into the attic later, but I need to open up my jewellery shop.'

Gemma cocked her head to one side. 'Yeah?' she said brightly. 'So that means I can stay, right?'

Benedict's spine stiffened and he felt the need to cough. 'Yes,' he said. 'You can stay.' Though as he said it, he wondered if he'd live to regret it.

4. Malachite

transforming, absorbing, soothing

Benedict walked briskly along the canal towpath towards the village and Gemma struggled to keep up with him. Her limbs weren't coordinated and her boots waggled on her ankles, reminding him of a newborn calf. Watching her made him feel motion-sick.

'You're going too fast,' she complained.

'Sorry,' he said and carried on, just as quickly.

Gossip in Noon Sun could spread like oil on water. If anyone spied him and Gemma together, the villagers might pounce like foxes on an injured rabbit. He didn't want the arrival of his niece to be the new topic of conversation in Bake My Day, the Deserted Dogs charity shop, or the Pig and Whistle pub. He bet that Veg Out greengrocers, Floribunda florists and the Soap'n'Suds launderette were hotbeds for tittle-tattle.

'Do you have nice customers in your shop, or are they crazy?'

Benedict shook his head at her bizarre question. 'I don't actually have that many customers, to categorise them.'

As Gemma pointed and asked what a canal lock was, and he took a moment to explain, Benedict couldn't help thinking of walking with Estelle, each Sunday. Not having children, they had slipped towards middle age quickly, embracing strolls along the canal and enjoying the scenery. They admired the horses in the fields, a flock of geese, or a kingfisher swooping down to the water. Sometimes they ended up back in bed, in the late afternoon, but it was difficult to be spontaneous, when the pressure of trying for a child weighed down on them.

'There are hills everywhere,' Gemma exclaimed, spinning around.

'If you climb to the top, you're on the Yorkshire moors.'

The moors made him feel uneasy. They were too wild, too deserted and too vast. The earth shifted, and the colour of the grass and sods of earth morphed from black to violet, emerald to mustard, so the landscape was never the same. One minute the air could be still and calm, and then black clouds descended and a storm could sail over the hills. Estelle said that the moors lured her to paint them, but Benedict shuddered at the thought of her walking up there, with her paints and drawing pad, without him.

'There's an interesting old quarry up there,' he told Gemma. 'They used to mine a gemstone called Blue Jack in the nineteenth century. It's indigenous to Noon Sun. Anyway, how did you get to my house last night?'

'I hitched a ride from a lady at the airport. I told her I'd lost my purse.'

'That's pretty lucky.' Benedict frowned. 'But you shouldn't accept lifts from strangers.'

'She looked nice.'

'Is this the first time you've travelled on your own?'

She shook her head. 'I went to Paris once, to see the Eiffel Tower.'

Benedict was amazed that Charlie allowed her to do this. 'I took Estelle there a few years ago, and it was lovely. What else did you see?'

Gemma stopped dead on the towpath and her teal blue eyes flashed angrily. 'Why are you asking me questions? Stop prying all the time.'

Benedict held up his hands in surrender. 'Okay, don't get mad,' he said. 'I only asked.'

She tutted and tossed her head.

Benedict sighed and carried on, looking up to see his friends Ryan and Nigel setting up their fold-up chairs on the canal bank. Two fishing rods stretched into the water. A pile of sandwiches wrapped in tinfoil sat between the chairs.

Benedict wondered if he could climb over the wall and take the longer route through the field, to avoid them, though he didn't fancy his chances in trying to clamber over.

But it was too late. Ryan raised his hand. 'All right, Benedict? Do you want to join us?'

'Not today, lads. I've got to get into work.'

Ryan was happy to share every detail of his marital

problems with his wife, Diane, who had asked him for a divorce. He lamented how sleeping on an inflatable mattress in the spare room gave him a sweaty back. Ryan always smelled strongly of the floral washing powder from Soap'n'Suds, and he ironed pin-sharp creases down the front of his black jeans.

'We're going to be here all day,' Nigel added. He worked at the newsagent's shop in the village and teamed his faded black Guns N' Roses T-shirt with a leather biker's jacket. His long, thinning strawberry-blond hair looked like strings of spaghetti escaping through a colander. Nigel's latest crush was Josie, the barmaid at the Pig and Whistle, though he didn't have enough confidence to speak to her. Instead, he bought far too many bags of crisps at the bar in a bid to get closer.

Ryan and Nigel sat back in their canvas chairs and stared at Gemma, as if she was an exotic zoo creature they'd never seen before. Benedict could see they were waiting for an introduction and he wasn't going to offer it.

'Maybe, I'll see you later, lads,' he said and placed his hand lightly on the small of Gemma's back, to usher her onward.

When they were out of earshot, Gemma scraped her feet. Benedict slowed down to allow her to catch up to him.

'What's wrong?'

'Are you ashamed of me, Uncle Ben?'

'No. Of course not.'

Her eyes told him that she didn't believe him.

'Look,' he sighed. 'Not much happens around here so, when it does, the villagers can latch onto it like leeches.'

'So you're happy I'm here?'

'Happy' was too strong a word, but he said yes anyway.

'So,' she said, 'I can have a job in your shop then, huh?'

Benedict held his fist to his mouth and coughed in surprise. 'Excuse me,' he said. 'Let's not rush things, eh?'

When Benedict and Gemma reached the high street, they neared Crags and Cakes. The café had undergone several refurbishments and now had an *Alice in Wonderland* theme, complete with a six-foot-tall angry-looking white rabbit on the pavement. The villagers said he looked so cross because of the cost of the cakes. Three pounds ninety-nine for a slice of Victoria sponge was extortionate.

Benedict's footsteps slowed down.

'Is this your shop?' Gemma asked.

'No,' he said quietly. He touched his wedding ring. 'It's where I met Estelle.'

'Yeah?' Gemma pressed a hand to her chest. 'Was it romantic?'

Benedict gave a quick grin. 'Kind of.' He told Gemma that each Sunday morning, the Noon Sun Walkers met outside Crags and Cakes for a quick coffee before going for a hike on the moors. 'My doctor told me to get more exercise and I thought walking would be easy. I bought some boots and a padded coat and off I went, thinking that I'd be like David Beckham within no time. And I saw this woman outside the café. She had hair like Cleopatra and she wore a purple coat and matching hairband. I couldn't look away.' He swallowed as he thought of Estelle's cobalt eyes and full lips.

'Aw. That's cute.'

'We hiked up to Dinosaur Ridge, a local landmark up high on the moors. The rocks are supposed to look like the profile of a stegosaurus. I was lagging behind but I heard a woman's voice say, "Quick. Shoulder." And it was Cleopatra. Well, Estelle. She had a stone in her boot and wanted to lean on my shoulder to steady herself. She said that I looked *solid*.'

'I suppose that's *one* word to describe you,' Gemma said.

'I thought she was gorgeous but I didn't know what to say.' He was aware that his words were flowing more freely than usual, because he wanted to talk about his wife. He thought back to that day and tried not to groan when he remembered his riveting first words to Estelle.

'My legs are killing me,' he said.

'You'll be fine. If you're not, I can always carry you over my shoulder.'

'Perhaps if you have a small crane…'

'I'm stronger than I look.' She rolled up her sleeve and flexed her arm. They both stared at the slight bump that appeared above her elbow. 'Pure muscle,' she laughed.

'I believe you now.'

'By the way, I'm Estelle.'

'And I'm Benedict.'

When they eventually climbed up and reached Dinosaur Ridge, the rest of the group sat on the stegosaurus scales, looking smug and eating their sandwiches. 'I have a joke,'

Estelle said as she rubbed her knees. 'It's completely rubbish. Do you want to hear it?'

'Go on.'

'Why are there no tablets in the jungle?'

'I have no idea.'

'Because the parrots eat 'em all. Get it? Paracetamol.'

'That's funny,' Benedict said, even though it wasn't.

'You tell me one.'

Benedict could only think of one that he'd overheard a couple of schoolboys sharing outside his shop. He regretted it as soon as he started to tell it. 'How do you get a fat guy into bed?' he asked.

Estelle frowned. 'I have no idea.'

'A piece of cake.'

She snorted and then laughed out loud. Her headband slipped off the top of her ears. 'I may bear that in mind,' she said.

Throughout the rest of walk, Benedict replayed his joke over and over in his head. It was so lame.

They agreed that a pint of cider in the Pig and Whistle would help to ease their aching thighs, and they talked so much that their cheese sandwich tea led into a pub quiz in the evening. They came second and, when Benedict walked Estelle home, they celebrated by kissing on the canal towpath in the moonlight.

Their dates from then on revolved around food – a new tearoom that Estelle had read about, over in York, or a new sandwich on the menu at Crags and Cakes. Except, whereas Estelle was sensible, choosing small dishes, salads, skipping a dessert, Benedict didn't have the willpower. He liked large meals and full oval plates, finding the heavy feeling in his stomach comforting. He couldn't resist a sticky toffee pudding, especially with custard.

They married almost two years later in the small church in Applethorpe, and began to try for a baby on their honeymoon in Santorini.

'I'd love to have two kids, standing on my knee, under the gem tree,' Benedict said, as the moon shone through the window, making the white bed sheets shine silver. 'Like Charlie and I did with our mum and dad.'

Estelle smiled. 'Who knows…in nine months' time…'

'We should stock up on nappies.'

However, the months rolled by and no double blue lines appeared on the pregnancy kits that Estelle bought each month, just in case.

For the first couple of years, it didn't concern them; they were having fun trying. But slowly, increasingly, it mattered.

'Never mind.' They smiled at each other. 'Next month, definitely.'

But still nothing happened.

They started to make love to a schedule, noting the days when Estelle was supposed to be most fertile.

Doctors' appointments and hospital appointments began to fill up their calendar. Benedict felt grubby as he sat in a small cubicle with a porno mag in one hand and a plastic cup in the other. But this was nothing compared to the invasive tests that Estelle underwent. She had sample tests and scans and blood tests, a hysteroscopy and a laparoscopy. Benedict stood and watched her disappear into rooms and behind curtains, and coming around, groggily, from her operations.

And the results were always the same. Nothing. Unexplained infertility.

Estelle started to look at the pregnancy tests in private, with the bathroom door locked. When she came out she was quiet and her cheeks were streaked with tears.

They still went out for walks, their pub lunches together, on holiday, to gigs over in Applethorpe. Benedict worked in the jewellery shop and Estelle started to paint.

They went through three rounds of IVF, which failed. The process gave Estelle excruciating headaches and made her feel lethargic, but she was determined to try again. Benedict sold his Ford Focus to pay for another go, but that didn't work either. There was nothing in the bank and the only thing left to sell was the house. They put it on the market for a year but prospective buyers deemed it old-fashioned, too much work to do.

Benedict and Estelle started to count the years, not celebrating the anniversary of when they met or married, but in terms of how long they'd been trying for children. 'It's been three years, since we first started'... 'It's been five years now'... 'I can't believe it's coming up to eight.'

Until they both, sadly, agreed that it wasn't ever likely to happen.

There were strangers missing in their relationship who had never been real. They had invented ghosts and pinned their hopes and futures to them. Benedict and Estelle had fallen in love with children who would never be.

Benedict had thought only of being a father and, without that dream, he felt lost, like he was only a husk of a man. What was his identity now? Being a jeweller or husband wasn't enough. He needed to be a parent.

A silence settled in the Stone household, like a fine layer of dust, coating everything.

When she was made redundant from the accounts department at Meadow Interiors, Estelle set up their spare bedroom as a studio. As her confidence grew, she started to walk on the moors on her own, with her sketchbook and paints. She travelled to York to buy new brushes and only told Benedict when she got home. She retreated to her studio for hours at a time.

Last Christmas, Benedict looked out of the dining-room window at the gem tree. It was coated in snow and children were laughing in the street, building a snowman. He swallowed and held his back straight. A deep longing welled inside him. 'I think it's time that we thought about adoption,' he said. 'There'll be a child who needs us, out there somewhere.'

Estelle stood beside him. She reached up and leaned on his shoulder, as she had done the first time they met. She didn't speak for a long time. 'I've thought about it,' she said, in a quiet voice. 'This isn't about raising *any* child. It's about us having our own.'

'It *would* be ours. Not biologically, but we have so much love to give.'

Estelle shook her head. 'I don't want to adopt.'

'Why not?' Having a family was all they had talked and dreamed of. How could they even contemplate a future without it?

'It would be a stranger's child. Not really ours.'

'I looked after Charlie when my parents died...' He tried to wrap his arms around her but she squirmed away.

'You had no choice. And your brother broke your heart...' Her words trailed off.

Benedict stared out of the window. 'That's different.' He'd never told his wife what happened between him and Charlie all those years ago. Or why his brother left. He wanted a family with Estelle, and he wouldn't mess up this time. 'This isn't about Charlie. This is about us,' he said, though he felt desperation tug inside him. 'Please let's consider adoption.'

'I have done, Benedict, but I feel that this isn't about you and me, and our family, any longer. It's about *you* wanting a child. Any child.'

'It's not like that.'

'It feels that way. We need to accept that we're not going to be parents, and to plan a future for just the two of us.'

'But I can't...we can't...'

'We've got to learn how to.' Estelle hung her head.

In the darkness, Benedict stared out at the snowy gem tree. It looked like its legacy, of the Stone children hanging gemstones into it, was about to end. Unless he could persuade Estelle otherwise.

After thinking about his wife, Benedict wanted to be alone for a while. When he and Gemma reached Stone Jewellery, he took all the money out of his pockets and told her to open her hands.

'What for?' she asked.

'If your purse is missing, you'll need some cash. You haven't brought many things with you.'

'I don't need them.'

'Well, go to the Deserted Dogs charity shop, anyway, to see if there's anything you like. They raise money to help unwanted dogs in the area. It's opposite the community centre. Look out for a large red-brick building with a big "*Closed. Keep Out*" sign on the door.'

'Why "*Keep Out*"?'

'The roof is caving in and the council don't have the funds to pay for a new one. It's a shame because it was sort of a village hub for things like yoga and baby groups.'

'That's real sad. What are you going to do?'

'I'll go into the shop, to do a few jobs. You can buy us some nice lunch, too.' His stomach gurgled at the thought of a chunky chocolate cupcake. 'Now, put the money in your pocket so you don't lose it...' He paused, realising this was something he used to say to Charlie.

'Don't forget that I travelled from America. On my own.' Gemma gave a withering sigh. 'I *am* capable.' She stared around herself hesitantly.

'Are you okay?'

'Yeah. It's a new place. I don't know anywhere yet.'

'It's a very small village.' Suspicion edged into Benedict's voice. 'I thought you went to Paris…on your own.'

'Yeah, well…' Gemma glared at him and scrunched up the money in her fist. 'Paris had a big tower, as a landmark.' She looked down the street again. 'You go and do your own thing, Uncle Ben. And I'll go and do mine.'

5. Amazonite

integrity, calming, aligning

The shop door scraped against a wodge of leaflets on the doormat. Picking them up, Benedict saw they were all the same. Four grainy faces glared back at him. Rock band, Restore the Hope, was playing a warm-up gig in Applethorpe before their UK tour. Benedict cursed and folded the leaflets in half.

Another leaflet had drifted farther into the shop, and he stooped down, immediately recognising one of Estelle's paintings of the moors. He read the white words:

Lawrence Donnington presents a preview of
'Moorland Escape' by Estelle Stone
at
Purple Heather Gallery, Noon Sun Village
6.30–8.30 p.m., 28th October

Benedict's heart dipped. He didn't know about this. Why hadn't she told him about her exhibition? Was Estelle embarrassed by him?

Purple Heather used to be a small tearoom, but local entrepreneur Donnington had renovated it and turned it into an art gallery, to display the work of Yorkshire artists.

Benedict had passed by and it was very modern, with white walls and polished floorboards. He spied Lawrence himself, standing in the middle of the gallery and waving his arms around as if conducting an orchestra. He dressed like a French mime artist, with slim hips in tight black trousers, and a Breton striped top.

The women of Noon Sun seemed to like him though. Benedict once overhead a small group in the Pig and Whistle gushing about him and fanning their flushed faces with the laminated menus.

From the shop counter, Lord Puss let out a short meow that sounded more like a bark, and his yellow eyes were like slits. From hearing the noise at least ten times a day, Benedict knew that His Royal Highness wanted food. 'Now I have a cat and a teenager to feed,' he said with a sigh. 'You'll have to wait a bit longer, Lord Puss. A bit of patience will do you good.'

He caught a glimpse of Estelle's purple anorak hanging in the store cupboard and he reached out to touch the vivid fabric. He allowed himself a moment to imagine his wife wearing it, then he withdrew his hand and furled it into a fist. What was he going to do to get her back? He wasn't particularly handsome, and he knew he ate too much. He might mention family too often, but he loved her with all his heart. He just didn't know how to express it.

He opened the back door and took a food sachet from his pocket. He squeezed it into the cat's bowl and threw the leaflets for the rock band in the bin. 'Here, puss, puss,' he said wearily.

Lord Puss jumped off the counter and walked as slowly as he could out into the yard. He barely sniffed his food bowl then sat down. A dapple of sunshine illuminated the paving flags with a circle of light so it looked like he was under a spotlight, waiting for applause. He turned his face away from Benedict, as if he had smelled something bad.

'Damn cat.'

Back inside, Benedict carried his laptop through to the workshop and flipped it open. After waiting ages for it to fire up, he was glad that Noon Sun had internet connection today. The phone and broadband in the village only worked intermittently because the surrounding hills blocked the signal.

Benedict had never made a proper effort to track down his brother before, for fear of what might happen. But this time, he Googled *Charlie Stone* and *Charles Stone*. He chewed his bottom lip as half a million results showed up.

Part of him wanted his brother's face to appear on the computer screen, but another part wanted it to remain hidden, so Benedict wouldn't experience the awful pangs of shame that kept him awake at night.

His fingers shook a little as he tried again, this time

typing in *Charlie and Amelia Stone* and then *Gemma Stone*. But there were still thousands of results.

It looked like Gemma's suggestion of sending a letter might be his only way of making contact with Charlie after all.

Next, Benedict phoned the airport and spoke to a young man who had a Northern Irish accent and who spoke at breakneck speed. He informed Benedict that there was no record of a purse with a passport inside it being handed in. He took Benedict's name and number and said that he'd call if anything turned up. 'Don't count on it though,' he added. 'Have a nice day.'

Benedict lowered himself into his chair. He opened his drawer and found half a packet of Polo mints pushed into the corner. He munched them one after another then crumpled the foil into a ball, tossed it into the bin and gave himself a small cheer. He opened another drawer and took out the anniversary necklace. Slinking it over the back of his hand and touching its tiny links, he hoped that Estelle would realise how much time and love he'd poured into it.

When his phone vibrated in his pocket, Benedict's heart leaped. A text from his wife? Finally.

'How R U Benedicto?' Cecil asked.

Benedict sighed. 'I should be asking you that! How did the op go?'

'Okay but a few complications. Visiting time is 6.00 till 7.30.'

'I'll be there tomorrow.'

'Any news on Estelle?'

Benedict hesitated. '**Not yet,**' he texted. He couldn't think of how to tell Cecil, in a few words, about Gemma's arrival.

Cecil replied, '☹. **How is Lord Puss?**'

'**He misses you.**'

'**Me too. Send my ♥.**'

Benedict couldn't think of anything worse than whispering gooey sweet nothings to the fluffy beast. '**I will do. Now rest up. All is great here.**'

'☺,' said Cecil.

While Benedict waited for Gemma, no customers came into the shop. He thought that he'd relish the quietness away from her, but when he picked up a length of gold wire to make more links, he squashed each one.

As he slid another batch of rejected links from his palm into the teacup, the electronic beep-bop in the showroom sounded. Gemma returning early, he pressed his lips tight.

'Hello,' he called out and walked into the showroom. And then his heart and time seemed to come to a standstill.

His wife stood in the middle of the shop.

'*Estelle?*' His word sounded raspy.

'Hello, Benedict,' she said.

He used to greet her with a big hug and a kiss on the cheek and he wanted to do that now. They'd shared twelve years of love and laughter, but they stood facing each other as if there was a thick pane of glass between them.

His wife used her arms and hands to express herself – a reassuring pat to his shoulder, a hug hello, a rub to his forearm as she spoke. This woman looked like Estelle and sounded like her, but she didn't move like his wife. It was like a clone had taken over Estelle's body but hadn't downloaded her personality.

He felt as if his limbs were held together by glue that was becoming unstuck. If he moved, then he might fall apart. 'Estelle,' he repeated. Words wafted around in his head and he couldn't pin them down to say them to her. If she came home, he would do whatever he needed to, to make things right. He didn't want to beg, but if that's what it took then he would do it.

Estelle touched her neck and he saw that she was wearing a bright resin necklace that looked like a firework exploding from beneath her collar. She followed his eyes. 'Oh, this? Friends bought it for me, to celebrate my exhibition at Purple Heather.'

'It's very bold.'

'It's nice to have a change sometimes.'

Benedict cleared his throat. 'Your exhibition looks very exciting. Congratulations. I found a leaflet on my doormat.'

Her brow furrowed in the middle. 'Sorry. I thought that you knew about it.'

'No.' He tried to say it without emotion but felt a tremble in his voice.

'Oh, I'm sorry,' she said again. 'Things have been so crazy recently. I hope that you'll come along.'

Benedict wanted to attend, but what part would he play? He wasn't sure if Estelle was inching him out of her life. He thought of Cecil's words about getting on his proverbial medieval horse to joust for her. But what could he do?

He felt like he was sitting on the beach when a huge

wave crashed, filling his nose and mouth with salt water. He might try to flail around and scramble away, but he was drowning. How had they come to this? It had happened so gradually – the niggles, the arguments, the silences had all reached a crescendo of awfulness, until his wife had felt the only option was to move away from him.

Estelle was coping with things much better than he was. She had a shiny new apartment to live in, friends to support her and a dazzling new career as an artist. And Benedict felt bereft, like a small child watching a circus driving away from town and not knowing if it would return.

Estelle looked around the shop. 'You don't have your lights on in here.'

'I just called in to feed Lord Puss.'

'Not much work on then?'

He couldn't tell if she said it with concern, or if there was a slight barb to her comment. 'Oh yes. No problem there,' he said, thinking about his empty appointment book. 'Busy, busy.'

Over his wife's shoulder, through the large front window, he saw Gemma lollop past on the opposite side of the road. She carried armfuls of coloured shopping bags and she stopped to wave at him.

Benedict looked away quickly, pretending not to see her. He rubbed the back of his neck, willing her to notice that he was talking to someone and to move on. He didn't want Estelle and Gemma to meet, until he'd had the chance to talk to Charlie, to find out what the hell was going on. However, Gemma waved again. She edged towards the kerb.

'I have other things to sort out today, with Cecil being in hospital.' He swallowed.

'How is he?' Estelle asked. 'Did his op go okay?'

'Yes, he's fine.' The stress of seeing Gemma made his words come out too quickly. 'I'm going to visit him tomorrow.'

'Good. Send my love.'

As Gemma crossed over the road, heading towards the shop, Benedict automatically shook his head.

'What is it?' Estelle asked sharply.

'I'll tell Cecil that you asked after him.'

'You're shaking your head.'

'Sorry.'

Gemma now stood outside the shop, looking at his window display.

'You seem distracted.' Estelle pulled her coat around her. 'I should go.'

'No.' Benedict reached out to touch her arm, but felt as if he'd made contact with an invisible force field. He slowly lowered his hand. 'Please don't go.' He opened his mouth to speak again, but the shop door opened.

Gemma heaved her shopping bags inside. 'Hi there,' she chirped. 'I'm Gemma.'

Benedict lost all of the words in his head, at the sight of his niece and wife in the same small space. His eyes flicked between the two of them as if he was watching a game of table tennis.

Gemma strolled around the shop, peering into each of the cabinets.

Estelle didn't look at her. 'I stopped by to ask if I can come over to pick up my paintings from the spare bedroom? Canvasses are expensive, so I'm going to paint over my old ones.'

Benedict's brain started to tick with possibilities. This could be the opportunity he'd hoped for. He could tidy the house, buy some fresh flowers, maybe attempt to make a shepherd's pie, and then casually invite Estelle to stay for tea. He'd open a bottle of expensive red wine to create a nice ambience for the two of them to discuss things.

But Gemma was sleeping in Estelle's studio.

His eyes darted over towards his niece again. Looking at her russet hair made him feel dizzy. 'I'll drop the paintings off at Veronica's apartment for you,' he said.

'Actually, Lawrence has offered to help me pick them up. He's an expert in landscape art, and I don't want to paint over any paintings that he thinks are worth saving. He's been so wonderful, helping me to set up the exhibition.'

Benedict thought of the clumps of bags, and piles of bills, on every conceivable surface in the house. He winced at the mention of Lawrence's name. 'It's not actually a good time…' he started.

'Oh. What's the problem?'

'Nothing. I'll drop the canvasses off for you tonight.'

When Estelle spoke again, her voice was cooler and low. She took a step back towards the door. 'There's really no rush,' she said. 'Don't go to *any* trouble.'

This is all going so wrong, Benedict thought. He wanted to stride over and stand in front of the door to stop her from leaving. He couldn't bear to see her walking away from him, again.

As he furiously thought what else to say, little by little, Benedict became aware that Gemma had turned away from the cabinets and was clearly listening into their conversation. She stood with her arms folded, gawking at Estelle.

At that moment, Benedict wished that he was psychic so he could send Gemma a message via his mind to stop her from staring. His own heart reverberated loudly in his ears, like there was a military drummer practising in his skull. He sensed that his niece was waiting for an introduction to his wife, and he wasn't ready to give it. How could he tell Estelle that Gemma had turned up unannounced? His wife would have more questions than he had answers.

Estelle noticed too. She gave Gemma a confused glance.

'I'll deliver your paintings tonight,' Benedict said.

Estelle gave a small, tight smile as she reopened the door. 'I'm leaving,' she said. 'I feel there's something going on here…'

'No, I…'

She held up a hand to stop his words.

'No, I want to say…' He didn't actually know what he was going to say. There were no ordered words in his head.

'Let's leave things alone, Benedict. If I'm not in when you call, leave the canvasses by the front door of the apartment. It's a communal hallway, so they'll be safe there.'

'I… I…' Benedict started again, but Estelle left the shop. He watched as she bustled past the shop window, her lips pinched together.

'About the text I sent you…' he shouted after her. But if she heard, she didn't turn back.

Gemma dropped her shopping bags onto the floor and gave a slow handclap. 'That went well. Way to go, Uncle Ben.'

Benedict couldn't stop all the frustration of the last few weeks from spilling out in his voice. 'What the hell did you come in the shop for?' he demanded. 'I was trying to talk to my wife.'

Gemma took a small step back and her ankle buckled in her cowboy boot. 'Hey. I didn't know it was Estelle, until I overheard your conversation. Then I figured it out.'

'You listened in,' he accused.

'Well, sorta.' She shrugged. 'Hey, are you worried about this Lawrence guy? Your nostrils flared real big when she mentioned his name.'

'They did not.'

'Yeah, they did.'

Benedict pictured the handsome gallery owner in his striped T-shirt and he suddenly felt exhausted. He wanted to go home and slump on the sofa, whether his wife was there or not. 'If you're going to stay with me then we need some rules,' he said grumpily.

'You don't have to worry about *me*.' Gemma pointed at her own chest. 'I think you need to focus on getting your wife back. Especially if this Lawrence guy is hanging around. Why didn't you introduce me to her? I knew that you're ashamed of me.'

Benedict opened his mouth to respond but then closed it again. He felt too emotionally drained to speak. It also wasn't fair to take his infuriation out on his niece. He waited until he felt a little calmer. 'I'm not ashamed of you, okay,' he sighed. 'I want to speak to Charlie first before I introduce you to Estelle. That's all. Sorry for getting cross with you.'

'That's okay. I get it.'

His shoulders slumped. 'I need to do something about Estelle.'

'Just do it then.'

'I'm not good at stuff like that. I can't think of anything to do for her.'

Gemma folded her arms. 'Hmmm.'

'Hmmm, what?' he asked suspiciously.

'We need a plan.'

'*We?*' Benedict said. As he plodded over to the counter, to lean against it, he felt like his feet were coated in tar. 'Need a *plan*?'

'Yes. A plan. An operation…to win Estelle back. Hey, Operation Win Estelle Back, that spells WEB. Well, OWEB really, but that doesn't sound as cool.'

'WEB?' Benedict repeated, feeling both scared and intrigued at the same time.

'Yes. WEB. You need a plan to get your wife back, Uncle Ben. And you need *my* help to do it.'

6. Peridot

protection, emotional balance, renewal

Benedict could kill for a chocolate éclair, or a slice of lemon drizzle cake. He wanted to eat and take his mind off Estelle. The sugar might stop his directionless thoughts from whirring around in his mind.

When Gemma tried to show him her purchases from Deserted Dogs, he scrambled in his head for an excuse to go into the kitchen and search through the cupboards for a stray bar of chocolate. However, his niece would probably be like a sniffer hound and know what he was up to.

He decided to slump on the sofa and let her chatter wash over him.

'I got some cool stuff. Here's this cute red dress and a plaid skirt. Oh, and a leather bag with lots of pockets. There was a box full of expensive underwear and pantyhose. It was all new, with the tags on and everything. I got us some good food too. Fruit. I put it in the fridge.'

'Lovely,' Benedict said. He pondered about what he could

have said to Estelle, in the shop. Perhaps he should have introduced Gemma…

Gemma shook out a pair of jeans and tried to hoist them on over her cowboy boots, managing to only pull them up to her ankles before they got stuck. She slid her legs back out and the boots remained jammed in the trouser legs. 'I'll show you these ones later.'

'That's fine.'

She tugged out her boots and dropped them to the floor with a couple of thuds. 'Are you even listening to me, Uncle Ben?'

'I am,' Benedict lied. 'You've bought some nice things. Well done.'

Gemma gave a small low growl, like Lord Puss when he saw another cat.

'Okay, okay.' He held up his hands. 'I was thinking of other stuff.'

'About Estelle, right? And my dad, I bet.' Gemma folded up her clothes into neat squares and set them on the armchair.

She sounded dismayed, but there was nothing he could do about it. 'Both. Now, will you write down Charlie's address for me?'

'You don't need it. I texted him before I lost my phone.'

'I'm sure he'll want to hear from you again. Can you remember any other phone numbers, so we can get a message to him?'

Gemma's pointed eyebrows twitched upwards. 'Nope.'

'Then I'll have to write.' Benedict picked up a pen and

scrap of paper from the table and handed them to her. 'Scribble down his address.'

Gemma flicked her hair, but she wrote on the paper and tossed it back to him.

'Sunnyside Farm,' he read. 'North Maine'.

The words made him feel a little calmer. He finally had a name, a place and a way to get in touch with Charlie, even if it was by letter. He smiled at Gemma, but her face was screwed into a scowl.

He addressed the envelope then added his own details, his phone number and email address to the top. Stuck for what to write, he brushed away a speck of imaginary dust from the paper with the side of his hand. Gemma peered over his shoulder, so Benedict couldn't write about his real feelings and worries and regrets, and he kept the letter short.

Dear Charlie
This is just a small note to let you know that Gemma arrived here safe and sound. I understand that she texted you to let you know, but I thought that you might like to hear it from me, too. Unfortunately, she's lost her phone so we don't have your number to call you.

We've agreed that she'll stay for a few days, maybe longer, depending on what you're happy with. I'll help her out all I can; however, it would be useful if you could contact me as soon as you can, so we can discuss her next moves. I'll keep

*this letter short and sweet, and I look forward
to hearing from you soon.*

Then he added:

*I hope you are well. Best wishes from your
brother,*
Benedict

'That sounds okay,' Gemma said. 'You'll need an airmail stamp.'

'I've got one, from when Estelle writes to her friend Veronica.' He sealed the letter into an envelope and set it on the kitchen table. 'Done.'

Gemma idly picked up her new bag. She unzipped its many pockets and peered into them. 'So, why did Estelle leave you? You're not such a bad guy.'

'Thanks.'

'Is it because of your…size?'

Benedict sucked in his stomach. In the ten years they'd been married, Estelle had never mentioned his weight as an issue. 'No.'

'Hmmm,' she said. 'So, she's just *gone*?'

Benedict cleared his throat. 'Yes.'

'And you don't have any children?'

It never ceased to amaze Benedict how often questions about kids rolled off people's tongues, as if they had no other dialogue in their heads.

'So, when will we hear the patter of tiny feet for the two

of you?' Margarita Ganza had asked Estelle as she picked up a bunch of withering daffodils outside Floribunda.

Ryan often told Benedict stories about his kids, over a pint at the pub. He finished his tales with a knowing, 'You have all this to come, Benedict.'

'No,' Benedict said. 'We don't have any kids.'

'Don't you want them?'

He didn't want to discuss this. His niece seemed to hook on to things like a prickly burr on a woollen sweater.

'I think that having children is probably overrated, anyway,' she said, before he could answer. 'It's a big responsibility. Do you and Estelle…?'

Benedict didn't want to answer another question about the family he and Estelle didn't have, so he tried to think of something, anything, to change her path of conversation. 'So, you want to look in the attic for your grandfather's gemstone journal?' he asked brightly. 'Shall we go up there now?'

Benedict stored the metre-long stick with the hook on the end, under his bed. It had been there, unused, for at least five years. The last time he ventured into the attic was when rainwater had leaked through the ceiling into the master bedroom. He had gone up through the hatch and patched up the hole in the roof, walking around his parents' wooden chest and pretending it wasn't there. Even a glimpse of the dark, curved box could make him feel shivery with emotion.

His parents had brought it home from one of their trips

overseas. Benedict and Charlie used to pretend that it was a pirates' chest and they crawled around it with plastic cutlasses clenched between their teeth.

When his mum and dad died, Benedict didn't want the chest in the house any longer, but he couldn't bear to get rid of it either so he gathered together their tools and belongings and stored them away in the attic.

In the studio, Benedict moved Estelle's canvasses to one side. He pushed the stick up, against the hatch, so the door creaked and opened up into the attic. 'Step back,' he warned Gemma. He let the door reverse down, so it hung back, perpendicularly, into the room.

In the darkness, he could just about see the ends of a wooden ladder, and he used the hook on the stick to tug them. They shuddered down, stopping halfway between the ceiling and floor. Specks of dust and grit showered onto the sheets of newspaper Benedict had laid down on the floorboards. He flicked a catch on the ladder and slid them all the way down to the floor with a thud.

'It looks spooky.' Gemma peered up into the dark space.

'The ghost who lives up there doesn't think so.'

Gemma's eyebrows grew more angled. Then she caught sight of Benedict's face, his lips twitching into a smile. 'You're kidding me, right?'

Benedict gave a short burst of laughter. 'Of course. There's nothing up there but piles of stuff.'

'It's *so* not funny. It's a long way up.'

'It's not as high as the Eiffel Tower.'

Gemma scratched her nose. 'Yes, but...'

'Well, if you want to know more about your grandparents and about the gemstones,' Benedict said, 'you'll have to be brave. Follow me.' He stepped onto the ladder and the rungs creaked and bowed as he climbed up.

Gemma didn't move. She stared at the ceiling.

'Are you coming?' Benedict squeezed through the hatch and hung his head over it.

'It's really dark up there. I don't like it.'

Benedict switched on a light. 'Come on. It's safe,' he said. 'I think.'

Gemma slowly climbed the ladder. One of her boots fell off and clunked down the steps, but she carried on. When she reached the top rung, her hands were black with dirt. She clambered into the attic on her hands and knees and Benedict handed her a piece of dusty paper towel to wipe them.

The attic had a pointed roof, and Benedict could just about stand up under its peak. There wasn't a proper floor, only pieces of chipboard that rested on the joists. There were rows of boxes stored along the rafters, and Benedict couldn't even remember what was in most of them. Some were labelled 'Mum' and others were labelled 'Dad'. He'd given all their clothes to charity, soon after they died, but some things he couldn't bear to get rid of, such as his mum's jewellery-making tools.

The wooden chest was larger than he remembered, reaching above his knees in height. His chin trembled slightly as he stared at it. He bent down to blow dust off its top and gagged as the particles went down his throat.

'It looks like a treasure chest,' Gemma said.

Benedict struggled to kneel down and Gemma sat down, too, on the other side.

She peered at the base of the chest. 'What's this piece of paper stuck under it?' she asked, plucking at something. 'OMG. It's an old photo.'

'A photograph?'

Gemma giggled.

'What's it of?'

'It's you, Dad and Mom. But you all look so young. Look at your hair. You look like a woolly mammoth.'

Benedict's heart beat faster at the mention of Charlie and Amelia. He nonchalantly reached out and took the photo from her.

The colours had faded to browns, mustard and pale pink. Charlie laughed and pointed at the camera. Amelia's eyes were closed and she rested her head on his shoulder. Benedict's mouth was open and his eyes shone red from the flash. The three of them looked like they were sharing a joke. 'Oh, yes. Funny,' he said lightly, but there was an iron-like taste of regret in his mouth.

'That is *so* ancient.' Gemma grinned but then her smile fell away. 'I suppose they were really young when they had me. Probably too young and that's why things didn't work out. Maybe they shouldn't have had me at all.'

'Don't say that.'

'It's true. Less trouble for everyone, huh?' She pressed her chin down towards her chest.

Benedict wasn't sure what to say and he looked at the

68

photo again. 'You said that your parents split up? Where is your mother?'

'Oh, Mom met someone else. He's a bit of a dork, but okay really. I don't wanna talk about it.' She peered through her curtains of hair. 'I want to find out more about my *other* family. What happened to my grandparents?' Gemma asked. 'I mean, my dad told me, but will you tell me too?'

Benedict took a deep breath and let his hands drop into his lap. He swallowed and it hurt his throat. He hadn't shared this story for a long time and he still found it painful. However, Gemma should know her family history.

'They went to buy gemstones, overseas,' he said. 'Me and Charlie sometimes went along but Charlie got it into his head that the school football team couldn't win an important match without him, so we stayed behind.' Benedict closed his eyes, remembering. 'I was half watching the news on TV at teatime, while Charlie played football outside. The report was about a tsunami in Sri Lanka. I didn't have the sound turned on, but I watched these huge grey waves sweeping houses and cars away, as if they were twigs in a river. People were running and screaming, clutching children to their chests. The sea even swilled around houses inland, reaching their second-storey windows. Mum and Dad were out there, and I just *knew* that things weren't okay.'

A lump formed in his throat and he gulped it away. He pushed his hand into his hair and stopped talking, unable to continue for a while. 'Charlie was only ten.'

Gemma sat still, listening.

Benedict looked down at the floorboards, watching as a spider scuttled towards his knee. 'I made Charlie his supper and tried not to worry,' he continued. 'But then, the next morning, one of my parents' business associates phoned the house. They said that Joseph and Jenny Stone had drowned. They were identified from documents in their rucksacks.'

'Oh God, Uncle Ben.' Gemma clasped her hands to her mouth. She shifted around the chest and sat next to him, the top of her arm pressing against his. 'That sucks.'

'The worst thing was telling Charlie,' Benedict said. 'He probably thought I was getting him up for breakfast. Instead, I told him that both his parents were dead. He cried out and I can still hear the sound.' He shook his head, as if to get rid of the noise. 'I felt numb and I can't remember anything else of that day, except me and Charlie huddled together on the sofa. We just stared into space.

'After that, friends and distant relatives offered help but they couldn't bring up two orphaned brothers. I took charge of everything.'

'You became, like, my dad's parent?'

'Yes, sort of. Our parents' rucksacks arrived back at the house a few weeks later. They were all white and crusty from sand and seawater. There was a small bag full of gemstones in the front pocket of my mother's rucksack. They're the ones you brought with you.' He gave a bitter laugh. 'They died looking for pretty coloured pieces of rock.'

He felt Gemma's fingers creep on top of his, and tightly hold the back of his hand.

'So now you know what happened,' he said.

'And why don't you and Dad speak? You sounded so close, when you were younger. You went through a lot together. What happened?'

Benedict shrugged. 'Your dad found a different life, in America, with your mum.' He could make it sound so simple.

'But *why* would he want to move away and never come back? Why couldn't he visit or something? He could have brought me to meet you.'

There was nothing that Benedict could say, without thinking back to what had happened between him and Charlie to break their friendship and family bond. 'I don't know,' he said, tight-lipped. 'Why did *you* come here *from* America?'

He felt her fingers tense and she pulled her hand away from his.

'I told you. I came here for an adventure,' she said frostily. 'Not to escape or anything.'

'Escape?' Benedict frowned. 'Who said anything about that?'

Gemma shuffled away from him, back into her own space on the opposite side of the chest. 'You're twisting my words, Uncle Ben.'

'I'm only asking you a question. What do you mean by escape?'

'Nothing. I picked the wrong word, that's all. Stop prying.'

'I'm not.'

'You are.'

'You barged into my shop and listened in while I was trying to reconcile with my wife,' Benedict said, exasperated. 'That's what I call prying.'

'Like you were doing *such* a great job there.'

'You didn't give me much opportunity.'

'Your great master plan to get her back is to do, well, zero.' She rolled her eyes.

'Unlike Operation WEB, or whatever it is you called it?'

Gemma's lips twitched into a small smile and, oddly, he found one too. It sounded so ridiculous.

'Yep, like that,' she said. 'Now can we look in this freakin' chest?'

Benedict was relieved to stop arguing. He placed the key in the lock and turned it. Together, they heaved the lid open. He caught his breath, unprepared for the wave of emotion that hit him as he saw the green-handled pliers his mother used to use and his father's rusty hacksaw. There was a battered wooden mallet and a roll of wire.

He stared and a memory came into his head, as vivid as the day it happened. His mother sat by the window in the dining room, the sunlight in her hair. She laughed as she heated and made delicate curls of silver wire. She always laughed – at birds hopping around the garden, if she burned their dinner, at her sons and their antics. As time went by, he recalled less and less of what his parents and Charlie looked like. He could look at photographs, but they were two-dimensional, a moment frozen in time.

'You're quiet,' Gemma said. 'Say something.'

He delved inside the chest, scooped up a handful of gemstones and held them out on the flat of his palm. Most were already polished and cut to shape, smooth or with their facets glinting. Others were dull. They looked like ordinary stones dug out of the ground, their potential not yet unleashed. Some had holes drilled through them, ready to hang in the gem tree. For a moment, Benedict wished he could be small again. Innocent. 'You're right. It's a treasure chest,' he said.

Gemma reached out and touched the gems. 'Cool. Can you use these in your jewellery?'

'Stone Jewellery has survived for long enough without gemstones.' He shook them back into the chest. Next, he pulled out a large ball of tissue paper. It looked like a cheerleader's pompom. This was something he hadn't seen for a long time.

'What is that?'

Inside it were separate bundles of soft tissue paper. Benedict took one out and peeled it apart. A silver clam-shell brooch nestled in the folds. It was a test piece he had made with his mother. Benedict was about to say that it was nothing, to crumple the tissue back up and hide it away, but Gemma snatched it from him.

'This is so cool.' She placed the clam shell on her palm. 'Did my grandmother make it?'

'No, I did,' Benedict said. 'It was a long time ago, when I was learning. You can see that it's clumsy.'

'It's different to the jewellery in your shop.' She turned it over in her hands. 'That's all kinda boring.'

'Thanks for your kind words.'

'I mean, compared to this.'

'I'm not sure that's any more complimentary.' He took it back off her. 'I was probably only sixteen or seventeen when I made this.'

'My age,' Gemma sighed. She shook her head. 'You know, everyone at home keeps asking what I wanna do next. All my friends are going to college, but I don't know what I want. I mess up everything I do…'

Benedict ran his finger over the edges of the silver. His niece's confidence seemed to have melted as quickly as an icicle in the sun. 'You're being too tough on yourself,' he said. 'What have you messed up?'

Gemma stared at him. She opened her mouth and slowly tilted her head from side to side, like a metronome, as if considering whether to tell him something. Benedict waited for her to speak, but her head came to a stop. 'Nothing,' she muttered finally. 'I was just saying, that's all.'

'When you're younger, things can seem worse than they really are.'

'Yeah, maybe.' She gave a short sharp laugh. She reached out and took hold of another ball of tissue. Inside this one was a silver blossom brooch, and a pendant set with a large, round, yellow Sunstone. She lifted the necklace over her head and patted it against her chest. 'You should display these in your shop.'

'They're not good enough.'

'Things don't always have to be perfect.'

'What's the point, if they're not?'

Gemma tugged off the Sunstone necklace and thrust it back out to him, at arm's length. 'Here. Take it.'

Benedict dangled the necklace back into a piece of tissue. 'What's wrong with you?'

'Nothing.' She folded her arms firmly. 'You only like perfect things, and I'm not one of them.'

Benedict wasn't willing to be drawn into another confrontation, so he pulled out all the balls of tissues and placed them behind him, unopened. Then he saw the item he'd been thinking about. 'My father's journal,' he said, as he took it out and set the heavy, burgundy leather-bound book on his lap.

The cover was faded and cracked. It creaked when he opened it. Inside, the paper was as yellow at Citrine, stained around the edges from age and thumbs wet from coffee and oil. The front page said:

Joseph Stone's Book of Gemstones and Crystals

Benedict swallowed as he saw his father's adolescent handwriting.

Gemma's eyes widened. Her arms slipped out of their tight fold. 'It looks like it's from when Jesus was alive.'

Benedict moved closer to her and opened it up.

Around a third of the pages featured sketches and photos torn from books and magazines, as well as notes and figures. His father started every few pages with a large italic letter of the alphabet. Some of the sections were full, 'A' for Agate,

Aquamarine, Amethyst… 'J' for Jade, Jasper and Jet. Other sections had hardly any entries.

'Even as a boy he was interested in gemstones,' Benedict said. He opened to a page on Peridot, and he and Gemma read the words.

PERIDOT

A rich green stone, sometimes called Chrysolite, Peridot is widely known as the birthstone for August. It can often be found in volcanic landscapes. It was used in ancient times to ward off evil spirits. It can assist us to recognise negative patterns in our lives, override unwanted thought patterns, help let go of the past and ease fear and anxiety. It enhances the healing and harmony of relationships of all kinds, but particularly marriage. It can lessen stress, anger and jealousy in relationships, and also helps us to find what is lost…

'That last sentence isn't complete,' Gemma said. 'It doesn't make sense.'

To Benedict, it did. It was silly, he knew, but it was as if his father had written the words just for him.

'You could *so* do with a piece of Peridot, Uncle Ben,' Gemma added. 'You need some harmony, with Estelle.'

Benedict was thinking the same thing.

'There are a lot of blank pages in that journal,' Gemma mused. 'If I stay with you for longer, I could fill in stuff about the missing gems…about my gems…'

'Hmmm.' It sounded like a long project. He looked at his watch and saw that it had already gone nine-thirty. 'Damn it.'

'What?'

'I said that I'd take Estelle's paintings around for her tonight. It's too late now.'

'She *also* said that Lawrence would help her to collect them.'

'I want to take them over. It will give us a reason to talk. I could perhaps take a small bunch of flowers too.'

'Flowers? You need to do more than that.'

Benedict closed the journal. What could a sixteen-year-old girl know about relationships that he didn't? But, her insistence that he do something echoed Cecil's words. 'Like what?'

'I dunno.' Gemma gave an exaggerated shrug. 'Like, show her that you love her. Where is she staying?'

'In her friend's swanky modern apartment. It has a balcony, overlooking the canal—'

'What?' Gemma interrupted. 'Like in *Romeo and Juliet* or something?'

'I suppose it's a bit like that.'

'Hmmm. Well, that's it then.' Gemma gave a big smile, pleased with herself.

'What is?'

'If you don't want this Lawrence guy sniffing around your wife, you're gonna have to take action.'

'I'm not really an action man. And I don't know what you mean...'

'Duh, Uncle Ben,' Gemma said. 'You gotta try to be like Romeo.'

7. Turquoise

healing, friendship, communication

Benedict caught the bus to Applethorpe Hospital and hoped that Cecil was okay. He rested his hand on his chin and stared at the green hills rolling past, but his daydreams soon turned to more unsettling thoughts. I wonder if Lawrence Donnington has any children, he mused. He looks virile, like he only has to glance at a woman to make her pregnant.

Benedict walked towards the rows of low stone buildings that reminded him of army barracks, through the entrance gates and past the maternity building. The windows of the middle floor were dotted with pink and blue helium balloons. They bobbed at the windows like blank faces. A baby cried out and Benedict stood still for a minute and listened. A wave of sadness overwhelmed him and he dug his hands into his pockets. The cries were a sound he might never get to hear.

He and Estelle had visited the antenatal clinic here often, for their tests and scans. Many times they had gripped hands tightly as they pulled open the heavy glass doors, took a deep breath and prepared themselves to hear the latest results, delivered with ever-increasing sombreness by the doctors and nurses.

All the posters on the waiting-room walls were aimed at women who were pregnant or who had given birth ... *don't smoke when you're expecting, breastfeeding is best, cut down on sugar, check your gums*...but there was nothing for anyone who *couldn't* get pregnant. That was like a secret, hidden away so as not to mar the happiness of those who could have children. It was only when you entered the realms of being unable to get pregnant that you heard the devastating stories of couples trying for years to have a baby, of miscarriages and of stillbirth. They were the tragedies that you might read about in a magazine and think that they happened to others and that you were okay, because you were one of the lucky ones. Then came the dull, creeping, painful realisation that you weren't.

And so with every visit, each appointment, each consultation, each reassuring hold of each other's hands, Benedict and Estelle learned that it was unlikely, very doubtful, they would ever be parents. What once was a possibility became uncertain and then improbable. And even though they sat with their fingers interlocked, Benedict felt very much alone, and suspected that his wife did too.

Estelle used to pore over leaflets and read out statistics to Benedict. 'Around one in seven couples struggle to get pregnant... That's 3.5 million people in the UK,' she said. 'It's not just us. I feel like a failure, but there are others too.'

Benedict often looked in the mirror and wondered what

was going on inside his body. He was like a clock that looked simple on the outside, but inside was a multitude of cogs, tiny screws and workings, and if just one was wrong, out of place, then the clock wouldn't work. Except that no one could ever find his bloody faulty cog, to fix it.

In the hospital car park, a man strode across, his face half obscured by a huge bunch of pink roses wrapped in cellophane. He grasped a bottle of champagne tightly around the neck. 'I'm a dad,' he announced to Benedict. 'My wife's just had a little girl. It's brilliant.'

Benedict said congratulations. It was so easy to imagine that Estelle might be in hospital, in bed on the maternity ward, holding their baby. He could almost feel the curl of tiny fingers around his own.

'I can't believe it. Me, a dad,' the man repeated. 'It's the best feeling in the world.'

'Well done,' Benedict muttered, his heart feeling heavy. He pressed on and looked for the sign for Cecil's ward.

Benedict had expected Cecil to be loafing around in his lilac silk pyjamas, entertaining the nurses with his stories about Lord Puss. He hadn't considered how weak and tired his friend might look after his operation. It was as if Cecil had been replaced by a paler, skinnier version of himself, even though his hair was still coiffed into its budgerigar quiff.

'Benedicto.' Cecil waved from his bed.

Benedict walked over. He gave his friend a brief hug then sat down on the plastic chair at the side of the bed.

He felt the legs splay under his weight and he reached into his shopping bag. 'I've brought *Hello!* magazine for you, and cupcakes.'

'Fashion, gossip and sugary treats. Fabby.'

Benedict felt a twitching sensation in his fingers when he handed over the cakes. The lemon icing on top was pleasingly shiny and topped with a ruby-red glacé cherry. *Cecil won't mind if you eat one of us*, they said. *Just ask him*.

Cecil tore them open. 'Want one?'

Don't do it, Benedict thought. He considered sitting on his hands, to stop himself, but he reached out for a cupcake anyway. He ate it in three bites but strangely it tasted a little too sweet. He batted the crumbs off his trousers with the flat of his hand. 'So, how are you feeling?'

Cecil sighed. 'Okaaay. I thought I'd be out and doing my Usain Bolt impersonation by now. I feel like I'm falling apart. How is my white ball of fluffy gorgeousness?'

'He's, er, the usual. White and fluffy.'

'But the two of you are getting on, aren't you? I worry about him not getting the love and attention he's used to.'

'We're getting on just fine.'

'And so...' Cecil prompted. 'Everything is just as it was?'

'Let's not talk about work – you're supposed to be trying to get better.'

'I mean, any progress with Estelle?'

Benedict shook his head. 'Not yet.'

'So you're still waiting and seeing?'

Benedict thought of Gemma's insistence that he should

be Romeo. He dreaded to think what that meant. 'There's something I need to tell you,' he said.

'What?' Cecil leaned forward in his bed.

'My niece, Gemma, has come to stay with me, from America. She's only sixteen and says she's here for an adventure.'

'Adventure, huh?' Cecil stared off into space. 'I remember that, once. A long time ago. You've not mentioned Gemma before.'

'She's my brother Charlie's daughter. Our family isn't close and Gemma just arrived out of the blue. It was a big surprise.'

'That sounds a bit strange.'

'I know.'

'So, what is she like?' Cecil picked up *Hello!* and took a quick glance at the cover. A soap star had given birth to quads.

'She's kind of infuriating. But she knows her own mind and she wants to learn. I'd forgotten what it's like to have a passion for new things.'

'Coolio. Like what?'

'She's interested in the meaning of gems.'

'Like gemstones?'

Benedict nodded. 'My father made notes on them in an old journal, and she brought some with her.'

'That sounds intriguing. And what is she up to now, this niece of yours?'

'I left her in the house on her own. So she can have some space to herself.'

'That's what you wanted to give Estelle.'

'I know.' Estelle's space had extended for much longer than he thought it would. 'Gemma says the same as you, that I need to *win* Estelle back.'

'She's right.'

'She says that I should try to be like Romeo,' he muttered, hoping that Cecil would agree with him, that the idea sounded absurd.

Cecil laughed, a machine-gun fire blast. 'Oh, Benedicto,' he said. Then he started to laugh again.

'I know that I have to do *something*.' Benedict shifted in his chair. 'Estelle came into the shop and we were like strangers. I can't let her go, Cecil.'

Cecil's laughter subsided. 'Well, if you don't try to be Romeo, what else are you going to do?'

Benedict pursed his lips. He had no other plans. 'Nothing, I suppose.'

'Exactamondo. Perhaps you should give Gemma's idea a go, whatever it is.'

He knew that his friend was right.

'And, I simply must meet her,' Cecil added. 'What does Estelle think about your niece's arrival?'

'Well, they kind of met but I didn't introduce them to each other.'

'So, your sixteen-year-old niece is staying with you, but you haven't told your wife. That's pretty brave.'

'Hmmm. Now you say it like that...'

The two men chatted for an hour, about Cecil's nieces and football, and how Ryan and Diane's marriage was doing.

'You might have to sweet-talk the nurses into letting me out of here,' Cecil said. 'They keep talking about complications and I don't want to let you down.'

'Take your time,' Benedict said. 'Come back when you're ready. The shop is doing fine.'

'It sounds like Gemma might be a good replacement for me...'

'No one could replace you, Cecil. And I'm not looking to.'

Cecil nodded with relief.

With visiting time coming to a close, Benedict was about to leave when he remembered something. He delved into his pocket then took out and placed a small mottled blue-green stone in Cecil's palm. 'Gemma asked me to give this to you.'

Cecil leaned in closer to examine it. 'Is it Turquoise?'

'Yes, it's one of the gems Gemma brought with her. She's copied some notes down, from my father's journal.' He gave an embarrassed cough as he handed the piece of paper to Cecil.

TURQUOISE

Early Europeans believed that this stone came from Asia Minor so gave it the name 'Pierre Turquoise' which means 'Turkish Stone'. Turquoise is formed by water acting upon copper and aluminium within rocks which causes the gem to develop and gives it its blue colour. The stone was used in protective amulets or rings to ward off accidents. It is said to speed up your recovery after illness and helps to alleviate pain and reduce infection. It should be given as a gift to bring good fortune and peace.

'Coolio. A miracle worker then?' Cecil said. He slipped the gem and note into his pyjama top pocket. 'Tell her, cheersy. And what gemstone has she given to you?'

'Me?' Benedict frowned. 'Nothing.'

'Perhaps you should ask her for one. If it will help you to get what you want.'

Benedict thought of the meaning for Peridot and how it sounded ideal for what he was going through. He recalled again Gemma's explanation for Moonstone.

He didn't believe for one minute that a small stone could make Cecil feel better, or help make Estelle fall back in love with him. Surely that would be crazy, wishful thinking.

8. Zircon

virtue, revealing, constancy

Benedict stood in Estelle's studio where her paintings were stacked against the wall. He picked a small one up and stared at the swooshes of emerald green and mauve. He remembered his wife pulling the studio door closed behind her, and the chink of brushes against glass jars. He touched a wispy, inky cloud and thought about their last conversation in the little room, as Estelle stuffed clothes into her purple suitcase.

'Leave me alone for a while. I want to stay in Veronica's apartment, to be on my own,' she said.

'Please don't go. You can think things through here.'

Estelle shook her head. 'It's like there's a constant buzzing in my head, with you talking about family, or my parents asking if I have any good news yet. They think their time is running out to enjoy grandchildren. I feel so guilty when I see them.'

'There is still hope for us,' Benedict said. 'We can keep trying.'

'We just need to accept that we can't have kids.' Estelle pushed the suitcase lid down, but her clothes bulged out of the sides. 'I feel like I'm a block of marble with a sculptor attacking me with a chisel, and soon there'll only be a small chunk of me left. When men don't have children, they're not looked upon with questioning and pity. Society just accepts it.'

'I don't care about society. It's me and you that I care about. If you're going to stay at Veronica's, can we at least still meet each day, for coffee?'

She opened the case again and tugged out a chunky sweater. 'I need a break, Benedict. You need to think about if it's me you really want, or a baby-making machine.'

Her words felt like knives plunging into his chest. Benedict didn't need time to think. He already knew what he wanted, his wife *and* a child. The three of them would be a family, a package. 'Of course I want you,' he said.

'But will you be happy with just me?' she asked.

Benedict didn't answer.

Benedict pulled an old trolley out of the shed to load up Estelle's paintings, ready to take them over to Veronica's apartment. Gemma's bare legs poked out from beneath the gem tree and it seemed odd to see someone other than his parents or brother sitting under the branches.

Even though it was cold outside, she had kicked off her cowboy boots. She leafed through the gemstone journal and sucked on the end of a pencil. At her feet was a bundle of clothes and a bunch of flowers. Benedict scratched his head when he saw something long and golden. He wondered if it was anything to do with WEB but didn't want to ask.

He brought most of Estelle's paintings down from upstairs, wrapped them in plastic bubble wrap, and secured them onto the trolley with a bungee cord. Out of breath, he went to the kitchen and made a cup of tea with three sugars in it for him, and one without for Gemma.

Back outside, he handed Gemma a cup. 'This is British tea,' he said. 'It's the perfect shade.'

'Beige?

'It's more golden than beige. Tea has its own unique hue.'

She shuffled along on her bottom, out from under the gem tree, and took it from him. Sitting cross-legged, she cocked her head on one side and took a sip. 'Yuck. I'm not sure about it.'

'You'll get to really like it.'

'Was Cecil okay?' she asked.

'He's fine but looks a bit pale. I gave him the piece of Turquoise.'

'Cool.'

'Who are the flowers for?' he asked. 'And, is that…a *sword*?'

Gemma nodded. 'The flowers are for Estelle, and the costume is for you.'

Benedict's fingers tightened around his cup and he took a nervous sip. 'Costume?'

'Uh-huh. It's for your Romeo.'

Benedict spluttered into his tea. 'What?'

'Uncle Ben,' Gemma said, 'we discussed this. While

you were visiting Cecil, I bought a hat and sewed a feather on it. There's a black mask for your eyes, and I got you a sword. It's amazing what you can get at the charity shop. I wanted to buy you a velvet tunic, but there was nothing in your size. Then there's flowers for you to give to her.'

Benedict rubbed at his neck. He stared at the items. 'A sword?'

'Sure. I think Leonardo DiCaprio has one in the film.' She looked him over. 'I know you're not Leo, but...' She jumped up and plonked the hat onto his head, then handed him the mask. 'All you have to do, when you take Estelle's paintings back, is to try to make it romantic.'

Benedict picked up the sword. This was a teenage girl's view of romance, not his. He looked at Gemma and her eyes were eager, like a friendly dog waiting to be patted. It was kinder to humour her and pretend to go along with her plan. Rejecting her efforts seemed a bit harsh, especially when she'd made quite an effort.

'Thanks,' he said and tested the tip of the sword with his finger. Thinking of what else he could add, he said, 'Ouch, that's sharp.'

'Be careful with it.'

Benedict nodded. He folded the eye mask and put it in his pocket, and tucked the plastic sword under his arm. 'Now, don't wait up for me. If Estelle invites me in for a talk, then I may be a while. You'll be okay on your own?'

'Why wouldn't I be?' Gemma sighed.

'No reason,' Benedict said. 'No reason at all.'

Benedict panted as he pushed the painting-laden trolley along the high street and past the crumbling community centre. It was a struggle to negotiate the kerbstones and he could only travel slowly. The sky was darkening quickly and an owl hooted. The waning moon reflected in the canal like a misshapen pearl. He focused on reaching the apartment block, intent on returning Estelle's paintings and sparking a conversation with her.

The mask, hat and sword sat in a shopping bag, balanced on top of the paintings. The flowers in the bouquet shook as he trundled along.

Veronica's apartment was the second one along, on the second floor. It had the largest balcony of the block, on which sat a wrought iron table and two chairs, and a metal sculpture of a heron.

Benedict pushed the trolley to the back of the apartment block, on the canal towpath. He positioned it next to a large bush and glanced inside the bag. The orange glow of a street lamp illuminated its contents and, as Benedict touched the feather on the hat, he tried to think of what to do next.

His biggest temptation was to about-face and go back home. He could lie to Gemma and say that Estelle wasn't in, even elaborating a little to say that he'd waited for a long time outside the apartment. Or, maybe he could tell his niece that he'd donned the outfit and that Estelle was impressed by his effort. Gemma would be pleased that he'd followed her idea, and they wouldn't have an altercation when he got home. She'd be none the wiser.

But Benedict also knew that if he didn't do anything,

then it would be his own fault if Estelle stayed away for longer, or didn't come back at all. How long could he carry on just waiting and seeing?

A small bolt of anger flared in his chest at his own uselessness, that he couldn't give his wife what she wanted, what they both wanted. As if a bloody feathered hat and mask would solve their relationship issues. It was ridiculous. How could waving a sword suddenly make being childless feel okay? He slid the sword out of the bag and plunged it into the ground. It was surprisingly sturdy and it shook as he let go of it.

He heard a swishing noise and lifted his head to see the patio doors to Veronica's apartment open up. He recognised Estelle's silhouette as she stepped out onto the balcony.

Not having prepared or rehearsed what he was going to say to her, Benedict automatically sidestepped behind a bush. It wasn't tall enough to conceal his height, so he bent his knees and squatted the best he could. Peeping through the leaves, he watched his wife move to the front of the balcony. She held a wine glass in one hand.

Adrenaline whooshed through his veins and he tugged the sword out of the earth, not wanting to use it, but to hold on to something. 'Go on, Benedict,' he said to himself, through his teeth. Step out there and say something. Shout up and offer her the flowers. Show her that you love her.

He steadied himself to pluck up courage to step out of the bush. He lifted his right foot, but then he halted as another figure joined Estelle on the balcony. It was tall and angular and, in the faint yellow light that shone from the apartment, Benedict could make out a striped T-shirt. Lawrence Donnington.

Lawrence stood next to Estelle at the balcony edge. Benedict cocked his head on one side and listened to the burr of their conversation, but he couldn't isolate any words. Estelle's laughter carried into the night, and it had been a long time since she sounded so carefree.

Benedict wondered what had been going on in Veronica's apartment. Had Lawrence called round for a quick chat, or had he been there for longer? Perhaps he and Estelle had made love and were enjoying a post-coital glass of wine on the balcony.

With that ominous thought, a wave of jealousy struck him and, within just a few seconds, Benedict managed to conjure up an alternative life for Estelle and Lawrence together. It was one where Estelle divorced Benedict and moved in with Lawrence. They had a child together and lived happily ever after.

Benedict tortured himself with his various imaginings of her new life, without him.

His and Estelle's story couldn't end this way, but he no longer felt in control. It was as if someone else had grabbed hold of a pen and started to write his life story for him, featuring a bolshie American teenager and a love interest for his own wife.

Lawrence and Estelle stood very close, side by side. They leaned against the balcony, facing the canal, their features highlighted by the moonlight.

A Jack Russell ran up to Benedict. It stared at him with

beady eyes then began to bark. Benedict's blood felt icy cold at the thought of being discovered, crouching behind a bush. He tightened his fingers around the hilt of the sword. 'Go away,' he hissed. 'Go.'

'Jimmy, come here,' a loud male voice ordered.

'Is anyone down there?' Estelle called out.

'Just walking my dog, love,' the man shouted back. 'Sorry for disturbing you.'

The dog stared at Benedict's ankle and then at its owner. It cocked up its leg and defiantly peed centimetres away from the toes of Benedict's loafers, before sloping away.

Benedict closed his eyes and held them tightly shut. He waited until his heartbeat slowed down. He reopened one eye and then the other, and he looked back up at the balcony.

It was now empty.

Springing onto his tiptoes, he lifted his head and tried to see inside the apartment, but the patio doors were closed, and the curtain inside pulled shut.

Benedict stepped out and stretched his back, cramped from hunching over. Hearing voices coming from the side of the apartment block, he moved quickly and peered around the corner.

Estelle and Lawrence stood under the street light. Lawrence placed a hand on her shoulder. Again, Estelle was laughing and Lawrence moved forward until his and Estelle's bodies almost touched. They stood close for a punishingly long time.

Benedict's throat grew so tight that he could hardly

breathe. He reached up to press and ease it. Please, don't let them kiss, he prayed. Please, not this. He didn't know whether to stride forward and demand that Lawrence take his hands off Estelle. He would grab the arty lothario by his shoulders and wrestle him away. His alternative was to walk away and slink off into the night.

Or, he could stay and wait.

Eventually, Estelle took a few steps back. Lawrence tried to take her hand but she continued to back away. He stared after her.

He's thinking about following her, Benedict thought queasily. He's going to make a play for my wife…

His feet felt like they were glued to the ground, but he had to get to Estelle.

He could go around to the front door, but Lawrence might be there, and Romeo didn't use an intercom buzzer.

Benedict thought quickly. What could he do to get her attention?

He waited, giving Estelle time to return to the apartment, then he reached down and picked up a small stone. He threw it up at the balcony, where it pinged off the glass door. After a few seconds, he picked up a handful of gravel and tossed that too. It showered through the air and hit his target.

The patio doors slid open and Estelle stepped out. 'Is anyone there?' she asked loudly. 'Lawrence?'

Her saying that name made him want to gag. Benedict stared at the hat and mask on top of the trolley. He had to do *something*, even if it meant making a prat of himself.

Without allowing time to talk himself out of it, Benedict put on the hat, he slipped on the mask and took hold of the sword again. It felt as if an invisible person gave him a shove in the small of his back and he stepped out from behind the bush.

'Estelle,' he called out, his voice echoing in the night.

She walked to the edge of the balcony. 'Hello...?'

'I'm here. It's Benedict.' He gulped.

'Benedict?' She sounded confused.

How did Romeo do it? Benedict racked his brain. What did he say? Did he get down on one knee? Did he have a skull, or was that Hamlet? 'I wanted to see you.' His voice wavered.

'What are you doing down there?'

'I've, er, brought your paintings.'

'Well, you startled me. Did you throw stones?'

'Yes,' he admitted, feeling foolish. 'I was on the canal towpath. I thought you might be...busy.'

She didn't speak for a while. 'Are you holding a *sword*?'

He stared at it. 'Yes.'

'Why?'

He ignored her question but took a deep breath and held it in his throat. 'I have to tell you something.'

'And you need a sword to do it?'

This was his jousting moment. He thought of Cecil's encouragement and Gemma's insistence that he fight for his wife. He wanted to tell Estelle that he was Romeo and that she was his Juliet, and that they should be together. He wanted her to invite him up to the apartment and for

96

them both to smile at his silly outfit. But the words began to stack up in his head like bowling balls lining up in an alley. He couldn't pick which ones to say first, or know which would have the most impact.

'Is that a feather in your hat?' she asked.

He gripped the sword more tightly. 'I want to say...' he started. Even though all the words were in his brain, about how much he wanted her back, none of them wanted to come out first. In the end, he said something. Anything. 'I need to tell you about...Gemma...'

His heart sank. Damn it. Those were the wrong words.

'Gemma? The girl in your shop said her name was Gemma.'

Benedict shook his head, dismayed at himself. But there was no going back. He didn't know when Charlie was going to get in touch, and he didn't want to pretend that Gemma wasn't staying with him any longer. His lies in the past had got him into enough of a mess. 'She's my niece, Charlie's teenage daughter.'

Estelle was silent for a long time. 'She was staring at us in the shop. Why didn't you introduce us?'

'I'm not sure. Her arrival was a surprise and I was still getting used to it. I didn't know how long she was going to stay, or what to say to you...' He felt that with every word, he was deflating like a tyre with a slow puncture. 'Anyway, I've brought your paintings for you.'

'Great,' Estelle said, though she didn't sound like it was great. 'Can you bring them to the front door?'

Benedict pushed the sword into the struts on the back

97

of the trolley and tugged off his hat. He pulled the trolley to the front of the apartment block and Estelle opened the door. Her cheeks were flushed and her hair was mussy. Benedict wondered if it was because of Lawrence, or from coming downstairs.

When Estelle saw him, she held her hand to her mouth and laughed. 'Why on earth are you dressed like Zorro, Benedict? Where is your cape?'

Damn. He was still wearing the mask.

It all seemed so stupid, to tell her that he was Romeo and that he wanted her back. He mumbled something about Gemma and a fancy-dress party at the Pig and Whistle, and it all sounded very garbled and not at all plausible. He imagined her picking up the phone to Lawrence after he'd gone and the two of them laughing about him.

He hitched the mask up onto his forehead. 'Shall I help you to bring the paintings up to the apartment?' he asked hopefully.

'No, it's fine. I can handle them. You go and attack the bad guys, or whatever it is Zorro does.'

Benedict gave a weak smile.

'So, how long is Gemma staying with you?'

He didn't know, so he conjured up something that sounded feasible. 'For a week or so. She's sleeping in your studio, if that's okay?'

'Sure.' She shrugged. 'It's certainly a surprise, after all this time.'

Benedict took the paintings off the trolley and stacked them against the wall. 'We're just getting to know each other,' he said and looked up hopefully. 'I'll introduce the two of you properly next time.'

'That would be good, and more suitable than our first meeting.'

'Sorry.'

'Well, at least I know now. I appreciate you telling me. Goodnight, Benedict.'

Benedict couldn't think of anything to say, so he said goodnight and started to push the empty trolley back along the Noon Sun high street. After a few steps, he realised that he wasn't carrying the bouquet of flowers, and he hadn't presented them to his wife.

'Estelle,' he called back as the front door closed.

'What?' She poked her head back around it.

Benedict looked over and saw the bouquet lying on the grass, the cellophane shining under the street lamp, as the Jack Russell scampered up and cocked his leg up on them.

'Oh, nothing,' he said, wondering if tonight could have gone any worse. 'Goodnight.'

When Benedict got home, he left the sword by the front door and stuffed the mask and feathered hat into the bin. The front room and kitchen lights were switched on but Gemma wasn't in either room. He locked the front door and turned off the lights.

As he made his way upstairs, it sounded as if someone had left a TV set on in one of the bedrooms. He could hear voices and muted laughter. But he didn't have a television upstairs.

99

He stopped, leaned against the bannister, and listened for a while. Though the sound was muffled, it was Gemma's voice. Now and again, he heard her laugh. He hoped that she hadn't invited anyone back to the house.

When he reached the landing, he stood and faced her door. It was shut, so he rapped on it. The talking stopped. Benedict felt a bit like a pupil waiting to be invited into the headmaster's office. There was a shuffling noise.

'Who is it?' Gemma shouted out.

'It's Benedict. Uncle Ben.' It was an absurd thing to have to say in his own house.

There was a thud and the door opened by a couple of inches. Gemma pressed an eye to the gap. 'Okay?' she asked, a little breathlessly. 'How did it go, Romeo?'

Benedict wanted to forget all about this evening. 'Fine. I heard voices from inside your room. Do you have anyone in there?'

'No. Of course not.' She tutted. 'I, um, talk to myself sometimes.'

'There was laughter too.'

'It was a funny conversation.'

They looked at each other through the gap.

She huffed loudly and opened her door wider. 'Go ahead. There. Take a look if you don't believe me.'

Benedict saw that she had a small lamp turned on. The duvet cover was folded over on one corner. The gemstone journal lay open on the bed. Everything looked normal and he felt guilty for questioning her.

'See?'

'Well, so long as you don't have any boys stowed away in there,' he half joked.

Gemma laughed also, rather too loudly. 'There's nothing going on. Goodnight, Uncle Ben.'

9. Aquamarine

openness, expression, clarity

While Gemma made a fruit salad for their breakfast, Benedict opened the curtains upstairs in the studio. He spotted that his niece had emptied the contents of her rucksack on top of the chest of drawers. There was her hairbrush, the teddy bear with the purple ribbon and a small heap of clothes. She had a half-used shower gel and a toothbrush. A phone charger was tangled around a grey vest top.

There was a small notepad and she had left it open. Gemma had drawn a heart in blue ink and inside it were the bubble letters *GS and DJ 4eva*. He smiled at it, remembering when he found similar doodles on the cover of Charlie's schoolbooks.

'D,' he thought. David, Derek, Dennis? Perhaps Gemma's boyfriend, or a secret crush?

He pondered on her belongings for a while, again wondering why she hadn't brought more things with her, especially as it was cold in England at this time of year. Surely a young girl would want things like deodorant and shampoo, and maybe perfume. It was almost as if she'd left home in a hurry.

Benedict went back into his own room and opened one of the drawers on Estelle's bedside cabinet. He took out a small scented candle, a can of hairspray and an eyeshadow with MAC written on the lid, then he carried them through and left them on top of Gemma's untidy clothes pile.

Later that morning, Benedict sat in his showroom and replayed the image of Lawrence and Estelle on the balcony over and over in his mind. He didn't feel like talking to anyone.

'Tell me what happened last night.' Gemma stuck her head around his door. 'Did Estelle invite you in?'

'No,' Benedict said. He studied the anniversary necklace. It was now half the length it should be.

'So, what happened? Did you wear the costume?'

'Yes.' He thought about the stupid hat and mask. How had he let Gemma and Cecil talk him into it? He felt like a total idiot now. But, he supposed, at least Estelle had laughed at him, which was preferable to the stony silences and stilted conversations they'd had over the last few weeks.

'And did it work? Was she surprised or amazed? Did she like the flowers?'

Benedict decided not to tell Gemma about the Jack Russell ruining the bouquet. 'It's not like we can fall back into each other's arms. Things are more complicated than that.'

'Why are they?' Gemma frowned. 'It's like when my

mom left my dad. He should have followed her and tried to get her back, instead of letting her go. Then none of this would have happened...'

Benedict heard frustration rising in her voice. 'None of what?' he asked, but she turned away from him.

'I don't want to talk about it.'

Benedict gave Gemma some space. He stayed in his workshop and made some links for the anniversary necklace. After half an hour of silence, he felt a bit fidgety and wondered what she was doing. 'I'd love a cup of tea,' he shouted.

'I don't know how to make one,' she called back.

'You don't? It's a British institution.'

Gemma appeared at his door. 'That's a place you lock people up.'

'You can't come to England and not know how to brew up.'

'Brew up?'

'Yes.' He stood, flicked on the kettle on the windowsill, and explained to Gemma that she should always put the teabag into the cup first and never the water, which had to be boiling. 'Stir the teabag until the tea looks nice and strong. The bag must stay in for at least three minutes. Then top it up with three glugs of milk,' he said. 'You're looking for a rich caramel colour. And, if you're ever making tea for me, I take it with three sugars.'

'That will rot your teeth.'

'It hasn't done yet.'

'There's still time.'

'Tea should be taken, where possible,' Benedict continued, 'with a digestive biscuit. You can dip the biscuit in and hold it for four seconds. That way, it's nice and soggy, but bits don't fall off in your drink.'

'I'll stick with water, thanks. Or juice.'

'You'll be missing out.'

Gemma raised a bushy eyebrow. 'So are you going to tell me about Estelle and the balcony?'

'No. Are you going to tell me more about your parents?'

She sighed heavily. 'There's nothing to say. You're prying again.' Lord Puss weaved around her ankles in a figure of eight. His purr revved like a Porsche engine. 'Good kitty.' She reached down to scratch him behind the ears.

The cat stood up on his two back legs and head butted her hand, then he jumped up onto the counter and trampled around on his purple cushion to find the perfect position. He tossed his head and glared at Benedict as if to say, *See,* someone *recognises my superiority.*

Benedict reached out to scratch the cat behind his ears but Lord Puss recoiled. He lifted his leg and proceeded to lick his nether regions, whilst holding Benedict's gaze.

'He can sense that you don't like him,' Gemma said. 'Cats are very sensitive.'

'It's not that I don't like him. It's just that he *hates* me,' Benedict said, aware of how childish he sounded. 'I let him live here, feed him nice food and clear up after him. I even made him a kitty den.'

'But you're giving off negative energy. Communication isn't always about words.'

Estelle had said something similar to this before she moved out, but Benedict hadn't understood. If communication wasn't about words, what was it about?

He thought it would be great if women came with an instruction manual or journal, so he could read and understand what Estelle meant by things. Then he would know what he needed to do to attract her home. He could turn to the page on *disillusionment* and know what to carry out to prevent it. Another page might give him tips on *satisfaction* or *communication*. Then he could have communicated his feelings up to Estelle on the balcony. 'I do my best,' he said.

'Hmmm.' Gemma reached into her pocket and took out a small browny-gold polished stone. 'Tiger's Eye.' She showed it to Benedict and placed it under Lord Puss's cushion. 'It stops animals from thinking they're the boss.'

'Great. Let's hope it works on him.'

Gemma walked around the display cabinets, trailing a wavy line with her finger across the glass. 'You have some nice things, though your test pieces are more exciting.'

'Why would you want to be excited by jewellery?'

'Because it says something to you. It makes you feel passionate, or surprised.'

The only inanimate thing that spoke to Benedict was food. In fact, he could smell Bake My Day from here. *Why not pop in and buy one of us*, he imagined a croissant saying to him. *We're all so flaky and buttery.*

'I make jewellery because I need to earn a living, because

my mother showed me how to do it and it was the only thing I could do when she died.' He could feel a touch of grumpiness setting in through lack of carbohydrates. 'Passion and surprise don't come into it.'

Gemma gave a deep sigh and her eyebrows twitched. She took Joseph's journal out of her bag. 'So, I'll read through this, and make some notes. I'll wait for customers to come into the shop.'

'Good. And I'll be in my workshop,' Benedict said. 'Working on my non-exciting jewellery.'

Benedict slumped at his desk and made sure that all his tools were nice and straight. The peace and quiet felt good.

Something rustled in his pocket and he took out the crumpled photograph of him, Charlie and Amelia. A memory emerged of him telling them a joke. It was something about an escaped gorilla. Amelia had laughed until tears ran down her face and it was the first time Benedict had seen his brother ruffled. Charlie's cheeks had flushed red. 'I'll leave you two jokers to it,' he said as he stormed out of the room. Amelia and Benedict stared at each other and dissolved into even more laughter until Amelia got the hiccups.

Benedict swallowed then reached out and regretfully touched his brother's mop of hair in the photo. 'I'll look after Gemma until you get in touch,' he said. 'But *please* hurry up.'

He opened a drawer and his heart leaped as his fingers wrapped around a half-eaten Mars bar. *Congratulations, you found me*, it said. It was a bit squashed, but with each bite and swallow Benedict felt calmer, and the stress of having to deal with his niece drifted away.

After he'd finished the chocolate, he took the anniversary necklace from the drawer and picked up a length of gold wire. He concentrated hard so he wouldn't think of Estelle and Lawrence, and of his own clumsy attempt at romance. He lost himself in the roundness and perfection of each link and hardly rejected any.

At midday Gemma knocked and poked her head around his door. 'No one has called in,' she said. '*Nobody*.'

Benedict lowered the necklace. 'Some days, the shop is quieter than others. In fact, most days. Here, take some money and buy us lunch.'

Gemma accepted a ten-pound note and reappeared just ten minutes later. She set some loose change down on the counter and handed him a bag. 'I don't know what the grass thing is.'

Benedict looked inside and took out a clear plastic carton. It contained lettuce, tomato, cucumber, red pepper, cress and a splodge of mayonnaise. There was a sprinkling of orange cheese across the top. 'It's cress. Is this for me?'

'Yes. Nice and healthy.'

Benedict stared at it. 'I need proper food. I'm a big bloke.' He patted his stomach and looked inside the bag again. There was a bottle of water, and no cake. Gemma sat on the edge of his workbench and he pointed his finger and flicked it to tell her to move away from his straight lines of tools.

She tutted and picked up a piece of cucumber, held it,

then gnawed around the edge like a squirrel nibbling at a nut. 'You want Estelle back, right?'

Benedict poked his finger into a slice of tomato. The yellow pips oozed out over his nail. 'Is this part of WEB?' he asked, suspiciously.

'I think you should try to shape up. We should go for a walk, up on the moors. That can be part of the operation.'

'Estelle likes me the way I am. I like me the way I am. Okay?' He bit into a slice of red pepper then screwed up his nose. He put it back in the box.

When Gemma finished her lunch and went back into the showroom, Benedict stuffed his half-eaten salad into the wastepaper basket then searched through his pockets, drawers and cupboards. Hunger seemed to run through his every vein and he needed something sugary.

In his drawer, under a wodge of sticky notes, he found an old humbug. He peeled the sticky cellophane off the brown-and-cream sweet and sucked on it gratefully.

When it reached mid-afternoon, Benedict's blood sugar levels had dropped, making him feel irritated and drowsy. He told Gemma not to disturb him in the workshop, where he started to ruin link after link for the anniversary necklace. None were good enough and he wondered when his quest for perfectionism had started. Maybe when his parents died and he tried to make everything right for Charlie growing up. Before then, he didn't recall striving so hard for everything to be in order. His current self-discipline seemed to be only for tangible objects and never for himself.

The electronic beeper sounded when the shop door

opened, and he looked through the gap in the showroom door to see Margarita Ganza come inside.

Even though she had moved from Italy to Noon Sun when she was eight years old, Margarita still had a soft Italian accent and, whenever she saw him, she said, '*Ciao*, Benedeect.'

Really, he should forget about his carbohydrate deficit and plaster a smile on his face. He should, at least, say hello to Margarita, even if he felt sluggish. But then he pressed his hands to his gurgling stomach. Gemma was handling this. She wanted to serve customers, so he should let her. Even so, he stood and sidled over to the showroom door to keep a secret eye on his niece.

Benedict used to hear Margarita singing Italian love songs as she placed fresh daffodils, roses and peonies into brightly coloured buckets outside Floribunda. '*Ore d'amore*,' she sang as she happily inhaled the scent of her flowers and waved to him.

But he hadn't heard her voice for a while now. The buckets that used to burst with blooms now housed a few straggly flowers. Floribunda sometimes didn't open until late morning, and anyone wanting flowers either did without, or travelled over to the garden centre in Applethorpe instead.

Benedict saw that, under Margarita's stained white Floribunda apron, she wore a turquoise silk dress nipped in at the waist. Her long, black curly hair had a singular wide streak of silver, which was the only clue that she had just turned thirty-five. Benedict thought that she looked more like a ballerina than a florist.

With her dark, exotic looks, Margarita attracted a lot of male attention in Noon Sun, but she had been dating fellow Italian Tony for almost a year.

Benedict thought that Gemma might greet their customer with a teenage grunt, but instead she said a lively, 'Hi there.'

'*Ciao*,' Margarita said, as she twirled a finger, nervously, through her hair.

The door opened again and Benedict saw Tony come into the shop. He was tanned and dressed all in black, but wore a white tie. He had a shaved head and a large diamond stud sparkled in his left ear. His shoulders were hunched with his hands shoved in his pockets. He was probably at least five years younger than Margarita.

'Hmmm,' Margarita said as her turquoise heels tapped around the floor. 'Hmmm.' She looked in each cabinet in turn.

'What about this?' Tony asked. He moved over to a tall cabinet and tapped loudly on the glass.

'It is lovely, but too plain.' Margarita brushed her black locks from her shoulder and clipped around the shop once more. 'I want something special, that I will love forever. But I'm not sure there's anything here.'

'Perhaps you're looking for something, like, more magical?' Gemma offered.

Benedict closed his eyes. Oh, God, Gemma. *Something magical*. This was a jewellery shop, not a fairy kingdom. He didn't sell jewel-encrusted magic wands.

'Yes. Yes, I am,' Margarita said. 'I want something

different. Unique. Maybe, as you say, even magical. Is Benedeect around?'

'He's busy working. I'm his niece, Gemma.'

'*Ciao*. So pleased to meet you. I am Margarita, and this is my fiancé, Tony. We're looking for an engagement ring.'

'For you? Congratulations. My uncle makes all the stuff in the shop and it's kinda traditional. But he can make anything you like.'

'Yes?' Margarita didn't sound convinced.

'Sure. Take a look at these.'

Peeping through the gap in the door, Benedict saw Gemma take a ball of tissues out of her bag and set it on the counter. His mouth fell open as he realised that she'd brought his test pieces into the shop. For a moment, he thought about storming through. His old jewellery had been for Gemma's eyes only.

But then Margarita spoke. 'These are so beautiful,' she said. 'I love this clam shell.'

'Me too. And there's a blossom brooch.'

'A flower? It's very gorgeous.'

As Margarita admired his pieces, Benedict lifted his chin a little. He hadn't heard praise for his work in such a long time. Even his commission pieces usually only garnered a smile and a thanks. Margarita's voice was full of warmth and…surprise.

'I've been to a few jewellery shops already but I haven't found anything. We were at a party and Tony twisted a piece of metal, from a can, into a ring. He gave it to me, so I am wearing that for now.' She presented the back of her hand to Gemma.

Tony smirked and looked at his watch.

Benedict leaned the side of his head against the door-frame. Margarita was too glamorous to be wearing a metal ring. She wanted passion and surprise in her jewellery, just as Gemma said customers wanted. His niece was right.

'Hmmm,' Gemma said. 'I think I have a special idea for you.'

'You do?' Margarita said.

You do? Benedict thought to himself in the workshop. He didn't think that the ball of tissues contained anything that would work as an engagement ring, and he didn't make and stockpile rings because of the multitude of different sizes needed to fit people's fingers. He did have a couple of gold bands set with solitaire diamonds on display; however he had a strong feeling that wasn't what Gemma had in mind.

'Uh-huh,' his niece said. 'We could copy your metal-twist ring, but make it in platinum. It would be, like, the same shape and style as the original, but in a precious metal.'

'Your uncle Benedeect, he could make this?'

'Yes. He's totally talented.'

Benedict almost laughed out loud. Talented! But then his eyes grew a little glassy. Feeling embarrassed, he blinked them hard and wished that Estelle was here to overhear the comment, to show that there were positive things about him.

Margarita didn't speak for a few moments. 'That is such a great idea.'

'We could set a small gemstone in the middle of the twist. It will look lovely.'

'I like it,' Margarita said. 'What do you think, Tony?'

He gave a small grunt. 'I dunno.'

'Let me get some gemstones to show you.' Gemma flung open the door to the workshop. It was too quick for Benedict to move out of the way and the door banged against his shoulder.

'Gemstones?' she buzzed as if she'd overloaded on caffeine. 'Where do you keep them?'

'I don't have any in the shop.'

'Right.' Gemma cast her eye around the workshop once more to make sure. She took the white cotton gemstone bag from her jacket pocket. 'I can use these though, right?' Without waiting for an answer, she flitted back into the shop. This time she left the door to the workshop open wider so that Benedict could see Margarita and Tony more clearly.

Gemma shook out the gemstones and they rattled onto the glass counter.

Margarita picked one of them up. 'I love this pale blue stone,' she said.

'It's an Aquamarine.'

'It's very pretty, the colour of my favourite flower, sea holly. I'm going to have them in my wedding bouquet.'

'Are you going to arrange your own flowers?'

'We'll hire a professional to do it,' Tony said. 'We want them to be perfect.'

'But, I am a trained florist,' Margarita said in a quiet voice.

115

'Your shop is more of a hobby. It doesn't make any money.'

'It is because I need to get to the flower market in York earlier. By the time I arrive, the best blooms are all gone.'

'You disturb me when you get up early.'

Margarita looked at Gemma. 'Tony works in a nightclub. He gets home late, but for my shop I need to rise early…'

'Why are we even discussing this?' Tony asked. 'We're here to find a ring. Engagement rings are gold with a diamond.'

'We don't have to follow tradition.'

'The ring I gave you was just a bit of fun. I didn't think you'd still be wearing that crappy bit of metal on your finger.'

'Oh.' Margarita looked down at the back of her hand. Her face fell. 'I didn't know you felt like that, and I really like Gemma's suggestion. Though, I suppose I like diamonds too. So, you think we should go for something more traditional?' She lifted her eyes, seeking out his approval.

'Sure. A simple band and a solitaire diamond.'

'Well, okay,' Margarita said. 'If you think so…'

Gemma let her breath out in a hiss. 'The Aquamarine suits you better.'

Tony fixed her with a glare. 'We want a diamond.'

'The Aquamarine is right. And Margarita wants platinum.'

In the workshop, Benedict felt the tendons tighten in his neck. *Gemma, you can't tell customers that they're wrong*, he thought. He'd obviously made a big mistake in letting her serve on her own and he should have interrupted sooner. He wanted to step into the showroom and take over, but didn't want to show her up.

An awkward silence followed.

'We can think about it,' Tony said curtly. 'No need to decide now.' He took hold of Margarita's hand and pulled her towards the front door. As she left, she looked over her shoulder and gave a small, quick smile to Gemma.

When the door closed behind them, Benedict entered the showroom. 'Why are you telling customers what's right and what's not?' he asked. 'You should just try to sell them a ring from the display cabinets.'

Gemma shook her head. 'I read about Aquamarine in Grandpa Joseph's journal this morning. Here.' She turned the journal so Benedict could see it. 'It's a good stone for Margarita.'

AQUAMARINE

A light blue gemstone, with good sources in Pakistan and Brazil. Its colour is determined by impurities of iron, meaning that the gem can range in hue from almost colourless to a deep ocean-blue-green. Aquamarine can clear blocked communication and helps you to express your ideas and imagination. It can give you courage to make dynamic changes. In ancient times, sailors regarded it as a lucky stone.

He read the description twice. 'But, they're just words in a book. It doesn't mean they're true.'

Gemma shrugged. 'Margarita will come back to the shop when she realises…'

'When she realises what?'

'That Tony is the wrong man for her, and to order her Aquamarine ring.'

'They're never going to come back into the shop again. And, how do you know he's not the right man for her?'

'The way he looks at her and speaks to her.' Gemma folded her arms. 'Did you know that the word "diamond" comes from the Greek *adamas*, meaning unbreakable, and *diaphanous*, meaning transparent, Uncle Ben? A diamond signifies honour and pure intention. I don't think Tony has that.'

'But, they were here to buy jewellery, not for you to interfere in their lives.' Benedict felt his cheeks growing redder, from having to defend what was right, in his own shop.

'You should read the journal some more.'

'It's not a bible. If any more customers come in, please try to sell them something we already have in stock. I have some nice triangular silver brooches that we need to shift.'

'I can't do that.' Her fierce expression was the same as when she hurled the bag of gemstones at him. 'Not if it's wrong. You asked me to help you out, and I am doing that.'

'It's my shop, and you're not exactly helping.' He regretted the words as soon as he said them. They were harsher than he meant them to be. 'What I mean is…'

But Gemma slammed the gemstone journal shut with a bang. She snatched it up and held it tightly to her chest. Blue veins popped up on her temples like gnarled twigs. 'Well, *you* obviously don't think I'm helping. So, I'll leave you to look after your own shop, huh?' She marched around the counter and towards the front door. After reaching out and tugging it open, a chilly blast wound around their ankles.

Benedict helplessly put out an arm to stop her. She didn't have a coat on, or have keys to the house. 'Where are you going?'

'What do *you* care?' Gemma wiped her nose with the back of her hand. She stood defiantly, holding the journal as if clasping a shield to her chest to protect her. 'You're just happy in your boring shop, shutting yourself away and not listening to anyone. You didn't even do the Romeo thing, I bet.' She lifted her nose in the air. 'I'm not surprised your wife left you.'

'Hey.' Benedict raised his voice at her sharp words. 'That's a horrible thing to say.'

'Well.' Gemma tossed her head and looked away from him, though she didn't make a move to leave.

On the counter, Lord Puss lifted his head, as if enjoying the drama.

Benedict stood for a moment. His head throbbed and there was a pain behind his right eye. The days of quiet, with only him and Cecil in the shop, seemed so long ago.

Gemma was right in that he didn't like change, and he supposed he didn't listen to other people much, but she couldn't go around trying to rule and change people's lives. Her words about Estelle leaving were cruel. He knew he was stuck in a bit of a rut. He couldn't deny that.

'Maybe,' he said finally.

Gemma stared out into the street, her hands balled into fists. 'Maybe what?' she asked, as if she didn't care.

'Maybe it's *not* a surprise she left me.'

When Gemma finally spoke, her voice was fragile. 'I shouldn't have said that.' She sniffed. 'But I *know* that you want *me* to leave.'

A car passed by and Benedict couldn't quite make out her words. 'I want you to, what…?'

Gemma span back and a tear trickled down her cheek. 'I said that I know you don't want me here. No one does.'

Benedict walked towards her. 'Who doesn't?'

'Anybody.'

'Are you crying?'

'No.' She rubbed her face with her sleeve.

The first thought in Benedict's mind was that it *would* be better if she wasn't here. Even though his life wasn't perfect, it was steady. But he supposed that was before Estelle left him. That's the life he really wanted back, not the one he'd been enduring for the last six weeks. So even if Gemma irritated him, provoked and challenged him, she was the only person who had come up with any ideas for how he could get Estelle back.

He tried to pin words down as they rampaged in his head, wanting to keep them simple. 'I want you to stay,' he muttered.

'Why?'

Benedict tried to think of some reasons, but there weren't

that many. 'So I can tell you about my Romeo episode. Okay?' he said.

Gemma scratched her nose. 'You said that you weren't going to tell me.'

He stepped towards her, feeling hurt prickle inside him as he again thought about his wife and Lawrence. 'It was a disaster, but I gave it a go.'

He told Gemma how he stood behind the bush and watched his wife and the gallery owner on the balcony. Gemma's lips twitched into the faintest smile as he explained how he threw stones up at the balcony, and about the dog peeing on the flowers. 'I wanted to do it. I wanted to be bloody Romeo, but I ended up telling her about you instead.'

Gemma pushed her hair over one ear. 'So, she knows about me? And that I'm staying with you?'

'Yes,' he sighed. 'Look, Gemma. I heard you talking to Margarita and you have more ideas than I could ever have. So, even if I don't always agree with you, I want you to stay. For as long as you need to, and so long as that's all right with Charlie. I just want you to try to be…less forceful, okay?'

She blinked at him as she considered this. 'I can try.'

'Right then.'

She let the door close and came back inside.

'Would you like a cup of tea?' he asked.

'Do English people think tea solves all their problems?'

He thought about this for a while. 'It makes things seem better.'

'Then I'd like a cup, please. We're going to make a great team,' she said. 'You know that, right?'

'I'm sure we will,' Benedict mumbled, as he made his way to the workshop to switch on the kettle.

'And I think we have another WEB operation,' Gemma called out to him.

Benedict stopped with his hand mid-air. He suddenly felt very cold. 'What's that?' he asked.

She walked over and jutted her head around the workshop door. 'You're going to introduce me to your wife, right?'

10. Lapis Lazuli

truth, relationships, enlightenment

Benedict allowed Gemma to bring all of his jewellery test pieces into the shop, in case she wanted to show them to customers. Some were only half-completed experiments but others, he had to admit, were not bad at all. There was a simple gold ring set with a Carnelian and a silver choker necklace with drops of lilac glass beads. Base metal daisy-shaped stud earrings had a centre of green and gold resin, and a filigree brooch was so delicate its swirls looked like handwriting. He grudgingly decided that he could let his quest for perfection slide a little but he insisted on storing the pieces under the counter, rather than put them on display.

Because they didn't have any customers, Gemma read out loud to him from the gemstone journal, though Benedict noticed that she moved it away from him if he got too close. She seemed to have assumed ownership of the journal and didn't allow him to look at it unless she was there to vet him. She turned some pages quickly and steered the conversation away when he asked about certain gemstones.

Even so, he learned that the ancient Greeks believed that Coral was formed from the severed head of Medusa, and that Jade changes colour, often to shades of brown, when buried with the dead. He knew that Jasper was one of the most popular stones for making seals and amulets, and that Mark Antony was reputed to own a Red Jasper seal ring with which he stamped his letters to Cleopatra.

Gemma brought a clear glass vase from the house into the shop and Benedict watched her take it from her bag, set it on the counter and give it a quick dust with her sleeve. She picked up a small cardboard box full of the gemstones they had uncovered in the chest, and shook them out. One by one she studied them, polished them with a cloth and checked if Joseph had noted anything about them in his journal. If the gemstone featured, then she dropped it into the vase, and soon there was an inch-deep layer of them, sparking like the most delicious sweets. For those gemstones not featured in the journal, or if Gemma didn't know what type of gem they were, she created a small pile on the counter, next to the phone.

Benedict delved his hand into the gemstone jar and swirled his fingers inside it. He felt fidgety today. Yet again, Charlie hadn't been in touch, and it was playing on his mind.

Surely if Charlie hadn't heard from his daughter for a few days, he'd try to contact Benedict? Even if Charlie didn't have his phone number, Benedict lived in the same house and worked in the same shop, so he was easy to trace.

'You're kind of annoying me,' Gemma said. 'Have you eaten enough breakfast?'

'No, and I haven't heard from your dad, either.' Benedict removed his hand, then bent down to take his laptop out from under the counter. He flipped it open and switched it on. 'Maybe you could show me your farm. We can try to find a phone number for your dad, too.'

Gemma closed one eye. 'Why do you want to see the farm?'

'Because I'm interested in where you live.'

'I can just tell you about it. I'm good at describing things.'

'Let's take a look together.' He tapped a button to try to hurry the laptop into action. 'What's the name of your farm again? Sunny something?'

Gemma's angled eyebrows danced a little higher up her forehead. 'Yeah, Sunnyside.'

Benedict flexed his fingers above the keyboard, but he noticed how Gemma held her breath as he typed in the words. 'Why aren't you breathing?' he asked.

'I am.' She blew out.

A list of searches appeared and Benedict scrolled down them, but he couldn't find any farms in north Maine called Sunnyside. He clicked on the images. 'Come closer and take a look,' he said to Gemma, who loitered a few steps back.

She hesitated then joined him.

Benedict scanned the photos. There was one of an orange

truck that stood out against the greens and golds of the other images. There was a logo on the side and he thought that he could make out the word *Stone* in pixelated letters. He squinted and moved his head closer. 'Is this…?' he started to ask.

'When can I meet Estelle?' Gemma interrupted. 'Where shall we go to?'

'I've not thought about it,' Benedict said, not moving his eyes away from the laptop. 'I'm looking at this.'

'Perhaps York,' Gemma said. 'It has those really old black-and-white buildings, right?'

'I'm trying to find…'

The screen suddenly went black.

Benedict hit a few keys but nothing happened. He blew through his teeth.

'What's going on?'

'The bloody internet connection is down again. The hills surrounding the village stop the signal from working.' He tapped again. 'It happens a lot.'

Gemma didn't say anything.

Finally, Benedict slapped his hand down. 'Damn it. We'll have to search some other time.'

'Ah, well,' Gemma said, as she traced a circle on the countertop with her finger. 'Never mind.'

The noise Lord Puss made sounded like someone being strangled. His mewling went on for most of the morning. 'What's wrong with him?' Benedict asked Gemma.

She stroked the top of the cat's head. 'I think he's missing

Cecil and he's trying to let us know. Can you take him with you to the hospital the next time you visit?'

Benedict pictured himself with the white fur ball tucked under his jacket, his lemon-yellow eyes terrifying everyone on the ward. 'You can't take pets in,' he said.

'Why not?'

Benedict was about to explain that hospitals had to be kept clean and sterile when he glimpsed Estelle through the window. He hurried across the showroom and watched through the window as she darted into Deserted Dogs.

Gemma slid alongside him. 'Why haven't you answered me?'

'Estelle.' He nodded. 'She's gone into the shop opposite.'

'Hey. I can go over and say hi.'

'No,' Benedict said.

'Why not?'

'Because I want to introduce you, properly.'

'Okay then.' She shrugged. 'Let's do it.'

'I didn't mean *now*.'

'Why not?'

Benedict rubbed his neck. Perhaps it was best to just get this out of the way. 'I don't know.' He moved over to the door and opened it.

After a few minutes, Estelle came back outside. She fastened her purse and put it inside her bag.

'Estelle,' he shouted out and beckoned her over.

She crossed the road. 'Benedict?' she asked coolly, but followed him inside the shop.

He cleared his throat and lifted an arm out to his side

as if he was a circus ringmaster presenting an acrobat. 'I thought that you might like to meet Gemma. Gemma, this is Estelle.'

Gemma stood up straight and karate-chopped out her hand. 'Hello,' she said. 'It's so very nice to meet you.'

'You too.' Estelle smiled. After Gemma had pumped her hand up and down a few times, she reached into her handbag. 'I'm sorry that Benedict didn't introduce us the last time I came into the shop. It must have been uncomfortable for you.'

'It was.'

They both flicked an accusing glance at Benedict.

'I was going to drop by anyway,' Estelle said. 'I have a few things for you, Gemma. There's some toiletries and make-up, and a couple of scarves too. In case you need them. How long are you staying in England for?'

'I don't know,' Gemma said.

Benedict's lips stiffened.

'Oh,' Estelle said. 'Benedict said that you were here for a week or two…'

'I've lost my passport.'

Estelle frowned. 'He didn't tell me…'

'Gemma's purse was stolen at the airport,' Benedict interjected. 'Her phone and passport were inside. We've both reported them missing but nothing has been handed in yet.'

'That's bad luck,' Estelle said. 'Have you contacted the network provider to stop calls being made on your number, Gemma?'

Benedict looked at his niece.

'No,' she said.

'Have you reported your missing passport to the passport office?'

'No,' Gemma murmured.

Benedict shook his head, feeling foolish for not thinking of these simple steps himself. 'We need to put a stop on your phone number,' he said to Gemma.

She gave a small shrug. 'It's probably okay.'

'Someone might spend a fortune making calls on your phone,' Estelle warned.

'Use the shop phone to ring the passport office,' Benedict said.

Gemma didn't move. 'I'll, um, do it later. Would you like a cup of tea, Estelle? I'm learning how to make it.' Without waiting for a response, she rushed into the workshop and closed the door.

'Not for me, thanks. I have to dash off,' Estelle called after her.

Benedict shook his head. 'I don't think she heard you.'

Estelle looked at her watch. 'I'm fine to stay for a couple more minutes, but I'm heading over to Purple Heather to finalise the plans for my exhibition.'

When Gemma re-emerged she carried two steaming drinks, and she wore a proud smile.

Benedict peered into the cups. 'You forgot to add milk.'

'Oh, yeah.' She vanished again. When she returned, she handed a cup each to Benedict and Estelle. The hot liquid inside was a murky brown, like damp wood.

Benedict tried not to wince as he took a sip. There was no sugar in his.

'This is lovely, Gemma.' Estelle raised the cup to her lips. 'But I'm afraid I have to leave now for an appointment.'

'Oh.' Gemma looked down. She kicked the toe of her boot against the base of the counter.

'I'd really like to meet you again, when we have more time.'

'Yeah?' Gemma blinked through her hair. 'Promise?'

'Of course.' Estelle took the toiletries out of her bag and put them on the counter, one by one. 'Just let me know if you need anything else.' She winked.

Gemma's eyes grew wider as she saw the shiny, coloured packaging. She reached out and caught a tube of mascara as it rolled off the edge of the counter. 'Thanks, Aunt Estelle.'

Benedict repeated the words in his head. *Aunt Estelle.* They sounded so strange. But they suited his wife too. They were so full of possibility, adding another dimension to his family. If he and Estelle couldn't be parents, then perhaps they could be an auntie and uncle together. The thought brought a small smile to his lips.

After his wife had left the shop, Benedict poured the cups of tea into the sink.

'Don't you like it?' Gemma raised an angled, bushy eyebrow.

'Yes, but I'm not very thirsty,' he said, to save her feelings. 'Now, we really should make those phone calls, as Estelle suggested.'

Gemma stared at him for a long time and Benedict

couldn't tell what she was thinking. Then she screwed her eyes shut and yelled, 'Oww.' She thrust her head down and her long russet hair fell over her face. Clutching her head with both hands, she cradled her skull. 'Aargh.'

Benedict reached out to take her arm. 'What is it? What's wrong?'

'A migraine,' she said through clenched teeth. 'It hurts really bad.'

Benedict recalled when the IVF drugs gave Estelle bad headaches. She used to lie in a darkened room with the duvet over her head and couldn't bear any sound or light. He used to tiptoe around, or hold her hand, until she felt better. 'Are you okay? Come and sit down,' he soothed and led Gemma through to his workshop. 'Take my chair.'

Gemma slumped down and pressed her cheek against the workbench. She shielded her eyes with a hand.

Benedict crouched down beside her. 'Are you okay? Can I get you anything?'

Gemma shook her head slightly. Her hair obscured her face. 'Just leave me alone,' she whispered. 'I'll be okay.'

Benedict tentatively stood up. He stared at the back of her head. 'Are you sure?'

She nodded again and gave a brave whimper. 'I think so.'

Benedict stood and watched Gemma for a while, to make sure that she was okay. When she fell asleep on his workbench he consigned himself to the showroom. He looked at the phone and thought about making the calls that Estelle suggested, but he didn't have enough details about Gemma's mobile or passport. It was probably best to leave it for today.

He sat behind the counter and wondered what to do. Margarita walked past the window and gave him a wave. She clutched a bunch of spiky blue flowers to her chest and he noticed that she was no longer wearing the metal twist ring, but neither had she called in to order her Aquamarine one. He reached out to stroke Lord Puss, but the cat hissed at him, jumped off the counter and swanked into the workshop to sit with Gemma instead.

Benedict gazed around the showroom and noticed that the walls were looking greyer than usual. There were black speckles of damp in one corner. There was no colour or energy about the room when Gemma and Cecil weren't in it.

The gemstone journal lay open on the counter and, although he knew Gemma didn't like him to look at it without her, he pulled it towards him. Gemma had drawn a pencil star next to one of the gemstones on the page and Benedict read his father's words.

LAPIS LAZULI
This stone was prized highly by the pharaohs of ancient Egypt, whose craftspeople used it to make treasures such as amulets and decorative scarab beetles. It is thought to increase mental clarity and intuition. Lapis is actually a rock rather than a crystal. It can give courage, and calms the nervous system. It helps you to adhere to your principles and rise above pettiness.

Below this, he saw that a passage of words had been added and, from the notebook in Estelle's studio, he recognised it as Gemma's looping handwriting. He wondered what else she might have discovered about Lapis and, without thinking more about it, Benedict read her words:

Lapis can bring contentment and a strong sense of family loyalty. It's supposed to help you to express your emotions. But who to? No one even wants me. Joseph Stone says that Lapis is a rock, not a crystal. I think it kind of looks like the Earth, when you stare down at it from space - blue and patches of yellow. I sometimes wish I could be up there, in the sky, so I can look down on everything but not be part of it. I thought that coming here would allow me to clear my head, but everything just feels more cloudy. Lapis is also supposed to help you to trust more... Yeah right. That's the last thing I'm going to do...

Benedict felt a prickly ball of guilt form in his stomach, like he had swallowed a horse chestnut. Gemma's words echoed the ones she'd growled at him when she threatened to walk out of the shop. '*I know you don't want me here. No one does.*'

But she had fired those words at him on impulse, hadn't she?

He frowned and his fingers twitched as he closed the journal and moved it across the counter.

He walked over to the workshop door – Gemma looked so serene as she slept. Her hair had fallen from her face so he could see her bushy eyebrows and her sticky-out ears. One of her boots lay on its side and she had curved her bare foot around on top of it.

It looked as if she didn't have a care in the world. But her own words told him otherwise.

11. Blue Jack

new beginnings, determination, change

Benedict stood in the doorway of the workshop until Gemma woke up. He felt like he was a soldier in a fairy tale, guarding a sleeping princess. His niece's eyelids were pale pink and her cheeks were ashen.

He wriggled his fingers, fidgeting as he thought about reading her words in the journal. He felt sensitive and exposed, as if the sun had burned off the top layer of his skin. He was tempted to leaf through the journal again to see if she had written anything else, but then he'd feel like he was spying. She might have been feeling vulnerable when she wrote her words.

He often took a quick peek at Charlie's schoolbooks, especially his English ones, to see what stories he'd invented. In an attempt at amateur psychology, Benedict tried to gauge, from Charlie's schoolwork, how his little brother was really feeling. He felt sure that their parents' death would adversely affect him in some way, whether that was his relationships with women, or resulting in deep-rooted insecurity. But he only found teenage scrawlings about what Charlie had done on Christmas Day, or his diary of the summer holidays. He wanted to fly to Australia and capture a koala bear to keep as a pet. His teachers said that Charlie had a vivid imagination, so that might help him to escape real life in his head.

Benedict was more practical. He couldn't afford to dream, or allow his imagination to run wild. He had to be strong, steadfast and provide routine. Benedict didn't think about his own needs when he cared for Charlie, only about keeping his brother safe and well looked after.

And, in his mind, when the two brothers grew older, they would both marry women from the village and have children. They'd all live close together and the two families would mingle happily. The Stone family would flourish again in Noon Sun. He'd never imagined the mess that might ensue.

As he watched Gemma, Benedict also felt guilty about another thought that crept into his mind. He tried to banish it, but it kept on coming back, like mould on a freshly painted wall. Had his niece feigned her headache to avoid chasing up the whereabouts of her passport and phone? Was he a bad uncle for thinking such a thing?

Gemma sighed, opened one eye and batted a stray lock of hair that had fallen across her nose. She wrinkled her brow as she saw Benedict standing there. 'What are you doing?' She raised her head slowly. 'What time is it?'

Benedict glanced at his watch. 'Almost four in the

afternoon. You've been asleep for a couple of hours. How is your head?'

She reached up and dug her fingers into her hair. 'A little better.'

'You still look a bit pale.'

'Hmmm. I feel kinda wobbly.' She looked around her and spied an unopened bottle of water at the back of Benedict's workbench. 'Can I drink that?'

'Yes.'

She yawned and unscrewed the top off the bottle. 'I need to get some fresh air.'

'That's okay. I'll lock up the shop early. We can walk home along the canal.'

She shook her head. 'I want to go farther than that.'

Benedict racked his brains for somewhere else to walk close by. 'How about the high street, then the canal?' he suggested.

Gemma took a big gulp of water. 'No. You need to get fitter for WEB. We talked about going for a walk on the moors, so let's go up there.'

Even the thought of climbing the hill, up to the moors, made Benedict's calves ache. 'You've been poorly,' he said. 'We should get you home.'

Gemma threw the bottle in the bin and pulled on her stray boot. 'I've decided,' she said. 'I need to be outside.'

'But, it's almost teatime,' Benedict tried weakly, knowing that his argument stood no chance.

'We agreed that part of WEB is for you to get fitter,' Gemma said firmly. 'No trying to get out of it.'

'I'm not trying to,' Benedict said, even though he was.

'Good.' Gemma glanced out of the window. 'It looks like it might rain. I'm going to need a coat with a hood.'

Benedict took Estelle's old purple anorak out of the store cupboard and handed it to Gemma, to wear. It had a slight tear to the sleeve so had been relegated as emergency-wear. 'Do you need to put some tights on? Your legs are bare.'

'Pantyhose? Nope, I'm fine like this.' Gemma flapped her arms like a penguin, the tips of her fingers peeping out from the bottom of the sleeves.

They left the shop and bought ham sandwiches from Bake My Day, then walked down the high street to the car park. A small pyramid of wood was taking shape on the expanse of tarmac, for Bonfire Night. The admission fee for the bonfire would help to raise funds for the community centre roof.

Benedict and Gemma walked past the bonfire stack to the foot of the biggest hill that overlooked Noon Sun.

'We should get you home,' Benedict tried again. 'I've got some paracetamol back at the house.'

'I don't take pills,' she said, looking up at the dome of patchy grass. 'Quit fussing. I'm okay.'

They started to hike up the hill. Gemma didn't zip up her coat, and she crossed her arms to hold it fastened. Her hood kept blowing off and her hair danced in the air like ticker tape. Benedict walked a few steps behind her, taking the walk slow and steady in his burgundy loafers. The ground was concrete-hard underfoot. The grass, flattened by the wind, had faded to a desert-yellow.

When they reached halfway up, Benedict felt a stabbing pain in his sides. He clutched them and stood, panting and looking up at Dinosaur Ridge, still at least a fifteen minutes' climb away. 'I think that's all I can do today,' he gasped.

'No way, Uncle Ben.' Gemma poked him in the side. 'Rest a minute and keep moving.'

'I really don't think I…'

But Gemma had already set back off without him. 'You're as slow as a snail,' she called over her shoulder.

Benedict looked back longingly at Noon Sun Village. The high street was the shape of a crooked arm, with the dilapidated community centre like a red boil on its elbow.

A cloud drifted over the setting sun, and banded shadows swept across the moorland, reminding him of Lawrence Donnington's bloody striped T-shirt. And Benedict told himself that he had to do this. No matter how ridiculous WEB was, it seemed like his only hope. He couldn't let Estelle fall into the slimy gallery owner's arms. Benedict flipped up his hood and began to march after Gemma. 'Hold on,' he shouted out. 'Wait for me.'

When they got a little closer to the ridge, Benedict pointed it out to Gemma. 'You have to lean your head to the side to see the rocks. They're supposed to form the shape of a stegosaurus.'

They both cocked their heads ninety degrees clockwise.

'I can see his scales,' Gemma said.

'We'll climb up to there. And then we'll go home.'

Gemma sighed at him and reached down to readjust her boot.

By the time they reached the top of the ridge, the sun was sinking fast. It sparkled fluorescent white behind the hill, and Benedict imagined Estelle up here, on her own, with her sketchbook, lost in her thoughts. Did she think about him, as she walked, or did she plan her future without him?

He read once that you should have a plan for when your kids leave home to avoid empty-nest syndrome. It was something that he and Estelle had never discussed – what they'd do if they definitely couldn't have children, and how they would live. He'd always assumed that she was content with their life as it was, but when she started to paint, he realised that she needed something else.

After a day in his shop, Benedict was happy to laze around and watch TV, or go for a beer at the Pig and Whistle. He hadn't considered if that was enough for Estelle, and now he knew that it wasn't. Just as his wife had found something that she was passionate about, he needed to find it too. But he didn't know what that was.

'I'm standing on the dinosaur's head.' Gemma hopped around and broke his thoughts. She lifted one leg in the air and, as her boot waggled on her ankle, Benedict couldn't help but smile.

They sat on the stegosaurus scales and rested their chins on their fists. The street lamps in the village twinkled below them, gold, orange and red, like underwater sea creatures. The clouds overhead were inky grey and the sky was turning deep mauve.

Benedict cast a sideways glance at his niece. They were up here alone without any distractions. There was no Lord

Puss to interrupt, no customers and no journal. It felt like a good time to try to talk to her.

'You don't say much about where you live…' he said.

'No.' Gemma picked up a small stone and threw it down the hillside, where it bounced down the rocks. 'There's not much to say.'

'Is your farm in the middle of nowhere, or are there shops and houses around it?'

Gemma shrugged. 'I suppose it's on its own.'

'With fields around it?'

'Yeah.'

Benedict felt like he was getting nowhere.

'When I think of the farm, I always think of yellow,' she said.

'Yellow?' he asked, surprised by her word. 'Like the colour? Like Citrine?'

'Yeah, like Citrine Quartz. The hay is yellow, and the sun is yellow, and there are yellow chicks. We have horses and cattle and there's always something going on, and Dad is always whistling. When my grandparents died, he took over running the farm.'

'So you have no grandparents left?' Benedict realised.

'No.' She stared off into the distance. 'All I've got is my dad, and my mom when I see her. And you and Aunt Estelle. That's why it's special that I'm here.'

Benedict opened his mouth to speak but couldn't think of what to say.

'There's this one horse.' Gemma threaded a piece of hair into her mouth. 'He's as white as an Opal, but real feisty.

Whenever Dad tried to saddle him, he kicked hard. I don't know what it was, but that horse liked me and let me get close. It's kind of easier with animals than it is with people, huh? They just like you, or they don't.'

Benedict thought of how Lord Puss hated him. 'Do you miss him?'

'Duh, how can I miss a *horse*? It's not like he could come with me.'

'I meant your dad.' Benedict tutted. He remembered the initials Gemma had penned in the notebook – *DJ*. He wanted to know more about her words on Lapis Lazuli and who she didn't trust. 'Do you have a boyfriend back home?'

'I did. Kinda.' She picked up a triangular-shaped stone and began to scrape marks onto the rock she was sitting on.

'What was his name?' Benedict waited until he realised that she wasn't going to answer and he asked something else instead. 'What about school?'

'What about it? I finished last quarter.'

'Did you like it?'

'No way. It sucked, though I guess I miss my friends. We used to hang out a lot, before…'

'Before what?'

'Nothing. I feel like I'm on some kind of quiz show.'

He tried again. 'So what do you want to do when you grow up?' The question sounded like something he'd ask Charlie, when his brother was five years old. 'A fireman,' Charlie used to say. 'I want to be a policeman, or a stuntman.' He never said that he wanted to be a farmer.

'I *am* grown up.'

'I mean, when you get older. Do you want to study more? Get a job?'

'Now you sound like Dad,' she said sharply. 'You ask too many things. I mean, it's not like I have choices.'

Benedict frowned. He picked up a stone, at first thinking it was a piece of Blue Jack. When he saw it wasn't, he threw it down the hill. 'You're only sixteen. You have lots of options.'

'Hmmm,' Gemma said.

Benedict felt like he was interrogating her, so he didn't ask anything else. They listened to the wind howling around the dinosaur scales.

'I like rock music too,' she volunteered, after a while.

Benedict didn't want to embarrass himself by saying *cool* or *coolio*, as Cecil might do. He didn't listen to music that much, unless he and Estelle went over to Applethorpe to watch a band, and they'd not done that for a long time. Estelle listened to the radio when she painted, but that was with the door closed.

'There's a few bands I like,' Gemma continued. 'The 678s, Orange Jackets, Restore the Hope…'

Benedict sat up a little taller. 'I've heard of Restore the Hope.'

'You have?' Gemma squinted with disbelief.

'I think they're playing a gig over in Applethorpe.'

'When?'

'I'm not sure of the dates.'

Gemma grew quiet. 'How far away is that?'

'Around ten miles from Noon Sun. Not too far.'

'I'd really like to go,' she said.

What would Charlie say, Benedict thought, if his daughter asked him if she could go to a gig? He'd probably be really liberal and say *yes*. If he didn't mind Gemma travelling to the UK on her own, then he'd certainly agree to her going over to Applethorpe.

But was Benedict in a position to grant such permission? Was it the norm for sixteen-year-olds to go to concerts? He couldn't ever remember Charlie going to one. He could hear in Gemma's voice how much she wanted to go, but he wasn't her father. If he had a daughter then he'd insist on taking her there and waiting outside the venue, like an embarrassing but loving dad.

'I could perhaps take you...' he started.

'*You?*' Horror flashed across her face.

'Well, I could wait outside for you.'

'Hmmm.'

'We can ask your dad when he gets in touch.'

He waited for her to say something else, but nothing came.

The wind blasted their hoods up over their heads and they looked at each other, laughed and pulled them back off again. 'Are you warm enough?' Benedict asked.

'Uh-huh.' Gemma stood up. She lifted her arms out to the sides and tilted her chin up towards the sky. Then she began to turn. She twirled slowly at first then grew faster and faster. Round and round she went, the purple coat flying around her like a cape.

Watching her spin, the shape of her Stone family chin,

her legacy of red hair, made Benedict's gut wrench. It could be his and Estelle's child up here, dancing in the wind.

He had always been able to picture himself and Estelle as elderly, with crooked backs and hair the colour of snow. He could imagine the laughter in their house on Christmas Day as their grown-up kids arrived. There would be opening presents, and cheeks growing too red from the fire and perhaps even grandkids sitting on his knee.

And the thing was, Estelle could still have that. She was a little younger than Benedict. It might not be too late for her. If he let her go, didn't persuade her to come back, she might find love and happiness and be able to have children with someone else.

He hated that idea. What if he bumped into her in five years' time and Benedict hadn't moved on? He still lived in the same house, ran the same shop, made the same jewellery, and time hadn't changed anything for him, except he didn't have Estelle. And she could be living with a new man, in a new house, with a child, and be immersed in making outfits for school plays and baking cakes.

Perhaps it was kinder to let her go.

He knitted his hand into his hair and tugged at the roots.

He looked over at Gemma and she was so unselfconscious, lost in the moment, laughing as she twisted. She was unaware of anything else. Benedict wondered when he had last felt that free. He'd always been a big brother to Charlie, then his guardian. He was a shopkeeper and a husband. As an adult, life was all about planning and responsibility and thinking things through. Of being careful and of wanting things you couldn't have.

He felt envious of Gemma's ability to not care, to jump on a plane if she wanted to, to spin around on the top of a hill at dusk. When did *he* ever do something on the spur of the moment? He'd spent all his life focusing on something in the future, trying to attain it – a child, getting his wife back and for the shop to perform better. He never thought about anything in the here and now, and enjoyed what he had at this exact moment in time. When he was with Estelle, they'd lost the art of just being together and relishing their friendship, love, jokes and togetherness. They both longed for something to make their lives complete when what they had was pretty perfect. To him, anyway.

More than anything Benedict had forgotten how to be spontaneous.

'Come on, Uncle Ben. Join in,' Gemma called out.

'No, I…'

'*Come on*. No one's watching.'

Benedict rose slowly to his feet and stood for a moment. Then he slowly lifted his arms out to the sides. He looked over at Gemma, who was still a whirl of purple. Oh, why not? he thought, and he began to turn too, gradually at first then picking up speed. It felt strange to be doing this, a grown man, dancing on top of a hill. What would the villagers say if they saw him? They'd think he'd gone mad. But he banished thoughts and questions from his mind as he turned even faster. The greenery surrounding him became a blur. His head grew light and the wind whistled in his ears. He was a whirling dervish, a spinning top, a bloody big dancer. He almost lost his footing but still he turned, until he was dizzy and felt a bit sick.

His feet stumbled, taking him in a wavy line, and he laughed as he used his hands to feel for a rock. When he plonked down, his head lolled and his eyes watered. Looking over at Gemma, he saw that she had flopped down too. His vision made it look like she was still moving even though she was still. They looked at each other and laughed.

Benedict tilted his face towards the inky sky. He closed his eyes and waited for the swirling feeling in his brain to subside. He felt the rock beneath him with his cold fingertips, to anchor him back to reality, before he shouted over to Gemma. 'I'll tell you about Blue Jack stone.'

'Yeah?' She stood and staggered closer to him.

'They used to mine it in the nineteenth century, but supplies ran low. No one is allowed to dig for it any longer. It's a blue and violet stone and used to be popular in Victorian jewellery. The old quarry is still there, but it's not used now. It's about half a mile down from the ridge.'

'Can we go there?'

Benedict looked at his watch. 'It will be dark soon. We should head back.'

'We agreed that you need exercise.'

'I didn't sign a contract with you, and I've done enough,' he said firmly. 'We have to walk all the way back home yet.'

He didn't expect her to agree so readily but she nodded her head. 'We can come another time, right?'

'Yes.' He walked towards her, studying the ground as

he went. 'If you look closely, you can still find bits of Blue Jack.' He crouched down and picked up a chip of stone. He wiped it with his thumb and held it out. 'Here.'

Gemma took it from him. She held it up to the darkening sky. 'It's translucent.'

'It's supposed to look like the sky when the sun goes down.'

'Like now?'

Benedict looked, and the stone was, indeed, the same colour as the sky.

'And what does it mean?'

Benedict laughed. 'I knew you were going to ask me that. I don't think anyone will have attributed a meaning to it. It's not in your grandfather's journal. You can be the first.'

'That would be a real honour, right?'

Benedict had meant it as a bit of a joke, but he saw from the determined line of her mouth that she was serious. And he thought to himself, why not? Why shouldn't Gemma be the one to give it characteristics? 'What do you think it should mean?' he asked.

'Hmmm. Do you have a pen and paper?'

Benedict tucked his hand into his pocket. 'I have a pencil and a receipt.'

Gemma took them from him and turned over the receipt, resting it on her knee, to write on the blank side. She poised with the pencil then began to scribble. When she finished, she turned it to show Benedict. He read:

BLUE JACK

A gemstone with indigo and violet striations, which can only be found in the hills surrounding Noon Sun Village, Yorkshire, UK. Mined in the nineteenth century, it is now in short supply. It means new beginnings, determination and change.

'They sound like good properties to me.' Benedict handed it back to her.

'I'll write this up in the journal. Will you tell me more about Blue Jack?'

'I'll tell you as much as I know,' Benedict said, as the sun finally slipped behind the silhouette of the dinosaur's head and the sky grew dark. 'Come on, let's head home.'

12. Carnelian

vitality, motivation, energising

That weekend, Benedict had a strange feeling, one that he had never experienced before. He found that he wanted to clean. He was fed up of the crumpled shopping bags on every surface of the kitchen, and the pile of pots on the draining board that didn't go down no matter how many times he washed up. He'd had enough of wallowing in his own mess.

As he tugged the vacuum cleaner out of the pantry, he wondered if this was what pregnant women experienced, when they felt the need to tidy the 'nest' ready for their new arrival. Except he didn't have anyone new arriving, he hoped that someone would be coming back.

He unravelled the power cable and plugged the cleaner into the socket. After pushing it into the front room, he switched it on and its motor roared into action. He pushed it back and forth, and around the sofa, banging it against the skirting boards.

'Your dad's not been in touch yet,' he shouted to Gemma,

who lay on the sofa. She said that she had a bit of a headache again but refused to take anything for it.

'I can't hear you over that noise.'

'*What?*'

Gemma stood up, stepped over and flicked off the switch on the cleaner. It juddered to a halt. 'I can't hear you over that noise.'

'Sorry.' Benedict crooked his elbow and leaned against it. 'I'm getting worried. We've not heard anything from Charlie.'

'He knows where I am, Uncle Ben. Stop worrying. I'm here, safe and sound. My dad does things his own way, in his own time. I'm sure you'll hear from him soon.'

Benedict never really believed those people who reckoned they could sense things, like they were going to have an accident or the weather might be about to turn, but this time he felt that something wasn't right. Yet he didn't mention this to his niece. 'How is your head?' he asked.

'Okay, until you switched the vacuum on.'

'Sorry.' Benedict wound the cord back around the cleaner and returned it to the pantry. 'I just want to speak to your dad, that's all.'

'You've got nothing to worry about.' Gemma stretched her arms up and yawned. 'You're trying harder with Estelle?'

'Yes.'

'And you're trying to be healthier?'

'I suppose.'

'And I've learned to make English tea?'

Benedict didn't answer that one.

'So, all is good, then?'

'Yes, all is good.' Benedict cleared his throat.

'So, what is there to worry about?' Gemma asked.

'Nothing,' Benedict said, trying not to think about Gemma's journal entry for Lapis Lazuli.

After tidying the house all day, Benedict felt stir crazy and needed to get out. He also wanted to eat something that wasn't colourful, round and healthy. He asked Gemma if she wanted to go out for tea and at first she screwed up her nose. But then she reconsidered and swung her legs off the sofa. 'Maybe Estelle will be there,' she said brightly.

When Benedict pushed open the door to the Pig and Whistle, he was greeted by the familiar smell of stale beer, musty carpet and vinegar. On the walls hung a wonky array of photos of Noon Sun from the nineteenth century. The village didn't look much different than it did today. Benedict led Gemma over to a seat at a small, circular, dark-wooden table with two-pence pieces glued to the top in a kind of mosaic. Benedict heaved it out further, so he could fit behind it.

Gemma read the menu. 'There's not much nutritious stuff on here,' she said.

'Nicholas Ledbetter, the chef, used to work for a top restaurant in London,' Benedict explained. 'He moved back to Noon Sun, to take over the Pig and Whistle when it became too much work for his parents to run. Everyone was really excited about what food he'd introduce. But he's not done anything. It's all still standard pub grub, like sausage and mash, and fish and chips. I think his younger twin brothers, Alexander and Alistair, are a bit of a handful too.'

Gemma looked over at Nicholas who was slumped against the bar. 'He looks totally bored.'

'He's supposed to have once conjured up roast figs with gorgonzola ice cream for Brad Pitt. It's a comedown, working here.'

Gemma glanced at the menu again. 'I suppose I'll have the cheese and onion pie,' she said.

Benedict watched as Josie the barmaid bent over and slipped off an orange-wedged sandal. She rubbed her foot with one hand as she slowly loaded the dishwasher with the other, picking up one glass at a time from the bar. Her cropped hair was bleached white, she sported a gold ring through her eyebrow and had a small heart tattooed on her neck. She didn't notice Benedict and Gemma waiting to be served.

In the kitchen, Alexander and Alistair Ledbetter batted each other across the head with pot towels. They both looked exactly alike, with black hair gelled into spikes like frozen grass.

Nicholas raised himself out of his slump. The frown lines on his forehead were like a concertina and his blond hair stuck up in tufts, greasy from standing over the chip fryer. 'Josie,' he snapped, 'don't play with your feet in front of the customers.'

Josie slipped her sandal back on. Her dishwasher-stacking grew even slower and she stuck out her tongue behind his back.

'What can I get you?' Nicholas shouted over.

'Two orange juices, please,' Benedict said. 'And can we order some food?'

'Can do.' Nicholas shrugged, as if he didn't care whether they did or not.

'Two cheese and onion pies,' Benedict said. 'Unless you have any specials on the menu tonight?'

'They *are* the special.' Nicholas poured orange juice into two glasses and set them on the bar. 'Ice?' he barked at Gemma.

'Uh-huh.'

Benedict cleared his throat. If Gemma was staying for a while, then he should get used to introducing her. 'This is my niece, Gemma. She's helping me out in the shop.'

'All right, love.' Nicholas jerked his head. 'Nineteen pounds fifty, mate.'

Benedict handed over a twenty-pound note.

'I hope that Benedict here isn't working you too hard, love,' Nicholas said, as he slapped down the change.

'I kinda like it.'

'You do, eh? Ha ha,' he said sarcastically. 'You'll soon grow out of it.'

'It's cool if you like what you do.'

'Hmmm.' Nicholas readjusted a beer tap. He thought for a moment. 'I don't think that I do like it. Noon Sun isn't the most inspiring place to live and work.'

Gemma tutted. 'Well, why don't you do something about that?'

'You've got a feisty one here.' Nicholas nodded at Benedict, ignoring her challenge.

'You can speak to me, you know. I have ears and a mouth.' Gemma rummaged in her pocket and took out the white drawstring bag.

Benedict threw her a stare. He didn't know that she was carrying it with her.

But Gemma didn't see him. She rummaged around inside the bag and placed a red stone, firmly, on the bar. 'This is for you.'

Nicholas eyed it with mistrust. 'For me? What is it?'

'It's a Carnelian. It's good for motivation and ambition. It can help you to find a new path in life.'

Nicholas gave a hearty laugh. He threw his head back so you could see four grey metal fillings in his teeth. 'Motivation and ambition, eh? I think you may be giving this pretty red stone to the wrong person, love. I'm not into all that airy-fairy stuff.'

'Put it in your pocket and see,' Gemma said. 'You might come to think it will look nice set in a ring.' She held his gaze.

Nicholas stared back at her. He tilted his head slightly to one side. 'You really remind me of someone…'

'Yeah?'

Nicholas's neck suddenly jerked, as if he was in a crash in a dodgem car. He shook his head, trying to unleash a memory. 'There was this head chef I worked for once, years ago. I burned a red wine jus and he yelled at me, in front of everyone. Your eyes remind me of his...a teal colour. And your stare is the same. He called me a bloody imbecile. I still dream about him.'

'Nothing to do with me.' Gemma shrugged.

Nicholas laughed nervously. 'Anyway. Whatever,' he said. 'Who cares. As if a bloody stone will fix anything.'

But he still pushed it into his trouser pocket anyway.

Gemma and Benedict had just finished eating their pies when Ryan and Nigel ambled into the pub. Nigel's eyes were pinned firmly on Josie and he didn't watch where he was going. His thigh connected with Benedict and Gemma's table, jolting it. Gemma's orange juice sloshed over the top of her glass and splashed her denim jacket.

'Sorry,' Nigel said, his eyes still on the barmaid as he and Ryan sat down. 'I'll ask at the bar for a cloth.'

'It's okay,' Gemma sighed.

'Bring it to the launderette tomorrow,' Ryan offered. 'I've got a new washing powder that smells of freesias and lime.'

'Thanks.'

Benedict introduced Gemma to his friends and they didn't mention their first strange sighting of her, on the banks of the canal. 'So, you're from America?' Nigel asked with wonder in his voice.

'Uh-huh.'

'Guns N' Roses are from Los Angeles. Are you from near there?'

'No. From the East Coast.'

'That's cool.' Nigel stood up and the zips on his biker's jacket jingled. 'I'll get us some drinks.'

In order to strike up conversation with Josie, Nigel worked his way through packet after packet of pork scratchings, crisps and peanuts. His chat never went further than, 'Are those a new flavour of crisp?' or 'I can't decide between salt and vinegar, or ready salted.' Josie would smile, serve him and then move on to the next customer without realising that Nigel was in love with her.

Ryan sat down, his floral aroma enveloping Benedict and Gemma. 'I'm still sleeping in the spare room,' he confided. 'The kids think my inflatable mattress is a great bouncy castle. Each morning they run in and jump on me. Diane stands in the doorway and watches as they bounce up and down, laughing their little heads off. She laughs too, and it's just me, on my crappy mattress, who's crying inside.'

Gemma gave a slow shrug and Benedict mouthed, 'Sorry,' to her.

'I found out that Diane's made an appointment to see Reggie Ramsbottom. That old crash-helmet head only smiles when he's dealing with divorces,' Ryan said glumly.

Benedict knew of the solicitor's ruthless reputation. Since his wife left him for the plumber who installed their new bathroom, Reggie homed in on other people's misery like a heat-seeking missile. 'What are you going to do about it?'

Ryan shrugged. 'She says I need to treat her like a woman more. She says she wants a hunter, like a caveman or something. For me to be more demonstrative. What can I do though? I own a launderette.'

'Have you tried flowers?'

'Yeah. And I bought a silver bangle from you, remember? She liked it but said her friend and cousin had one exactly the same.'

'They have good taste.'

'Yeah, but what should I do, Benedict?'

Benedict swallowed. He felt like the last person who could give advice on affairs of the heart. He was a few years older than his friends and they sometimes thought him wiser than he was. If he knew a way to get Ryan's marriage back on track, then he'd use it on Estelle.

'Maybe you should commission a pendant,' Gemma suggested.

'Hmmm.' Ryan stared at her. 'That's a nice idea.'

Nigel returned from the bar. He set down three pints of lager, an orange juice and a bag of onion bhaji and coriander flavoured crisps. 'I didn't fancy them,' he said, nodding at the vivid orange packet. 'I wanted to show Josie that I'm open-minded.'

'Did you ask her on a date?' Ryan asked.

'No. I can't do.'

'Of course you can,' Ryan said. 'It will put you out of your misery. You'll know one way or the other.'

'I can't,' Nigel said. He glanced at Gemma then decided to overshare anyway. 'Josie is my fantasy woman, and if I ask her out, it will become real world. If we go to the cinema then she'll want to watch something lovey-dovey with Jennifer Aniston in it, and I'll want to watch Liam Neeson knock the shit out of bad guys. I'll have to keep quiet about my love for Guns N' Roses, because she's probably into Justin Bieber. I bet she has a boyfriend named Mason who has sleeve tattoos and is into mixed-martial arts. He drives a red BMW and takes her to expensive restaurants.'

'Don't keep torturing yourself,' Benedict said. 'She might not want to go anywhere fancy.'

As he said this, he couldn't remember the last time he had taken Estelle out anywhere other than Crags and Cakes, or the Pig and Whistle. He wondered where Lawrence might take her. Probably somewhere with live jazz and starters that cost more than ten pounds.

At the start of their marriage, he and Estelle had tried to impress each other. They took ages to find nice restaurants and dressed up for a night out. But they soon relaxed into a comfortable tempo of being together.

The danger of being cosy was that complacency could set in. A romantic dinner for two could easily change into a quick bowl of pasta balanced on your knee in front of the TV. Just as a favourite comfy cushion could suddenly become too soft and careworn, a marriage could too. Benedict supposed that's what happened with him and Estelle. The familiarity and softness of their being together had left her wanting something new.

For him, that new thing would be a child. A son or daughter would give their marriage a new focus and meaning. Instead of being husband and wife, they would be a mum and dad. They would be together, raising another person. They'd go shopping for brightly coloured plastic toys and install a sandpit next to the gem tree.

But what new hopes and dreams could he find when his existing ones were becoming redundant? Could he simply conjure up new ones and forget that the original ones existed? Wasn't the whole premise of dreams that they gave you something to wish for, and try to achieve? And if you no longer tried to attain them then did you simply give up?

As he thought, again, of his wife with Lawrence on the balcony, a lump formed in Benedict's throat. He picked up his pint and gulped it down.

'For our first date, I took Diane to McDonald's,' Ryan said. 'It was nice.'

'And that's probably why you're sleeping on a blow-up bed in your spare room.' Nigel sighed. 'I don't have the confidence to ask Josie out. She can find someone better-looking and with more money than me. So if I just admire her from a distance then I'm not going to be disappointed.'

Ryan nodded. 'Middle-aged man has a tricky place in society these days. Everyone takes teenage spots and moods for granted. We accept that old people can start to lose their minds and topple over. People know that women can get a bit hot and bothered when they hit the menopause. Except, no one is sympathetic to the plight of the thirty- and forty-something bloke. When us men have done our duty, getting married and having kids, we can get lost in the wilderness. What's our use any longer?'

Gemma shuffled in her seat.

Ryan carried on regardless. 'Women have their friends and family, and facials, and clothes shopping, and make-up.

Middle-aged men have, what? We have ear hair, baldness and football.'

'And Guns N' Roses,' Nigel chipped in.

Ryan ignored him. 'I think about what will happen to the kids if Diane and I don't patch things up. I won't get to read stories to them at night and tuck them in bed. I want to put milk and cookies out for Santa on Christmas Eve, and be there when they open their presents in the morning. It kills me to think of us splitting up. Diane's an attractive woman and could easily get a new man. Then I'll be obsolete, like Arnold Schwarzenegger in the last *Terminator* film.'

'What do you mean?' Nigel asked.

'In the first *Terminator* film,' Ryan explained, 'Arnie comes back from the future, and he's like this shiny, unstoppable ruthless killing machine. He's got these red shiny eyes that mean business. That was like me when I met Diane. I knew what I wanted – marriage, a wife and kids. Then, one day, you wake up and you've achieved all that, and you're ready for the next stage in your life, but you have no idea what the hell that is. You feel…lost. In the last *Terminator* film, Sarah Connor even calls Arnie "Pops". He's got old and technology has moved on. He might insist that he's not obsolete, but he's not bloody far off.'

Nigel lowered his pint. 'I've never watched any of the *Terminator* films,' he said.

'Me neither,' Benedict admitted.

The three men looked into their drink glasses.

'Well, thanks for killing that conversation,' Ryan said. He

turned to Benedict, his eyes pleading. 'It's Diane's birthday next week and I want to get her something special to show that I love her. I need my family. Maybe this pendant, as Gemma suggested...'

'Pink gemstones are good for this kinda thing.' Gemma nodded.

'I'm willing to give anything a go.'

Benedict knew that Diane was a stylish woman, all walnut-shiny bob, pencil skirts and crisp white blouses, with a taste for oversized designer handbags. A simple statement necklace, which looked unique and expensive, would look great on her. 'Perhaps a pendant set with a singular stone?' he proposed.

Gemma took out her gemstone bag and selected a smooth translucent petal-pink stone, the quarter size of a postage stamp. 'This is Kunzite.'

'It's said to be a symbol for romance and marriage,' Benedict added, surprised that he was able to recall what Gemma had told him about the stone.

'You remembered, Uncle Ben.' Gemma patted him on the back.

'Make me something for Diane,' Ryan pleaded. 'Help to make her love me again...'

When they left the pub, Gemma exhaled noisily. 'I am never getting married. Ever,' she said to Benedict. 'Are your friends always like that?'

'Mostly. Noon Sun is the kind of place that lulls you into a relaxed way of life. You can slip into a sort of coma and then wake up when you're eighty years old and realise that you haven't done anything with your life. You only come around when something happens and shakes you out of it. But by then it can be too late.'

'It's not too late for you and Estelle, though, huh?' Gemma asked.

Benedict didn't know if it was or wasn't. All he knew was that he didn't want to end up in the same melancholic state as Ryan. Gemma and Estelle were his family and he had to try to make it work. The thought of Gemma returning to America and things slipping back to exactly as they were, before she arrived, made him feel twitchy.

'Hopefully not,' he said, as they turned off the high street and headed towards home. 'And this time you don't have to nag me about WEB. I know I have to do something.'

'So, what's that?'

Benedict took a deep breath. 'I'm going to call Estelle…'

'Yeah?'

'I want to invite her out for lunch, the three of us.'

'Cool.'

'It will be our first outing together, as a family.'

13. Blue Lace Agate

sensitivity, understanding, nurturing

'Estelle said yes,' Benedict told Gemma as they stood in the kitchen together, making toast for supper. He felt like his internal organs were having a party. 'It's amazing.'

'I'd say yes if someone invited me out for a free lunch.' Gemma smiled. 'She must really want to meet me.'

'She has a meeting with an art gallery in York tomorrow, and suggested that we meet her afterwards at 11 a.m. We could go somewhere first, before we eat. It was great timing that I called her.'

'You have me to thank for that.' Gemma nodded.

'It was both of us. A team effort for WEB.'

'Will Cecil be out of hospital, to look after the shop?'

'No. He's stuck in there for a while longer. There's complications, so he won't be back on his feet for a while. I'll shut up the shop for the day. I've only got Ryan's commission for the pendant in the appointment book.'

'Okay,' Gemma said. She drummed her fingers lightly

on the kitchen table. 'So, can I choose where we go, with Estelle?'

Usually such a suggestion would make Benedict feel nervous, a plan that he hadn't made himself, especially coming from Gemma, with her teenage view of romance and relationships. However, York was a lovely city, so whether she chose a walk around the city walls, a trip to see the majestic Minster, or a browse around the shops in The Shambles, it was all good.

'Okay,' he said. 'We'll do whatever you think best. Pick somewhere nice.'

Even the sight of Reggie Ramsbottom's crash-helmet of white hair coming through the door couldn't dampen Benedict's spirits. As the brusque solicitor swept around the showroom in his grey cashmere, knee-length coat, Benedict knew that Gemma wouldn't be able to handle this customer on her own.

He scribbled a note and passed it to her. *I'll deal with this one. Solicitor. Divorced. Difficult.*

Gemma's bushy eyebrows arched. *I think I can handle it,* she wrote back.

After briskly surveying the display cabinets, Reggie took out his wallet. 'I'll take the oval gold earrings, third cabinet from the door, second shelf down,' he barked and pulled out a wodge of ten-pound notes. 'Can you gift-wrap them, pronto?'

Gemma frowned as she opened the cabinet door. 'Who are they for?'

'For my daughter Laura's birthday, so make the wrapping, er, feminine.'

'How old is she?'

The solicitor sighed dramatically and lowered his money. 'She's eighteen. Now, please hurry up. I have a job to go to.'

'I have a job too.' Gemma folded her arms. 'To find the right gift for *your* daughter.'

Reggie glared at her insolence and slowly raised his left eyebrow.

Benedict knew about the *Ramsbottom Raise*. Lifting one eyebrow, slowly and challengingly, was a gesture that Reggie was known for in legal circles, and it struck fear into the heart of many a young lawyer opposing him in court.

Benedict had always found Reggie to be curmudgeonly; however, since his wife and daughter moved out three years ago, the solicitor wore a permanent scowl. He strode around Noon Sun with his eyes fixed to the pavement so that he didn't have to make eye contact with anyone. He reserved his words for those who paid for his time.

'If I select something and pay for it then it is by default the right gift,' Reggie said.

Gemma shook her head. 'You need something younger and prettier for an eighteen-year-old.'

'*Younger?*' Reggie's intimidating raised eyebrow remained in action, but then it slowly crept back down. He looked at the earrings again and grunted. 'I suppose they are rather plain. What do you suggest?'

'My uncle Ben can design something for you.'

'I'd prefer to buy off the shelf. I don't have time for design.'

'But you want something special for Laura, huh?'

Reggie considered this. He glanced around the shop again and pushed up the sleeve of his coat to reveal a white-haired wrist and a gold Rolex. 'You have ten minutes.'

Gemma rolled her eyes. She tucked her russet hair behind her ears so they stuck out. 'What things does your daughter like?'

Reggie opened his mouth to say something but nothing came out. He shook his head and tried again. It was as if Gemma had asked him the most baffling legal question in the world. 'Er, I don't actually know what amuses her these days. I don't see her so often.' His shoulders slumped a little. 'Is it completely necessary to know such things?'

'Um, yeah,' Gemma said. 'How can Uncle Ben create something special if he doesn't know the details?'

Reggie hesitated then flipped open his wallet and proffered a photograph of Laura. She had long, straight, auburn hair with a blunt fringe that skimmed her Sapphire-blue eyes.

'She's real pretty,' Gemma said.

'Rose gold would look stunning with her hair,' Benedict added.

'What makes her different? What makes her laugh?' Gemma asked.

Reggie blinked slowly. 'I…I'd need to ruminate on the answer.' He waved his wallet. 'Look, I just want to procure a piece of nice jewellery…'

Benedict noticed that beads of sweat had begun to form on his brow, as if the solicitor found it physically painful to discuss his true feelings. 'What else can you tell us about her?' he prompted.

Reggie cleared his throat. 'She's around five feet six inches tall, and I'd describe her as *sporty*. She hopes to be a novelist one day, though I told her that's not a real profession and that practising law is a far more suitable career option. I'm afraid that we had a disagreement over this, and regretfully...' He trailed off his words and looked down at the floor. 'We haven't spoken for a while. So the present is...'

'Very important?' Benedict asked.

'Yes. Undoubtedly. You know, Benedict, I handle divorces all the time in my profession. I keep a box of tissues on my desk because people break down in front of me.' He shrugged one shoulder. 'And I used to look down my nose at them. I thought they were weak...that is, until Susan took Laura...'

'Sorry,' Benedict said. He wanted to reach out and pat the solicitor on his arm but felt sure that he'd jerk away. 'It must be tough.'

Reggie gave the slightest nod of his head, which Gemma didn't seem to notice.

'But, you must know what kind of things she likes,' she insisted. 'Even *my* dad knows that stuff. It's your job to know.'

Benedict flashed her a warning glance. He could hear the emotion in Reggie's voice and saw that his knuckles were white, gripping on to his wallet. It was ironic how Gemma was ordering Reggie to be more open, when getting any information from her was like mining for Black Opals.

'My relationship with Susan is less than amicable, so our communication is…lacking.' He took a deep breath then rapped on the counter. 'Now, enough is enough. My time is money. I want to buy some bloody earrings.'

'You should try harder,' Gemma said gruffly. 'Then you and Laura could be friends.'

'What gem would work best?' Benedict asked her hurriedly, to stop her from riling their customer.

Gemma blew into her hair and walked over to the counter. She pulled the journal towards her, flicked through the pages and stopped at the 'B' section. 'Blue Lace Agate is good for families.' She turned the journal so Reggie could read the description.

BLUE LACE AGATE

Agate can be many colours but Blue Lace Agate's bands of violet-blues, white and greys give the impression of the gentleness of a calm, cloudy sky. The gem can bring peace, understanding and contentment and gently soothes emotions. Blue Lace Agate is a protective and encouraging stone and is particularly good for children and families. It can help you to de-stress and keeps family members from arguing. Writers can use the stone to help them to develop inspired ideas. It's an excellent stone for starting afresh.

'It could help Laura with her writing,' Gemma said. She found a sample of the gem in the glass jar and passed it to Reggie.

'Laura is going to study law, not creative writing,' Reggie growled. He examined the stone. 'She likes the colour blue, though.'

'So, we're getting somewhere,' Gemma said. 'Long, rose gold earrings, set with Blue Lace Agate.'

Reggie nodded. He stared for a while at his manicured fingernails then rubbed his fingertips together. 'Before you make them,' he muttered, 'I want to make sure that you both understand...'

'Understand?' Benedict asked.

Reggie coughed. He held his fist to his mouth to cover it. When he spoke, his words were quiet and muffled. 'I may not tell her, but Laura is, um, the best thing in my life.'

Gemma froze, as if a stranger had just grabbed her ankle. Her lips puckered into a small circle. 'You should tell her,' she whispered. 'Instead of saying it to us. Look at what a mess you've created.'

'Me?' Reggie performed the *Ramsbottom Raise*.

Gemma thrust her face away from him. 'Can I sit at your bench, Uncle Ben?'

'Is there something wrong?'

She held her breath, her ribcage expanding. 'No,' she said in a small voice. Then she sped away and slammed the workshop door behind her, so hard that the gems rattled in the jar.

Reggie and Benedict glanced awkwardly at each other.

'Young people, tsk. They can be so unpredictable,' Reggie said.

'I'm discovering that for myself.' Benedict stared at the closed door.

He decided the best option was to leave his niece alone, to give her time out and so he could sort out Reggie's commission.

'I trust you know what you're doing with these earrings,' Reggie said. 'And you know their importance. Will Laura know the significance of this gemstone?'

Benedict considered this. 'No, but I'll write down its meaning for her.'

Reggie looked at his watch. 'You took eleven minutes. Not bad,' he said.

'Thanks.'

Reggie took a long time to fasten the top button on his coat. Before he opened the door, he paused on the doormat. 'If you ever experience marriage difficulties,' he said, 'you'll find that Ramsbottom Solicitors offers a wide range of services. We don't offer tea and sympathy, but we do have the most efficient divorce provision in Yorkshire.'

'Thank you,' Benedict said. 'Though I hope I won't need it.'

'You can't be too sure. It happened to me.'

Benedict promised himself there and then that he would try to brush up on his own communication skills. 'Thanks for your offer,' he said.

After he watched Reggie return to his practice, Benedict went into the workshop. Gemma sat in his chair, swivelling to and fro, as she picked up and examined each of his tools in turn. This would usually make Benedict's throat restrict, but he noticed that her eyes were pink and swollen so he didn't tell her to leave them alone. 'What's wrong?' he asked gently.

'Nothing.'

'I can tell there is.'

Gemma shrugged her shoulders. The corners of her mouth turned down and she suddenly looked younger than she was. 'Don't know.'

'Did Reggie say something to upset you?'

'No.'

'Then, have I done something?'

'No…it's not that.'

She spun the chair around so she had her back to him. Her knees were pressed together and her ankles splayed. She picked up a pair of pliers from the bench and toyed with them.

Benedict shuffled towards her, thinking that she looked like a little girl who had lost her favourite doll. 'Are you sure?'

She hung her head for a while. Her hair straggled over her face as she ran her fingers over the pliers. She tested the sharpness of their jaws, closing and opening them using the spring-loaded handles. When she eventually spoke, her voice was quiet and trembled a little.

'That man said that his daughter was the best thing in his life. He's the most awkward person I've ever met and he can say something like that. Yet my dad's *never* said anything like that about me.' She jabbed a finger at her own chest. 'I wish he felt that way about *me*.'

Benedict paused for a moment before he reached out and placed his hand on the back of the chair. 'Of course your dad cares about you.'

She gave a suck in of breath, and then noisily let it go. 'Then why am I here? Why am I sitting here in your shop, and he has no idea where I am?'

'He does know where you are,' Benedict said softly. 'And he knows that I'll keep you safe, just as I looked after him, when he was younger.'

Gemma left the pliers on her lap. She took a lock of her hair and ran it through her lips. She was quiet for a while, and Benedict stood, motionless, waiting for her to reply. 'I guess,' she said finally.

'Look.' Benedict sat on his bench. 'If your dad hasn't told you how he feels, then it's not because he doesn't feel it. He might not know *how* to tell you. I find it difficult to express my feelings too. It's hard to find the words sometimes, to open up to Estelle…'

Gemma let the piece of hair drop from her mouth. 'Yeah?'

There was a huge number of times when Benedict had wanted to say things to Estelle, to tell her that he was devastated too, when they received bad news after their hospital tests. He always felt that he had to be the strong one in their relationship. So he tried to be solid and positive, because he thought that's what his wife needed. Perhaps he should have shown his softer side too.

He summoned up Gemma's scrawled words in the journal for Lapis Lazuli. *No one even wants me.* 'There's something you wrote in the journal…' he started tentatively.

But she had already stood up, batted her hair from her shoulders and headed back into the showroom.

14. Jade

connecting, belonging, serenity

Gemma's idea for the first Stone family outing was a visit to the York Crypt. She handed Benedict a leaflet that she'd picked up from a tourist information booth. '"See Olde York brought to life before your eyes",' Benedict said aloud. '"Live actors, history, gore...and more."'

The logo was red against a black background and there was a spattering of blood. The photo showed an old woman who wore a grey smock and headscarf, smiling and baring her blackened teeth.

'Gore?' he repeated. He'd thought that Gemma would have chosen a park or a river cruise instead. 'How about tea and a scone in a nice teashop? Or a walk and an ice cream?'

'We can do that afterwards,' Gemma tutted. 'This will be a fun date. It's dark in the crypt and a bit scary, so if Estelle gets frightened, you can protect her.' She gave him a sideways glance. 'I bet Lawrence Donnington would never think to take her to the crypt.'

'No,' Benedict said, as he imagined his wife and Lawrence

sipping champagne in a wine bar with chrome stools and neon signs. 'I bet he wouldn't.'

They met Estelle outside Brenda's Tearoom. She was already waiting, standing in front of the window. She wore a purple dress that Benedict hadn't seen before, and a plum-coloured coat. The firework necklace burst with colour from under her scarf.

Benedict's heart thumped so loudly he was sure that Gemma and Estelle would be able to hear it. It felt like he was on his first ever date. His wife looked beautiful and he thought how lucky he was, or rather how lucky he *would* be if she came home.

'Hi,' he said, as casually as he could.

He'd made a special effort in getting dressed that morning. He took the suit that he saved for special occasions out of the wardrobe, and polished his loafers. He trimmed his stubble and was surprised to find that he had to fasten his belt in a tighter hole.

Even though Gemma pushed Benedict to make contact with Estelle, she was acting strangely shy, lagging behind and allowing her russet hair to swing over her eyes. He wondered if she was still mulling over Reggie's visit to the shop, and her own reaction to it.

'How did this morning go?' Benedict asked, as they started to walk together along the cobbled street, with Estelle and Gemma on either side of him. The autumn sun sparkled on the river like silver bottle tops, and tourists strolled along the turreted city walls. An ice-cream van tinkled past.

'Really well. The gallery liked my work. After the exhibition at Purple Heather, they've offered me space there, alongside some other landscape artists. Some of them are quite well known. It's a bigger gallery than Purple Heather too, and it's in the city centre. I'm really excited about it.'

Benedict felt a little childish, secretly revelling that the gallery was better than Purple Heather. 'That's fantastic. Well done.'

Gemma was uncharacteristically quiet. She shuffled along in her cowboy boots and chewed on her hair.

Benedict tried to link her into the conversation. 'Gemma has found us somewhere exciting to go, before we eat,' he said and handed the leaflet to Estelle. 'We're, um, going to the York Crypt.' He wanted to add that they didn't have to go and could choose somewhere else, but he didn't want to embarrass Gemma.

'Oh.' Estelle stared at the leaflet. She read through it as they walked and it seemed to take an age.

Benedict thought about how loud their footsteps sounded.

'This looks fantastic,' Estelle said. 'Some of the girls from Meadow Interiors went there and I couldn't make it. They said it was hilarious. Great idea, Gemma.'

Gemma peeped out from behind her hair and smiled. 'Thanks, Aunt Estelle,' she said, and Benedict sighed with relief.

They were greeted at the door by a man dressed in a ragged brown monk's habit and his face marked with black spots. 'Don't get too close to me,' he hissed, as Benedict handed over their entrance fee, 'or ye'll get the Black Death.'

Benedict shuddered. The room was dark and he could make out a broken stained-glass window and some chains hanging from the wall. This was not an ideal place to bring his wife.

Estelle and Gemma seemed to be enjoying it though. Gemma's eyes were wide and Estelle wore a huge grin. They giggled and chatted to each other as the monk ushered them into a makeshift pub. A woman wearing a black wool cloak told the story of a drunken landlord who murdered strangers by putting poison in their beer and Benedict wished he could hear what his wife and niece were talking to each other about.

After the pub, they witnessed a fake leg amputation, a burning of a witch – really a member of the audience who unwisely raised her hand as a volunteer – and the execution of Guy Fawkes.

'Guy Fawkes was born in York and was part of the plot to burn down the Houses of Parliament,' Benedict told Gemma, as he caught up with her. 'It's why we have Bonfire Night in the UK, on the fifth of November, to remember the event.'

'I know,' Gemma said. 'Estelle told me.'

They ducked, in single file, to squeeze through a small doorway and found a man with his head on a chopping block. The mock-executioner wielded a huge axe and wore a crazed expression.

'Just do it, man,' a teenager shouted out.

'This is sick,' his friend said.

Gemma covered her face with her hands.

The executioner cackled. 'This is how they carried out justice in the court of Edward IV, in the fifteenth century.' He swung his axe and the lights went out, leaving the room in total darkness. There was a thud and Benedict felt something spurt, warm, against his cheek.

'Blood,' Gemma shrieked.

In the darkness, Benedict felt her grasp his sleeve. 'It's just water.' He laughed. But when the lights blinked back on, and he looked down, it was Estelle who had a hold of his arm. He wanted to cover her fingers with his, but he kept his arm still, enjoying her touch.

After the dinginess and unexpected fun of the York Crypt, Benedict wanted to treat Estelle and Gemma, and they returned to Brenda's Tearoom. It had a gilded sign over the door and swirly lettering that announced its establishment in 1895. A group of middle-aged ladies sat at a table in the window. They all wore crisp white trousers and held their expensive handbags between their gold-pumped feet. They nibbled at tiny triangular sandwiches and scones, displayed on tiers of floral bone china plates.

'We're going in here?' Gemma asked.

Benedict tried not to wince when he glanced at the

menu, on display on a gold box on the wall, and saw the price of the salmon sandwiches. 'It looks nice, doesn't it?'

'Yes, but...am I dressed okay?' She looked down at her cowboy boots and bare shins. 'Will they let me in?'

'Of course they will. You're not exactly Kate Moss, but you'll do.'

'Who is Kate Moss?'

'You look lovely, Gemma,' Estelle soothed. 'Of course they'll let you in.'

Benedict asked for a table for three and the bow-tied waiter led them to a corner. The wood-panelled walls were the colour of acorns and the chair seats were covered in thick burgundy leather. The waiter slid out a chair and Estelle sat down first, winking at Gemma. Benedict tried not to smile as he noticed his niece trying to position herself elegantly. She sat with her hands on her lap and her back rod-straight.

'I keep thinking they're going to ask me to leave,' she whispered, as the waiter glided away and she opened her menu. She peered closely at it. 'What's Eggs Benedict? Are you named after it?' she hissed. 'What is Welsh rarebit? Is it like a rabbit?'

'It's a kind of posh cheese on toast,' Estelle explained.

'Be patient and read the descriptions,' Benedict said. 'And I'm not named after an egg dish.'

'Oh, okay.' Gemma read through the menu twice then closed it. 'Can I have a cake?' She looked over at a large rounded glass cabinet. 'They look amazing.'

'That's usually my line.' Benedict smiled.

Gemma glanced quickly at Benedict then focused on Estelle. She gave a tiny cough. 'You know, Estelle, Uncle Ben has been trying to eat real healthy, with fruit and all,' she said earnestly. 'We even walked up to Dinosaur Ridge, so he could get some exercise.'

Benedict didn't know whether to glare at Gemma, or to smile at his wife.

'Oh,' Estelle said. 'That's good. I'm glad you're getting to see more of Noon Sun than the inside of Benedict's shop.'

'He's making a *real* effort,' Gemma said.

Benedict was glad when the waiter returned.

'And are you ready with your food order, sir?' the waiter asked.

Order me. I'm so sweet and gorgeous, a pancake topped with blueberries and maple syrup, being whisked past by a waitress, said. *I contain fruit, so I'm quite good for you.*

Benedict focused on the menu and used all of his will-power to order scrambled eggs on toast instead.

Estelle pointed to the smoked salmon sandwich and requested it on brown bread.

'Thank you. And for your daughter?' the waiter asked.

Benedict's fingers grew rigid and he dropped the menu. Estelle gave a small, embarrassed smile. But Gemma laughed out loud, a blast so huge that a white-trousered lady threw her a stare.

The waiter's smile stiffened when he realised he might have made a mistake. 'I'm sorry, I—'

'Duh. He's my uncle, not my dad,' Gemma interrupted.

'And I'm capable of ordering for myself. I'll have a cup of English tea, with plenty of milk, and a slice of strawberry cheesecake, please.'

'Yes, of course,' the waiter murmured. 'Is that everything?'

'Yes thanks,' Benedict said. He was surprised to find that he felt like he had a marble stuck in the back of his throat. It was a small lump of emotion, a reaction to a thought that dropped, unwanted, into his head. He and Estelle didn't have, or wouldn't ever have, a daughter of their own to take out for lunch.

He coughed, rubbed his Adam's apple and looked around the tearoom. There was a lady feeding honey on a spoon to her adorable toddler daughter. Three beefy men, devouring full English breakfasts, were obviously a father and two sons; they all shared the same flat nose and jutting chin. Two young sisters played a game of peekaboo with the pepper pot and their Monster High dolls.

They were all happy families, and Benedict sat there with his wife, who had moved out, and the daughter of his estranged brother.

He tried to anchor himself back in the moment. He looked at the beautiful swirly writing on the menu, the heavy silver forks and the chandeliers, but it was still a struggle to escape his original thoughts.

'Are you okay?' Estelle asked.

'Yes, just a tickly throat,' Benedict said. 'I could do with my cup of tea.'

After lunch, Estelle bought Gemma a slim, lilac-coloured

box of six macarons. When she eased off the lid, they were set in a line in the colours of English beach huts.

'They're almost too pretty to eat.' She leaned closer and sniffed them. 'I'm not sure what they are.'

'They're like a posh biscuit made with almonds,' Estelle said.

'I think I like posh,' Gemma said. When they reached the pavement outside, she offered the box to Estelle, who took a pink one. Gemma took out a lemon-coloured one and insisted that Benedict take the green one. 'I don't like the look of it. The colour reminds me of caterpillars.'

They nibbled their macarons and walked down towards the river. When they found a spare bench, Gemma kicked off her boots and wriggled her bare toes in the cool air. 'Did you guys ever come here together, before you got married?'

'I remember bringing Estelle once, when we first started dating, to York for afternoon tea,' Benedict said. 'I didn't really know what it was. I thought it was just a cup of tea that you got in the afternoon. So when the waitress brought out a tier of plates stacked high with tiny sandwiches, and scones and cakes, I thought they'd got the order wrong.'

Estelle laughed. 'I didn't know that. I thought you were really sophisticated.'

'You did? I thought you'd think me an idiot if I told you.'

'Don't be silly. You can tell me anything. You know that.'

Benedict's chest tightened and he patted his hand against it. He instinctively thought about how he pushed the bag of gemstones into Charlie's rucksack, and the secret that burned in his heart. Could he really tell his wife *everything*?

He glanced at a passing boat, and a seagull swooped down and stole a flake from a Japanese man's ice-cream cone. Benedict tossed a tiny piece of macaron onto the floor where it was pecked by three pigeons. 'Do you and your dad go out to restaurants?' he asked Gemma.

'Oh, yes,' Estelle said. 'I want to know all about your dad, Gemma. I've seen photos but I've never met him.'

Gemma gave a quick smile. 'He used to take me out for meals, like on my birthday and stuff. But not so much now. He has Janice to replace me.'

It was the first time Benedict had heard this name. '*Janice?*' he asked.

Gemma's face fell. Her toes stopped wriggling and she picked up a boot and stuffed her foot back into it. 'Oh, she's no one,' she said breezily. 'My dad doesn't like to travel much. He likes to stay close to home.'

'Is Janice your dad's girlfriend?' Estelle asked simply.

Gemma looked up. 'Um, yeah.'

'I noticed that you screwed up your nose, a tiny bit, when you said her name,' Estelle said.

Benedict felt full of admiration for his wife; she was so perceptive and subtle. If he'd asked Gemma something so sensitive, it would probably have resulted in the two of them having a stand-off argument. 'Your dad has a girlfriend?' he asked.

'Yeah. The *adorable* Janice.' Gemma stood up and stamped her feet. She looked off into the distance. 'Mrs Freakin' Perfect.'

'Oh,' Estelle said. 'Are things difficult between you?'

The sides of Gemma's mouth drooped low. She wrapped her too-large denim jacket across her chest. 'We were doing all right until *she* came along. She kinda bewitched my dad and…' She stopped mid-sentence and shook her hair. 'Anyway, I'm having a good time and I'm not going to spoil it by thinking about *her.*'

'Bewitched him?' Benedict repeated. He imagined a faceless woman swooping down on a broomstick to cast a spell on Charlie.

'Let's go somewhere else,' Estelle said, casting a quick glare in his direction. She stood up. 'Shall we head to York Minster, and do a bit of sightseeing along the way?'

'Yeah.' Gemma ran ahead. 'Can I go in this bookstore?' she asked, over her shoulder. 'There's a book on gems in the window.'

'Sure. You go inside,' Benedict said.

He thought this would be a good chance to spend a few minutes alone with Estelle, but before he could say anything, she asked, 'What's going on, Benedict?'

'What do you mean?'

'Gemma's a sixteen-year-old girl, on her own in England. You don't find that odd?'

'She's with me. I'm looking after her.'

'But what about her father? Where is Charlie?'

'Don't worry. He's at home in the US, but it's all okay.'

'It seems strange that she's here alone. Especially when you've not spoken to your brother for years. I don't feel comfortable about this.'

Benedict's heart began to beat faster. He suspected that

things were far from fine but he didn't want his wife to know that. 'I think Charlie sees it as part of her growing up. He wasn't much older when he moved away.' He was aware that he was inventing things here, on behalf of his brother and niece.

'That jacket she's wearing is too big, and she has bare legs.'

Benedict rubbed his neck. 'She's a young girl looking for an adventure, and it's a big step towards me getting reacquainted with Charlie,' he said.

'Hmm…well, I suppose that's a good thing.'

Benedict wanted to try and keep his wife happy. 'Yes it is. I'm not concerned in the slightest,' he lied.

15. Fire Opal

individuality, awakening, progress

Benedict felt flashes of excitement in his stomach for a couple of days after the trip to York. His niece and wife got along well; it had been a fun day; and when he said goodbye to Estelle, when they got back to Noon Sun, she had kissed him on the cheek.

His positive feelings made him optimistic for the day ahead. He actually felt in the mood for creating something a bit different today, that wasn't a simple brooch or bangle.

As he reached up to touch the spot on his cheek where Estelle had pressed her lips, Benedict told himself not to worry about his wife's questions. She was caring and was sure to think of Gemma's needs.

He just had to hold out until Charlie got in touch, then he could sort everything out with his brother, without Estelle having to know a thing.

No customers came into the shop until Alistair and Alexander Ledbetter tramped in after lunchtime, both wearing too-white, too-large training shoes and with their hair stiff and spiky. They pointed at the display cabinets and chatted to each other in a strange language that reminded Benedict of *Planet of the Apes*.

Gemma seemed to understand them, though, and the three teenagers stood chatting while leaning with their elbows on the counter. Gemma handed a large oval-faceted Amethyst to Alistair and he peered through it. 'Everything looks purple,' he said. 'It's cool.'

Alexander snatched it from him. 'I can see lots of Gemmas.' He spun it between his thumb and index finger. 'I reckon this is how insects see the world.'

They hung around, mumbling and giggling, and Benedict busied himself straightening necklaces in his window display. When he saw Margarita locking the door of Floribunda and heading towards the shop, he raised his head. 'Margarita,' he said to Gemma. 'She's coming over.'

'Yeah?' She stood up straight.

'We have a customer, lads,' Benedict said to Alistair and Alexander. 'Scoot off back to the Pig and Whistle to help Nicholas.'

Alistair rolled his eyes. 'Nah,' he said. 'Nothing we do is good enough for him.'

'We always get it wrong,' Alexander added.

Gemma pressed the Amethyst into Alistair's hand. 'Take it,' she said. 'It's good for deeper understanding, and helps to soothe anger.'

'Cool.' He rubbed it against his chest then opened the door for Margarita. 'Thanks and see ya around, Gemma.'

'Thank you.' Margarita smiled. Her black-and-silver hair was swept into a loose bun with tendrils falling over her face. She wore an emerald-green fifties-style dress and no apron. '*Ciao*, Benedeect,' she said, then proffered a small bunch of sea holly and white roses to Gemma.

Gemma smelled them and offered them to Benedict to do the same.

'They are my favourite flowers. Sea holly is very tolerant,' Margarita said. 'It can grow anywhere there is sunshine but, like all flowers, a bit of love and attention helps it to thrive.'

'Thanks. They're lovely,' Gemma said.

'I have been waking early, to go to the flower market. It is wonderful there. I missed the smell of the lilies.' She closed her eyes and inhaled. 'The flowers make me feel 'appy.'

Gemma frowned. 'So has Tony changed his job?'

Margarita gave a small laugh. 'I have changed Tony,' she said. 'And so, I am here to order my Aquamarine ring.'

Gemma performed a small fist pump under the counter. 'Great,' she said. 'You won't be disappointed. My Uncle Ben is a genius.'

'I think you're exaggerating,' he replied.

'Nope.'

'Well, I loved your idea for the ring, Gemma.' Margarita's black curls bobbed as she spoke. 'It's a shame that Tony didn't feel the same way. Everything we did seemed to be a compromise. What he was 'appy with, I was not, and the other way too. I had my doubts, but our differences suddenly seemed too much. I told him that I need to be with flowers and he said no.' She took a tissue from her pocket and dabbed at the corner of one eye.

'Oh,' Gemma said. 'Sorry. Are you okay?'

'Yes. When I asked him to leave, I knew he would not take it very well. I hoped he might change but…no.' She shook her head. 'He threw a few things around, but he missed me, this time.'

'*This* time?'

Margarita touched a faded bruise on her arm then moved her hand briskly away. 'It does not matter now.' She pressed her hands to her heart. 'I've come to my senses. So, I want to order my own ring instead. I have a photograph from a magazine.' She took a folded page from her bag and handed it to Benedict. 'It is for me to start afresh.'

Benedict flattened down the creases with his fingers and studied it. The band of the ring was made from polished platinum, wide and flat. A garland of delicate flowers wove around it, each with a tiny Aquamarine centre.

'The name Aquamarine comes from the Latin meaning *water of the sea*, because of its colour,' Gemma said.

'Ah, sea holly,' Margarita said. 'See. It all fits together. So, can you make this for me, Benedeect?'

Benedict stared at the photo. It was intricate, using techniques that he'd not practised for a long time. He ran his finger over it, trying to imagine how the ring might feel. Slowly, his mind cranked into action and he started to think about how he could create the flowers and set the stones.

When he made jewellery with his mother, they would

both sketch and discuss a piece, how it might look and feel, but for years he had worked on autopilot, producing what was easy. Margarita was asking if he could make something special and he wasn't sure if he had the skills any longer to create something that wasn't a bangle or a simple brooch.

He also thought of his own efforts, since Gemma arrived, to take chances. He was useless at playing Romeo, but he had given it a go. He'd invited Estelle out and they had a good time, even though he'd told her a lie. He should try to make this ring, because he might not fail. 'I can try,' he said.

'I know you can do it.' Gemma nudged his arm.

Margarita handed her makeshift metal ring to Benedict. 'This is the size I need. Then you can throw this away.'

Benedict took out a ring mandrel from under the counter. He slid Margarita's ring onto it and made a note of its size against the measurements. He estimated how much platinum he would need and how much time he would take to make the ring. When he had a figure in his head, he took twenty-five per cent off, because he wasn't totally confident he could deliver what Margarita wanted. He wrote the figure down and showed it to her.

'Wonderful.'

'And you need it by…?'

Margarita looked at her bare finger then lifted her chin. 'As soon as possible, please, Benedeect.'

'I'll start work on it today.'

Benedict put the mandrel back into the cupboard under the counter. 'So, you said that you weren't good at anything, and that you always mess up…' he said to Gemma.

'What do you mean?'

'You found the right stone for Margarita. So I think that you've just proved otherwise.'

Benedict's big fingers shook a little as he picked out a small sheet of platinum. He had programmed himself to automatically cut, file, shape and solder his jewellery, but this piece was going to be very different. He knew the meaning behind it. Its story. It wasn't just a ring. It was something important for Margarita to wear, to symbolise her fresh start.

There were no stories behind the pieces of jewellery he usually made or, if there were, then he didn't know them. He had created rings and necklaces and bracelets for milestones in people's lives – birthdays, Christmas, christenings – and he hadn't thought what they might mean to someone. He had been too self-absorbed, thinking only of his and Estelle's problems, about paying the bills and about children.

He avoided other people's emotions, even if they were happy or celebratory. He shut himself away in his workshop, because he didn't want to feel what his customers did.

Benedict stared at his face, reflected in the platinum sheet, and took a long look at his wavy image. He couldn't carry on like this, moping about, putting on weight and yearning for his wife to come home. Gemma had called him talented. Margarita trusted him to design her ring. Perhaps he should listen. Maybe he wasn't a husk of a man after all. There might be something more inside him that he wanted to find and demonstrate, to himself and to Estelle. Perhaps not all his cogs were broken.

And if he tried and failed, then at least he'd had a go.

He propped Margarita's photo, from the magazine, against a wooden block, and he smoothed his hand over the platinum sheet, imagining his mother pressing the snips into his hand and telling him to take care.

His hand flowed as he marked out the shape of the ring onto a piece of masking tape, which he then adhered to the platinum sheet to use as a template. He slipped on his white cotton gloves to handle the platinum then pierced out the ring using his saw.

When it grew darker outside and Benedict reached out to re-angle his lamp, he glanced at his watch and saw that it had already gone six o'clock. He had worked on the ring for five hours, but it only seemed like five minutes.

He peeled off his gloves and placed them neatly on his bench top. The ring he'd created was a good replica of the one in the magazine. The finish he'd achieved was as shiny as a puddle. The flowers looked almost real.

His heart rate and breathing were slow and he felt relaxed and calm, as if he'd devoured a slice of sticky cake, but he hadn't eaten or thought about food since lunchtime. He took a deep breath and exhaled slowly, not noticing a stray piece of cress lying on top of his pliers. *This* is what it feels like to be interested in my own work again, he thought.

'Have you seen the time?' Gemma asked, as she opened the workshop door.

'I was engrossed with making the ring.'

'Is it finished?'

'I think so.'

Gemma edged forward. She gave a small gasp as she caught sight of it. 'Wow,' she said. 'You've done it.'

'I know.'

They both admired it for a while until Benedict switched off his lamp. 'I hope Margarita likes it,' he said and wheeled his chair away from his bench. He sat and stared straight ahead. Even though he was happy with the ring, there was a small niggle in his head and he couldn't get rid of it.

Somehow, Gemma managed to detect it. 'What are you thinking?'

'Hmmm. I've created the ring for Margarita and it's perfect for her. But am I really pouring all the passion I can into making the anniversary necklace for Estelle? Or am I doing what I always do, and creating something beautiful but with no soul?'

'So that could be a challenge for WEB, Uncle Ben,' Gemma said. 'Turn Estelle's necklace into something wonderful.'

'Hmmm,' Benedict said again, and he began to wonder how he might do it.

16. Kunzite

love, mood-lifting, frees emotions

Benedict and Gemma stood in the kitchen together, making a stew for tea. He chopped up some lamb and vegetables then dropped them into simmering water with a handful of fresh herbs.

While they waited for the stew to cook, Gemma made a fruit salad on a plate, cutting and arranging the fruit so the colours fed from one to another – the red of strawberries and watermelon, running through to slices of banana and yellow apples. *We look like a beautiful sunset*, the fruit said to Benedict. *Eat as much of us as you like.*

They dined at the table and Gemma nibbled on a piece of bread, turning it around and around. Benedict ate his stew slowly whilst thinking about the pendant for Diane.

'The Aquamarine ring was right for Margarita, and I want to make the perfect piece of jewellery for Ryan to give to Diane,' he said. 'I think the pendant should be a circular shape, in silver, with a square-cut Kunzite set in the bottom third, rather than in the middle.'

'That sounds cool.'

'But it's not different enough.' Benedict broke off a chunk of bread and dunked it into the last of his stew. 'It's too simple. Ryan wants to demonstrate to Diane how much he loves her, and to show her that their marriage is worth fighting for.'

'Is the gemstone not enough?'

'I don't think it is.'

Benedict considered Ryan's talk of Terminators and bouncy mattresses. He stared into his empty bowl. He couldn't keep relying on Gemma to deal with customers, and he had to prove to himself that he could do this. If he could create something wonderful then he might be worthy of Estelle.

The pendant had to be the equivalent of a love letter from Ryan to Diane. And with that thought, Benedict let his spoon drop. It clattered into the ceramic bowl. *A love letter.* 'I have an idea,' he said slowly.

'What?' Gemma cupped her hands around her face. 'What is it, Uncle Ben?'

'Where is Joseph's journal?'

'In my bag, in the front room. Do you want me to look something up?'

'Yes. K for Kunzite.'

Gemma scraped back her chair and skipped out of the kitchen. When she returned, she set the journal down on the kitchen table. Flicking to the K section, she turned it so Benedict could read the page.

KUNZITE

This gem was named after G. F. Kunz, who discovered it at the start of the twentieth century. This beautiful crystal appears pale pink from the side, but if you look at it down its length, its striations can make it appear a pinky-violet. Kunzite can enhance self-esteem and help us to be patient and understand other people. It protects, helps to bring resolution to conflict, heals the heart, and helps love to grow.

'Aw, that's real sweet,' Gemma said.

Benedict's mind began to tick. 'Perhaps…' he said.

'Perhaps what?'

'Well, if the pendant is going to be a love letter to Diane then it should actually feature some words on it. I think I'll engrave the meaning of the gemstone onto the pendant, and then Diane has it in writing, how Ryan feels about her. *Love, protect, understanding* and *heart*. I want to make a sketch of it first.'

'That sounds cool. Way to go, Uncle Ben,' Gemma said. 'I'll get some paper.'

'And some pens too,' he said.

They shared a smile.

Benedict shut himself away in his workshop and worked on the pendant for Diane.

He took a small sheet of silver and cleaned the surface with a piece of emery paper. He marked the middle of a circle by gently tapping a centre punch once with a hammer, and then placed the silver sheet on a piece of paper. He picked up his dividers and set them to the radius he wanted and turned the paper around to form a circle, which was easier than turning the dividers themselves. Using his snips, he cut out the circle, following the marks.

After filing the edges of the pendant, he measured the Kunzite and annealed a small strip of silver to make into a square setting. After sawing through the strip where there was an overlap, he used pliers to squeeze the seams shut. He painted borax onto the seam and placed a pallion of hard solder onto it, then heated it with his blowtorch until the solder flowed through the seam.

Gemma came into the workshop a couple of times, but Benedict didn't speak to her, or even raise his head to acknowledge her presence. He ignored the shushing open of the door and her offers of cups of tea.

He polished the silver with a steel brush to produce a matt finish, and then set about engraving the words. They appeared shiny against the matt background. When he was finished, he cleaned the pendant with a cloth.

After concentrating so hard, his neck and back were stiff. He was still a little hunched over when he walked back into the showroom, but that didn't matter. Ryan had something beautiful to present to Diane.

Benedict opened the door on one of the display cabinets and selected a fine silver belcher chain. Sliding it through the jump ring of the pendant, he hung it up for Gemma to see. 'What do you think?'

'It's gorgeous, Uncle Ben.'

'I hope Ryan will be pleased.' He closed the cabinet door and headed back to his workshop.

'Are you going to take it to Soap'n'Suds now?'

'I'll wait until I next see him.'

'Can I take it?'

'You?'

'Yeah. A pendant was my idea and I want to see his face when he opens the box. I also want to call on Aunt Estelle.'

'You do?'

'Yeah. I've made her a bracelet out of small gemstones.'

'Oh.' Benedict's nostrils flared a little. He didn't know that Gemma had started to make her own things too. He placed the Kunzite pendant in a box. 'Why?'

'Duh. Because she's my aunt. She lives in the apartment block by the canal right?'

Benedict nodded. 'What gemstones did you choose for her?'

'I just picked pretty ones for confidence and security.'

'Confidence and security?' Benedict repeated. They weren't the gems he'd automatically think of for his wife.

'All people need that.'

'And is it something you're looking for too?'

Gemma's eyes hardened. 'Who said that *I* need it?'

'I don't know.' He thought about the initials 'DJ' in her notebook. 'Are you missing anything or anyone from home?' he asked.

'Like who?' A frost seemed to settle over her features.

'Your ex-boyfriend perhaps?'

'Boys are a waste of time,' Gemma snapped. 'And you're

prying again.' She snatched up Ryan's Kunzite pendant and put the box in her pocket. After peering out of the window she headed to the storeroom and pulled out Estelle's purple coat. 'It's raining.'

'When will you be back?'

Gemma tossed her head as she left the shop. 'When I'm finished.'

A strange noise made Benedict's ears pick up and he realised that Lord Puss was purring. He tentatively reached out and gave the cat's head a gentle stroke as he nestled down on the pillow. Perhaps he's mistaken me for Gemma, Benedict thought but then he caught sight of the Tiger's Eye gemstone poking out from under the purple cushion.

The journal lay on the counter and, even though he knew Gemma liked to be the one to read it, Benedict pulled it towards him to see what it said about the small browny-gold stone.

TIGER'S EYE

A member of the quartz family, the stone is so named because it looks like the eye of a tiger. Its brown and gold stripes seem to shift and change when the stone moves. Tiger's Eye is supposed to impart a tiger's fearlessness, so Roman soldiers carried it into battle to give them courage. In ancient Egypt, the stone offered the protection of the sun god, Ra. It is said that Tiger's Eye reduces anxiety caused by feelings of insecurity and inadequacy, and encourages contact with others. It's a good stone for assisting animals in adapting to new changes.

He noticed that Gemma had again added her notes underneath. He was cautious about reading them, but curiosity simmered inside him.

I need to check if she's okay, he told himself. She doesn't tell me a lot of things, so there's no other way I can find out. She keeps the journal away from me, but it's mine, not hers.

He pressed his finger against the brittle page and read on.

Tiger's Eye is supposed to reduce feelings of anxiety, but my emotions are still crazy. This gemstone is good for dilemmas, so I hope it will help me with mine. I miss D more than I thought I would. I wish I'd told him where I was going. There's no way he'll find me here. What am I going to do?

The letter 'D' again. The initials 'DJ' in Gemma's notebook must refer to her boyfriend. And what was her dilemma?

When Charlie had girlfriends he always fell hard for them, exclaiming he was in love after only a few dates. Perhaps Gemma was like that too.

Benedict was more cautious. He believed that love was something that grew and blossomed. A person's looks might hit you between the eyes, but it was their personality that had to seduce you. He liked to take his time.

There was only once when he hadn't followed this instinct, when he had been so overwhelmed by a moment that he lost his self-control, and it was something that ricocheted and affected every area of his life, and his relationships, from then on.

He closed the journal and hoped that Gemma wasn't living through anything like it.

17. Azurite

memories, release, mysteries

Eighteen years ago, Benedict Stone made the biggest mistake of his life. Since then it had weighed on his mind, it broke his sleep, and it might ruin his marriage. It made him want to eat, to dull the heavy regret that he carried with him like a wooden yoke across his shoulders.

Before Charlie left for America, Benedict always exercised control in his life. He organised everything, from Charlie's packed lunches, to the sorting out of the insurance to pay off the mortgage on the house after their parents' death. He ensured that Charlie was on time for his football practice each week, and that his school clothes were freshly washed and pressed each Sunday night.

When Charlie grew older and started to bring girls home for tea, Benedict cleaned the house beforehand and brought out the best plates for the sandwiches he'd made. Afterwards, when Charlie didn't offer to do the washing-up, Benedict did it. And he never complained once, because he wanted to do the best for his brother.

Whether this influenced Charlie to grow up to be carefree and spontaneous, and rather ignorant of other people's feelings, Benedict didn't know. He supposed he gave his brother a safety net, so that if Charlie ever tried and failed at anything, Benedict was waiting to catch him.

But then everything changed.

It was one of those rare English summer days, when the evening was as hot and sticky as the daytime, when events set in motion.

Charlie had been flopping around the house all day in his shorts and flip-flops, bored and too hot. The sun had burned his shoulders the same reddish shade as his hair.

'Phone Amelia up,' Benedict suggested. 'The three of us could drive up to Scarborough and have a picnic on the beach this evening.'

'A picnic with you?' Charlie sniffed. 'I'm eighteen, Benedict, a bit old for all that.'

'It's up to you. I thought it would be nice.'

Charlie lolled around some more, then shrugged and said, 'Sure.'

When they got in the car, Benedict knew that his brother had something to say. Charlie had a *tell* when he was pondering. Around exam time, when he was stressed over his revision, Charlie licked his top teeth over and over. And now, in the car, his tongue moved from side to side like a windscreen wiper.

Benedict stole a glance at his brother. Just look at the size of him now. The spindly white limbs that once smelled of talcum powder were filling out. His freckles were showing, rust coloured, on his nose. His eyes were blue, the same as Mum and Dad's. Benedict always felt the odd one out with his dark grey eyes.

He looked down at his own body, bursting around his seat belt. He'd always been thicker set than Charlie, but recently he'd noticed a band of fleshiness that curved over his waistband. Running the jewellery shop and sorting Charlie out meant he didn't get as much exercise as he should do.

They picked up Amelia and arrived in Scarborough at just past 8 p.m. There were still families on the beach, kids paddling and dogs running into the sea to retrieve soggy tennis balls. Charlie brought their old cricket set along, but the bat was too small, and after half an hour of playing, Benedict had a stiff back from being bent over double. He flopped down beside Amelia while Charlie continued to run around with the bat and ball on his own.

'You're not as fast as you used to be,' Charlie shouted at him. 'You're putting on a lot of weight there.'

Benedict adjusted his T-shirt.

'Ignore him,' Amelia said. 'You look fine.'

Afterwards, they lit a fire at the quiet end of the north bay, where only a few dog walkers roamed by.

Charlie picked up a long piece of spindly driftwood off the beach. He poked at the fire and his tongue began to swipe his teeth again.

'Do you have something to say?' Benedict asked.

'How do you know?'

'I can tell when you have something on your mind.'

'Years of bringing me up, eh?' Charlie took the driftwood out of the fire. He blew on the smouldering end. 'I've decided to go to America with Amelia,' he said. 'We'll stay on her parents' farm out there for a while.'

'Oh,' Benedict said, not expecting this.

Amelia curled up her legs on the rug. 'It's only for a few months or so,' she said. 'We want an adventure.'

Benedict watched the fire crackle, black embers floating like small flying beetles into the night air. 'America? Well, that's a surprise. Why?'

Charlie laughed and slapped him once hard on the back. 'Man of few words, Benedict. I tell you I'm going to live in America, and you respond with *why?*'

'It's a good question.'

'I suppose it is.' Charlie shrugged. 'The thing is, *why not*? I feel like I need to get out of Noon Sun, away from the house. Away from you.'

'Thanks.'

'Not in a bad way.' Charlie scratched his head. 'Everything feels so claustrophobic and I need time out.'

Benedict liked Amelia. She was tall with tanned caramel limbs and had the same easy, laid-back manner as Charlie, as if neither of them could get flustered about anything life threw at them. She looked comfortable when she came over to the house and chilled out on the sofa, and she showed an interest in Benedict's shop and jewellery.

Benedict took sausages out of a plastic box and speared them onto a wooden skewer. He handed them to Charlie and Amelia, then prepared one for himself.

'I want to take a chance,' Charlie said. 'I wonder how things would have worked out if Mum and Dad hadn't been killed. What happened to our parents, well, it changed us. It made you more careful, I know that.'

'I had to look after you. I wanted to look after you.'

'And I love you for it.' Charlie gave Benedict's leg a punch. 'I just want to go and see other places, meet new people. Staying with Amelia's family will give me that option.'

Benedict felt a lump rising in his throat and it was difficult to swallow away. It must feel like this being a parent, when kids moved out of the home to go to college. One day they broke out of their cocoon and they were ready to fly. 'It sounds like a great opportunity,' he said. He tried to think of how this was good for Charlie, not how alone he'd feel with his brother gone.

'Thanks. I knew you'd understand. And you can also do what you like. You've been stuck, looking after me for eight years. There must be things you want to do, want to see.'

Benedict shook his head. 'I have the shop to run. There's the house, and I like it in Noon Sun.'

'Well, you should still think about it. I'll miss you. But I know we'll stay in touch. Stone brothers forever, eh?'

'Stone brothers forever,' Benedict said quietly.

After they'd eaten, and the sun began to sink in the sky, Benedict and Charlie kicked sand onto the smouldering fire. Benedict carefully collected their beer cans, tinfoil and napkins, and rolled up the picnic blanket. As usual Charlie didn't help. He studied a blister on the underside of his foot then performed a clumsy cartwheel. Amelia threw an empty beer can at him, which skimmed his shoulder. 'Missed,' Charlie laughed.

Benedict shook his head and carried on tidying up. Amelia helped him.

Back in the car, Charlie yawned loudly. 'God, I'm tired now. I want to go to bed. Could you drop me off first, Benedict, then drive Amelia home?'

'I can do, but...'

'Thanks, Benedict.'

Charlie swaggered up the path and waved from the door of the house. Amelia raised her hand back and laughed. 'He's so lazy,' she said, when Benedict started the car again. 'I think staying on the farm will be good for him.'

'You do?'

'Sure. My mom and dad will make him work, but don't tell him that.' She winked.

When they arrived at Amelia's apartment, she invited Benedict inside. 'Let's grab a beer,' she said. 'My room-mates are out and Charlie can pick up the car in the morning. You've done all the work tonight and deserve a break.'

Benedict was glad that she'd noticed, because Charlie never did. 'Maybe just one beer,' he said.

He and Amelia sat on the squashy sofa and chatted. They drank three bottles of Budweiser each. Benedict told himself he should get home, but it felt good to be away from the house and Charlie.

She showed him photographs of when she was young,

with her family back in the States. 'You can come over and visit,' she said. 'It'll be fun.'

'I have the shop to look after.'

Amelia sighed. She sipped her beer and studied him. 'Don't you ever have fun, Benedict?'

'Yes,' he said, though he wasn't sure that kicking a football around with Charlie was what she meant. 'Sometimes.'

'Hmmm.' She blew into the neck of her bottle.

'Very musical,' Benedict said.

'I have lots of secret talents.' She laughed. 'Did you also know that, when I first met you, I got a little crush on you?'

Benedict gave an embarrassed laugh and picked up another photograph.

'I did,' she said. 'You're so protective and caring, and kinda mature. You made me feel welcome. Hey,' she said, noticing that he'd finished his Budweiser, 'do you want another beer?'

'I should go,' Benedict said. 'It's late.'

'Aww, stay a while.' Amelia moved closer and gave his T-shirt a tug. 'We can talk some more.'

Benedict glanced out of the window and knew he should leave. Something had switched in the air and he wasn't sure what it was.

Amelia took his bottle from him and set it down on the floor. She inched her head towards his, and Benedict didn't move his away. Her breath smelled sweet, like toffee. She smiled and studied him, and he didn't know what to do. Her face was too close for him to turn his away. 'I've drank a little too much,' she whispered.

'I think I have too,' Benedict said.

It was the prompt that told him to feign naivety and resume conversation about America, and her photos, but he ignored it. The hairs sprang up on his forearms, one by one. Their faces remained so close that Benedict could see that her eyelashes were sun-kissed on their tips and she had a tiny mole next to her left eyebrow.

'Benedict,' she said, smiling. 'I'll miss you.'

'Amelia, I...' he said, not sure what he was going to add to his words.

She pressed her lips against his and they were soft and firm. He hadn't experienced the closeness of another person for such a long time, and he had just a couple of seconds to make his decision. He could pull away, or kiss her back.

And, in the heat of the moment, he made the wrong choice.

When Amelia opened the front door for Benedict to leave, they both knew it had been a mistake. They didn't need to say anything. Amelia's eyes were low as she said a quick, embarrassed 'Bye', and Benedict's feet felt like lead when he walked home.

In the early morning light, he found the white drawstring bag full of gemstones that had returned in his mother's rucksack after her death. The gems represented Benedict and Charlie's happier times under the gem tree and, heavy-hearted and full of regret, Benedict pushed it into the front pocket of Charlie's rucksack.

And he never saw Amelia again.

Charlie and Amelia moved to America within a few days, and Benedict never knew if Amelia told Charlie about what she and Benedict did. But he guessed that she must have done, because the two Stone brothers never spoke again.

Charlie wrote twice after he left. One postcard said that he and Amelia had married and had a child. In a second letter, Charlie told Benedict that he never wanted to see him again.

He never left a forwarding address.

Benedict's foolhardy half-hour on the sofa with Amelia, on that hot July night, was one reason why having a family of his own was so vitally important. He wanted to bring up a child and not mess up this time. He could try to compensate for his mistake with Charlie, and start a new untarnished version of the Stone family.

Benedict also thought that if Gemma was hiding anything and if she was in any kind of trouble then he wanted to know, so he could try to help her.

And, in doing so, he could make some kind of amends for what he'd done to his brother.

18. Red Aventurine

attraction, action, perseverance

Noon Sun Manor was situated at the end of a dirt track, around half a mile's steep climb up a hill from the high street. Benedict huffed as he trudged towards the grey square building, with its overgrown topiary and cracked Georgian windowpanes.

'Think of WEB,' Gemma said, beside him. 'You're getting fitter.'

Benedict grunted and pressed on the stitch in his side. In his hand he held a lilac envelope, and inside that was a small handwritten card which smelled of violets.

> I, *Violet de Gama, seek the company of Mr Benedict Stone on October 26th, at precisely 11 a.m., to discuss items of jewellery*

'Who is Violet de Gama?' Gemma asked. 'I like her name.'

'She was born in Noon Sun, in the forties, and starred

in a few Hollywood romances. She had an affair with the head of the studio, and his wife made sure that Violet never worked again. After that, I think she started to drink too much and had a series of affairs with married men. She stayed on in America but moved back here over a decade ago.'

'How do you know all this?'

'Estelle read a magazine article about her once. Before that, I didn't even know who she was. She's a real recluse.'

'But she's interested in your jewellery. Way to go, Uncle Ben.'

When Violet opened the door, Benedict's senses were accosted by a flourish of heady rose and patchouli perfume. He could hardly see Violet's face because her hair and forehead were hidden under a voluminous purple paisley turban. The lenses of her sunglasses were black, large and round, making her look like a bluebottle under a microscope. She wore a man's red silk dressing gown over an emerald-green top and trousers, and three strings of chunky pearls around her neck. The only unglamorous thing about her appearance was her sturdy black shoes which were each fastened by three straps of thick Velcro.

'Come in,' she croaked, her voice sounding like she smoked and drank whisky all day long.

Benedict and Gemma treaded along the frayed woven rugs lining the hallway and into a room lit only by candlelight. It was small and square, with the only furniture a leather sofa, a chair and a round table upon which lay playing cards, mapped out in a game of Solitaire. The walls were covered with black-and-white photographs in thick black frames. They were mainly of men, posing, smiling and smouldering for the camera. Lawrence Donnington wouldn't have looked amiss amongst them, Benedict thought.

Then he told himself that he should try not to worry about Lawrence. He'd managed to convince himself that Estelle's conversation with the gallery owner on the balcony was purely platonic, about art.

'I received your note,' Benedict said, as Violet nodded curtly for them to sit down.

Benedict and Gemma sank into a battered black leather sofa with a criss-cross of duct tape on the arm. The room was so cold Benedict could see his breath, and Violet's perfume did little to mask the smell of damp. Gemma picked up a fading ochre velvet cushion and put it on her lap.

'Of course you did,' Violet said with a prickly tone. 'I posted it myself.'

'You did?' With her theatrical clothes, it looked like she might be more used to being chauffeured around.

Violet gave an exaggerated sigh. 'You should ignore stories about my decline and my death, Mr Stone,' she said. 'It is all fantasy made up by others to enhance their own boring little lives.'

Benedict had never heard anyone discussing her, and he doubted that many villagers even knew of her existence. The main topic of conversation in Noon Sun at the moment was Bonfire Night, and maybe Estelle's art exhibition.

'People can be so jealous,' she continued. 'It's why I keep myself to myself, then they can talk about me all they like, and I can't hear them.'

'Okaaay,' Benedict said. 'How can I help you?'

'I want to sell some of my jewels,' Violet announced. She said it as if it didn't matter to her, but he heard a tremble in her voice. 'I have no need for them any longer and I have bills to pay.' She picked up a small worn tan leather suitcase, positioned it on her lap and flipped open the lid. Inside was an array of smaller boxes, each with an embossed name on top – Tiffany, Chanel, Cartier, Bulgari.

She opened a red velvet box and took out a string of pearls. 'Davis Hamilton gave me these. He was my most voracious lover,' she purred. 'Heathcliff Matterson was supposed to be well endowed but I couldn't see what the fuss was about, and Taylor Benjamin left his wife for me. He gave me a pink sapphire ring to mark the occasion.'

Gemma stifled a giggle. 'I've never heard of these people.'

Violet gave her a withering stare. 'I'm sure you can see them on TV all the time, my dear, their films are timeless.'

'I could look them up on YouTube.' Gemma shrugged.

Violet's face was expressionless behind her sunglasses. 'Maybe on video cassette.'

'I'd love to see the pink sapphire ring,' Benedict said.

'I'm afraid that I gave several precious items away to a young lover many years ago. He was most attentive and I was foolish then. These are what I have left and I want to sell them. I have no one to pass them on to.' She tapped a finger on the suitcase.

Benedict opened up a Tiffany box, but the necklace inside had paste jewels. He suspected that a pearl necklace was fake, too. A few of the items were real, though, and looked to be of good quality.

'I think Aunt Estelle might like this stuff,' Gemma said. 'It's real classy.'

'These are beautiful, Ms de Gama,' Benedict said, as he examined them by candlelight. 'But I'm afraid that I only sell new jewellery, my own work.'

'And this one was from Barney Banks, though you may know him as Vincent D'Artagnan. He changed his name for Hollywood.' Violet nodded. 'As did a lot of the stars.'

Gemma caught Benedict's eye and angled her bushy eyebrows. 'What's your real name?' she asked.

Violet's expression didn't alter. 'There's no need for you to know, child.'

'I'm sorry,' Benedict tried again, 'but I don't trade in old jewellery.'

'But of course you do.' Violet pushed her glasses down her nose so she could see over the top. 'You're a jeweller.'

'I don't know anything about antique jewellery.'

'It's not antique – it was new when I received it.'

'If it's from the fifties and sixties then it's classed as antique.'

'Hmm,' she said, as if this surprised her. 'I suppose it is. Time moves so quickly, yes?'

She was right, Benedict thought. It didn't seem long since

he and Estelle met and walked down the aisle together. When you were a child, life passed by slowly, with the gap between one birthday and another seeming to stretch out forever. But when you reached adulthood it was as if an invisible finger and thumb turned the winder on your watch so time spun faster.

Benedict also imagined that, if you were older and alone, you could easily get cut off from everything going on around you, caught up in your own world.

Violet ran her hand over her pearls. 'I grew up in Noon Sun, but now I no longer recognise the place. It only seems like two minutes ago when I was a child and used to go to watch plays in the community centre with my parents. I loved the glamour, the ladies in their jewels and the men with their cigars. The building reminds me of a Moroccan riad from *Sultry Nights*, a film I starred in with Butler Jacobson. I saw that it was all boarded up when I delivered your note. So very terrible, and sad.'

'There's a bonfire taking place in the village to help raise funds for repairs,' Benedict said. 'But it will only go a small way towards paying for what's needed.'

'Hmmm.' Violet patted her turban. 'Anyway, I have myself to think of. What am I to do about my jewellery?'

'I'd suggest a specialist auction house,' Benedict said. 'Or there may be an antique shop in Applethorpe.'

'Tsk. I don't travel over there. It's a larger town and I'd certainly be recognised. And I know nothing of auction houses. It's all too much to worry about. I need to sell this house too. I can't look after it any longer.'

Gemma put down the cushion. 'I don't think anyone will mob you,' she said. 'And hiding away up here must be lonely.'

Violet pursed her lips. 'I have my men to keep me company.' She swept her hand around the room at the photos on the wall. 'I have my memories.'

She removed her sunglasses and her eyes were startlingly lavender. Her fingers, knobbly and stacked with large rings, crept over onto Benedict's knee. 'I'm sure you could make an exception for me, Mr Stone,' she said coquettishly. 'Wouldn't you like to buy my lovely jewellery?'

Benedict spied an old photograph of Violet on the wall. She wore a polka dot swimsuit and a white scarf around her hair. She stood on tiptoes and held a beach ball aloft. He realised that the sunglasses she had just taken off were the same ones she wore in the photograph. 'I'm sorry, but I can't sell it,' he said.

Violet's hand slid off his knee. 'Well, if you're not interested in buying from me' —she clicked her fingers— 'then we shouldn't waste each other's time any longer.'

'It's not been a waste of my time. It's been fascinating to meet you. I also know of a solicitor in the village who might be able to advise on selling your property.'

'Hmmm.' She offered the back of her hand, for him to kiss.

Benedict stood and lightly brushed a large fake-ruby ring with his lips.

Gemma stood up too. 'You shouldn't lock yourself

away. People in the village won't bother you. They might want a selfie, but that's all,' she said.

'A selfie?'

'A photo with you, on their mobile phone.'

'I don't do modern technology. Or posing.' Violet sniffed.

'You could come along to my wife's art exhibition, at the Purple Heather Gallery,' Benedict offered, trying to inject some positivity to the conversation. 'You can meet some of the other villagers there.'

'Hmmm.'

'And if you do ever visit my shop, ask Gemma for a piece of Golden Beryl.'

Gemma nodded her approval at his choice.

'Beryl?' Violet said offhandedly. 'Mr Stone. I've owned rare diamonds. Why should I want a common gemstone?'

'It can help you to release old emotional baggage and give you hope and optimism.' Benedict folded her note and put it in his pocket. 'It's like letting the sun in on a winter's day. I think it would be a perfect gemstone for you, and it would be a gift from me to you.'

'Hmmm,' Violet said. 'I'll bear it in mind.'

Benedict and Gemma walked past Frank Winterson's farm as they made their way down from Violet's manor house.

Benedict once read a newspaper article that claimed people who owned animals often resembled them. It was accompanied by a photograph of a glamorous red-haired model hugging a Red Setter. In the case of farmer Frank Winterson, this statement was definitely true.

Frank always wore pale-grey corduroy trousers and a dark-grey sweater with holes in it. With his long face, large square teeth and wispy shoulder-length white hair, tied in a ponytail with a child's pink bobble, the farmer had a distinct look of llama about him.

'Why are we stopping?' Gemma asked.

'Just to say hello to Frank the farmer. He's over there, feeding the white horse. I thought you could meet another Noon Sunner, if you're staying a while.'

Gemma wrinkled her nose. 'This place doesn't look much like a farm. It's kinda ramshackle.'

'Frank used to grow and sell plants, but a new garden centre in Applethorpe opened up with a posh café in a conservatory, and a gift shop. It took away a lot of his business, so he just owns a few animals now.'

Benedict waved to Frank and the farmer gave the horse a pat and joined Gemma and Benedict at the gate.

'Aye, Benedict,' Frank said, by way of a greeting.

Gemma stood on tiptoes to look at the white horse that he'd been feeding.

'Does it remind you of your horse, back at Sunnyside?' Benedict asked.

'I don't have a horse. They're scary. You can't tell what they're thinking.'

'You said that you were good with them.'

'No, I didn't.'

'Gemma.' Benedict pinched the bridge of his nose. 'I never know if you're making things up or not.'

'Sorry,' she said. 'A horse on my dad's farm did like me, a little. I forgot about it.'

He opened his mouth to press her further, but Frank sidled up on the other side of the gate. 'Aye,' he said, jerking his head to indicate that Benedict should come closer.

Benedict was still frowning at Gemma, but he stepped forward.

'Nicholas showed me his red stone,' Frank said.

'The Carnelian?'

'Aye. Can you help me out? I need to perk things up.' He sighed.

'Um, perk things…?'

'Aye, you know. Put a sizzle in the sausage, or eggs in the pan.'

Benedict blinked, wondering what the hell Frank was asking for. It sounded like he wanted Viagra. He lowered his voice. 'Perhaps you should try a doctor…'

Frank laughed and it sounded like a horse braying. 'Aye, it's for the llamas, not me. I sell their wool and I need more of them, but they're not frisky this year. I've got the missus and three kids to feed and I'm not making any money. I don't want to have to get rid of my beauties. Look at 'em in the field over there…just lovely.'

Benedict and Gemma looked over to where four llamas stood in a line, peering over a fence with doleful eyes. 'Have you given up growing plants?' Benedict asked.

Frank nodded. 'I tried my hand at cauliflowers but they

didn't grow large enough, and my tomatoes didn't taste of much. I prefer things with faces anyway. But when those llamas look at me in the morning, when I feed them, I can see they're not happy. I thought that you might be able to help. With yer gemstones.'

'Maybe.' Benedict scratched his head. 'So you want something for…?'

'More llamas,' Frank said. 'And, while you're at it, making plants grow better.'

Benedict tried to recall stones that he and Gemma had talked about. 'Perhaps Aventurine…'

Gemma nodded in agreement. 'Red or green?'

'Both. Red Aventurine can boost feelings and emotions, so is sometimes used to encourage pregnancy and enhance fertility. It's also said to bring prosperity and lessen negativity.'

'You can bury Green Aventurine in the soil and it's supposed to help plants grow healthily,' Gemma added.

'Aye, well, I'm willing to give anything a try.' Frank took out his wallet. 'Things are getting desperate. The kids had to go back to school in their old uniforms and my window frames are rotten, need replacing. I'll take some of the red and green, please.'

'Are you going to Estelle's art exhibition, the day after tomorrow?'

'Aye, maybe.'

'I'll bring the gems for you then. We've just called on Violet de Gama and told her about the exhibition too.'

'She seems lonely,' Gemma said.

'Aye. She should come out more. And that big old house is crumbling around her. I bumped into her recently, on one of her midnight walks, and told her about those nice, modern apartments by the canal, but I don't think she listened. She prefers to dwell in the past.'

'If we give you a gem for her, can you pass it on?' Benedict asked.

'Aye.'

The white horse neighed and trotted over towards them. Gemma recoiled from it and stepped back. Benedict recalled Cecil's words about getting on a white charger for Estelle and an idea began to twinkle in his head. He told himself that it was silly, because trying to be Romeo certainly hadn't worked, but it wouldn't go away.

He didn't want to end up like Violet, living in the past with her memories, and he still had to prove his intentions to Estelle. 'Any chance you could bring the white horse along on the night?' he asked. 'With a saddle on him?'

Frank didn't question this. 'Aye,' he said.

'I'll pay you for him.'

'Nope. I'll do you a swap for the gems.'

'Agreed. Purple Heather at 8 p.m.?'

'Aye.'

'Why do you need a white horse?' Gemma asked as they walked back to the shop.

'It's an idea I have for WEB.' Benedict explained how Cecil agreed with her, that he should be more proactive in trying to win Estelle back. 'I mean, I've never actually ridden a horse, and I don't know if I'll attempt it, but the thought is there.'

Gemma's bottom lip protruded into a small cushion. 'But I'm supposed to come up with the challenges, Uncle Ben. Operation WEB is *my* idea. I want to help you and Estelle to get back together.'

Benedict nodded. 'Yes, but I should try to make more effort too. I don't need to wait for you to have ideas, when I have my own. And isn't WEB a joint affair, between us?'

Gemma looked down at her boots and sucked in her lip with a pop. But Benedict didn't notice. He was too busy thinking about his next plan of action.

19. Tourmaline Quartz

unity, positive energy, enlivens

The next morning Gemma didn't eat her breakfast. She toyed with her spoon, stirring it around in her cereal bowl until the clinking noise made Benedict clench his teeth. 'Is anything wrong?' he asked.

She screwed up her eyes. 'I have a headache. My brain hurts.'

'You'll want to feel well for Estelle's exhibition tomorrow, so why don't you rest up for the day?'

She lifted her chin. 'I can do that?'

'You don't have to come into the shop. It's not compulsory.'

Gemma considered this for a while and pushed her bowl away. 'Okay. I might go back to bed. Can you cope without me?'

'I'll try my best.'

'What are you going to do about the horse?'

'What about it?'

'Don't you have a plan?'

Benedict frowned. 'Frank will bring him along on the

night, and it will be a nice surprise for Estelle. I'll invite her outside to see the horse and tell her that I'm ready to joust for her.'

'Without you doing any actual horse riding, or jousting?' Gemma frowned.

'It's the gesture that counts. I'll explain it all to her.'

'I think you need me to help you, but my head hurts even more now.'

'Gemma,' Benedict said, 'go to bed and rest up. I'm fine doing things on my own. I hope you feel better soon.'

Benedict walked along the Noon Sun high street, and the grey clouds and drizzle made the village look like an old black-and-white etching. The cherry scones in Bake My Day sang out his name, but he ignored them, eager to get into his shop.

Once inside, he reached into the gemstone jar and picked out a pleasingly round piece of Golden Beryl for Violet, and a few stones of Red and Green Aventurine for Frank.

He spent the morning making the Blue Lace Agate earrings for Laura and wrote out the meaning of the gemstone for her. He left a message for Reggie, saying that they were ready to collect.

After that, he took his test pieces out from under the counter. He studied them for a while and they didn't look as rough as he remembered. In fact, they were rather stylish.

He spent the next couple of hours, reaching into his window display to remove his bangles and brooches, and replacing them with the clam shell, blossom brooch and Sunstone pendant, amongst others. He unfolded the tissues and discovered a series of gemstone stud earrings and a couple of silver link bracelets with dangling heart charms. He put these inside a cabinet. Some of the pieces he vaguely remembered making and others he didn't.

When he'd finished, he was pleased with the result. His window and cabinets looked less uniform. More magical even.

At lunchtime, he bought a salad and ate it while sitting at the counter. He jumped when Estelle knocked on the window and came into the shop. It was raining outside and she held her coat tight to her neck. Once inside, she smoothed a hand through her damp hair.

'How is Gemma?' she asked.

'Gemma? She's okay. Well, she has a headache.'

'I know. She phoned me this morning.'

'She did?'

'That's okay, isn't it? I gave her my number when she called around. The bracelet she made is so sweet.' She held out her wrist to show Benedict. 'She's a clever girl.'

'It's lovely,' he said. 'Did the two of you, er, talk for long?'

Estelle frowned and shook her head like a wet dog. She felt around in her bag. Drips of water fell from the leather strap onto the floor. After producing a small, clear packet of tissues, she pulled one out and dabbed at her hair. 'Not really. We just had a chat. She talked about you mostly.'

'Really?'

'Don't worry. It's all good.' She smiled. Her dabs grew

slower as she noticed something different about the show-room. She unfolded then refolded the tissue and moved towards the nearest cabinet. 'Are you displaying work made by other jewellers now?'

'No. It's all mine.'

'Oh.' She tilted her head and her lips parted. She pressed her fingers against the glass as if she wanted to reach inside the cabinet, to touch the silver blossom brooch. Her eyebrows lifted by just a fraction. 'Yours? All of it?'

'I'm trying to diversify. I've made an Aquamarine ring for Margarita and a silver pendant for Diane, though it's a surprise for her birthday, so please don't tell her. The old jewellery pieces in the cabinets are ones I made with my mother, years ago. I told Gemma that they weren't good enough to display, but I thought I'd give it a try. We discovered the gemstones in the bottom of the old wooden chest in the attic.'

'Your parents' chest?'

'Yes.'

'I don't think I've ever seen inside it.'

Benedict wondered if he detected a touch of surprise in her voice that he had shown something so personal to his niece. 'I told Gemma about her grandparents, Joseph and Jenny,' he said. 'She wanted to find out more about her family.'

Estelle walked over to the counter. As she leaned over and peered inside it, her black bob swung down and obscured her face. Benedict took the wet tissues from her and put them in the bin. He wanted to reach out and push back her hair, over her ear, as he used to do when it fell onto her cheek. He spread his fingers out against the glass to stop the temptation.

'Has Gemma talked to you any more about Charlie?' she asked.

'What about him?' Benedict felt the hairs on the back of his neck bristle.

'About where he is and what he's up to?'

'He's at home on the farm. It must be difficult to get away from work.'

'I suppose it is. I just worry about Gemma.'

'She seems fine. I think she's enjoying it here.'

'Yes,' she said, as if to convince herself. 'I'm sure she is.' She looked around the shop again. 'I actually came here to buy a present. Veronica has got a promotion, out in the States.'

'Does this mean that she'll stay out there a while longer?' He wondered if it meant that Estelle would also stay away from him.

'I think so,' Estelle said lightly. 'She's not sure yet.'

'If I remember correctly, Veronica wears a lot of black and white...' He held back from saying that he thought that Veronica looked like the type of person to weigh her breakfast cereal before eating it, and would wear stilettos around the swimming pool on holiday. 'She's very... style-conscious.'

'Yes, she is, so choosing jewellery for her is tricky.'

Benedict moved his eyes from cabinet to cabinet. He wanted to choose something that would suit Veronica but that would also impress Estelle. A brooch with gemstones could be perfect.

His eyes settled on the cabinet at the far end of the counter. He walked over to it and found his hand instinctively hovering over a piece of Tourmaline Quartz. He wished Gemma was here to help him to verify that it was a good stone for Veronica, but he picked it out anyway and placed it on a sheet of white paper. The clear stone was shot through with fine streaks of black.

Without looking up at his wife, Benedict picked up a pen and started to sketch a brooch. At first his strokes were short and sketchy, but they soon grew thicker and bolder as his confidence grew and his idea took shape in his head, and on the paper. He didn't have to think too deeply about the design, it's like it was there fully formed in his head and waiting to escape.

He drew a five-sided star crafted from silver wire. Within the outline of the star, he added a series of abstract scrolls and curls of wire, soldered to each other. These were punctuated with small, round gemstones.

When he was satisfied with the sketch, he turned it around to show it to Estelle. 'Tourmaline Quartz is supposed to bring you luck,' he said. 'It combines the luckiness of both Quartz Crystal and Tourmaline. It can help to give you a positive attitude and attracts inspiration.'

He looked up and expected her eyes to be trained on the drawing, but instead she looked directly at him. Frown lines were etched on her forehead. 'When did you learn all this?' she asked.

'From my father's gemstone journal. Gemma's enjoying reading through it and has been adding her own notes. I've learned about some of the gemstones too.'

For a second he considered showing Estelle some of Gemma's notes in the journal, to ask her what he should do about them. But then he'd be admitting that there might be a problem. And he wanted to sort everything out himself, first. 'I can add additional stones, but I think the Tourmaline Quartz should be the main one. The star is a lucky shape, and Veronica can wear a brooch with anything.'

Estelle didn't speak for a while. She studied the drawing and held the clear and black gemstone up to the light. 'I think it's a wonderful idea,' she said. 'You've certainly been keeping busy.'

Benedict would usually make a joke, to lighten up the mood, but he fought against it. He didn't want to make general chit-chat, or pretend with her any longer. He met her eyes with his. 'It helps to be busy,' he said, 'when you're not here.'

Estelle took a small, sharp intake of breath.

They both reached out to touch the drawing at the same time, to talk about the star. As they did, the tips of their forefingers touched and they both laughed, nervously. Their hands remained there, on the paper, with their fingers resting on the star. Benedict felt electricity prickle along his forearms and he wondered if she felt it too. After so long apart, being this close to his wife again felt delicious.

'I think that…' Estelle started to say, but her words trailed off.

'Yes?'

'I think that, we…'

'Yes?' He placed his index finger on the top of her wedding ring and watched her throat as she swallowed. Her cheeks began to redden.

The moment was interrupted when the shop door beep-bopped open.

'Good afternoon, Benedict,' Reggie bellowed and strode inside.

Estelle quickly moved her hand away, but Benedict kept his in place, already missing her touch. He looked longingly at her before forcing his gaze towards Reggie instead.

From the neck down, Benedict wouldn't have recognised the solicitor. He had abandoned his suit and cashmere coat and instead wore a navy Adidas hooded top and indigo jeans. They still had creases, worn fresh from the shop shelves. His white hair was still as domed as ever.

'I've come to collect the earrings,' he said. 'I only have one minute.'

Benedict passed the box to him and opened the lid.

Reggie peered into it. 'They're fine,' he said and took out his wallet.

'I'm glad you like them.'

Reggie reached out and touched the blue gemstone for a few seconds. 'I think Laura will, um, love them,' he said awkwardly. His lips grew tighter as he thought about something else. 'I'm taking her out for dinner today and we usually go to a fish restaurant in York. I wondered if

Gemma might have more of an idea about where to take a young woman to…'

'She's at home nursing a headache, I'm afraid.'

'Ah, well. Never mind.' Reggie's eyebrow twitched.

'The three of us enjoyed Brenda's, a lovely tearoom in York,' Estelle said. 'I think that your daughter might like it there.' She put her bag on her shoulder. 'Now I must go. You and Gemma are coming to my art exhibition, Benedict?'

'Yes, we'll be there.'

'And I love your star brooch idea,' she said.

They gave each other a secret smile.

'And you're welcome to come along too, Reggie,' Estelle said, as she opened the shop door. 'Bring Laura along, if you like.'

Reggie stared after her. 'Oh, okay. Art? Yes… Thank you.' After Estelle left, he lowered his voice. 'Do young people enjoy that sort of thing?' he asked. 'And I thought that your wife had moved out…'

'Yes, but we're trying to make things work,' Benedict said, as he watched Estelle turn and wave to him. 'So don't try to make an appointment for me at Ramsbottom's just yet.'

Benedict phoned home and left a message for Gemma, to tell her that there was something he wanted to do.

He took out the anniversary necklace from his drawer, picked up a pencil and sketched it onto a piece of paper. Except this time, he didn't just draw the necklace, he drew the outline of his wife's face and her neck. He took extra care when he drew her eyes, shading in the irises until he felt that her true image was looking and smiling back at him.

Her necklace sat just below her collarbone. What could he do to it to make it more special? He dipped his hand into the glass jar and took out a handful of gemstones. Then he shook out more onto his bench and sifted through them, looking for ones with significance and meaning for Estelle. Just as he'd had the idea for engraving Diane's Kunzite pendant with words, a picture slowly emerged in his head and he saw how the anniversary necklace should be.

He chose twenty-five gemstones, rejected seven then deselected six more, then another two until he was left with ten – one for each year of his and Estelle's marriage. Then he set to work.

He only set down his tools when the necklace was finished and when he heard the Noon Sun village clock strike 11 p.m. Time had run away with him again. The street lamp outside lit the jewellery shop with an orange glow, like a Halloween pumpkin.

He thought briefly about Gemma at home; she was surely in bed asleep by now. Then he turned his thoughts back to the necklace and how he'd completed another WEB challenge. He lifted the necklace up and it twinkled in his hands. His eyes might be bleary but it was perfect at last.

20. Bloodstone

courage, guidance, instinct

As Benedict approached his house, he saw that it was all lit up. Each room seemed to be illuminated. Light streamed through the glass panels in the front door, making the path look like a yellow carpet. The gem tree's leaves shone as if they were made from gold foil.

Benedict once owned a Christmas lamp. It was a fibreglass house with a light inside. The windows and door lit up and he liked the glow the house gave; it was yellow, warm and homely. When he was a child he switched it on and read by the lamplight.

Charlie used to press his eye against the windows, wanting to see the bulb and the wires inside. He flicked the switch on and off until Benedict told him to stop it. The lamp eventually broke after Charlie manhandled it once too often.

And now, Benedict's own house reminded him of that lamp.

Speedily, Benedict took his key from his pocket and opened the door. The hall light was so bright it made him squint. He listened but couldn't hear any sounds. 'Gemma?' he shouted up the stairs, but there was no reply.

All the doors leading off the hallway were open, and in each room the light was turned on. Benedict thought of the night that Gemma first arrived, when everything was in darkness. Now, everything was too bright.

He looked around the kitchen and switched off the main light. The light over the cooker was on and he turned that off too. The dining room was empty, as was the front room and the cupboard under the stairs. He switched off the light in each.

He circled around downstairs again and found a small reading lamp and a wall light that he had missed on his first time round.

Striding upstairs, he shouted again. 'Gemma?'

He went into the bathroom, then into his bedroom. All the lights were on up here too – a bedside lamp, a reading lamp, his torch, at the top of the stairs, which highlighted a mound of fluff on the carpet. It was as if someone had searched the house, from top to bottom, but not moved anything out of place. Then they left, leaving everything illuminated.

His pulse quickened. This was very strange. There was nothing to indicate that Gemma wasn't still here. The front door was locked. He didn't sense anything was amiss. She might be asleep, but why were the lights on?

He came to Charlie's old bedroom last. 'Gemma?' He pushed open the door. As with the others, the pendant light in the middle of the ceiling flooded the room with a golden glow.

Gemma sat, hunched up against the wall. She wore

Estelle's flowered pyjamas and her own cowboy boots. Her knees were tucked up to her chin.

'Gemma,' Benedict exclaimed. 'Is everything okay?'

'Uh-huh.' She hugged her legs.

'All the lights are on.'

'Huh?'

'I mean *every* single light in the house.'

She rested her cheek on her knees. 'It's late,' she said. 'Where have you been?'

'I stayed late to work on Estelle's necklace.'

'You didn't tell me that.'

'I rang the house and left a message.'

'I didn't hear it.'

'Sorry. I thought you'd probably be in bed, with your headache.'

'I've not been in bed all day. I got up.'

He held out his palms. 'What has happened here? Why are you sitting on the floor?'

'Someone came to the house.'

'Someone?'

'You didn't come home, and there was this knock at the door and I thought it was you. But when I answered there was no one there. There was this face at the window and it was horrible, white and black.'

'It was probably kids, out trick-or-treating early, for Halloween.'

'It freaked me out. Then I kept thinking I could hear noises in the house. It was all dark and I was on my own. You said there was a ghost in the attic.'

'That was only a joke.' Benedict crouched down beside her. 'You know that. Are you okay now?'

She nodded.

When Charlie got scared or worried, Benedict used to wrap a comforting arm around his shoulders. They would cuddle up and talk. But putting his arm around Gemma didn't feel right.

He usually recalled when Charlie was younger as being a fun and lovely time. Over the years, he chose to forget how damned difficult it was too. Bringing up a child wasn't all cosy suppers and putting plasters on grazed knees. Exasperation, exhaustion, stress and loneliness could accompany parenthood. Sometimes you felt lonelier than if you were alone.

Benedict didn't think of these things when he tried to persuade Estelle to adopt. All he could see were the good parts.

He and Gemma both remained crouched on the floor until he felt his ankles lock up. 'Sorry again,' he said. 'I should have phoned the house again, to speak to you.'

She shrugged and stretched out her legs. 'Sorry about the lights. I'm a dumbass. I'll go and turn them all off.'

'It's okay. I've done it.'

She lifted her chin and pushed her hair away from her eyes. 'Can I have a cup of tea, please, Uncle Ben?'

'Sure,' he said, studying her face for a moment. 'I'll make us one now.'

21. Tiger's Eye

sociability, vigilance, bravery

Benedict was surprised to find a steady stream of people heading inside the Purple Heather Gallery. He felt rather ashamed that he'd assumed Estelle's exhibition might attract only a handful of villagers. However, there were at least eight people queued in front of him, including Reggie.

'I invited Laura, but she's busy doing something else, a creative writing class,' he said. 'She did love the earrings though. She showed them to her friends, so you may enjoy an influx of teenage girls to your shop. Hmmm,' he said, as though as he'd thought of a good idea. 'Perhaps we could discuss commission, for referrals.'

Benedict blinked at him incredulously. 'I don't think so, but I'm glad she liked them.'

He turned away and thought that he glimpsed someone standing outside the community centre, and the streetlight glinting off a pair of dark, round sunglasses, but a surge in the queue swept him into the gallery foyer.

Margarita sat at a wooden desk behind a huge bouquet of flowers in a green glass vase. They filled the air with a sweet, heady scent. Her Aquamarine ring sparkled on her finger as she took an orange rose, snipped off the stem with a small pair of shears and handed it to Benedict. 'For the buttonhole on your jacket, Benedeect. I have arranged these for Lawrence and he will not miss one bloom.'

Benedict smiled and pushed it into his lapel.

She handed him a piece of paper. 'Here is some information about the artist, although you're probably an expert already,' she said with a laugh. 'The exhibition is at the top of the stairs.'

Before he followed the chink of glasses and rumble of conversation upstairs, Benedict read the paper:

> The Purple Heather Gallery is delighted to host local artist Estelle Stone's debut exhibition, 'Moorland Escape'. Full-time artist Estelle is self-taught. She is influenced by the Yorkshire moors, where she enjoys walking alone with her sketchbook and camera. She uses oils, pastels and acrylics to create her abstract canvasses.

Benedict's throat grew dry as he read it again. He wasn't mentioned in the résumé. A big part of Estelle's life, *her husband*, was missing. He wondered if there was some ominous meaning behind this and asked Gemma what she thought.

'They probably ran out of space.' She shrugged. 'Why should Estelle mention you, when this is about her work?'

He supposed she was right. 'You're kind of wise sometimes,' he said.

'I know I am.'

Estelle's paintings lined the stairwell and were alive with colour. Benedict viewed the moors as bleak with miles of nothingness, but his wife saw flashes of exotic green and turquoise. Her sheep were lilac daubs of oil paint. The old Blue Jack quarry became smears of mustard and terracotta.

They seemed to come from a part of her that Benedict didn't know any longer, or wasn't privy to. He wondered what else she hid away, and which was now being released, and he thought about his own secrets too.

There were so many times over the years that he could have confided in his wife about his relationship with Charlie. And the thing was, she would probably have listened and tried to understand. She might have persuaded Benedict to contact his brother again, and Benedict could have been part of Gemma's childhood. He had missed out on watching her grow up. Perhaps that was his punishment for his mistake with Amelia.

In not telling Estelle about what had happened, it was no longer just his secret. It was over a decade of lies.

'What are you thinking of?' Gemma nudged him.

'I'm feeling a little nervous,' he said, trying to banish thoughts of Charlie from his mind. 'I hope Estelle likes the white horse that Frank's going to bring along.'

'Are you going to ride him, and pretend to be a knight or something?'

'I don't know yet. My plan didn't go into that much detail.'

Gemma tutted. 'You should let me deal with WEB. You only have half an idea.'

'Okay, I get it. Let's go and say hi to Estelle. I think she'll like the horse anyway.'

Firstly, they headed for the drinks table. There were wine glasses set out in blocks of colour – red, white and rosé, and orange juice. Benedict picked up a glass of red. The gallery was full and when he finally caught sight of his wife, through the crowd, he held his breath.

She looked beautiful, radiating a holiday-in-Greece like glow. She wore a knee-length purple dress with a deep scooped neck and the firework necklace. With a churn of his stomach, Benedict noticed that she wasn't wearing her wedding ring. He crooked his thumb into his palm and spun his own ring around.

Estelle chatted to a man whose beard would make a suitable home for small birds to nest in. She pointed to a large square painting of the moors, moving her hands to show the rise and fall of the hills. Then a lady dressed in jeans and a flowing psychedelic-print top tapped her shoulder. Estelle was in demand and, for a big bloke, Benedict felt invisible.

He had always seen marriage as a robust thing, like a boulder. And that boulder might become weathered, or the earth might shift, but it would always be there. But now he was beginning to think that it was delicate. Perhaps more like an orchid, which needed care and attention or else it might die. He hoped there was still a chance for his marriage to re-flower.

Of course there is, he told himself as he reached out for another glass of wine. He just had to keep trying. He dipped his hand into the peanuts and took a handful. A gooey chocolate cupcake whispered to him from a plateful of others. *Hi, Benedict. Look at our lovely silver sprinkles.* He took one and munched it.

'Uncle Ben,' Gemma scolded, 'put that down.'

'What?' He stared at the cupcake in his hand, and couldn't remember picking it up. 'Sorry.' He threw it into a bin and wiped his hands on a napkin.

Gemma wanted to look at the artwork on her own, so Benedict circled in the opposite direction. He admired the paintings and thought of Estelle walking on the moors, without him.

He moved slowly, not wanting to be too obvious with his glances over at her. Ryan and Nigel stood in the corner of the room, drinking bottles of beer, so Benedict joined them. 'Did you give Diane her pendant?' he asked Ryan.

'It's her birthday this weekend. I'll save it for then.'

'It's gorgeous,' Nigel said. 'She'll love it.'

'I hope so.' Ryan gulped from his bottle.

'You're the Terminator, remember?' Benedict said. 'You're tough.'

Ryan straightened his back. 'Yes, I am,' he said.

Gemma joined them. She took Benedict's glass of wine off him and handed him an orange juice instead. He shook his head and took a sip.

'I'm also thinking about booking a small break in Paris, for us, without the kids,' Ryan said. 'Nigel saw a great deal in the newspaper. Have either of you been?'

Benedict nodded. 'It was a long time ago, but it was beautiful.'

'I've never been,' Gemma said.

Benedict frowned. 'You said that you went there, to see the Eiffel Tower, on your own.'

'Oh, yeah.' Gemma shuffled on the spot. Her boots waggled on her ankles. 'I did go once. Sorry.'

'How could you forget something like that?' Benedict felt the tips of his ears reddening. 'You forgot about befriending the white horse, and then about the Eiffel Tower. They're pretty big things to drop out of your brain.'

'Hey, it's not a problem,' Ryan butted in. 'I'm always forgetting stuff, my keys and wallet.'

Benedict remembered that when Charlie reached the age of thirteen or fourteen, he developed a lethargy that found him unable to crawl out of bed in the morning, a voracious hunger and a new passion for arguing. He left his school books at home and forgot to set his alarm clock, but he wouldn't ever have blanked out that he'd been to France.

Benedict wasn't sure whether to be suspicious, or if this was all part of Gemma being a teenager. He gulped his juice. 'It's not the same,' he said.

'I want to look at that painting.' Gemma pointed at one, without looking, and she sloped off.

'How are things going, with a teenager in the house?' Ryan asked.

248

'Don't ask.' Benedict set his glass of juice down and picked his wine glass back up. Estelle was now talking to four people.

She had always attracted attention; an admiring glance from a male passer-by, or a brush of the arm from her boss at work. Benedict once sat in the Pig and Whistle and watched as a handsome guy, probably ten years younger, chatted up Estelle at the bar.

When she sat back down, Benedict said brightly, 'It looks like you have an admirer.'

'What? That boy?' Estelle laughed and rested her face on his shoulder. 'I need a proper man. Like you.'

Breaking his thoughts, a fork clinked loudly against a glass and a hush fell over the room. Benedict watched Lawrence Donnington make his way to the centre of the gallery. He wore black jeans and his customary striped T-shirt, though this one was tighter than ever, clinging to his firm chest. His coal-black hair was swept back off his forehead, which made his eagle-beak nose seem even more majestic.

Everyone turned to look at him.

'Good evening. I'm Lawrence,' he said in his treacly voice. 'I'm the proprietor of Purple Heather and, tonight, I'm delighted to present the work of the very talented local artist, Estelle Stone.' He held out his arm and Estelle, smiling coyly, joined him.

As she lifted her head, Benedict caught her eye. She cast him a small quick smile and wriggled her fingers.

'And to mark this wonderful occasion,' Lawrence continued, 'here's a bottle of champers from Purple

Heather.' He whispered something in Estelle's ear and she held a hand to her heart.

'Ew, he's touching Estelle.' Gemma appeared beside Benedict. 'What time is Frank arriving at?'

'At eight o'clock.' He smiled to himself. 'And that's better than a bottle of champagne.'

Friends flocked around Estelle, patting her on the arm, kissing her on the cheek, and Benedict felt proud.

When the congratulations petered out, he made his way over to her. He wanted to kiss her on the cheek, but he held back. 'I have something for you, too,' he said.

'You do?' Her eyes flicked to his pocket, as if expecting him to produce an item of jewellery.

'It's outside.'

'Outside?' Estelle smiled and frowned at the same time.

Benedict looked around for Gemma, but she was talking to Nigel. 'Come with me.' He didn't take her hand, but he led the way down the stairs.

Lawrence stood leaning against the table, talking to Margarita. He bent over to bury his nose into her flower arrangement.

Damn it, Benedict thought. He wanted to be alone with Estelle.

Lawrence stood upright as he noticed them. 'Estelle. Are you leaving? So soon?'

'No, I'm not going. Benedict wants to show me something, outside.'

'Does he?' Lawrence said slowly. 'Outside? Well, that sounds intriguing. Is it private, or can we all take a look?'

Benedict cursed under his breath. He couldn't say that it was for Estelle's eyes only when there was going to be a bloody big horse standing on the pavement. Besides, he thought as he puffed his chest a little, he'd let Lawrence see that he was fighting for Estelle, and that Benedict could come up with something more inventive than champagne. 'Anyone can see,' he said.

He opened the door first, feeling the weight of expectation on his shoulders. Estelle stood close behind him and he could feel the warmth of her body. Margarita moved out from behind the table and Lawrence followed her.

Benedict stepped out onto the pavement first.

'Aye,' Frank greeted him.

Benedict felt like his heart might stop. He wished that the pavement flags would crack open and swallow him up.

On the pavement stood a grey llama.

Estelle crinkled her brow and then laughed. 'Is this for me...?'

'Er, yes, but...' The words queued up in Benedict's head, about Cecil's talk of white chargers and about how he wanted to bring a white horse to her exhibition. He could tell her that he wanted to joust for her, but that there had been a mix-up. But before he could find the right thing to say first, Lawrence roared with laughter.

'A llama?' he guffawed. 'Is this *your* gift?'

Estelle raised a questioning eyebrow at Benedict.

The door opened and Gemma came outside. 'Where's the white horse?' she asked and this made Lawrence laugh even more. He slid his arm around Estelle's shoulder and gave her a tight squeeze. 'Your husband is hilarious,' he said. 'Come inside and I'll get you a glass of wine.'

Estelle lowered her shoulders to move out of his grip. She stood on her own then looked at Lawrence and then at Benedict.

Benedict's arms dangled by his sides.

Estelle walked over to the llama and patted it on the head. 'She's lovely. What's her name?'

'Bernard,' Frank said. 'It's a *he*. We've got some problems in that area. Did you bring the gemstones, Benedict?'

Benedict closed his eyes and held them shut for a while to muster some strength. 'Yes,' he sighed. He took a small bag of Red and Green Aventurine from his pocket and pressed it into Frank's palm. 'I hope this helps. And will you give this piece of Golden Beryl to Violet?'

'Aye,' Frank said. 'I've seen her wandering around the village tonight. I told her to come over to the gallery, but she said that she didn't want any attention.'

'What gemstones do you have?' Margarita asked, looking over Frank's shoulder. 'Mine is Aquamarine.'

'Red Aventurine for the llamas, and the same in green for growing plants.'

'Ah, this is something I want to do, to grow and sell my own flowers in Floribunda.'

'Aye? Come up to the farm one day and take a look. You're welcome to use my land.'

Estelle stroked the llama behind his ears. 'I don't know what this means, Benedict, but he's adorable.'

'I'm glad you like him,' Benedict muttered and he patted

the llama on his back. 'There's a story behind it, but I'll tell you another time.'

Alexander and Alistair sidled up and whispered to Bernard. The llama seemed to listen to them and flicked his ears. 'Can we take him for a walk, Frank?' Alistair asked. 'He's gorgeous.'

'Aye, not really, lads. It's dark and he's not used to being out on the streets.'

'Can we help to walk him back home then?' Alexander asked.

'Aye. You can do that. If it's okay with Nicholas.'

'I'll ask him,' Alistair said and sped off.

Estelle smiled at Benedict. 'I look forward to hearing your story. But, for now, I'll go back inside to see my guests.'

'And I'll go and try these out.' Frank rattled the gems in his hand.

Gemma yawned. 'Can we go home, Uncle Ben? I'm really tired.'

'Okay. Let's walk back,' he said with a sigh.

Benedict said goodbye to Frank and Margarita, and his legs felt heavy as he and Gemma walked away from the gallery.

The street was dark and gloomy, with no cars or people around. He felt that he should chat to Gemma, about how great the exhibition had been, but his thoughts kept switching back to the grey llama and his woeful effort to impress his wife.

'Lighten up, Uncle Ben,' Gemma said. 'Estelle liked Bernard.'

'I'm fine.'

'It was funny.'

'Lawrence thought so.'

'He's a jerk. He just displays other people's art but you actually create stuff. You're more talented, and you're kinda nicer looking too.'

'I don't think so.'

'You have a kind face.'

'Thanks.'

They walked in silence for a while longer. 'So, do you think I can go to that Restore the Hope concert in Applethorpe?' she asked.

'Gemma,' he said, 'you are so obvious.'

'Okay. Just asking. I still think you look kind,' she said with a laugh. 'But next time leave the WEB ideas to me, huh?'

22. Sunstone

self-empowerment, benevolence, radiance

When he wasn't occupied in his workshop, Benedict sat on a stool with Gemma behind the counter in the showroom, as she looked through the pages of the journal. When he saw his father's handwriting and read his words, Benedict felt there was a hand clasped around his heart, squeezing tight. He thought what might have been if his parents had survived. They would have met Estelle, they would have been around to raise Charlie, and Benedict would have never made his huge mistake.

Sometimes, Gemma insisted on skipping a page or she placed an arm or a hand, slyly, across the words. Benedict pretended not to notice, but it was obvious she was hiding something and he had read enough of her entries to know why.

Her enthusiasm, when she read out loud to him about gemstones, was like osmosis and Benedict learned more of their stories too.

The jar of gemstones sparkled on top of the counter

and Benedict began to think less about his brother on the other side of the world. If any thoughts of Charlie and his whereabouts did niggle him, he silenced them by assuring himself that he'd done all he could to make contact, and what kind of father allowed his young daughter to travel on her own to England, anyway?

He no longer tried to Google Sunnyside Farm and he hadn't cajoled Gemma into phoning her mobile provider and the passport office again.

Benedict let Gemma's slips about forgetting the Eiffel Tower and her friendship with the white horse slide, and he began to look forward to any future commissions that the Noon Sun villagers might bring his way.

He worked on the Tourmaline Quartz brooch for Veronica and it turned out better than he imagined. He made the star shape with variations on the length of the points to make the brooch less uniform and more unique. Alongside the gem he originally selected, he added a small Ruby for the achievement of goals, and Malachite for success in business.

As he gave the brooch a final polish and placed it into a grey box, he thought how beautiful it was, but that the box it sat in was dull. His eyes swept around the shop and everything was so grey.

Estelle's paintings livened up the blank white walls of the Purple Heather Gallery, and people flocked to it, but Stone Jewellery needed an injection of colour and a lick of paint. He wanted it to live up to its blossoming reputation.

Benedict had left a few paintings behind, before he

transported them over to Veronica's. He stared at his blank walls and imagined how they might look dotted above the cabinets.

It felt strange because he was used to *not* having ideas, and to creating his work without any thought, working automatically and without emotion. So it felt rather intriguing when a picture began to form in his head. The hairs on his arms stood on end, and his fingers tingled with anticipation.

Perhaps he could create jewellery inspired by Noon Sun, to complement Estelle's paintings. Using Peridot, Amethyst and Malachite, he could reproduce the colours of the moors. He'd scour marks into silver to represent dancing grass against grey sky. Rather than tucking himself away to make his jewellery, and Estelle shutting herself away in her art studio, they could work together. Stone Jewellery could be their family business.

It might work.

Benedict got swept away in his imagination, and despite Gemma's insistence that she should be the one to generate ideas for WEB, the seedlings of his next challenge were already growing in his mind.

A few days after Estelle's art preview, Nigel called in to the shop on his way home from work. He drifted around like a goldfish in a bowl that was too small.

Benedict noticed his listlessness. 'What's wrong?'

His friend scratched his head in bewilderment. 'I kind of asked Josie out on a date,' he said. 'I was in the pub, on my own, and she was on her break. She was eating a bag of bacon and brown sauce flavoured crisps and she offered me one. We got chatting, and she loves crisps, and American rock music too. She's *not* got a boyfriend called Mason and she's absolutely perfect.' He sighed. 'Well, except for the habit of picking her feet. That's a bit nasty.'

'Well done.' Benedict reached out and gave his friend's hand a firm shake.

Nigel gulped. 'I'm not sure I can do it though.'

'Why not?'

'Because, she's gorgeous and I'm just…me.' He brushed his hands down his biker's jacket. 'She's out of my league, and I think I'm just going to end up looking stupid.'

'Don't be daft. She said yes.'

'I don't know why. Perhaps she has nothing else better to do. Perhaps she feels sorry for me or something.'

'Or maybe she likes you.'

Nigel shrugged. His eyes flicked to the gemstones on the counter. 'Have you got one that might mean something for me?'

Benedict looked at the gems and picked up a circular piece of Citrine. It looked like a small piece of sunshine and already had a hole pierced through its centre. He found a small offcut of round black leather thong and deftly fashioned it into a bracelet.

'Hold out your wrist,' he said and tied it in place. 'Citrine attracts love and happiness and helps new pursuits. It gives you optimism and boosts your confidence.'

'Oh, mate, it's cool,' Nigel said, admiring it. 'What do I owe you?'

'Nothing,' Benedict said. 'Have a great time with Josie. Just be yourself and you can't go wrong.'

'You're like some kind of doctor,' Nigel said. 'But instead of medicine you prescribe gemstones.'

'I'm happy with that.' Benedict smiled. 'Feel free to tell others.'

His enthusiasm and happy feeling slipped a little when the next customer through the door was Lawrence.

The gallery owner shook the rain from an oversized red-and-yellow umbrella and propped it against the door. He casually strolled across to the counter in his black jeans and striped T-shirt.

Casting his eye over Lawrence's lion-like frame, Benedict felt as bulky and awkward as a buffalo.

'Benedict,' Lawrence boomed. 'Hello there.'

'Hello,' Benedict muttered back.

'Don't worry. I'm not here to berate you for the mess the llama left on the pavement after Estelle's exhibition. Such an unusual, er, gift, for your wife.'

'She seemed to like it,' Benedict said through gritted teeth.

'Estelle seems more of a champagne kind of woman, to me.'

'We've been married for almost *ten* years,' Benedict emphasised. 'So I think I know her pretty well.'

'Ah, yes. She said that your anniversary is approaching. Is she, er, still living in Veronica's apartment?'

'Yes,' Benedict said. 'I think I saw you there the other night.'

The two men stared at each other.

'I like to help my artists out.' Lawrence grinned. 'They appreciate my input.'

Benedict wanted to shoot out his fist to thump the smug gallery owner on the nose, but he had to keep calm. Even if Lawrence was trying to provoke him, he was also helping Estelle with her art, and to realise her potential. He took a deep breath to steel himself and was grateful when Gemma placed her hand, lightly, on his wrist.

'Did you want to buy anything?' she asked Lawrence.

'Oh, I want something.' Lawrence placed both his hands flat on the counter. When he moved them away again, he left finger-shaped halos of condensation on the glass. 'I rather fancy a new pair of cufflinks. I understand from Margarita that you do commission pieces, using gemstones. So what do you recommend?'

Benedict thought he knew the perfect gemstone for Lawrence. Sunstone. It was a bright orangey-yellow and ideal for self-discipline and humility. It might help the gallery owner to exercise some self-restraint.

He took a piece from the jar and set it down on the counter. 'I think this will suit you,' he said.

'Very vibrant.' Lawrence smirked.

Benedict sketched a pair of sunshine-shaped cufflinks and Lawrence agreed to the design, though he wanted them made larger.

When he left the shop, Benedict sighed deeply. 'Do you think that Sunstone is the right gem for him?' he asked Gemma.

She shook her head. 'Hmmm, I'm not so sure.'

'You're not?'

'You've been getting them right, Uncle Ben, but I don't know about this one.' She grabbed out for the journal as he reached out for it at the same time. Benedict took hold of it first. 'Give it to me,' she said. 'I'll read to you about Sunstone.'

Benedict flicked his eyes at her. It looked like she was hiding something from him again. He placed his arm across the counter as a barrier between his niece and the journal. 'I can read it for myself,' he said.

SUNSTONE

Believed to actually be a piece of the sun, Sunstone was highly prized by ancient magicians. Found in Norway and the USA, the gemstone is associated with the legendary phoenix who is said to rise from ashes and anew every five hundred years. Vikings believed Sunstone to be an aid to navigation and it has been found in Viking burial mounds. Sunstone can warm the heart and lift your spirits. It is said to enhance male sexual potency.

Benedict groaned aloud at the last few words. But he read on, not noticing that his father's words turned into Gemma's.

Sunstone can give you a feeling of self-worth and it promotes positive self-image. The gemstone helps you to believe that everything

> *will turn out well in the future. You should enjoy*
> *the present without worrying if the good times*
> *are about to end. That's something that I'm*
> *trying to do too. If I think about the future,*
> *I don't think I can handle it.*

Benedict turned to Gemma and his eyes narrowed. She might gloss over it, but he had to understand her words. She sounded so troubled.

He could leave this be and tell himself that she'd written them in an angst-ridden moment. Or he could demand to know what she meant.

His niece's thoughts about the future and her not being able to handle it tipped the balance. If she was in trouble, or was upset about anything, then he wanted to know and help. He didn't want any more secrets to pull the Stone family apart.

He tapped on her words about Sunstone.

'What?' she asked cautiously. Then her eyes fell upon her own handwriting. 'Oh,' she said.

'What can't you handle?'

'Nothing.' She shrugged. 'I don't know what you mean.'

'These are your words in the journal, Gemma.'

'They don't mean anything,' she tried.

Benedict read her passage aloud, then he found her ones for Lapis Lazuli and Tiger's Eye, and reminded her of them. All the while, Gemma looked at the floor.

'I think they do mean something, and we need to talk about this, once and for all.'

23. Garnet

initiating, life-force, self-confidence

'It's just silly scribble,' Gemma said. 'Honestly, Uncle Ben. In fact, I didn't even write that stuff. Joseph must have used a different pen.'

Benedict folded his arms. He couldn't ignore her excuses. He had to find out what was going on. 'The handwriting is the same as in the notebook in your room.'

Her eyes flickered upward and to the right, as if she was running through every explanation in her head. 'You read that?'

He didn't speak.

'I thought I could trust you. Why are you prying?'

Still Benedict didn't say anything. He wondered how else she might try to distract him. She sucked on a piece of hair and studied her boots. And still he waited.

Finally, she spat out the lock of hair. 'Okay, I wrote it. But I was pretending to be a character. Like in a book or something. It doesn't mean anything.'

'What can't you handle about the future?' he repeated.

'Nothing.'

Benedict studied her and, with her bottom lip protruding, she looked like a small child sulking in a supermarket because she'd been refused a bar of chocolate. He supposed she was still only a young girl, and with her friends living thousands of miles away and her mother gone, she had no one to share her feelings with. He was a forty-four-year-old man and couldn't pretend to understand a teenage girl's emotions.

'Sorry, Gemma,' he said firmly but kindly. 'This time you've got to tell me the truth. I've read other parts of the journal that tell me things aren't okay for you.'

'You shouldn't read it. It's *my* project.'

'I want to know what's going on. You're not going to get a sudden headache, or a need to be anywhere else but here.' To show her that he meant business, he walked over and locked the front door. 'No more.'

Gemma kicked one of her feet with the other. She ran her hand through her hair and tugged on the ends. 'Okay,' she said finally. 'You win. I suppose I didn't just come here for an adventure.'

'No?'

'I wanted to get away from home too, and to think about stuff.'

'But Charlie knows you're here?'

'Yeah,' she said. 'But it helps for me to be gone.'

'Why?'

'I dunno.'

Benedict sighed. 'Why don't you trust me and tell me the truth for once?'

She blinked through her russet hair. Her eyelids were pale pink, like seashells.

'I want to help you.' He gave her a small encouraging smile. 'You're my family.'

Her head ticked slightly like a metronome for a while and then it stopped. 'I like the f-word,' she said.

'Family?'

'Yeah.'

'So, tell me.'

'My dad's girlfriend…' she started.

'Janice?'

'Yeah. Well, she's having a baby.'

Benedict felt his jaw slacken.

'I'll have a new brother or sister soon, and it sucks.' Gemma shrugged as if she didn't care, but he could see from her expression that she did. 'It's been me and Dad for years. We stuck together when Mom left, like we were twins or something. Then Janice rocked up and everything changed. Dad has less time for me. He wanted the three of us to go and stay with Janice's parents, in New York, and play at being a happy family, but I didn't wanna go. So he said I could come here instead.'

'He must trust you, and think that you're grown-up enough to come on your own.'

'Maybe. Or perhaps he was happy for me to leave…so he can be with *her*.'

'I'm sure that's not the case.'

'You don't know that,' she said, tears pricking her eyes. 'I get so confused, so I write stuff down. I really wanted to come here, but I also kinda wanted him to put his foot down and stop me.'

'Why didn't you tell me this before?'

'Because I don't want you to discuss it with him. We need some time apart. I bet you don't understand.'

Actually, Benedict did. Just as Estelle needed to stay away from him for a while, Gemma wanted that too, from Charlie.

He remembered when he and Gemma stood on Dinosaur Ridge. Getting away from the village allowed him to think more clearly and take a different perspective. He was relieved that she had shared what was wrong. 'I think I do understand,' he said.

'I feel that Dad doesn't need me anymore, so I like helping you out, and the customers. It makes me feel useful. Like I'm finally good at something.'

'I'm glad you've told me all this.' He reached out his arm and rubbed her shoulder.

She stood still for a while and then stepped towards him. She wrapped her arms around his waist and briefly pressed her cheek to his chest before awkwardly pulling away. 'I'm kinda glad I've told you too, Uncle Ben.'

'So, no more lies or strange behaviour?'

'No more.'

'So, what should we do about your dad?' After spending so many days willing Charlie to get in touch, Benedict was beginning to feel ambivalent. It was up to his brother to make the next move.

'Can we wait until he gets your letter? Then he'll reach out to you, right? And we can all talk then.'

Benedict told himself that it wouldn't make much difference to wait a few days longer.

Gemma tried a small smile. 'I don't want Estelle to leave you for good, like my mom left me. That's why I want the two of you to get back together.'

'Operation WEB?' Benedict asked.

'Yeah. Stupid, huh?'

Benedict closed the journal. Wanting to win Estelle back had taken on another dimension. It was no longer something personal, just for him. There was Gemma to think of too. With Amelia leaving, and Janice on the scene, she needed a strong female role model to look up to. Estelle could be the perfect match.

'It's not stupid at all,' he said. 'You've done more to make me think about my life than anyone before. If you want to wait until the letter arrives with Charlie, then I trust you, okay? Though you did give me an address for a farm in Maine, not New York...'

'He should be back home by now.' Gemma sniffed.

'No more lies?'

'I promise.'

'I'm glad we've sorted things out. And do you still want to help me move forward, with my efforts to get Estelle back?'

'More than anything.'

'Good, because I have an idea for my next challenge, and I want you to help me, so that WEB is a team effort this time.'

'Okay.' Gemma's lips switched into a tiny smile. 'What is it?'

Benedict thought of how much his life had changed over the last two weeks and how relieved he was that Gemma had been so honest. He unlocked the front door and told her of his plans. 'I want the shop to shine as brightly as the jewellery and gemstones inside it,' he said.

24. Poppy Jasper

enthusiasm, enjoyment, fresh energy

Benedict put on his black tracksuit and found an old grey shirt for Gemma to wear over her clothes. He opened up his shed and took out all the cans of paint and paintbrushes, and loaded them onto his trolley. He folded up some old white sheets, and added a plastic bottle of turpentine. He'd bought a lot of the stuff a couple of years back, when he promised Estelle that he'd redecorate the house. His intentions had been true but his spirit was weak back then.

'This will be a fresh start,' he said to Gemma. 'For you and me, and Stone Jewellery.'

They trundled the decorating materials along the high street down to the shop, and Benedict ushered Lord Puss into his cat carrier. 'We'll move you into my house for a few days, to keep you away from the paint,' he said. Gemma pushed the piece of Tiger's Eye under the cat's cushion in the carrier.

When they let Lord Puss out at home, the cat instantly made himself welcome. He strolled around the kitchen with his head held aloft, as if he owned the place. 'There's a cat flap in the back door, so no smelly presents from you,' Benedict warned.

Lord Puss looked at him as if to say, 'Maybe I will, maybe I won't.'

Benedict hand-wrote a sign and taped it into the shop window. *Closed for Refurbishment.*

He and Gemma moved all the cabinets from the showroom into the workshop, and covered the floor with the old sheets. He stored the jar of gems, the cash till, the appointment book and phone in the cupboard under the counter, and covered that up too. He wrestled his ladder out of the store cupboard and set them in the middle of the floor. Standing with his hands on his hips, he took a deep breath. It was time for change. 'Okay. Let's do this.'

He climbed up the ladder, carrying a can of white emulsion paint in one hand, and his paintbrush between his teeth. He worked on covering the ceiling with a fresh coat of white paint, whilst Gemma painted the walls.

After he'd finished the ceiling, Benedict tackled the skirting boards next, and he and Gemma conducted a strange kind of dance as she moved clockwise, and Benedict worked in the opposite direction, crouching and crawling along the floor.

His niece proved to be a determined worker, not tempted by Benedict's suggestions to stop for a cup of tea or a trip to Bake My Day for a chocolate éclair. 'We're doing really well,' she said firmly. 'We'll eat later.'

It was past two o'clock when they took their first break. Benedict handed Gemma some money. 'I'd like something more substantial than salad.'

'You've earned a nice ham sandwich today,' she said.

As she headed towards the door, Benedict glimpsed a flash of white on her face. 'Come back here a minute.'

Gemma let go of the door handle. 'What?'

'You have paint on your cheek.'

She reached up and touched both sides of her face. 'Where?'

He took a clean tissue from his pocket, stepped over a can of paint then dabbed gently at her face.

She closed her eyes. 'Is it gone?'

'Yes. You'll do fine.' He smiled.

They ate their sandwiches sitting on the floor, on a paint-specked sheet, with their legs outstretched and their backs against the counter. Gemma had bought a chocolate éclair and broke it in half, to share. 'You've earned this,' she said. And Benedict felt that, actually, he had done.

After eating, they both gave the walls a second coat of paint and, within a few hours, the dolphin-grey of the showroom had gone, and it shone wet with a coat of brilliant white.

As Benedict and Gemma made their way home, Nicholas Ledbetter hurried along the canal towpath towards them. The chef wore his white apron and had a bundle of leaflets under his arm. When he saw Benedict, he peeled one off and thrust it into his hand. 'Here,' he said gruffly. 'Take one of these.'

'What is it?'

'It's my new pub menu. I've been planning to do it for ages.' He glanced quickly at Gemma and looked away again before their eyes could meet. 'And before you say anything, it's nothing to do with that Carnelian stone thing you gave me.'

'Of course not.' Benedict tried not to smile.

'I mean, as if a bloody stone could have that effect on anything or anyone,' Nicholas grunted and walked away, muttering to himself.

'Look at this,' Benedict handed the menu to Gemma. 'Plain old cheese and onion pie, chips and peas, is now farmhouse cheddar, red onion and ale pie with thrice-cooked chips and pea purée. I wonder what the villagers will think of that.'

'He's found new motivation from somewhere,' Gemma said. 'Whether that's shaped by the stone or not.'

'Hmmm,' Benedict folded the menu and put it in his pocket. 'Have you ever thought that perhaps it's you, Gemma, who influences people, rather than the gemstones?'

'Don't be silly.' She threaded a piece of hair into her mouth. 'I don't inspire anything.'

Yes, you do, Benedict said to himself. You inspired me.

The following morning, Gemma uncovered a tin of red emulsion in the shed, and one of yellow. Benedict had no idea why he'd bought those colours, but she sat on the lawn and mixed the two together, adding a touch of blue, until she created a coral shade.

'That's rather bright,' Benedict said.

'A bit of colour won't kill you.'

'That's what Estelle said about my shoes.'

Gemma eyed up his berry-coloured loafers and nodded, approvingly. 'Your wife is so smart.'

Benedict again loaded up the trolley with the paint and extra sheets, and he and Gemma pushed it along the high street. The village was quiet, not yet awake. Only one shop, the newsagent's, opened in Noon Sun on a Sunday, and Nigel closed up at lunchtime, when he'd sold out of the *Applethorpe Times*. Crags and Cakes opened up at 11 a.m., ready to welcome walkers inside for a cup of coffee.

He used to relish lazy Sundays such as this. His parents used to call it their 'family day'. It was a break from work when Joseph and Jenny took Benedict and Charlie out to play or for a picnic. Benedict still remembered the sound of children's laughter as they approached the park. As soon as they walked through the gate, Benedict and Charlie ran as fast as they could, their knees reaching almost as high as their chins. Charlie threw himself down the slide, on his belly, head first, and spun around on the roundabout until he felt sick. Benedict begged rich tea biscuits from Jenny, then took them down to the paddling pool, where he sat and dipped them into the gritty water before eating them. Everything stopped for family on Sundays.

Families were changing these days anyway, Benedict mused, as he and Gemma reached the shop. Back then it was pretty much the norm to have two parents and two kids. Now there were more step-families and extended families, single-parent families, and same-sex families.

He wondered if a family could ever be just two people, like him and Estelle. Did you have to have children to be a family? Could having Estelle and Gemma in his life be enough for him?

If he was honest then he didn't know. He still wanted a child of his own so badly.

He unlocked the shop door, and the interior looked like the inside of an expensive shoebox. Everything was white except the door through to the workshop, which had dried to a streaky grey.

Again he and Gemma worked quickly.

Benedict found a signal on his phone and selected the Applethorpe FM radio station. He and Gemma laughed at the cheesy pop music played by the DJ. Gemma held out both her hands to invite him to take them. They both shook out one leg and then the other in an uncoordinated but enthusiastic dance.

They painted the walls with a second coat of emulsion, and gave the skirting boards an extra layer of white gloss. Benedict tackled the streaky grey door.

When a knock sounded on the window, Benedict wobbled on the top of his ladder. 'We're closed,' he shouted out.

'Benedicto. It's me.'

'*Cecil.*' Benedict clambered down.

His friend waved through the glass.

Benedict rushed to the door to unlock it and Cecil came inside. His eyes widened as he stared at the showroom, bright white and empty except for the ladder, sheets and cans of paint. 'Benedicto,' he said, 'what's going down?'

'We're redecorating.'

'Well, I can see that, Einstein.'

'Gemma is helping me. Gemma, this is Cecil.'

Gemma stood and karate-chopped out a speckled white hand. 'Hello.'

'Aloha. I'm so pleased to meet you.'

'How are you feeling?' Benedict asked.

'I'm okay. Maybe a bit wobbly. I just got out of hospital this morning and I'm still finding the feeling in my body.'

'Should you really be out and about?'

Cecil rolled his eyes. 'You sound like the nurses.' He held up his piece of Turquoise. 'I have this to help me. Now...' he looked around the shop '...where's my gorgeous white fluff ball? Is he camouflaged against the walls?'

'I moved him into my house, while there's paint around.'

'Fabio. Thanks for that.'

Benedict set down his paintbrush. 'Do you want to come and see him? We can finish up here for the day.'

'I can't wait to see his little furry face,' Cecil said longingly. 'But can I come tomorrow instead?'

Benedict noticed the tiredness and fragility in his friend's eyes. 'Are you really sure that you're okay?'

'I'm doing my best.' Cecil popped the gemstone into his pocket. His face grew serious. 'Can I ask you a big favour?'

'How big?' Benedict asked with a smile.

'Ooh, ginormous.' Cecil held his hands wide apart to demonstrate. 'One of my sisters has invited me on hols, to Majorca, for a few days. I can rest up and catch a bit of late sun. There's the shop and Lord Puss to think about, but I just want to feel well again.'

Of course Benedict didn't mind Cecil taking time to recover properly, but he sucked through his teeth and shook his head to tease his friend. Then he laughed and patted Cecil on the arm. 'We can cope without you for a while longer. His Lordship has already decided he's the king of my house, and I have Gemma to help out here.'

'So, you don't mind?' Cecil said with relief in his voice.

'No. You could do with some colour in your cheeks. Come and visit Lord Puss tomorrow, and I'll give you a hand to pack for your holiday. Gemma will be okay here, on her own, or she can take a day off.'

Cecil looked at Benedict and then at Gemma. 'And it's okay, for sure?'

'Leave it all to me.' Gemma batted her hands together. 'If Uncle Ben moves the cabinets back into the showroom today, I can arrange all the jewellery tomorrow. And I've got a few ideas on how to make the shop look amazing.'

'Amazing?' Benedict questioned and Cecil raised an eyebrow.

'You know that you can trust me, Uncle Ben.'

Now that they'd talked about her words in the journal, and about Charlie and Janice, he felt that he could. 'Definitely,' he said. 'Of course I trust you.'

25. Citrine

warming, generosity, uplifting

Cecil and Lord Puss got reacquainted by rubbing heads and noses in the front room, whilst Benedict went to put the kettle on. He made Cecil a cup of tea, and when he made his own, he spooned in just one sugar. When he returned with the drinks, Lord Puss rolled onto his back, showing off his fluffy belly. He purred loudly and pawed at Cecil's hand and nuzzled his nose into his palm.

'I'll only be away for a few more days, my fine furry friend,' Cecil said. 'Then I'll be all tanned, relaxed and healthy again, and ready to take you home with me. I will treat you like the prince you are.'

'When you get back from holiday we can chat about your return to the shop,' Benedict said.

'I can't wait to get back to work.'

'I know that, but you must be sensible.'

'That's not the best way to describe me,' Cecil sighed.

'Now, look at this.' Benedict slowly reached out and

scratched the back of Lord Puss's neck. The cat closed his eyes with pleasure.

'Wowser,' Cecil said. 'Wonders never cease.'

'Tiger's Eye,' Benedict said knowingly.

After feeding Lord Puss, the two men walked to Cecil's house. He lived in a small stone terrace behind the community centre. The outside looked plain, rather ordinary, but inside was an explosion of colours and textures, with teal velvet throws, sheepskin rugs and hand-printed floral wallpaper.

Once there, Cecil insisted that he make Benedict a shepherd's pie. 'I love cooking, but my nieces only want beans on toast. Where is the adventure in that?'

They ate together at the kitchen table and Cecil laughed when Benedict told him about his efforts to woo back Estelle on the balcony, and about Bernard the llama. 'So you're really trying to joust for her?' he asked.

Benedict closed his eyes and imagined himself wearing a full suit of armour. 'I'm attempting to pick up my lance.'

'Well done, Benedicto. Let's hope it works. Have you spoken any more about adoption?'

'No. But, when the time's right, we will do.'

Benedict spent the whole day with his friend. He helped to do Cecil's ironing and pack for his break in Majorca, and it was almost teatime when he arrived back at the shop.

The first thing he noticed was the new logo on the coral-coloured back wall. Gemma had painted the words *Stone Studio* in her own handwriting, in two-foot tall, rose-gold letters.

'Do you like it?' she asked, as she wiped her hands on a piece of paper towel.

Benedict's mouth fell open. 'It looks so stylish.'

'What do you think about the rest of the shop?'

Gemma had rearranged the cabinets more haphazardly, so instead of you having to circle the showroom like a caged tiger, the new display took you on a journey, from one cabinet to another. She had rescued a wooden chair, with peeling turquoise paint, from the shop's backyard and set it at the end of the counter, for customers to sit down on.

Benedict always displayed his jewellery in straight lines, like barcodes, but Gemma had laid it out in a more spontaneous way. A silver belcher chain bracelet dangled from a piece of driftwood. His silver clam-shell test piece sat within a real clam shell. His recent work – the triangular brooches – didn't look as *Star Trek*-like displayed on a small broken tree branch. His geometric platinum triangle earrings lay in contrast next to the organic shape of his silver blossom brooch.

Gemma had added small heaps of gemstones to the glass shelves, and they glimmered under the tiny white fairy lights strung along the top of the cabinets, so they connected like stalls at a fairground.

A silver seahorse pendant hung on a piece of navy leather cord and Gemma had positioned it so it emerged from a small plastic chest. 'A miniature treasure chest,' Benedict said, pointing at it.

Gemma nodded. 'I bought it from Deserted Dogs. It's from an aquarium, but no one will know.'

A silver necklace with a teardrop-shaped pendant was draped over a pebble next to a bangle Benedict had made, and forgotten about, for his mother. He caught a lump in his throat as he saw it. He never had the chance to give it to her.

'Are you okay?' Gemma asked. 'You look weepy.'

'The wind outside made my eyes water a bit.' Benedict suddenly felt like laughing at this huge change in his shop. He leaned his head back, baring his teeth, and an unadulterated roar came out.

'You're laughing at it?' Gemma asked in a small voice.

'No. Not at all. It looks so…brilliant. I was just thinking about what Estelle will think, when she sees this change.'

'Are you going to invite her over?'

'Yes, but there's something else I want to do first.'

'Okay. And there's another thing,' Gemma said, reaching into her handbag. 'It's something I bought for you, for looking after me and stuff.'

'For me?'

'Yeah. Don't get too excited though.'

'I'll try not to.'

'Close your eyes.'

Benedict expected her to press a gemstone into his palm, but the thing he felt was soft and light. When he opened his eyes he saw a folded silk handkerchief, the same colour as the coral wall, rested on his open hand.

'It's for the top pocket of your suit jacket.'

Benedict had never worn a handkerchief before, and he wouldn't have chosen an orange one, but he pushed the small square of silk into his pocket anyway. And when he patted it, he felt as if he'd finally begun to sparkle as brightly as the jewellery he made.

26. Blue Topaz

learning, honesty, inspiration

A few days later, after plucking up courage, Benedict phoned and invited Estelle over to the shop, at 6 p.m. that evening. This gave him and Gemma enough time to add the finishing touches to the shop's interior.

Whilst sorting out the newsagent store cupboard, Nigel had discovered a large roll of coral-coloured ribbon and given it to Benedict. Gemma fashioned it into a large bow and Benedict adhered it to the door using sticky tack.

Time until Estelle's arrival passed by too slowly. Benedict and Gemma shuffled around the shop, straightening up necklaces that didn't need to be straightened, and rearranging piles of gemstones into different shapes on the shelves.

Eventually, with five minutes to go before Estelle's arrival, they stood behind the counter with their arms folded and their backs straight.

When Benedict caught sight of his wife's plum coat, he nudged Gemma in the ribs. 'She's coming.'

'Ouch. I'll open the door.'

'No. I'll let her in.'

He moved to the window and watched as Estelle stopped still on the pavement. Her eyes widened as she stared at the huge coral bow on the door. Then she peered through the window into the shop and shook her head as if she couldn't quite believe what she saw. She pressed her hand to her chest as she came inside. 'Benedict,' she said. 'It looks beautiful.'

The small white shop, rechristened Stone Studio, was alive with the colours of the moors.

Benedict had hung any paintings left behind in her studio on each of the walls. A canvas, with daubs of navy and powder blue, depicting stormy skies, reflected in the glass cabinet closest to the door. Rolling emerald and lime hills contrasted with the sharp shapes of Dinosaur Ridge on a slim, wide canvas near the till.

Benedict knew that he'd struggle to find words to say to her, so he kept them simple. 'It's for you,' he said. 'This is your shop too.'

'Mine?'

He nodded. 'I eat too much,' he said, as he picked up a bottle of prosecco off the counter and poured her a glass. 'And I need to help out more in the house. I don't have a llama to show you today, or a hat with a feather in it. I know that you need space, and that's okay. I just want you to consider if my jewellery and your paintings could work, side by side. For this to be our family business.'

Gemma sighed and rested her chin in her hands.

Estelle touched her neck. 'When did you do all this?'

'We've both spent a few days working on it,' Benedict said.

'It looks amazing.' Estelle turned to Gemma. 'I hope you didn't do too much.'

Gemma yawned and covered her mouth with her hand. 'I'm exhausted.'

'You should rest up.'

'I will. I'm going to bed after this.'

'Oh,' Benedict said. 'I was going to invite the two of you over to the Pig and Whistle for a drink, to toast Stone Studio, and to try out Nicholas's new menu.'

Gemma rubbed her eye with her fist. 'You two go. I need to sleep.'

'Are you sure?' he asked, though he liked the idea of spending time with his wife alone.

Gemma nodded. She took Estelle's old purple coat out of the store cupboard and draped it over her shoulders.

'We'll walk you back home,' Estelle said.

Gemma shook her head. 'It's only fifteen minutes away.'

'It's dark outside.'

'I'm fine.'

Benedict looked at his watch. 'It's only six-thirty. Just stick to the high street instead of the towpath.'

'Yeah. I will.'

'Take care, won't you,' Estelle called after her, as she left the shop.

Benedict and Estelle walked over to the Pig and Whistle

where they ordered Nicholas's fancy new version of cheese and onion pie. The pub was fuller than usual, with a buzz of conversation and laughter in the air.

At a table in the corner, Benedict spied someone facing the wall. She wore a paisley turban and dark glasses. 'I'll be back in a few minutes,' he said to Estelle and headed over to see Violet.

She sat with her hands clasped around a glass of whisky. Her elbows were stiff in her bottle-green velvet coat. A pile of black-and-white photographs lay on the table.

Benedict placed a hand gently on her shoulder and she immediately shot up the back of a hand, like a target springing back into place in a funfair shooting game.

'No photos,' she said.

He curved to the side of her. 'Violet. It's me. Benedict Stone.'

'Oh, Mr Stone.' She lowered her dark glasses to peer over the top. 'It's very lovely to see you again. I thought you must be a fan.'

'So, you've been brave and ventured into the village?'

'Frank suggested that I might like to look at the old photographs on the wall in here, and Nicholas the chef passed me some, too. It's poignant to remember Noon Sun as it was.' She took a sip of her whisky and her hand shook a little. 'Surprisingly, no one else has approached me yet, though I am well covered.'

Benedict smiled. 'It's great to see you out and about. I'm here with my wife, Estelle. Would you like me to introduce you?'

'I don't intend to stay for long. And women can be a little jealous of me.' She shook her head. 'Frank passed the yellow stone on to me. I don't know what I'll do with it, but it was a nice gesture. He's hoping that the gemstones you gave him will work wonders.'

'I hope so too, but it's the person who owns the gem that makes the changes.'

'Hmmm,' she said.

'Have you had any luck selling your jewellery yet?'

'Frank knows of an auction house who may be able to help. And solicitor Reggie Ramsbottom is advising me on the sale of the manor. Both such charming gentlemen.' She smiled.

From the corner of his eye, Benedict saw Estelle waving, to tell him that their food was ready.

'I have to go, but it was nice to see you again,' he said.

'You too, Mr Stone.'

Alistair carried the pies over for Benedict and Estelle but forgot the knives and forks. Alexander batted him over the head with a napkin, and the two boys reappeared seconds later with Alistair bringing the forks, and Alexander the knives.

Estelle and Benedict tucked in to their food and when Nicholas came over to ask if they were enjoying their meal, Estelle proclaimed it was, 'Absolutely delicious.'

As Nicholas mumbled his thanks, his cheeks flushed as red as the small Carnelian in his pocket.

Benedict and Estelle stayed in the pub, after their meal, and joined in a quiz. Estelle answered a tricky one about

David Hockney's swimming pool paintings, and she nodded, impressed, when Benedict knew the answer to one about Blue Jack.

They placed first and Alistair and Alexander Ledbetter sidled over. The teenagers nudged each other before Alistair handed Benedict and Estelle their prize envelope. Inside was a handwritten note, inviting two people to sample Nicholas's new Christmas menu.

'Oh, yeah, Mr Stone,' Alexander said, before he walked away. 'We have a spare ticket for a gig over in Applethorpe and we wondered if Gemma wanted to come? Nicholas is driving us there and we'll get a taxi back.' He took a crumpled piece of paper from his pocket and offered it to Benedict.

The ticket was for Restore the Hope.

Benedict's heart flipped. Could today get any better? 'I think she'd love that,' he said. 'Thanks, lads.'

'Do you think that Gemma will be okay at a concert?' Estelle asked, as Benedict walked her back to Veronica's apartment.

'The ticket states that over sixteens are allowed,' Benedict said. 'Gemma did travel here from America on her own, so she's really independent.'

'Still, those places can get very crowded.'

'I'm sure she'll be fine,' he said. 'She'll be so excited when I tell her.'

They reached the apartment block and Estelle took her keys from her handbag. Benedict glanced at a couple who were locking lips on the steps of the community centre. He remembered how he and Estelle had kissed, that first time on the canal towpath. It had been such an innocent moment, without any hint of what troubles might lie ahead in their future.

'Thanks, Benedict. It was so lovely of you to display my work,' Estelle said. 'I had no idea you were planning such a thing, and the shop looked wonderful.'

'The paintings brought it to life.' Benedict stuck his hands in his pockets. 'I always saw the shop as just mine, but it could be our family business…'

Estelle smiled and selected her key. 'There's a lot to think about. I still need time. But thanks again.'

She reached out and opened the door, then stepped back and gave him a peck on the cheek.

''Night, Estelle,' he said. Then he added, 'I love you' so quietly that he didn't think she'd hear.

'And I love you too, Benedict,' she said, over her shoulder.

27. Onyx

gives strength, old sorrows, letting go

The following evening, Benedict asked Gemma a dozen questions and gave lots of instructions before she went to watch Restore the Hope that evening.

'What time will the gig finish?' he asked, as she sat at the kitchen table, in front of Estelle's make-up mirror, trying to apply black eyeliner. She wore jeans, a baggy black T-shirt and her too-large denim jacket. She'd backcombed her hair so the roots were mussy.

'Around 10 p.m.'

'Do you usually wear that stuff around your eyes?'

'No. Aunt Estelle gave it me.'

'Make sure that the taxi drops you off right at the door. No walking anywhere,' he said. 'And no drinking alcohol, you're underage.' He wrote down his mobile number on a piece of paper and passed it to her. 'Put this in your pocket.'

'Stop fussing, Uncle Ben. It's just a gig.'

Benedict felt that he still didn't have the authority to tell her what to do, and what not to do. 'Just take care, okay?'

'What are you doing tonight?' she asked. 'Are you seeing Estelle?'

'I'm staying here, waiting for you to come home safely.'

She gave him a look, that said *Really?* 'You should look out for Lord Puss. Kids are setting off fireworks early and he might be afraid.'

'I'll keep him inside.'

'Good. Well, I think I'm ready to go.'

A car horn sounded outside and Benedict pulled aside the curtain to see Nicholas's car pull up. Benedict waved to the chef and he felt a small lump in his throat. It was the same feeling he'd got when he waved Charlie off on his first day at high school.

Don't worry, he told himself. She'll be back soon, safe and sound.

Lord Puss didn't like the fireworks. He wedged himself into a corner of the sofa and his eyes were wide. 'There's hardly any going off tonight, you soft cat,' Benedict said. 'Wait until Bonfire Night, and then things really go with a bang.'

Benedict had forgotten what it was like to have the house to himself. He never enjoyed being alone with its creaks and crackles and squeaks. But tonight he relished it. He took a bottle of Budweiser from the fridge and helped himself to an apple. He kicked off his loafers and put his feet up on the coffee table. Turning on the TV, he started to watch a programme about ancient Egyptian jewellery and discovered that Tutankhamun's burial mask was inlaid with Turquoise, Lapis Lazuli and Carnelian.

After a few minutes, Lord Puss edged towards him. He stood on the cushion then he lifted and pressed one foot against his leg. Benedict looked at the cat and Lord Puss stared back at him. 'Do you want to sit on my knee?'

Lord Puss winked.

Benedict moved the TV remote control to allow the cat to climb onto his lap. Lord Puss circled twice then settled down. The cat began to purr, and Benedict flicked the channels on the TV. This is it, he thought. This is what it feels like to be satisfied.

In an ideal world he'd have a proper family – a wife, a child and a pet. Instead, he had a distorted model of that – a wife living in her friend's apartment, a stray American niece and a lodging cat. But that was okay. He was determined to enjoy it for what it was.

A firework went off and Lord Puss pricked up one ear. 'It's okay, puss,' Benedict said and placed a reassuring hand on his back. 'Nothing to worry about.'

The cat looked around him warily, but when the next bang came, he jumped off and backed under the coffee table.

'Come here.' When Benedict reached out for the cat, the TV remote control slipped onto the floor with a thud and the noise startled Lord Puss. The cat ran out of the door and into the hallway.

'Sorry,' Benedict called out. He followed the cat, but he wasn't there. His heart skipped a beat as he saw Lord Puss sitting by the front door. It was ajar and the white cat peeked furtively through the gap.

'Come on, puss, I'll look after you,' Benedict said.

'Gemma mustn't have closed the door properly when she left.' He padded towards the cat, whose ears were now pinned right back to his head. Reaching out, he felt his fingers brush lightly against white fur.

There was another blast of noise outside. Lord Puss jumped and then he was gone. The white tip of his tail vanished out of the open door as he fled into the garden.

'Damn it,' Benedict said and looked around for his burgundy loafers. 'You come back here.'

He followed the cat outside. Lord Puss ran across the lawn, under the gem tree and out the other side. Benedict felt stupid shouting out 'Lord Puss,' so instead he hissed, 'Come on, kitty.'

There was a flash of white and the cat squeezed under a bush in the corner of the garden. Benedict trekked after him. 'Cecil will kill me if I lose you.'

He crept towards the bush so he wouldn't startle the cat. Through a gap in the leaves he saw Lord Puss pressed up against the wall. Benedict kneeled down and the damp grass soaked through the knees of his trousers. He held his face away from the scratchy branches and reached in with his hand. His fingertips skimmed the cat's chest. 'Damn cat.'

He tried again but Lord Puss edged backwards, wedging himself further against the wall. It was then that Benedict noticed something else, furry, beneath the bush. It seemed to hover a couple of inches above the ground. It was small with long arms, a creature with a smiling face.

Benedict frowned. What was it? He turned his attention away from Lord Puss and reached out to touch the furry thing. Under the orange glow of the street lamp, he saw it was a small cheeky-faced chimpanzee attached to a key ring. His fingers crept along it, over its body and face, until they touched something ridged and shiny. He patted around and it felt like sequins. There was a loop of fabric, a strap.

He used it to pull the item towards him and it swept out of the bush bringing a few leaves and twigs with it. It was a large, black purse. It had a zip and a single wrist strap. Benedict frowned at it and wondered how it had got into his garden.

Perhaps someone at the airport had found and returned Gemma's purse, he thought. Though why hadn't she told him about it?

Lord Puss edged out and sat beside Benedict.

'I'm not playing games with you. You can do what you like.'

The cat licked his paw and brushed it over his face.

Benedict unzipped the purse. Inside were dollar notes, folded around something else. He eased them out and found himself looking at a passport and a phone.

Opening the passport, he saw the person in the photo staring back at him. She was younger and her hair was a little darker and shorter, but her chin, triangular bushy eyebrows and the ears that poked through her hair were the same. Gemma.

He leafed to the back page and the contact address wasn't for Maine or New York. He frowned and pushed it back inside the purse. As he held the bag against his chest, his heart felt as though it had dropped down to his stomach.

'We should go back inside,' he said to Lord Puss distractedly. 'Let's keep you away from the fireworks.'

As if obeying him, the cat stood up and trotted ahead.

Benedict set the purse down on the coffee table and rubbed the back of his neck. How had anyone at the airport got in touch with Gemma? He'd given his own contact details when he called them.

He took out the phone again. It was shiny and white, an old-model iPhone. The screen was dark, blank. He pressed the button on top of it, not expecting anything to happen but rows of icons appeared.

One of them was green with a white speech bubble and there was a small number five beside it. Benedict hesitated as he paced out of the room and into the kitchen. He switched on the kettle but didn't make a drink. If this was Gemma's phone, who had been trying to get in touch with her? Would she be able to tell, if he stole a quick glance at her messages? Perhaps it wasn't hers, but why was it stored with her passport?

He caught his breath in the back of his throat. Had his niece been using her phone the night she said she was talking to herself in her room? He thought about the phone charger he'd seen, wrapped around her grey vest, on the top of the chest of drawers in the studio.

As if it was a cupcake that Benedict couldn't resist, he pressed on the icon. A list of text messages appeared and they were all from the same name.

Dad.

His hand trembled as he pressed the top message. It opened up and he read it:

'Gemma. Please let me know that you're safe. Where are you? Dad x'

'Just leave me alone, okay? I'm fine. Will be back when I'm ready,' Gemma replied.

Benedict read the other four messages in the inbox and each was from Charlie. One apologised to Gemma for shouting at her, and another said that he was thinking of contacting the police. As Benedict read them, his throat tightened and he thought he might wretch.

Gemma had lied to him yet again.

He returned to the front room, edged back towards the sofa and sank into it. He set the phone on his lap and stared at it. He switched off the TV so the room was silent apart from the tick of a clock and the electric motor of the fridge whirring on and off. Lord Puss gave a bored yawn, showing off his pink tongue. He smacked his lips then headed off to his food bowl.

Whether Gemma had truly lost her purse at the airport, or whether she'd placed it under the bush the very first night she arrived, Benedict didn't know. What he did understand was that somewhere, maybe on the other side of the world, his brother might be sitting in the very same position that Benedict was now. Worried, bewildered and waiting for Gemma to come home.

Gemma had assured Benedict she'd told him everything, the truth, about why she was here. But now he knew that she'd been lying to him from the very first moment she'd knocked on his door. When he confronted her about her words in the journal, she could have told him the truth about her passport and phone then, that they hadn't been stolen. But she'd carried on misleading him.

Charlie and Janice having a baby together was going to mean a huge change to her life and he understood why she might need to get away from home, to think things through. Yet, he felt so stupid too. After all their conversations, and poring over the gemstone journal together, he now felt as if he didn't know her at all.

He'd thought that they were family, but she had played him for a fool.

For a moment, he considered phoning Estelle, to see if Gemma had told her anything. But this would stoke his wife's suspicions and it would become apparent how little Benedict knew about his niece's arrival. And if he confronted Gemma again, she would probably spin him more lies. He imagined that she'd have a ready reason about why her phone and passport were hidden in the garden.

He ran his finger over the sequins on the purse and felt that he didn't have a choice.

He remembered his brother's words in the letter in which Charlie told Benedict that he never wanted to hear from him again. But he had to do this. Whatever bond he had with Gemma, the one with his estranged brother was still greater.

He picked up Gemma's phone and copied Charlie's number into his own mobile. Then he pressed Dial. It rang several times and Benedict was about to hang up, when he heard his brother's voice for the first time in eighteen years.

Benedict gazed into space as a slug of sadness hit him. How could he have hurt his brother so badly?

'Hey, this is Charlie Stone. Leave me a message, yeah?'

Benedict pulled the phone away from his ear, as if it was scorching hot. His mouth suddenly felt as dry as sandpaper and he ran his tongue around inside his mouth. He felt torn apart, wanting to demand from Gemma what was going on. But he also wanted to find out directly from Charlie.

He covered her purse with a newspaper so he couldn't see it.

He just wanted to hear the truth. He was so weary of all this and he needed to try to take back some kind of control.

Just as he made a snap decision when he returned Amelia's kiss, Benedict made one again.

'Charlie.' He cleared his throat. 'It's Benedict. Gemma is staying with me, and I think she may have been lying to both of us… We desperately need to talk. Please call me back.'

28. Amethyst

inner strength, transition, sobriety

The noise was a squealing sound, like kids make when they're on holiday and run into the sea. There was a girl's voice and Benedict heard deeper ones too. They were coming from the garden. He swiftly stood up and Gemma's mobile phone slid to the floor with a thud that seemed to echo around the room. He picked it up and tucked it into his jacket pocket.

He switched off the light so he could see outside more clearly, and edged over to the window. Lord Puss lay asleep on the windowsill with his tail and whiskers twitching. As Benedict's eyes adjusted to the darkness, he saw three figures in the garden – Gemma, Alistair and Alexander. His niece stood still with her back to the house as the two boys ran around the garden, shouting to each other.

The sound of his niece laughing made his neck bristle. She had lied to him, yet she was acting as if nothing was wrong. Was she laughing with her friends at him, thinking that he was stupid?

The security light outside pinged on and off intermittently, so sometimes the scene was illuminated and sometimes not. The boys both wore skinny black jeans and their arms were bare in their Restore the Hope T-shirts. They used a rolled-up sweater as a rugby ball, throwing it to each other. Gemma tried to join in too, making small attempts to reach out and catch it.

Benedict hesitated for a moment, wondering if he should tell her to come inside. He unfastened the catch on the window and opened it by an inch so he could hear, more clearly, what was going on in the garden. He told himself that he'd done the right thing by calling Charlie.

'Hey, what's this dangling from the tree?' Alexander shouted.

Benedict watched as the branches of the gem tree bowed and then sprang back into place with a rustle. He heard Gemma say something but couldn't make out her words.

The tree arched again and this time there was a crack as a branch broke. Alexander wrestled with it, tugging it away from the tree. He brandished it like a sword and chased his brother, thrashing the broken branch at him. Again, Gemma just watched.

Benedict felt something snap inside him as he witnessed the damage. He couldn't stand and watch his family history being vandalised. He yanked the window shut, hurried to the front door then flung it wide open. 'Stop that, right now,' he yelled. 'Gemma, get inside.'

The three teenagers turned to look at him. Their arms dangled by their sides.

'Your uncle says you have to go in.' Alexander nudged her.

'Yeah. It's bedtime, Gemma,' Alistair laughed. He kicked a can of lager over on the lawn.

Gemma looked at the two boys then at Benedict. Her expression was blank, impossible for him to read. 'I'll be inside in five minutes, Uncle Ben.'

'I want you inside *now*.'

Her lips curled into a snarl. 'We're just having a bit of fun.'

'No, you're not. You're damaging the gem tree.'

Alexander strode forward. He placed an arm in front of Gemma as a barrier. 'Ignore your uncle. Come and play,' he said.

'Yeah, come on.' Alistair took hold of her hand and tried to drag her with him.

But Gemma stood firm and his hand slipped away from hers.

'Alistair and Alexander Ledbetter.' Benedict took his own mobile from his pocket and held it aloft. 'I'm asking you nicely to leave before I phone Nicholas and tell him to come and get you. Does he know that you've been drinking?'

The two boys seemed to shrink in size, their bravado diminishing quickly. 'Don't tell our brother,' Alexander pleaded. 'He'll kill us.'

'Yeah, he's scary when he's angry,' Alistair added.

'It's time for you both to go home.'

Alistair jerked his head towards the garden gate. 'Come

on, Alex. Let's get out of here. See ya soon, Gemma,' he said, and the two boys trudged out of the garden.

'Thanks for taking me to the gig,' Gemma called after them.

As soon as the boys were out of sight, Benedict heard them begin to shout and whoop again.

Gemma refused to look at him. Her eyes were narrow and angry. She tossed her hair and marched past him into the house without acknowledging him.

He strode after her. 'Gemma, we need to talk.'

'Yeah? Well, thanks for embarrassing me, Uncle Ben,' she snapped. 'Did you *really* need to come outside and scold me, like I'm a child? I said I was only going to be five minutes… You made me look like an idiot.'

Benedict let out his breath in a whistle. 'Alexander and Alistair were attacking the gem tree.'

'It was an accident.'

'They'd been drinking.'

'It was a bit of fun, that's all.'

Benedict folded his arms. 'That tree has stood there since my family planted it over thirty years ago. How could you stand by and let them damage it like that?'

Gemma lowered her head for a few seconds. She rubbed her eye with her fist and stared at her boots. 'Sorry about the tree,' she muttered eventually. 'I didn't mean for it to get broken.'

Benedict closed his eyes. He told himself to accept her apology, so they could calm things down and move forward. 'Let's go into the kitchen. I can make us a cup of tea and we can talk,' he said. From the hallway he could see the edge of her purse poking out from under the newspaper on the coffee table.

'I don't want a drink. I wanna go to bed.'

'How was the concert?' he asked, but his question was hollow.

'It was great.' Gemma took off her jacket, hung it on the banister and tramped up the stairs in her cowboy boots.

'*Gemma*,' he called after her.

She raised the back of her hand. 'We'll talk in the morning, huh?'

Benedict stood rooted to the spot. Then he followed her up the stairs. 'Gemma,' he repeated, his temples throbbing with tension.

'*What?*' She turned to face him on the landing and her make-up, black and smudged around her eyes, made her look tired and vulnerable.

'There's something I need to ask you.'

'What is it?' She sighed and flapped her arms by her sides.

Words swam in Benedict's head. He thought about her throwing the bag of gemstones at him and the thwack as it hit his cheek. He recalled her switching on all the lights in the house, and her threatening to walk out of the shop. What would she do if he confronted her about hiding her phone and passport under the bush? She might fly into a rage or perhaps she might break down and cry. She'd accuse him of prying again, that was for certain. He combed a hand through his hair.

He could tell her that he'd discovered her things, and

demand to know why she'd hidden them, but he'd already set other wheels in motion. Charlie would call him back soon. And, at this moment in time, Benedict trusted his brother's words more.

He felt like a wrecking ball that kept hitting a wall, but which only managed to knock down small parts of it, to give him a tiny glimpse of what was on the other side. Gemma'd had plenty of opportunities to tell him the whole story of why she was here, but she'd only fed him scraps. And now he didn't know what was true and what wasn't. Only Charlie could tell him that.

'Lord Puss escaped…' he started.

Gemma's eyes flicked to the bottom of the stairs. 'He escaped? Is he okay?'

Benedict nodded. 'He was frightened by a firework and ran under a bush in the garden…' He let his words trail off, still wondering whether to confront her or not.

Gemma's eyes widened. 'Oh…'

It's best to leave this be, Benedict told himself. But was he able to prevent himself from demanding to know why she'd lied to him? He had let Gemma stay and had cared for her. He'd introduced her to Estelle and developed an image in his head of them becoming a happy family together.

He looked at Gemma as she stood before him. She was a paradigm of contradictions, bolshie yet caring, young but almost an adult. He knew that whatever he asked her, he couldn't be sure that she was telling him the truth. And he also felt guilt gnawing inside him that he'd already betrayed her trust, by phoning Charlie.

In the end, he decided that he couldn't confront her tonight, not without thinking more about it, and trying to find the right words. 'Lord Puss is fine,' he muttered. 'We must take care to keep the front door closed.'

Gemma's shoulders slumped and she sighed with relief. Her eyes looked fat with tears. 'Good.' She swallowed. 'I'm tired and I wanna go to bed. I'm really glad that he's okay.'

'Fine.'

'And I'm sorry about the tree, Uncle Ben,' she said quietly.

'Goodnight, Gemma,' Benedict said. 'Let's leave everything until tomorrow. We can talk about it all then.'

29. Smoky Quartz

grounding, acceptance, potential

Benedict couldn't sleep. He could hear Gemma snoring along the corridor, and the noise made his body feel skewer-stiff. Every one of his nerve endings seemed to be alive, heightening all his senses. He could taste the apple he'd eaten at teatime still sweet on his tongue, even though he'd brushed his teeth. His hearing seemed to home in on the slightest noises – a car alarm going off in the distance and the creak of the gate swinging in the wind. His eyes picked out shapes in the bumps of plaster on the ceiling – sneering faces and roads that led to nowhere.

He tried to force his eyes to remain open, so that surely they'd grow tired and close, but it didn't work. He glanced at his phone to see the time, and when he looked at it again, over an hour had gone and he was still wide awake.

He lay, twitchy and alert, waiting for his phone to ring, or for the ping of a text from Charlie, but there was nothing. He didn't even know what time it was in the US. It might be hours until Charlie picked up and listened to the message.

If there had been sweet, sugary food in the fridge it would have called out Benedict's name, and he wouldn't have been able to resist it. He would have crept downstairs to gorge and force it down. But there was only fruit and salad, and a home-made soup that he and Gemma had made together.

Thoughts and questions swirled around in his head in a psychedelic pattern, yet he couldn't focus on any of them for long enough to pin them down to answer or solve them.

When he closed his eyes, he saw Gemma's bare shins in her tan cowboy boots, and gemstones sparkling and shining in the gem tree, almost blinding him with their brightness. He saw Estelle and her black bobbed hair, and Amelia with her caramel skin.

When his parents died, Benedict had thought that things couldn't get any worse, but when he slept with Amelia, they did do. It was like he lit a match that night, and started a forest fire where everyone he loved got scorched, and the flames were still flickering.

He felt like he had a coil of pythons in his stomach, writhing around his organs. It was difficult to resist the urge to jump out of bed and storm into Gemma's room. He could throw something at her to grab her attention, just as she'd done with the bag of gemstones. Then to demand that she tell him her story. Yet he knew he had to kill time until his brother got in touch.

Benedict was used to playing the waiting game. When Estelle left, that's what he'd done to give her the time and space she needed, but this was a different matter. This was about waiting to speak to his brother, so he could unravel Gemma's web of untruths.

All he could do was wait.

When morning finally came around, Benedict was bleary-eyed and groggy from his restless night. His pyjamas stuck to his back as if they were coated with jam, and he reached up to pluck them away from his skin. His footsteps were slow and heavy as he headed to the bathroom to wash his face.

'Uncle Ben,' Gemma called out, her voice feeble and slow.

He froze, motionless outside the bathroom door. 'Yes?'

'I, um, don't feel well. I have a migraine. So, I'm not gonna come into the shop today. Okay?'

Benedict pressed his tongue against the back of his front teeth. One part of him wanted to storm into her room and confront her, but the other part didn't want to see her face. 'Okay,' he said to her closed door. 'You stay home and rest up.'

The showroom felt chilly. Benedict turned up the heating but couldn't seem to get warm. His hands were cold and felt bigger than ever. He checked his phone intermittently to see if Charlie had replied, but there was nothing. He called Estelle too, but her phone rang out, unanswered. He tried three times over a couple of hours and then gave up, not wanting to worry her with a string of missed calls.

He headed out to Bake My Day and the jam doughnuts

in the counter spoke to him. *Yay, you're back*, they said. *Buy three of us and get one free!*

Benedict bought four and sat at his workbench where he ate them, one after the other, not caring if sugar and crumbs flecked his tools.

He shivered and wrapped his jacket around him, and the stodgy, sweet food in his stomach, and his lack of sleep, made him feel drowsy. Slowly, his head dropped down until the front of his hair touched the bench. Maybe just a few minutes' sleep, he told himself... That will make me feel better.

It was late afternoon when he woke again. He'd rested his cheek against a small pair of pliers and, when he reached up, he found an imprint of the tool in his skin.

He gave his face a quick rinse under the tap and patted it dry with a towel, still feeling disorientated and lethargic. Picking up his phone, he saw there were still no messages from his brother or wife.

He sighed and opened the gemstone journal to flick through it. This time he actively looked for Gemma's words. Scanning page after page, he read the notes she'd written about Lapis Lazuli, Tiger's Eye and Sunstone, wanting to see if he could find any more. He ran his hand over his father's handwriting, photos and drawings, and his niece's descriptions of the gems. Then he read through again and spotted something that he'd missed.

SMOKY QUARTZ
Smoky Quartz is found where granite exists, within

volcanic rocks or in mountainous regions. It is a protective and grounding stone and is excellent in guarding against negative energy. It can calm the mind and assist the prioritisation of emotional needs and wants, and bring wisdom to everyday life.

Under the passage, Gemma had written:

Smoky Quartz is supposed to help relieve stress, fear, jealousy, anger and other negative emotions by transforming them into positive ones. It's a good stone for encouraging courage and inner strength, and I really need that right now.

Because when everyone finds out about me, there's going to be trouble.

'You're so right, Gemma,' Benedict said out loud. 'I don't know what it will be, but there *is* going to be trouble.'

He knew that, as soon as Charlie made contact, Gemma would have to go home, and he'd have to explain everything to Estelle. Not just about his niece, but about his past and why his brother had walked away from him. Things that had remained buried for years would burst to the surface. How much longer could he hide them for?

And did he still want to keep everything from his past stowed away, anyway? Wouldn't it be better to be honest? He had carried his secret around for years, and it felt like a noose around his neck, growing tighter and squeezing the life out of him. He had to do something to set himself free.

And he knew what it had to be.

Benedict had done all he could to show Estelle that he wanted her back, but what he had to do next was nothing that llamas or plastic swords could help him with.

Because if he wanted a future with his wife, then he had to tell her about his past.

He didn't know what her reaction would be. Surprise, that was for sure. Upset and even dismay? But, whatever the outcome might be, he was going to have to live with the consequences.

Feeling cold again, Benedict tugged his jacket to try to cover his wide chest. He put Veronica's star-shaped brooch in his pocket, and set off to find his wife.

30. Diamond

intention, commitment, purity

Benedict pulled up his jacket against the rain as he headed towards Veronica's apartment. He walked slowly but steadily, aware of the squelch of his burgundy loafers in the puddles on the pavement. A car drove past too quickly, splashing his ankles with dirty water. He reached down and brushed the gritty specks on his trousers with the flat of his hand.

As he trudged past the community centre, he spotted Estelle heading towards him. Even though she was holding a large red-and-yellow umbrella low over her face, he recognised her plum coat. When he drew closer, he noticed that the umbrella was Lawrence's and he wanted to wrestle it from her hands, throw it to the ground and stamp on the spokes.

'Benedict,' she called, waving. 'I was coming to see you. Are you free for a coffee?'

'I've been trying to reach you,' he said.

'I was over in Applethorpe and forgot to take my phone. What did you want me for? Where's Gemma?'

'She has a bad headache so didn't come into work today.'

'Oh. Poor thing.'

This wasn't the right time and place to explain things to his wife, not here in the street. He didn't want to go to Veronica's apartment, where he had seen her with Lawrence on the balcony, and he presumed that Gemma was still back at the house. 'Can we go to the shop?' he asked. 'I need to talk to you about something.'

'I'd prefer to celebrate with cake instead.'

'Celebrate…?' He frowned.

'Yes. Let's go to Crags and Cakes.' She linked her arm through his. 'I'll tell you when we get there.'

'Yes, but…'

However, Estelle started to walk and chat, and Benedict found himself being swept along with her, towards the little café.

The white rabbit on the pavement at Crags and Cakes held a toffee apple as well as his stopwatch. Shooting rockets, and sparkles of fireworks and stars decorated the windows.

As Benedict opened the door and went inside, his legs felt wavy. 'Let's sit in the corner,' he said.

The tables were situated close together and he had to hold in his stomach to squeeze between them. He chose a seat that faced the wall.

He inhaled the smell of caramel and coffee and thought back to when he'd first met Estelle. When was the first time he lied to her and invented a story of why he and his brother no longer spoke? He couldn't even remember what excuses he'd used. Even if it was uncomfortable, he should have told her the truth.

'I'll be with you in a few minutes,' a waitress called over.

Estelle propped the umbrella against the wall and Benedict wondered how she came to be using it. He tried to think of something light to say, to prepare the way for his heavier words. 'You need muscles like Popeye to carry that thing,' he said, with a nod.

'Good job I have them.' She flexed her arm. 'Remember when I offered to carry you over my shoulder, when we first met?'

'I never did take you up on it.'

'Perhaps another time.'

He noticed that she was wearing the firework necklace but that one of the shards was missing. There was a hollow of yellow base metal instead of a pink resin spear.

'Oh, yes.' She noticed his gaze and touched it. 'A bit fell out and I've lost it. Never mind. I don't think it's an expensive one.'

'But you like it…'

'It's a bit too bright for me, really. Too dramatic. Anyway, I overhead a terrible joke today. Why didn't the skeleton go to the ball?'

'I don't know.'

'Because he had no *body* to go with.'

Benedict tried to smile. 'What's a ghost's favourite fruit?' he asked.

'No idea.'

'Booberries.'

'Ha,' Estelle said.

When the waitress came over, Estelle ordered a latte and an apple tart. Benedict asked for a black coffee with no sugar.

'Aren't you having a cake?' Estelle asked.

After devouring the doughnuts, Benedict couldn't face eating anything else. They seemed to have set like cement in his stomach. 'No. The slices are too big.'

'Ah, you're still trying to be healthier.' She smiled. 'I'm impressed.'

'Thanks.' He reached into his pocket and took out a small coral-coloured box. 'I've brought Veronica's brooch for you. I didn't want to give it to you in front of Gemma.'

'Why not?'

'I'm not sure.' He shrugged. 'I just want to make sure that it's right. Sometimes you think things are all sparkly and lovely, but then they tarnish quickly and a bit of polish isn't enough.' He met her eyes with his and thought that, in twelve years, she hadn't changed a bit. She was every bit as beautiful now as when they first met. He felt such an idiot for keeping secrets from her. 'I want to try to make things shiny again,' he said.

Estelle nodded and opened the box. The star-shaped brooch glinted inside. 'This is so beautiful,' she exclaimed as she unpinned it from the white satin lining. 'If it does need a polish, then hopefully it's only a small buffer, to bring up the shine again.'

Benedict gave a small smile. 'You were going to tell me your news…'

'Oh, that will wait. It's just about the gallery in York and another exhibition. What did you want to talk to me about?' She sat back in her chair.

Benedict reached over the table and put his hand on the back of hers. He took a deep breath and held it in the back of his throat. 'I need to...' he started.

The waitress set a tray down on the table. She placed their drinks, the tart, two plates and two cake forks in front of them. 'Enjoy,' she said.

Estelle moved her hand away from his. She stuck her fork into the tart and held a piece to her lips. 'Do you want to try it?' she asked and opened her mouth.

He shook his head. 'Estelle, I...'

'Mmm. It's delicious, not too sweet.'

'Estelle...' He pushed his empty plate away and pressed his fingers together into a steeple. He rested his chin on the point. 'I need to tell you something.'

She swallowed and put her fork down. 'Is it about Gemma?'

Benedict shook his head. 'It's more about me and Charlie.'

'Your brother?'

Benedict felt as if he was tumbling down from the top of Dinosaur Ridge and couldn't find anything to hold on to, to break his fall. He squeezed his eyebrows together, his emotions already flooding over him before he spoke.

Estelle studied him. 'What's wrong?'

Benedict didn't need to worry about his words jumbling up, because, after so long, they spilled out of him like rubbish tipping from a garbage truck. He stared at the

317

star-shaped brooch, not able to bear looking in his wife's eyes.

And he began to talk.

He told Estelle that, after caring for his brother for over eight years, when their parents died, Benedict had betrayed him. He explained how he, Charlie and Amelia had gone for a picnic on that hot July night, and how he'd dropped Amelia home and stayed to drink beer. 'I didn't mean for anything to happen. I don't know what came over me. It was as if nothing else existed, for that short while…' He lifted his eyes.

Estelle's face looked like a mask. Her features were frozen but her eyes bored into his. 'Are you telling me that you slept with your own brother's girlfriend?' she whispered.

'Yes.' The word strangled him to say it. 'It happened one time and it was a huge mistake.' He reached across the table to take hold of her hand again.

She snatched it away and sucked in her breath. 'Does Charlie know all this?'

Benedict nodded his head once. 'I think it's why he broke contact with me, and we haven't spoken since.'

Estelle screwed her napkin into a ball. She shoved her half-eaten tart away. 'Why haven't you told me this before, Benedict? I felt sorry for you, that you had this ignorant brother in the States who didn't stay in touch. And all the time, he stayed away because of you. You lied to me.'

'I was so ashamed.' Benedict swallowed. 'I didn't have the words.'

She closed her eyes, taking this in. Then they snapped back open. 'Oh my God. Gemma,' she said. 'Is she your daughter?'

Benedict shook his head. 'No. The dates don't add up. Charlie left eighteen years ago and Gemma is sixteen. She can't be mine.'

Estelle ran her tongue over her front teeth, digesting this. 'Well, that's something,' she said. 'I suppose that you hoped you had a daughter, seeing as I can't give you one.'

'No,' Benedict exclaimed too loudly and the waitress stared over at him. 'It's *us* who can't have children, not *you* or *me*. No one is to blame. We're a couple.'

'We *were* a couple.'

'We still are, I hope.'

Estelle pushed her hand down on the top of the jewellery-box lid and the cardboard splayed and split open. She picked it up and stuffed it into her pocket. 'We've tried our best, Benedict. But we keep going around in circles and not getting anywhere. And now you've made things even worse.'

'I didn't mean to lie to you, Estelle... I just didn't tell you the whole truth.'

'But you did lie. For all the time we've been together, you've lied to me.'

'I'm not perfect, I know it. But I've tried to show you that I love you. It might not have worked that well, but I've tried. I should have told you about Charlie, but I didn't. I kept putting it off, until it seemed too late to raise it. It was easier for me to pretend that it hadn't happened. We can still make things work between us. Please come home,' he pleaded. 'Let's start again.'

Estelle held her neck at a crooked angle, as if she was stooping to walk through a doorframe that was too low. 'Benedict, I…'

'The house is empty without you. I miss our walks and our jokes. I miss the smell of your perfume on the towels, and your hairgrips on the windowsill in the bathroom. I need to see your face on the pillow next to me, in the morning and at night. I've messed up, but I can try to make things better.' He laid his hands on his heart.

'Why are you telling me all this now, after all this time?'

'I don't want any secrets between us. I want you to know that you can always trust me, and I'll always trust you.'

She pursed her lips into a straight line.

'So I have to tell you something else too,' he said quietly.

'What the hell is it this time?'

Benedict gave a deep sigh. 'I found Gemma's passport and purse under a bush last night and I don't think that Charlie knows she's here. I called him and left a message. I'm waiting for him to get in touch.'

Estelle edged to the front of her chair. 'Charlie doesn't know that his sixteen-year-old daughter is here?' she repeated.

'I always suspected something wasn't right, but I ignored it.'

'I asked you, and you told me that everything was fine.'

'I know. I'm sorry.'

'You did it because you wanted a family so badly, right?'

'I suppose that's true,' he said. 'I'm going to sort this out, Estelle, but I wanted to let you know what's going on.'

Her hand shook as she picked up her latte and took a sip. 'It's going cold,' she said. 'You should drink yours.'

'I'm not thirsty.'

She peered in her cup, thinking of her next words. 'I'm not going to ask you anything, because this is between you and Charlie to sort out. But can I be there for Gemma at all?'

'Let me speak to my brother first.'

She swallowed and hung her head. 'I can see that you're trying to change.'

'I am. If you come home then we'll take things as slowly as you like. I know things have been crappy but we're meant to be together, like jam sponge and custard, or bonfires and fireworks.'

Her lips flickered into the smallest smile and then her face was still.

'I know I messed up and there's a lot to discuss and think about, but, do you ever think about coming home?'

She picked up her handbag and set it on her knee. 'Sometimes.'

'So, there's still hope?'

She ran her hand through her hair and gave one tiny nod of her head.

'Perhaps we can talk about family again,' he tried, thinking this might help to sway her decision.

'Family?'

'*Our* family. We've started to bond with Gemma, and we've only known her for a couple of weeks.'

Estelle furrowed her brow as if she couldn't comprehend what he was saying. She leaned a few centimetres closer and lowered her voice. 'Are you talking about adoption again?'

Benedict gave a small nod. 'I think it could work for us.'

'*What?*' Estelle scraped her chair back and the sound made him want to cover his ears with his hands. Her handbag fell off her knee and onto the floor with a thud.

Her eyes flashed as she bent down to pick it up. It was upside down, so her purse fell and money spilled out of it. Pennies rattled and spun around on the lino. She felt around for them blindly, batting Benedict's hands away as he tried to help.

When she sat back up, her posture was hunched as if she was crammed into a small space. 'Bloody adoption? We've been through all that. Is this what your confession has been all about? And the stupid mask, and displaying my paintings, and the llama. So you can butter me up so you can try to have a child. I thought that it's me you wanted back, Benedict Stone.'

'It is. I just thought…' He felt like he was clinging on to a cliff face by his fingertips, and the cold, dangerous sea was sloshing around beneath him, waiting for him to fall so it could swallow him up.

'And I was beginning to fall for it too,' Estelle seethed. 'I admired how you were trying to get fitter, and I was touched when you displayed my work, but all the time you had a strategy.' She tugged her coat off the back of her chair, nudging the table and causing a salt pot to topple over. 'I thought you wanted me, not some phantom child.'

'I'm sorry. I just thought…'

'No, Benedict Stone. What you need to think about is *why* you want a family so badly. Is it because you want to be a parent, or to make amends for what you did to Charlie?'

His mouth dropped open. Her reply felt like a smack in his face, but her question was one that he couldn't answer truthfully. Had he been so focused on making amends that his desire to be a parent had overwhelmed him, blinded him? He tried to find the words to respond but they jumbled in his head.

'Don't say anything. I can see now that everything you did for me was all about *you*.'

'No.' This time, he didn't think about trying to find the right words, and he spoke from his heart. 'I did it because I want you, Estelle. The two of us are a family, whether we have a child or not. I don't need or want anyone else.'

She fastened her coat with the buttons in the wrong holes and picked up the umbrella. 'Get away from me,' she said.

'Can't we…?'

'No.'

He stood up. 'I'm so sorry. For everything. It's not what I meant…'

She looked away.

'Is there still hope for us?' he asked.

'Not if you're chasing a dream.' She turned, marched and slammed the café door shut.

Benedict stared after her, aware that everyone in the café was looking at him. He threw some money on the table and left the café too. As he walked out into the rain, it speckled his face and ran into his eyes so that he couldn't see clearly where he was going.

He hoped that telling Estelle the truth might make him feel lighter, but he felt nauseous and heavy, as if he'd been forced to eat a truckload of brownies.

Where the hell did they go from here?

31. Black Obsidian

past life healing, revealing, purpose

Benedict needed to lie down. He wanted to get into bed and pull the covers over his head. He would let his shoulders relax, his legs unstiffen, and he would listen to nothing other than his own breathing. He wanted to pretend that he was an Egyptian mummy in a sarcophagus, so he couldn't feel the emotions that were churning his stomach and needling his brain.

He hadn't expected Estelle to simply accept his story. He thought that she'd be upset and angry with him, and dismayed too. But he didn't think he'd see disgust in her eyes, when she thought that he only wanted a child, and not her.

His mind reeled as he stumbled towards his house and through the garden gate. What could he do to stop himself from unravelling? He wanted to shout and storm around the garden, but Gemma was inside and might hear, so he made a fist and pushed it against his own mouth. He had messed up, yet again.

The gem tree stood before him, stooping like an old woman, in silhouette against the darkening petrol-blue sky. His fingers felt stiff as he reached out and trailed them over its leaves, feeling them soft yet prickly. He remembered them scratching his forearms as he pushed through the branches, to sit down with Charlie and thread gemstones.

As he stared at the leaves, the shape of tiny surfboards, he didn't see the figure lurking under the tree.

The dark shape moved quickly beside him and the punch swiped through the air. It connected with Benedict's cheek, jolting his head to the side. He stumbled backwards, and hit the ground with a thump. Finding himself in sitting position, he realised that the fall had jolted his spine, and he had to place his hands down flat to steady himself. The grass was damp and slimy beneath his fingertips.

He shook his head and tried to stand up, but he was winded. He took a few gulps of air. Then he saw his assailant.

His brother.

Charlie's eyes were fierce and his fists were still raised. He hesitated for a moment and lurched forwards again.

Benedict hunched over with his elbows covering his knees. He held up his forearms to shield his face as his brother's blows rained down on him. They caught the sides of his ribs, his shoulders, his ears. The wallops made his head jerk and his body dance.

'How could you do…it…to…me…?'

Benedict felt one of his front teeth crumble as Charlie's fist crunched into his chin. He tried to spit out the hard pieces but they stuck to his lips.

'Go on, hit me back,' Charlie demanded.

Benedict shook his head. 'No,' he said between his brother's punches. He was bigger, and stronger. If he managed to stand and retaliate, then he might knock his brother out cold. He kept his forearms in front of his face and let Charlie's blows rain down on him. 'I won't hit you.'

Charlie wiped the back of his hand against his forehead and glared at Benedict. He drew his fist back again, ready to thrust it forward, but something made him hesitate. Benedict followed his eyes and saw that his brother had spotted the gemstones hanging in the tree. For a moment, Charlie watched them glinting.

This gave Benedict the opportunity to lurch forwards onto his belly. He grabbed hold of Charlie's shins, holding them tight and bringing his brother crashing to the ground onto his back. Charlie flailed with his arms and tried to right himself but Benedict held on. 'Enough,' he said, through gritted teeth. 'That's enough.'

Charlie tried to kick out and wrestle himself free. His knees shuddered but he couldn't move properly. Like a fish on the deck of a boat, running out of air, he floundered for a while and then was still. Benedict felt the tension ebb away from his brother's body and they both lay panting on the grass.

Charlie wiped his cheek with his hand. 'You're not worth it.'

His voice had an American drawl mixed in with his Yorkshire accent and, now that his brother was still, Benedict could see him more clearly.

He was bigger than Benedict remembered; must have put on a few stones of muscle. His languid arms and legs were now thick and solid. He wore faded jeans, a denim jacket and a red checked shirt. His hair was the colour of straw.

Benedict pressed his lip and looked at the blood on his finger.

'Even when we were young, you didn't have any guts,' Charlie accused as he sat up. 'Why didn't you fight back?'

'Because I deserved it,' Benedict wheezed. He curved to the side and sat up too. 'I've always regretted what I did, Charlie. I'm so sorry. But I did have guts. I needed them to care for you for all those years, after our parents died. I made one mistake.'

'But it was a massive one, huh?'

'We could have talked. We could have sorted it out.'

'Sorted it.' Charlie gave a short laugh. 'You had sex with Amelia.'

The men sat with their arms wrapped around their legs, staring straight ahead, not wanting to look at each other.

Benedict screwed his eyes shut and felt his brother's pain as if it was his own. 'You were like my own child and I threw everything away. I lost my self-discipline that night but it was one time, Charlie. Just once. Thirty minutes of madness. I don't need a punch from you to tell me that.'

Charlie stared over at the tree for a long time. He wiped

his cheeks with his fingers and studied the dirt on them. 'Do you have any kids?'

'No. I've driven Estelle away, because we can't have them. I ruined my life too, as well as yours.'

'Is that supposed to make me feel better?' Charlie picked up a stone and threw it at the tree. 'We'd only been in America for a few weeks when Amelia found out that she was pregnant. That's when she told me, about you. I might not have found out otherwise.'

Benedict clutched his stomach. He felt like Charlie had punched him again. 'She was pregnant?'

'Uh-huh. I was ecstatic. You know, we were young and all, but that was okay. It was time for me to grow up. After what happened with our parents, I was going to be a dad and I loved that. But Amelia was quiet, cagey, about it and I knew something wasn't right. She admitted that she slept with you, and she didn't know whose baby it was. When she had an early miscarriage, I think she was relieved. I hate to say it, but I was too.'

'So, you never knew?'

'No. I could have maybe forgiven you for sleeping together, but I went through years of wondering if it was my baby or yours. How could I even grieve for it when I didn't know if it was mine?'

Benedict slumped over further.

'Amelia said she'd had second thoughts about us moving away together,' Charlie continued. 'She was young and wanted to test how she felt, and you were there. I hated you…for a long while.'

'And now?' Benedict whispered.

Charlie glanced at him then looked away. 'I don't know. I tried to forget about you. I blocked you from my head for years, but you always had a way of creeping back into my brain. When you rang and left the message about Gemma, it brought everything back to the surface. I'm not here because of you. I don't even know if I want you as my brother again. I've flown here to see my daughter.'

Benedict clambered onto his knees then to his feet. The seat of his trousers and knees were caked with soil. 'She was feeling unwell today, so I left her in bed.'

'I want to see her.'

Benedict swallowed. 'She doesn't know that I called you.'

Charlie stood up and batted grass from his jeans and shirt. 'Well, I figured that from your call. That's why I jumped on the first plane out here. Gemma runs. It's what she does. She hated it when I told her about me and Janice, and the baby. I thought that she was staying with friends.' He jerked his head towards the house. 'I didn't think that she'd come *here*.'

'She told me that you'd agreed for her to stay with me.'

'Ah,' Charlie said. 'That sounds like my daughter.'

The two men went inside and Charlie dumped his rucksack on the kitchen table.

'This old place looks exactly the same,' he said, as he looked around the kitchen.

Benedict nodded and listened out, but he couldn't hear his niece. 'I'll tell Gemma you're here,' he said.

330

The studio door was open and Gemma was curled in bed, fully dressed, with her back to him. Her boots were pushed up against the wall and the small white bag of gems lay in the middle of the floor. Benedict stood and watched her for a while, guilt creeping through every pore. 'I'm so sorry, Gemma,' he whispered. 'I had to tell him that you're here.'

Back downstairs, he told Charlie that Gemma was sleeping and his brother sighed with relief. 'At least she's okay.'

'She's fine. Do you want to wake her up?'

'No. Leave her. Let her rest.'

The two men stood in silence for a while. Charlie picked up his rucksack and threw it onto his back.

'So, do you want to stay, for the night?' Benedict offered.

Charlie shook his head. 'I'll get a room someplace else.'

'There are no hotels around here.'

'Oh, don't you worry about me, Benedict,' Charlie said. 'It's not your job any longer. Call me tomorrow when Gemma is awake, and I'll come straight over. Don't tell her I'm here before then.'

'What should I say to her?'

'Oh, I'm sure you'll think of something,' Charlie said. 'You must be used to covering your tracks by now.'

32. Emerald

equilibrium, patience, honesty

Benedict sleepily turned his head and glanced at his alarm clock, then he sprang upright in bed. His eyes opened wide. He had slept straight through the night and it was almost eleven o'clock in the morning. He groaned as he recalled his punch-up with Charlie and flopped back onto his pillow.

Every joint and inch of his body ached, and was sore, from his brother's punches. The blood had dried, tight across his bottom lip, and his forearms were dappled with blue and black bruises.

He lay there for a while, wincing with pain each time he tried to move. Through the gap in the curtains, he could see that the weather was as dark and gloomy as his mood. The sky was flint grey and the clouds were bilious and black. He wondered why Gemma hadn't woken him, but then remembered it was Sunday.

His head was stuffed too full of thoughts. Of him and Estelle, of Charlie and Amelia, and of Gemma. He reached up and rubbed his stiff neck. Should he tell his niece that her father had arrived in England, or should he message Charlie and ask him to just show up? Questions zipped around his head like cars in a Formula One race, and he wanted to wave a chequered flag to stop them.

Wanting to distract himself, he reached out and picked up Estelle's amber perfume bottle. He sniffed it and closed his eyes, for a moment transported back to their holiday in Greece, but images of Gemma and Charlie kept creeping into his head.

He placed the bottle back on the bedside table. Family was so confusing. It should be a warm, enveloping thing that made you feel safe and secure. But inside that one word, 'family', were different dimensions and fractions. There were people who loved, and sometimes hated, and those who made mistakes.

Now, after yesterday's events, he would have to watch everyone leave him again. Charlie would take Gemma back to America, and he was sure that Estelle wouldn't come home now. There had been hope, precious and delicate, and he had stamped on it, because he'd made his wife think it was only children he wanted, not her.

Why had he pushed so vehemently for adoption? Why couldn't he listen and hear that wasn't what Estelle wanted? But he kept pushing and nudging, until she felt she had no other option but to escape from him.

He understood now that it wasn't a new family that he was desperate for, it was for his existing one to be whole again. He wanted Estelle back so badly, but had he broken things beyond repair?

More than anything, he needed to hear her voice, so he could apologise once more. He picked up his mobile phone from the bedside table, dialled her number and screwed his eyes shut. To his surprise, she answered the call.

'Please don't hang up,' he said. 'Please listen to me.'

'I'm so tired of this, Benedict,' she whispered.

'I know. And I wanted to say that I'm sorry, again. I've been a total idiot. What I said in the Crags and Cakes, about adoption...I didn't mean it.' He stared at her empty side of the bed. 'They were words of desperation, a last-ditch attempt. We've been married for almost ten years, and I don't want that to end. My words slipped out and I'm so sorry for making you feel that way. You've always been enough for me.'

Estelle's voice was small. 'I appreciate your call, Benedict.'

'Do you believe me, though? I couldn't bear it if you didn't believe me.'

'Yes, but...' Her voice cracked.

'But?' he asked.

There was a click and the phone went dead.

Benedict eased himself up into sitting position on the edge of the bed and slipped on his loafers. He pressed a hand to his stomach — it felt hollow, but it was an emptiness that he could never satiate with food. He manoeuvred his sore arms into his dressing gown.

He paused outside the studio, ready to rap on the door. It was ajar and he could see that it was dark inside, the curtains still drawn. There was no sound and he lowered his hand, deciding to let Gemma sleep for a while longer. She would feel more refreshed for when Charlie came over.

He tied the belt on his dressing gown and trudged downstairs.

In the dining room, Lord Puss lay on the windowsill and raised his head drowsily. Benedict stroked the cat's back and tried to convince himself that Gemma would be okay about Charlie's arrival. She'd surely be pleased to see her father.

He opened the top drawer in the freezer, ready to take out two slices of bread to make some toast. Then he closed it again and opened the fridge door instead. He wasn't hungry but had the urge to eat something, to fuel his body. Gemma had made a fruit salad and put it in a plastic pot. He took a spoon and carried it over to the window to look out at the gem tree. He took off the lid and ate the fruit directly from the container. The cherries were juicy and sweet and a trickle of juice ran down his chin.

At first Benedict thought that the sparkles on the grass were morning dew, but then he squinted. They were too big for droplets of water. He lowered the fruit salad and set it on the windowsill beside Lord Puss. The sleepy cat smacked his lips. Marching into the hallway, Benedict took the front door key from his dressing gown pocket and slid it into the lock, but the door was already open.

The first thing he spotted on the lawn was a pair of scissors. The orange handles stood out in contrast against the green of the grass. He picked them up and studied them for a while, wondering what on earth they were doing out here.

He narrowed his eyes as he spotted threads fluttering up from the grass like fine jellyfish tentacles, then he realised there were more and more. There were strands and strands of gemstones strewn on the grass.

He snatched one up and studied it, noticing that the end of the thread had a neat, sharp edge, as if it had been cut. It didn't have the curl of a knot, tugged undone. He stared at it for a moment then strode towards the tree. He pushed his way through the branches and looked up.

Hundreds of trails of short lines hung down, like silk worms. All snipped.

He reached up and ran his hand through them. Every strand of gems had been cut down and all that remained were knots and short threads. The tree had been butchered.

Benedict pushed back out from under it and rubbed the back of his neck. He blindly looked around him. The gems had all been hanging when he fought with Charlie last night. A stranger surely wouldn't have done such a thing. And he couldn't imagine that Charlie or Estelle had returned to attack it.

That just left Gemma.

Benedict almost threw up as he began to pick up the gems. Doing so brought back memories of his mother and father, of his childhood and of Charlie. Tears rolled down his cheeks as he relived the phone call to tell his brother that their parents were dead. He pictured Charlie's eyes, wide and scared. 'It's not true, Benedict, is it?'

He stooped, picked up the strands of gems and carried them back to the house. He laid them neatly in the hallway and they looked like hundreds of tiny, glittering fish caught in a fisherman's net.

He stood on the front step with his hands on his hips choking back his sobs. The tree looked naked without the gemstones hanging between its yellowy-green leaves. No longer a family tree, just a normal one. He gulped and hung his head. What had Gemma done?

He turned and looked up the stairs. He couldn't wait any longer to speak to her.

He pounded upstairs and stood outside her room before knocking loudly. When she didn't answer, he slowly pushed it open. 'Gemma?'

Her blankets were screwed up in a heap on the floor, as if she'd thrown them off the bed.

Damn, where was she?

Benedict walked briskly from one room to the next, opening doors and patrolling around. He sped downstairs and into the front room where Lord Puss sat up on the windowsill. 'If only you could talk. Have you seen Gemma?'

Lord Puss turned to look into the garden.

Benedict marched around the kitchen. He went out into the garden and opened the shed door but she wasn't there either.

He conducted a full circuit of the house again, this time flinging open wardrobe doors and peering under the beds. He checked her wardrobe and some of her clothes hung there, but he couldn't see her denim jacket, or the blue dress she'd arrived in. He peered up at the hatch to the attic but it was firmly shut.

Her rucksack seemed to be missing and half her belongings had disappeared too, from the top of the chest of drawers. Her teddy bear and notebook had gone, but her hairbrush remained.

He thundered back downstairs and into the front room. The black sequined purse had vanished from the coffee table. 'Where are you, Gemma?' he hissed to himself.

Then, on the coffee table, he saw a scrawled note. With a shaking hand he reached out for it.

Uncle Ben

I saw what happened last night.
You and Dad are better off without me.

Gemma

33. Sugilite

integration, spirituality, forgiveness

Benedict phoned Charlie and told him that Gemma had gone missing. He tried to keep his voice calm. 'I can't find her in the house and her purse has gone.'

'I'm staying at a hotel in York. I'll be there as soon as I can,' Charlie said. 'Wait for me and we'll look for her together.'

When Charlie arrived, the two men strode into Noon Sun. It was raining again, and the puddles on the pavements shone like mirrors.

'It's Sunday, so there are no buses out of the village. She can only travel by hitching a lift, or on foot,' Benedict said.

'Or by cab?' Charlie suggested. 'When did you notice that she was missing?'

'When I got up this morning. I woke up late and she was gone.'

Benedict took out his mobile and rang Applethorpe Cabs, immediately recognising Toby Entwistle's lisp. The two men used to go to school together. Toby confirmed that he didn't have any bookings pencilled in for the day but would let Benedict know if an American girl called.

Benedict and Charlie pressed on past Deserted Dogs. The clothes in the window were all orange, yellow and red, hung around a makeshift bonfire constructed from cardboard and coloured cellophane.

'If we argue, Gemma usually heads out for a long walk, or to a friend's house,' Charlie said.

'Does it happen often?' Benedict asked, thinking of Gemma's temper flares.

'If she doesn't get her own way or when things are rocky, her first instinct is to get real mad or run. She squats at a friend's house, and then shows up after a day or two, as if nothing has happened. I try to reach out to her, but it doesn't work. I suppose she gets her stubbornness from me. She's been hanging around with these older kids and got kinda attached to this boy called Daryl.'

'She wrote the initials "DJ" in her notebook.'

'Yeah, Daryl Jones. I think she was more interested in him than he was in her.'

'Do you ever call the police when she runs away?'

'Gemma's not your normal sixteen-year-old girl, so we don't treat her like one. She's vanished a few times and always comes back, but never for as long as she's been staying with you.'

'But there's nowhere for her to run to from here,' Benedict said. He tried to think straight, not to panic. 'She's taken her rucksack, and we don't know if she wrote the note last night or this morning.'

'Do you think she saw and heard everything?' Charlie asked. 'Her dad and uncle fighting, like stray dogs on the lawn?'

Benedict dipped his chin. 'I hope not.'

They tried Crags and Cakes next. Benedict scraped his knuckles on the wooden white rabbit's stopwatch as he reached out for the doorknob. He prayed that Gemma was sitting inside. She'll be sipping a cup of tea, or eating a bowl of soup, he told himself. She'll raise her pointed eyebrows and ask what the fuss is about.

Charlie followed close behind.

Each of the tables was occupied and no one turned to look at them. Benedict brushed his wet hair off his forehead and quickly scanned the room.

Nigel and Josie sat opposite each other at the table nearest to the door. They both wore Guns N' Roses T-shirts and were examining a bag of crisps. 'Ham and mustard seed,' Nigel said, his yellow Citrine bracelet glinting in the daylight. 'I'm not sure about this flavour.'

'Far too exotic,' Josie agreed.

Ryan and Diane occupied the table in the window. They held hands over their cheese sandwiches, and Diane wore her Kunzite pendant.

Benedict asked Ryan if he had seen Gemma.

'Yes, she was walking through the village this morning.' He nodded.

Benedict felt a brief whoosh of relief. 'How long ago?'

'A couple of hours. Is there a problem?'

He didn't want to raise an alarm if there was a chance that

he and Charlie might find Gemma quickly and easily. 'No.' He stood up straighter, to compose himself. 'No problem.'

They headed next to the Pig and Whistle. Nicholas was chalking on his blackboard – *Bonfire Night Special – honey and herb sausages, hickory-smoked mash and minted mushy peas*. 'All right, Benedict. Are you coming to the bonfire tonight?'

'I don't know. Where are Alexander and Alistair?'

'What have they bloody well done now?' Nicholas folded his arms.

'Nothing,' Benedict said, not wanting to tell the chef about the kids in the garden. Finding Gemma was more important. 'We wondered if they knew where Gemma is.'

Nicholas cupped a hand to his mouth and shouted up to the top floor of the pub. 'Alistair. Alexander. Get out of bed, now.'

Two faces appeared at the window. It pushed open. 'What?' Alistair, said rubbing his eyes, then he spotted Benedict. 'Oh. Hello, Mr Stone. Sorry about the other night.'

'What did you do?' Nicholas yelled.

'Nothing,' Benedict said. 'The kids were a bit boisterous, that's all.'

Nicholas crinkled his brow. 'Benedict is looking for Gemma. Have you seen her today?'

They shook their heads.

'Sorry, mate,' Nicholas said. 'I bet she'll come along to the bonfire later on.'

'Yes,' Benedict said firmly, to assure himself. 'I'm sure she will.'

He led the way to the canal towpath and tried the buzzer for Veronica's apartment, but there was no reply. The patio doors were closed. He tried to phone Estelle but there was no signal. 'This is where my wife has been staying,' he explained to Charlie. 'Since she left me.'

'Has she gone for good?'

'I don't know. She moved out, and then I told her about what happened between me and you. She didn't take it well.'

'Not surprising, huh?' Charlie said.

'I'd kept it secret from her since we met.'

Charlie didn't answer. He looked up at the patio doors again. 'Do you remember that time when you thought that I was missing?'

Benedict was about to shake his head and say that he didn't recall, but the memory started to take shape in his mind. 'You didn't arrive home from school and I thought you might have had an accident. I phoned round your friends' parents and on the fifth call...'

'Yeah. Ian Smith's mom asked if you'd forgotten that I was sleeping over.'

'I was so busy that it slipped my mind. I was really embarrassed.'

'You took a lot on, huh? Looking after me and running the shop.'

'If you were the older brother, you'd have done the same for me.'

Charlie shrugged. 'Maybe not as much.'

Benedict spied the bouquet he'd brought for Estelle, the

345

night he attempted to be Romeo. It was muddy, crushed into the ground. 'Perhaps we should call the police.'

Charlie shook his head. 'She's real nervy around them. We should try to find her first, just you and me.'

They reached Benedict's shop and he used his hands as a visor to look through the window. He couldn't make anything out in the dark interior, so he unlocked the door.

Stepping inside, it felt cold and empty. There were no lights on and the door to the workshop was closed. 'Gemma?' he said aloud and walked through. His bench was just as it always was, with his tools laid out in straight lines. He looked out into the yard and checked in the store cupboard.

'It looks different in here,' Charlie said. 'Real classy.'

'Gemma helped me to revamp it. She's changed lots of things for me.' Benedict picked up a towel and roughly dried his hair, before passing it to Charlie, who did the same.

Charlie walked over to the counter where the gemstone journal lay open. His eyes widened. 'Oh, God. This is Dad's.'

'We found it in the attic. Gemma's been reading it and making notes about the gemstones.'

Charlie ran his fingers over the cover. 'I'd forgotten all about it.' He was quiet for a while, thinking. 'We had a good little family, didn't we, Benedict? Until Mom and Dad…'

Benedict cleared his throat. 'I know.'

The brothers shared a look, heavy with loss.

'When Amelia and I got married,' Charlie said, 'we were both trying to erase what happened, between you and her. When we had Gemma I thought we were starting afresh, but it was always there. We got on by until Gemma was twelve, then Amelia met someone else and walked out on us. Since then I raised Gemma alone, just as you did with me.

'I hated you for a long time, Benedict. But the longer I looked after Gemma, the more I kinda grew to understand what it was like for you, caring for me. It was like her life overtook mine. It was relentless and pretty lonely.'

'I've regretted what happened every single day,' Benedict said. 'Estelle's gone because I was obsessed with having a family. I wanted to prove I could raise a child and not mess up.'

Charlie moved first. He swiftly wrapped his arms around Benedict's back and gave him a quick, thorny hug. 'We should have said what we needed to all those years ago and not let things fester. I should have punched you then.'

Benedict spoke into his brother's neck. He grasped on to his shirt and held him close. 'I'm so sorry for what I did. I just wanted to feel close to someone.'

Charlie's grip tightened for a moment, then he released Benedict and stepped back. 'Whatever happened, we need to forget about it, for today.'

'We need to be united for Gemma,' Benedict agreed. He looked at the page in the journal, left open on Sugilite.

SUGILITE

This gemstone is good for anyone who feels they don't belong or fit in. It helps you to live in the present rather than the past. It protects you from disappointment and shocks, and encourages forgiveness and meaningful conversation. It assists with acceptance and self-belief. Its soothing qualities mean that it's an excellent stone to use for headaches…

Benedict stopped reading. He traced his finger over his father's handwriting, pausing on the word *headaches*. 'I think I know where Gemma is,' he said.

'Where?'

'She had a migraine one day, and we went for a walk on the moors, to clear her head. She liked it up there.' He walked over to the window and looked up over the roofs at the rolling charcoal and ochre hills. 'I think she's headed up to the moors.'

Charlie joined him. 'But it looks like a storm is brewing out there,' he said. 'The skies are getting real dark.'

'That's what I'm worried about,' Benedict said. 'I'll get you a coat.'

Nicholas was shifting barrels of beer outside the pub, ready to roll them down to the car park for the bonfire. Alistair and Alexander brandished chair legs like lightsabers and chased each other, playing *Star Wars*.

The rain began to lash down more heavily so Benedict and Charlie put up their hoods and collars, and all you could see were their eyes. Old chairs, a few doors and a broken wardrobe had been thrown onto the giant wooden pyramid on the car park. A piece of rope was strung across the entrance with a sign hanging on it. BONFIRE LIT AT 5 P.M. FIREWORK DISPLAY AT 6 P.M. FUNDRAISING FOR NOON SUN COMMUNITY CENTRE.

The moors loomed before them and Benedict could see the shape of the stegosaurus. 'Gemma liked dancing on the rocks at Dinosaur Ridge.'

'I'd forgotten how high the hills are. The scale of the moors,' Charlie said. 'It's scary.'

'I know,' Benedict said. 'Let's climb.'

The bleached grass was the colour of sweetcorn. The clouds hung heavy, casting long shadows that shifted, black, across the landscape, like giant crows had flown across the sun. A wild wind howled over the crags and whipped Benedict's coat around him. The cold caught the back of his throat as he navigated over marsh and rocks.

Charlie walked slightly ahead, stopping occasionally to look around him.

They climbed to the top of a small rocky crag and stopped for a while, both out of breath. A kestrel swooped overhead.

'Gemma gets so full of emotion that she doesn't know what to do,' Charlie said. 'They blast out of her. That's why she runs. You know, she always sensed there was something wrong about our family. She knew that beneath the surface, things weren't right.'

Benedict faltered over a rock. 'And what did you tell her?'

'I suppose I lied, like you must have done with your

wife. I told her that we were never close, that we never got along. It was easier than telling her the truth.' He jumped over a tree stump and Benedict followed.

'We'll always be family,' Benedict said.

'Just not the one we all hoped for.'

'We can try to change that, and put the past behind us.'

'You make it sound real easy.'

Benedict stopped walking. He paused and pressed an arm against Charlie's stomach. 'I think there's someone out there. I can see a figure.'

The person was moving closer, heading towards them. It was a woman and her hood was pulled up. She wore a purple scarf.

'You'd better head back,' she said. 'The weather is turning.'

Benedict recognised her voice, even with her face almost covered. 'Estelle?' He tugged off his own hood. 'What are you doing up here?'

'*Benedict?*'

Through the wind and rain, Benedict blinked at his wife. Her eyes were pink and puffy, like she'd been crying. It was difficult to tell with the raindrops running down her cheeks.

'I was up here walking and drawing,' she said, avoiding meeting his eyes with hers. 'I was trying to think things through. Then the weather changed' —she snapped her fingers— 'just like that.'

Benedict saw her glance at Charlie. Her eyes narrowed a little, trying to place him. There were photos of Charlie as a boy in frames around the house. 'Estelle, this is my brother,

Charlie. Charlie, this is my…' He hesitated, not sure of how to describe her after their conversation in Crags and Cakes.

She looked searchingly at Benedict but then shook Charlie's hand. 'I'm Benedict's wife, Estelle. Have you travelled here from America?'

'Benedict called me. We'd not been in touch for a long time, but we needed to talk…'

'We're searching for Gemma,' Benedict said. 'She's run away.'

Estelle clamped a hand to her chest. 'Oh, no. Can I help? I know the moors well.'

'Yes.' Charlie squinted against the rain. 'Help us, if you can.'

'We think she may have climbed up to Dinosaur Ridge,' Benedict said.

The three of them tramped upwards until the ridge stood before them in profile. The plates of the rock were black against the grit-grey sky. Charlie and Estelle treaded easily, with sure feet across the rugged landscape. Benedict trailed a few steps behind, trying to catch his breath.

'I know an easier path up there,' Estelle said. 'It's a route that walkers take.' She led them over a mound of rocks to a trail that had been worn away by walkers' feet over the decades. It curved and weaved up to the horizon like a roller-coaster track.

'Be careful,' Benedict said.

'I will, but it's Gemma we need to worry about.'

Benedict watched as his wife moved deftly and quickly ahead, until she became a dark shape that merged into the landscape. After a minute or so she shouted out. Her voice carried on the wind. 'Quick. I've found something. Come here.'

Charlie and Benedict shared a look, and then hiked speedily towards her. Charlie jumped over a marshy bog and traversed the uneven ground.

Benedict tried his best to follow. 'What is it?'

His brother and Estelle had their heads bowed. Charlie held something in his right hand. He used his mobile phone to shine a light on it.

At first Benedict thought that it might be an injured animal. In the yellowy light, he could see it was a light tan colour. But, as he drew closer, he saw what it really was.

Gemma's muddy cowboy boot.

34. Jet

guards, heals grief, stabilises

'She can't be up here, walking around with one boot on,' Benedict said. 'We have to find her.'

'It was stuck in the bog,' Estelle replied. 'I had to tug it out.'

The three of them stared at the mud-coated boot. They now knew that Gemma was up here, but whereabouts?

Charlie tucked the boot into his belt. 'Perhaps it's time to give the police a call, Benedict.'

Benedict took out his phone and swiped the screen. 'There's no signal again.'

'She can't be far, can she?' Charlie looked wildly around him.

'We need a plan,' Benedict said. 'Let's carry on up to Dinosaur Ridge. It's the highest point on the moors. If she's not there, then we'll have a good viewpoint.'

'Okay.' Charlie nodded. 'Let's go.'

It took an additional fifteen minutes until they reached the jagged stones that formed the scales. In the distance an orange light lit the sky, like a setting sun. The bonfire in Noon Sun was alight.

Charlie stood with his hands on his hips and scanned the moors. It was getting too dark to see properly. '*Gemma!*' he shouted into the wind. 'If you're out here, call out to us. This is all my fault. Not yours.' He stopped and listened, but the only sound was the whistling of the wind through the grass. 'Just let us know you're okay, honey.'

She's got to be here, Benedict thought. His eyes watered from the wind and his hands were sore and raw. He could barely feel them and he pushed them into his pockets. His fingertips hit something small and hard and he pulled it out. It was the piece of Blue Jack he had picked up. He recalled Gemma's joy at coming up with her own properties. *Determination, change and new beginnings.* 'She's not at Dinosaur Ridge,' he said aloud. He hurried towards Charlie.

'What?'

'I think she's gone to the Blue Jack quarry.'

This time, Benedict led the way. He focused on his feet, finding his weight and sturdiness useful. As the wind buffeted against him, he felt solid, as if nothing could topple him. After every few steps, he looked back to check on Estelle. 'Are you okay?' he shouted out to her.

'Don't worry about me. Focus on your niece,' she said.

'*Our* niece,' he corrected.

Charlie leaped over a stream running down the hill and Benedict went next. The ground was marshy and he reached out to help Estelle across. She hesitated for a moment, refusing to take his hand. 'I don't need your help, thanks,' she said.

Benedict felt his fingers fall back through thin air.

They carried on until they reached the disused quarry. The dark grey of the rock was the same colour as the sky. 'Gemma,' he shouted out, his throat tight from the wind. 'It's Benedict. Uncle Ben. Let us know if you can hear us.'

'Gemma,' Charlie hollered. 'You're not in trouble. We just want you home safe.'

Benedict heard something below, several feet down in the quarry – stones tumbling. 'I think she might be down there.'

They reached the edge of the quarry and looked down. The drop was around twenty feet. Estelle grabbed hold of Benedict's and Charlie's sleeves tightly, as if they were small boys. 'Be careful. There are some rocks further along you can use as steps.' She showed them where to go.

Charlie clambered down first, sending small stones skittering down into the quarry. Benedict followed. At the bottom, he instinctively held his hand out again for Estelle. This time she took it briefly and jumped down.

The wind dropped, the bowl-shape of the quarry keeping it sheltered. It was warmer too. Benedict felt a little relieved. If Gemma was here, she'd be more protected against the elements.

Benedict, Charlie and Estelle stood and listened. There was movement behind a rock and Benedict froze. A sheep sauntered out and it stared at them for a moment before wandering off.

'*Jesus*,' Charlie said. 'I thought that was her. Where the hell is she?' Panic rose in his voice. 'We're going to have to go back and get more help. I should have listened to you, Benedict.'

Benedict narrowed his eyes. 'I still think she's here.' It was then he noticed something amiss. As he looked at the sharpness of the rocks against the sky, he saw that one area didn't have angled edges. It was soft and more rounded.

'Over here,' he said, heading towards it, staggering over the uneven ground.

And finally, there she was.

'Gemma,' he gasped. He dropped to his knees and reached out, touching her arm. He could feel that it was floppy, like a pram toy. 'Gemma.'

She opened her eyes, and their whites shone against the black of the rocks. 'Uncle Ben,' she said, her voice weak and full of relief. 'You came for me. I'm so cold. I've… Ouch.' She reached down and grasped in the air, in the direction of her ankle. 'I think I've broken it.'

Benedict saw that she was wearing her denim jacket and blue dress. Her legs were bare. He tugged off his own coat and wrapped it around her. 'We're here now. You'll be okay.'

'Is my dad here? I want him.'

'Yes. And Estelle.'

'*Gemma*.' Charlie crouched and circled his arms around his daughter. He held on to her tightly. 'Don't you worry, okay? You're going to be fine.'

Gemma closed her eyes and pressed her cheek against his shoulder. 'Dad. You came for me. All this way.'

'Of course I did, honey.'

'I saw you and Uncle Ben fighting. I heard you shouting.'

'We were idiots, honey. But we're all good now.' He looked up at Benedict and nodded. His expression indicated that there was more for the brothers to say to each other, but this wasn't the time to do it.

'I've been stupid. I've hurt my ankle. I lost my boot.'

'Why'd ya run away?' Charlie asked gently.

Tears rolled down her cheeks. 'There's no room for me any longer.'

'What do you mean?'

'At home.' She wiped her face with the sleeve of her denim jacket. 'When the baby comes. You and Janice will have a new family. Mom didn't want me, and you don't want me either.'

Charlie shook his head. 'Now, that's not true,' he said. 'There will be changes, no doubt about that, but you'll always be my little girl. I'll always love you more than you can ever know. We can talk things through. But we can't do that if you keep running away. Okay?'

'Okay,' she squeaked.

Estelle looked at Benedict and gave him a wry smile.

'I've got your boot here.' Charlie tried to slip it onto Gemma's foot.

'Ouch. It hurts. I can't wear it.'

'That's fine. I'll carry you.'

Benedict could sense the love flowing between Charlie and Gemma, a strong blood bond. It made him feel suddenly helpless, as if he was no use to either of them any longer. They only needed each other. He was just a conduit for reuniting them. He'd provided shelter and support for Gemma when she needed a break from her family, but now it was back, intact.

Estelle stood beside him, her bobbed hair flapping in the wind. She didn't need him either. He was alone and it was all his own fault. He had driven her away by his constant longing for something that they couldn't have. He'd betrayed Charlie all those years ago, and Gemma was a confused teenager who needed to go home to rebuild her own family.

Benedict dug his hands into his pockets. How could he hope to return to his normal life after Gemma helped to open his mind, to people and finding his passion? He could carry on creating jewellery in his shop and discover more about gemstones, but what was the point if he didn't have Estelle to share it with?

The rain pelted down more heavily, stinging his cheeks and dribbling down his neck. His shirt was sodden and clung to his chest and shoulders. He watched Charlie whispering into Gemma's hair, as if they were only aware of each other and nothing else mattered.

Estelle crouched down and refastened her shoelaces. The corner of her sketchbook and a paintbrush poked out of her coat pocket. He should have supported her more with her painting and offered to come on walks with her, but he couldn't keep his mouth shut about wanting a family. That's why she'd had to escape him, to find some peace. With her acceptance of not having children she'd been able to adapt, to look forward instead of back. She had found something else to drive her onward. And he hadn't been able to follow.

All Benedict had seen was the rosy glow of past family life, with his mother, father and Charlie, and he'd wanted to create a carbon copy of it. But that only brought disappointment, because nothing like that could be replicated. It could only influence. And if Benedict couldn't recreate his old family, then he could still nurture his love and support for his wife. If there was still a chance…

Being up here, on the hillside, had a way of clearing your head, and Benedict knew without question that it was Estelle he wanted, not a fantasy family. He had to let go of any dreams of children and focus on what was real, and what was within reach. He had to accept that his vision of kids standing on his knee under the gem tree was just that. An image in his head. It didn't mean that he had to keep trying to make it real.

The rain rolled down his cheeks and there was no point wiping it away. 'Let's go…back,' he said to Estelle. He had been about to say the word *home*, but Estelle's home was elsewhere now, away from him.

Charlie wrapped Gemma's arm around his shoulders but she yelped with pain. 'Sorry. I'll carry you instead.' He bent down and effortlessly elevated her over his shoulder in a fireman's lift. 'You go first,' he said to Estelle and Benedict. 'We'll follow you down.'

Estelle led the way and Benedict felt that, when he followed, he was stumbling in the darkness.

The four of them walked slowly and steadily back to

359

Dinosaur Ridge and then down the hillside. Their boots sank into rabbit holes and boggy grass. Gemma murmured and Charlie whispered to her that everything was going to be all right.

As they reached halfway down the hill, fireworks burst into the sky over Noon Sun. Hemispheres of blue, green and gold sparkles showered down. Benedict saw another set of lights at the bottom of the hill. There was a stream of orange flames, moving in a line.

'It looks like help is on the way,' Benedict shouted over to his brother. 'I think the villagers are coming.'

They carried on, traversing down the hillside, and Estelle reached the line of people first.

Frank led his white horse with a pile of blankets on his back. 'Aye, are you all okay? I heard you'd set off for the moors, but no one saw you return. We thought we'd better come and look for you.'

'How did you know?' Benedict asked.

'Oh, you know what Noon Sun is like,' Frank said. 'Gossip spreads like wildfire.'

Charlie lowered Gemma to the ground. She stood like a flamingo on one leg and sobbed softly against the arm of his coat.

'Don't cry. You're safe now,' he hushed.

The small snake of villagers caught up with them. Most carried a chair leg or a long piece of wood as a torch, with a flame on the end. Alexander and Alistair came next, arguing in a language no one else could understand. Margarita walked with them.

Ryan and Diane followed. They had their arms wrapped tightly around each other and looked up as a firework exploded overhead. The sparkle reflected in Ryan's eyes, so they glowed red for a moment, making him look a little like an unstoppable Terminator.

Nicholas pressed sausages wrapped in tinfoil into Benedict's hand. 'In case she's hungry,' he said. 'They're my new recipe. Nigel and Josie are looking after the pub for me.'

The orange light from the torches glinted off a pair of dark, round sunglasses and Violet de Gama wafted forward. She wore her paisley turban, and her long velvet coat skimmed the top of her Velcro shoes. 'Frank and Reggie escorted me to the bonfire tonight and no one bothered me,' she said. She held out the crook of her arm.

Frank slipped his own arm through it. 'Now, you take care, young lady,' he said.

As Reggie took Violet's other arm, Laura appeared by his side and smiled proudly. Her Blue Lace Agate earrings swung beneath her long auburn hair.

Violet smiled coyly and turned to Benedict. 'There'll be an auction for my jewellery next week and I've decided to donate all the proceeds to the renovation of the community centre. Us villagers need somewhere to come together,' she said. 'I'm thinking that a private viewing of *Sultry Nights* would make for a wonderful opening evening. I could perhaps give a small performance.'

'I'm sure that everyone in Noon Sun would love that,' Benedict said.

'Perhaps you could charge people for your autograph.

Your time is money,' Reggie suggested, but then dropped his chin as Laura shook her head at him.

Charlie lowered his hands and wove his fingers together to form a step for Gemma to climb onto the back of the white horse. He helped her up and she took hold of the reins. Estelle handed her a blanket to wrap around her shoulders. Frank passed a rope to Charlie so he could lead the horse down the road, back to Noon Sun.

'I will send Gemma some flowers, when she is feeling better,' Margarita said.

'It's a good job I didn't bring Bernard the llama instead,' Frank said, as the sound of horse hooves echoed around the moors. 'But Alistair and Alexander Ledbetter came up with a great idea...'

'Yes?' Benedict said.

'Aye. People love my llamas, and the llamas love people. Bernard seemed so much happier after his trip out to the gallery. So, I'm going to investigate opening a small petting farm, for people to meet and feed the animals. If the Red Aventurine kicks into action, they'll be sure to love the babies too.'

Benedict and Estelle followed the rest of the villagers. They walked in silence and lingered a few metres behind. Benedict rubbed his wet shirt and it sucked against his skin. His trousers clung to his thighs.

'You were brave,' Estelle said, as they reached the high street.

'Thanks. You were too. Perhaps I'll never be a dad but I can try to be a good uncle.'

Estelle nodded her head slightly. 'And I like the idea of being an aunt.'

Charlie helped Gemma down from the horse and Benedict found a signal on his phone. He ordered a taxi to take his brother and niece to Applethorpe Hospital. 'It's only a twenty-minute drive away. You'll be there in no time,' he said.

'We'll drop you back home, then get Gemma checked out,' Charlie offered.

'It's fine. I can walk.'

Charlie shook his head. 'You're soaked to the skin.'

Benedict felt water dribbling down his back. 'Thanks. It's on the way.'

'I don't know how long we'll be at the hospital for so we'll check back in to my hotel afterwards. My stuff is still there. You get some sleep, brother, and I'll call you tomorrow. I appreciate your help tonight.'

'Stone brothers forever,' Benedict said quietly.

Charlie gave a brief nod. 'Stone brothers forever.' He turned to Estelle. 'Are you going back to the apartment, or to the house?'

'To the house, please. I need to talk to Benedict.'

Benedict felt a small flicker of hope in his heart.

'No worries,' Charlie said.

Benedict, Estelle, Gemma and Charlie said thanks to all the villagers and got into the taxi.

In the back seat, Gemma threaded a piece of hair into her mouth. 'I'm so sorry for what I did to the gem tree, Uncle Ben. I saw you both fighting, and I spoiled something that we all love.'

'The tree is still standing,' Benedict said. 'We can put the gemstones back.'

'All of us,' Charlie said. 'The Stone family should hang the gems back onto the tree.'

Benedict glanced at Estelle, but she turned away and looked out of the window at the silhouette of moors and the White Opal moon.

35. Golden Beryl

illumination, independence, insight

'I never knew if the weeping willow represented happiness or sadness for you,' Estelle said, as she and Benedict got out of the taxi and walked into the garden. 'It's sad because there's the memory of your parents, but there's the happiness of the loving family that planted and tended to it.'

'The family that I tore apart?'

'Your family were pulled apart long before then, when your parents died.'

Benedict swallowed. He reached out and touched a leaf. 'I thought that one day our children would look after the tree,' he said softly.

'Me too.'

'I've finally accepted that it won't happen now.' Benedict's words hung in the air. 'It's taken a long time and I should have come to terms with it earlier, without causing you more stress.'

'You placed all your hopes and dreams with me, Benedict, for us to have a baby, or adopt a child. It's too heavy a load for me to carry. You need to be responsible for your own happiness. Not pin it on me.'

'I'm sorry.'

She looked at his sodden clothes. 'You should get changed.'

'I think you're right. Do you want to come inside? The house is clean and tidy.'

'Really?'

'I'm a bit of a demon with a feather duster.'

'Who would have guessed? I'll stay outside though. I'll wait by the tree for you.'

Benedict frowned. 'Why?'

'I just feel the need to be close to it.'

'But you're cold.'

'A hot drink will warm us up.'

Benedict went into the house. He got changed and made two cups of tea. He set them on a tray and tucked a blanket and a rug under his arm.

Pushing through the branches, he joined Estelle and they spread out the rug and leaned back against the tree trunk. The steam from their tea curled up into the night air. Fireworks burst in the distance and the leaves of the gem tree spread around them, in a cocoon.

'I'm sorry for everything. Truly,' Benedict said.

'A marriage has to be built on trust.'

'I know. I swear there's nothing else, Estelle. I know I'm not good with words, but I want you to come home.'

She lowered her head.

'You do believe me?'

'Yes, but what if it's too late?'

'It might be. But I'd like to try.'

She lowered her cup and swallowed. 'If we're being honest with each other, then I have to tell you something too.'

'What is it?'

She touched her hair. 'It's...'

Benedict waited patiently, wondering what she wanted to share.

'I'm afraid it's about someone else...'

Benedict felt his stomach crunch. He immediately thought of Lawrence and he could hardly bear to speak his name. 'Donnington?'

'Yes... I...'

Benedict blinked hard at her.

'I want to be truthful with you,' Estelle said. 'As you were with me.'

'Go on,' he said, dread already creeping through his veins.

Estelle took a deep breath. 'The night you came to the apartment, wearing the mask and with the sword, Lawrence had called around beforehand.'

Benedict nodded. He remembered watching his wife and the gallery owner on the balcony, in the moonlight.

'There's a landscape exhibition in London and Lawrence said that my work was good enough to enter. I was flattered by his attention and belief in me.' She adjusted her scarf, pulling it further up her chin. 'He brought champagne. I was wearing the colourful necklace, and it made me feel different somehow.'

A wave of agony hit Benedict. He wanted to bend over double and clutch his middle with both arms. He thought that something might have happened between Estelle and Lawrence, but had managed to convince himself otherwise.

No wonder Lawrence had smirked about the llama. He must have thought it a feeble gift. When he bought the Sunstone cufflinks, he taunted Benedict, too.

Benedict clenched his fists and imagined marching up the stairs of the Purple Heather Gallery and punching the eagle-nosed lothario in the face. But he knew that fighting didn't solve anything. He respected Estelle too much to do something like that, but it felt like she was about to confirm his worst fears.

'One thing led to another.' Estelle breathed. 'I was confused about me and you, Benedict. I wanted you, but not the part that made me feel that I couldn't satisfy you.'

'You've always been enough for me.'

He wanted to tell her to stop talking about Lawrence. He understood now how Gemma felt when she threw the gemstones at him. Anything to stop the words. But he had to find out what happened. There had been too many secrets in the Stone family, and he didn't want another one spreading like fungi on a damp wall.

And Estelle needed to tell him too. He could see the desperation in her eyes, that she was carrying a burden. So he had to listen.

When they said their wedding vows, they'd promised to be there for each other, for better and for worse. And if this was the worse, he had to be strong. He knew how easy it was to succumb to temptation. For you to make a decision in a few seconds that would affect the rest of your life, and other lives too.

He took her cup and set it on the lawn. 'And, now you want to be with him?' His voice shook.

Estelle held her hand to her mouth. 'He helped with the exhibition – he told me my work was brilliant. I got swept away… All you and I had talked about for months and years was babies, and children and adoption. I'm so weary of this constant longing for something we can't have. I felt like I was in a fog, merely getting by. And when Lawrence kissed me, I tried to say *no*. But I was numb, and he was there, and he wanted me.'

Benedict wanted to clamp his hands over his ears but instead he dug his big fingers into the soil. 'I understand.'

'No.' Estelle took hold of his hand and smoothed away the dirt. 'I want to tell you this, even if it's painful for me to say, and for you to hear.'

Eventually, Benedict nodded. He screwed his eyes shut. In his mind he saw Lawrence in the apartment, moving towards Estelle, standing behind her, reaching up and unfastening the firework necklace and placing it on the bedside cabinet, before pulling her towards him. The two of them would make a fine couple, both slim, dark and artistic. Perhaps there was a chance for Estelle to have the child she longed for. Without Benedict.

He felt a maelstrom of emotion. Anger at Lawrence, and at himself for not being honest with Estelle for all those years. If only he'd told her sooner about Charlie, then everything might have turned out differently. He was sure she'd have encouraged him to make contact and try to repair their relationship. Benedict might have got to meet Gemma as a young girl, watched her growing up and been present at those birthday parties and school plays that she'd accused him of being absent from.

And Benedict might have been more accepting of his and Estelle's circumstances in not being able to have children. He wouldn't have become obsessed and driven his wife away, into finding someone else.

'I know you're no longer sure about us,' he said. 'But it's hard for me to hear about you and Lawrence…if you want to be with him.'

Estelle shook her head. 'No,' she said. 'It's not like that. I've never wanted to be with him.'

Benedict felt the tiniest bit of optimism flicker inside him. 'You don't?'

'I didn't sleep with him, Benedict.' She swallowed. 'I couldn't do it. We kissed and I wondered what it would be like. I had this voice in my head, compelling me to do it, but it wasn't because I wanted him. It was because I was challenging my own feelings for you. To test myself. To see if I still wanted you, even though I'm a disappointment to you—'

'Oh God. You've never disappointed me,' he interrupted.

She shook her head. 'When I was with Lawrence that weight lifted. I could forget about it for a while. I was so close to tumbling into the bedroom with him, but you're my husband. I couldn't do it.'

'I don't want to lose you.'

'I feel that we've lost ourselves.' She placed a hand against her chest. 'I want to be myself, Benedict. Not a version of me that can't have children. I think you *need* them and I can't give them to you. I want to hold my head up high and simply tell people that I'm child-free and okay with that. I'd have loved to be a mother, but I don't need parenthood in the way that you do. It doesn't define me. It's not a bloody disease and I want to stop feeling guilty about it. I've not failed at anything. It's just the way it is. I think I can still be happy.'

The leaves of the gem tree swayed around them like a hula dancer's skirt and Benedict looked up at the moon. 'I think that having a family would have been wonderful. But it's you and me, Estelle. People say that you can't choose your family, but we can. We did.'

'We can work on being a great aunt and uncle to Gemma,' Estelle said.

'And I can try to be a good brother to Charlie again. From the moment I saw you in your purple anorak, Estelle, I felt that you were my family. But what happened to my parents, and with Charlie, made me constantly search for something else. I thought that I could only be happy if there were generations of the Stone family under one roof, in Noon Sun. And I was wrong. I had this ideal in my head but it was like something in a glossy Hollywood film. It wasn't real. Instead of obsessing over a family I don't have, I want to concentrate on the one that I do have.'

Estelle nodded and soaked in his words. 'If people judge

us for not having children then that's their problem, not ours. And I'm sure that we'll go through painful times, but if we're together, and we're strong, I can deal with that.'

'Me too. Every family is different. Ours is just a little smaller than some others.'

'And a bit more dysfunctional.'

They sat quietly for a while, listening to the rustle of the leaves and the Noon Sun clock striking in the distance. Benedict flexed the fingers of one hand, watching his wedding band glint in the moonlight. He turned his hand over and held the flat of his palm out to Estelle. After hesitating for a few moments, she placed her hand in his.

A firework cracked and exploded overhead, sending pink sparks twinkling down and Estelle shivered.

'You're cold. We should have talked inside instead.'

'I'm glad that we're here, under the tree.'

'Come on.' He stood up. 'Let's go inside the house. I'll make you another hot drink and phone a cab. Or I can walk you home.'

'Veronica's apartment isn't my home. Our house is.'

Her words warmed Benedict's heart. 'I've washed the bedding in the studio,' he said.

'Thank you.' She smiled. 'I'll stay the night, in there.'

36. Alexandrite

realigns, longevity, compassion

Benedict woke in his bed alone again, but this time he didn't feel lonely. He heard the covers swishing in the studio and Estelle pulling the curtains open. He knew that they still had lots to talk through, but having her home made him smile.

His phone pinged with a text and he sat on the side of the bed. His ribs were still sore from Charlie's punches and he rubbed them as he opened the message.

'Hey, Benedict. Gemma is fine. She has a small fracture in her foot and is taking it easy. We'll come over to the house around noon, if that's okay?'

'That's great. I'll make lunch,' Benedict texted back.

He slipped on his dressing gown and loafers and met Estelle in the kitchen.

'It's a whole new world in here,' she said, peering into the fridge and examining the contents. 'So you really have changed?'

'Gemma's into healthy eating. She's got me hooked on it too.'

'Don't go too mad on fruit though. You're fine just the way you are.'

'I'll always be the way I am, just more solid.' He smiled. 'Now, would you prefer muesli or yoghurt for breakfast?'

Later that morning, Benedict chopped the apples, grapes and melon that he and Estelle had bought from Veg Out, and dropped the chunks into a bowl. He inhaled and they smelled so fresh. *Look at how juicy and healthy we are*, a chunk of melon said to him. He chuckled and popped it into his mouth. He arranged a bunch of flowers, which Margarita had thrust into his arms for Gemma, into a ceramic vase that Estelle had bought in Greece.

Rummaging in the freezer, he found some sausages, which he cooked and cut into small pieces to put on cocktail sticks. He emptied the kitchen cupboard of crisps and tipped them into brightly coloured plastic bowls.

He and Estelle were still chopping vegetables, pouring orange juice and polishing cutlery when he heard a car outside.

Benedict sped to the front door. He opened it and Gemma waved as she and Charlie got out of the taxi. Charlie had his arm around her waist and helped her to hobble up the garden path.

'Sexy, huh?' Gemma pointed at her ankle, which was bandaged and encased in a protective blue boot.

'It doesn't matter how it looks, honey,' Charlie scolded. 'You should rest up.'

Benedict thought how odd it was to hear his brother sounding so responsible. It was as if their positions had switched. He helped Gemma to take her coat off and she mouthed a meek 'Thanks.'

'The food looks amazing.' She eased herself into a chair at the kitchen table.

'You two have been busy,' Charlie said.

'We thought you might be hungry,' Benedict said.

'No cakes, though?' Gemma surveyed the various plates and bowls. She stared at Benedict and then at Estelle. 'You two look happy.' She pointed her finger and dotted it between them. 'Are you…?'

'We're trying to work things through,' Estelle said.

'I'm glad to hear it.' Charlie nodded.

When they ate, Benedict noticed how his brother reached out for the brightly coloured food, the tomatoes and the mango, just as he was attracted to the bright gemstones. Benedict piled up his plate too.

'Noon Sun kind of reminds me of Sunnyside,' Charlie said. 'We've been staying with Janice's folks near New York, but I want to move back to Maine.'

'That's really the name of the farm?' Benedict asked, pleased that Gemma had told him the correct one all along.

'Sure. It's a kind of smallholding, but it earns me enough to get by. I miss looking after the animals.'

'Me too,' Gemma said.

'You know' —Charlie bit into a slice of watermelon— 'we have this white horse on the farm and it looks like the one that carried Gemma last night. It's feisty and only lets her near it. I never know how to train that darn horse.'

Gemma looked over at Benedict. 'Tiger's Eye.' She nodded.

When they had finished eating, Gemma rubbed her eyes. 'I'm so tired,' she said.

'Why not go for a lie-down in the studio?' Estelle suggested.

'There's something I want to do first. Can we do it, Dad?'

Charlie gave her a disapproving look. 'You should be in bed.'

'I know. But first, I want to hang the gemstones back in the tree, where they belong.'

Charlie and Benedict and Estelle protested. They told Gemma that the gemstones would wait, but she wore a determined glint in her eye and her bushy eyebrows were high and angled. Knowing they'd be fighting a losing battle in trying to persuade her otherwise, Benedict and Charlie gathered the gemstones from the hallway and carried them outside.

'The tree sure looks smaller,' Charlie said, as he laid the gems on the grass. 'I thought it was huge when I was little, like a room in a mansion or something. Why are all the gems cut down?'

Benedict caught Gemma's eye and she cast him a pleading glance. He gave a small cough. 'I, er, took them down so I could prune the tree a little. It was getting a bit overgrown.'

'You may have overdone it, brother.' Charlie thumped him on the back. 'That tree looks naked.'

Charlie stooped to pick up a strand of gems. 'I always thought that the red, orange and yellow ones were more valuable,' he said. 'Now I know it was never about their value. Our family, hanging them together, was the precious thing.'

'I always went for the dull stones,' Benedict replied. He reached out and picked out a strand of yellow gems. 'But not any longer.'

'Can I hang the first string?' Gemma asked. She hobbled over to the tree and picked one up, tied with green and blue stones. 'Blue Lace Agate helps harmony in families and Peridot helps you to understand relationships.' She lifted up her arms and tied it into the tree.

'I'll choose the pink ones,' Estelle said. 'I don't know the names, but I love the colours.' She selected a branch and looped the end of her thread around it.

'You go next,' Benedict said to Charlie. 'You're too big to stand on my knee, though.'

Charlie grinned and selected a strand of red stones. He tied it in with a firm knot. 'What do these ones mean?'

'Fire Agate is for courage, protection and strength, and Red Beryl gives you confidence to change your mind,' Gemma said.

Benedict went last. As he reached up, he felt like this was some kind of ceremony. When he tied the end of his thread around the sturdy branch, it felt as if he was tying his family back together again. Lemon Quartz was said to bring positivity, and Fire Opal was ideal for hope and progress.

Benedict, Charlie and Estelle worked quickly and quietly.

Only Gemma spoke, telling them which stones to hang, and where, and soon there were no more strands left on the grass.

'Finished,' Gemma said. The weak November sun shone through the gemstones and reflected flecks of red, orange and yellow light onto her face. 'The Stone family tree is complete again.' She moved and winced at her ankle.

'Are you okay?' Estelle rushed to her side. 'Don't try to do too much.'

'Let's go inside,' Charlie said.

Gemma stayed still. 'There's something I gotta say first.'

'Do it later,' Charlie said. 'Come and rest up.'

'I want to tell Uncle Ben that I'm sorry.'

'You don't have to say anything,' Benedict said.

'I wanna do it.' She turned to him. 'I just want to say how sorry I am, Uncle Ben. I showed up on your doorstep in the middle of the night, I threw gemstones at you, I lied to you. I told you that I was chatting with myself when really I was on the phone to Daryl, the boy I used to hang out with. And all the time you were really kind and looked after me. Even when you got mad at me, it made me feel like I mattered. I wish I could have met you before, but I feel lucky to know you now. When we were in the attic and I didn't understand that Peridot helped you to find what was lost, well, I understand that now. When we learned about those gemstones together, it made me feel kinda special.' She shrugged. She hobbled forward and wrapped her arms as far as they'd stretch around his waist and pressed her cheek onto his chest. 'Thanks, Uncle Ben.'

'No. Thank you,' he whispered into her hair. 'Thanks for changing things for this family.'

She pulled away and her cheeks flushed pink.

'Everything is out in the open now,' Charlie said.

'Except for one thing,' Gemma said.

Benedict reached up and rubbed the back of his neck. 'What's that?'

'Now that my dad's here, what's the real story behind the white bag of gemstones?'

Benedict and Charlie exchanged a quick glance.

Charlie curled his fist and coughed into it. 'What exactly did you hear, when we were brawling on the lawn?'

'Did the two of you have a fight?' Estelle frowned. 'So that explains your swollen lip.'

Benedict nodded.

'It was my fault,' Charlie said. 'I started it.'

'I heard you fighting, then talking,' Gemma said. 'I couldn't hear much over Lord Puss mewling.'

'Oh, right.' Benedict exhaled noisily.

Charlie nodded at him. 'When Benedict gave me those gemstones, it was his way of sending a reminder of home and what it means to me.'

'I thought it might be something more than that,' Gemma said.

The two brothers looked at each other again and shook their heads. 'No.'

'Good,' Gemma said. 'I don't like secrets.'

'Me neither,' Benedict agreed.

37. Rose Quartz

unconditional love, forgiveness, trust

Benedict cleaned his teeth whilst Estelle changed into a fresh pair of flowered pyjamas. She used the bathroom while Benedict put on his own pyjamas. For a reason that he couldn't explain, he pushed the orange handkerchief into the breast pocket.

On the landing, they found themselves facing each other and Benedict felt a warm glow in his chest. He wanted to step forward and slip his arm around her waist, to hold her close and press his lips against hers, but he held back. Their relationship felt as delicate as spun sugar and he didn't want to risk snapping it. There was still a barrier between them but they were going to try to hurdle it, together.

'Goodnight, then,' he said. 'I hope you sleep well.'

'Thanks. Goodnight, Benedict.'

They hesitated then parted without touching.

In bed, Benedict might not have Estelle's feet to rub against his, but knowing she was sleeping along the corridor was enough. He stood and listened to the noises in the house. The creak of the floorboards and the crackle of the radiators sounded musical. He sat on the edge of the bed and could smell Estelle's amber perfume bottle. Operation WEB was almost accomplished.

After a few minutes there was a knock on the bedroom door.

His pulse quickened. 'Yes?'

Estelle poked her head around. 'Can I come in?' she asked. 'I'm suddenly not at all tired.'

'Me neither.'

She sat down on the opposite side of their bed. 'It's nice to be home,' she said.

'Veronica's apartment must be so lovely and modern.'

'It's a little clinical, a bit like a hospital waiting room. And I've had enough of those.'

'Me too. Do you remember what day it is today?' he asked tentatively.

Estelle gave a small nod. 'It's our tenth wedding anniversary. I thought that you'd forgotten.'

'No. I've been thinking about it for weeks,' Benedict said. 'I've made something for you.'

'Oh. Thanks. I wasn't expecting anything.'

'It's not as bright as the necklace your friends gave you, or as bold...' Benedict started.

'Now, you've told me what it is,' Estelle laughed. 'A necklace.'

'It's a good job that it's unique, then.' Benedict tutted at himself. He opened the drawer on his bedside cabinet and handed the long, shiny, coral-coloured box across the bed to his wife. He had tied it with a matching ribbon. 'This is for you.'

'I love this colour,' Estelle said. 'It's the same as the bow tied on the shop door.'

'I know.'

'Shall I open this now?'

Benedict nodded.

Estelle untied the bow. She lifted off the lid and peeled back the tissue paper. Inside the box lay the anniversary necklace. She gasped as she saw it, and then looked up at Benedict. 'It's gorgeous. It's so different.' She took it out and held it up.

Benedict had always known there was something missing from the necklace. On the night he spent working late in his workshop, he added a rainbow of tiny gemstones, each set in precious metal and fastened with a small link to the necklace, so they dangled and sparkled in a line. There were ten in total, one for each year they had been married.

They swished as Estelle held the necklace to her neck. 'It's beautiful. I absolutely *love* it.'

'Each of the gemstones has a meaning,' Benedict said. 'Lavender Amethyst brings light and love. Yellow Topaz is for good fortune. This grey gem is Goethite. It banishes the dark clouds and brings hope and light to your life.'

He continued touching, naming and describing each of the stones to Estelle. When he finished he saw that her eyes were glassy with tears.

'I'll wear it every day,' she said and gently placed it

back in its box. 'Thank you. I haven't got you anything though...maybe I can bake a cake.'

'Do you remember the awful joke I made when we first met?' Benedict asked.

'About how to get a big guy into bed?'

'A piece of cake,' he said. 'But a slice of pineapple does it for me these days.'

'I don't have a pineapple,' Estelle said. 'But I would like to get into bed.'

Benedict felt as if he'd been waiting to hear these words forever. 'Are you sure?' he asked.

'Yes.' She peeled back the sheets.

Benedict switched off the bedside lamp and they climbed under the covers together. He reached out an arm and Estelle snuggled under it, and they fitted perfectly together. She rubbed her feet against his to warm them up and Benedict thought that this might be the happiest he had ever felt.

He turned to face her but felt something small and hard under his leg. 'What's that?' he asked aloud and lifted the sheet.

'What is it?'

'I think that there's something in the bed.' Benedict turned the lamp back on and reached down, under the duvet, to take hold of the strange object. His fingers wrapped around it and he held it up for Estelle to see.

'A gemstone?' she asked.

Benedict broke into a smile. It was a piece of Rose Quartz, in the shape of a heart. 'I think it's a present from Gemma.' He handed it to his wife.

She held it on her palm. 'And does this one have a meaning too?'

Benedict thought about his father's journal and his entry for the shiny pink stone. 'If I remember correctly, the story goes that in Greek mythology, Aphrodite's lover, Adonis, was attacked by the god Ares, who disguised himself as a boar.'

'Really?' Estelle said. She lay back on her pillow and held the Rose Quartz up to the light.

'Really.' Benedict lay back down beside her. 'In rushing to save Adonis, Aphrodite caught herself on a briar bush. Their blood stained the quartz pink and it became known as Rose Quartz. It's the crystal of reconciliation and eternal love.'

'Hmmm. So do you think the meanings behind the gemstones are all true?' Estelle leaned over and switched off the bedside lamp. In the darkness Benedict felt her breath against his neck as she moved closer. Her eyelashes flickered against his cheek.

'Rose Quartz is for love, peace, emotion and appreciation.' Benedict sought out her lips with his. 'So I think, in our case, it's definitely true. Happy anniversary, Estelle.'

'Happy anniversary, Benedict.'

And, as they kissed, the little chunk of heart-shaped Rose Quartz fell from Estelle's fingers and dropped gently to the floor.

Author's Notes

The tsunami in Sri Lanka, that killed Benedict and Charlie's parents, did not take place as described. I devised the date and location to suit the story.

Blue Jack gemstone is loosely based on the Blue John gemstone, which is still mined to this day, in small amounts, in Castleton, Derbyshire, UK.

There are many sources for information on gemstones and their meanings in books and online. From source to source, I found many of the gemstone meanings to be the same, but many differed also. Benedict and Gemma discovered most of their material on gemstones from Joseph Stone's journal, which may or may not collaborate other information available.

If the reader is interested in gemstones, I hope they find the right stone for them and enjoy discovering their own meaning behind it.

Reading group questions

1. Benedict keeps a past mistake hidden from his wife, Estelle, throughout their marriage. Is he right to have kept this to himself, or should he have shared the secret with her?

2. Are close family ties important to your own happiness?

3. Cecil is a flamboyant and helpful assistant to Benedict. Why doesn't Benedict listen and act on Cecil's words of advice? Do you listen to advice when others offer it to you, or are you more likely to do your own thing?

4. As a woman, Estelle feels pressured by her parents and society in general to have children. Do we automatically expect women to have children, or are attitudes and times changing?

5. Benedict is stuck in a rut with his work in Stone Jewellery. Do you ever feel this way about your job or workplace? Do you plan or hope to do something about it? If not, why?

6. Benedict and his brother Charlie haven't spoken for eighteen years. Are there any unresolved rifts in your family? Do you let them be, or do you take action?

7. The villagers in Noon Sun like to gossip. Do you think that gossip is a bit of harmless fun to pass the time, or can it be more damaging?

8. The internet and phone connection in Noon Sun is problematic. How would you react if you didn't have access to your phone or computer for a day? Would this be a problem for you? Do we depend too much on technology?

9. Joseph Stone writes in his journal about gemstones having different meanings and the ability to influence. Do you believe in this?

10. Benedict's friend Ryan believes that men find middle age tricky to deal with, and that women adapt more easily. Do you think this is true and why?

11. Which gemstone featured in the book appeals to you most? Does it have any significance for you?

12. Benedict and Estelle's marriage has become comfortable, like an old sofa. Do you think it's important to keep a spark going in a relationship? Or do you think it's inevitable that relationships change over time?

13. Benedict can't bear to get rid of his parents' belongings, stored in the attic. Do you think that, now he's resolved

his relationship problems with his wife and brother, he'll be able to let go of these things? Or do you think he'll still hold onto them? How do you personally 'let go' of sentimental items?

14. Benedict comes to realise that people want passion and surprise in their jewellery, and for it to mean something to them. Which pieces of jewellery mean the most to you and why?

15. Benedict turns to food for comfort in times of need. Why do you think he does this, knowing that he'll feel worse afterward? Is there anything you turn to, when life is a bit rocky?

16. What would you do if a young relative turned up unannounced on your doorstep in the middle of the night? Would you be worried, scared, suspicious, relieved, irritated...?

17. Hanging gems into the gem tree is a Stone family tradition. Does your family have any unusual traditions?

18. Benedict tries some strange methods to win his wife back, including attempting to be Romeo and wooing her using a white horse. Has anyone ever done anything out of the ordinary to attract your attention?

19. How do you picture Benedict and Estelle in five years' time? And how do you imagine Gemma's life to be?

Acknowledgements

A big thanks to my family and friends, who encouraged me through the good times and the more challenging ones while writing this book, especially Mark, Oliver, Mum and Dad.

Thanks goes to my lovely, perceptive and encouraging agent Clare Wallace at Darley Anderson, and the rest of the brilliant team, including Mary Darby, Emma Winter and Sheila David.

To all at HarperCollins in the UK and US, in particular my super editors Sally Williamson and Erika Imranyi, who combine razor-sharp instinct, tact and loveliness to help make my writing better.

Finally, thanks to readers, bloggers, libraries, retailers and reviewers for their support and feedback. It means a lot to me.

Keep reading for the first chapter from another spellbinding tale from Phaedra Patrick

The Curious Charms of Arthur Pepper

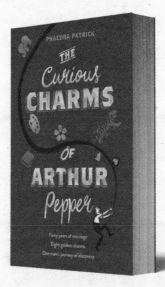

ONE PLACE. MANY STORIES

The Surprise in the Wardrobe

Each day, Arthur got out of bed at precisely 7:30 a.m. just as he did when his wife, Miriam, was alive. He showered and got dressed in the grey slacks, pale blue shirt and mustard tank top that he had laid out the night before. He had a shave then went downstairs.

At eight o'clock he made his breakfast, usually a slice of toast and margarine, and he sat at the pine farmhouse table that could seat six, but which now just seated one. At eight-thirty he would rinse his pots and wipe down the kitchen worktop using the flat of his hand and then two lemon-scented Flash wipes. Then his day could begin.

On an alternative sunny morning in May, he might have felt glad that the sun was already out. He could spend time in the garden plucking up weeds and turning over soil. The sun would warm the back of his neck and kiss his scalp until it was pink and tingly. It would remind him that he was here and alive—still plodding on.

But today, the fifteenth day of the month, was different. It was the anniversary he had been dreading for weeks. The date on his *Stunning Scarborough* calendar caught his eye whenever he passed it. He would stare at it for a moment then try to find a small job to distract him. He would water his fern, Frederica, or open the kitchen window and shout 'Gerroff' to deter next door's cats from using his rockery as a toilet.

It was one year to the day that his wife had died.

Passed away was the term that everyone liked to use. It was as if saying the word *died* was swearing. Arthur hated the words *passed away*. They sounded gentle, like a canal boat chugging through rippling water, or a bubble floating in a cloudless sky. But her death hadn't been like that.

After over forty years of marriage it was just him in the house now, with its three bedrooms and the en-suite shower room that grown-up daughter, Lucy, and son, Dan, recommended they had fitted with their pension money. The recently installed kitchen was made from real beech and had a cooker with controls like the NASA space centre, and which Arthur never used in case the house lifted off like a rocket.

How he missed the laughter in the home. He longed to hear again the pounding of feet on the stairs, and even doors slamming. He wanted to find stray piles of washing on the landing and trip over muddy wellies in the hallway. *Wellibobs* the kids used to call them. The quietness of it being just him was more deafening than any family noise he used to grumble about.

Arthur had just cleaned his worktop and was heading

for his front room when a loud noise pierced his skull. He instinctively pressed his back against the wall. His fingers spread out against magnolia woodchip. Sweat prickled his underarms. Through the daisy-patterned glass of his front door, he saw a large purple shape looming. He was a prisoner in his own hallway.

The doorbell rang again. It was amazing how loud she could make it sound. Like a fire bell. His shoulders shot up to protect his ears and his heart raced. Just a few more seconds and surely she'd get fed up and leave. But then the letterbox opened.

'Arthur Pepper. Open up. I know you're in there.'

It was the third time this week that his neighbour Bernadette had called around. For the past few months she had been trying to feed him up with her pork pies or home-made mince and onion. Sometimes he gave in and opened the door; most of the time he did not.

Last week he had found a sausage roll in his hallway, peeking out of its paper bag like a frightened animal. It had taken him ages to clear up the flakes of pastry from his hessian welcome mat.

He had to hold his nerve. If he moved now she would know he was hiding. Then he'd have to think of an excuse; he was putting out the bins, or watering the geraniums in the garden. But he felt too weary to invent a story, especially today of all days.

'I know you're in there, Arthur. You don't have to do this on your own. You have friends who care about you.' The letterbox rattled. A small lilac leaflet with the title

'Bereavement Buddies' drifted to the floor. It had a badly drawn lily on the front.

Although he hadn't spoken to anyone for over a week, although all he had in the fridge was a small chunk of cheddar and an out-of-date bottle of milk, he still had his pride. He would not become one of Bernadette Patterson's lost causes.

'*Arthur.*'

He screwed his eyes shut and pretended he was a statue in the garden of a stately home. He and Miriam used to love visiting National Trust properties, but only during the week when there were no crowds. He wished the two of them were there now, their feet crunching on gravel paths, marvelling at cabbage white butterflies fluttering among the roses, looking forward to a big slice of Victoria sponge in the tea room.

A lump rose in his throat as he thought about his wife, but he held his pose. He wished he really could be made of stone so he couldn't hurt any more.

Finally the letterbox snapped shut. The purple shape moved away. Arthur let his fingers relax first then his elbows. He wriggled his shoulders to relieve the tension.

Not totally convinced that Bernadette wasn't lurking by the garden gate, he opened his front door an inch. Pressing his eye against the gap, he peered around outside. In the garden opposite, Terry, who wore his hair in dreadlocks tied with a red bandanna and who was forever mowing his lawn, was heaving his mower out of his shed. The two redheaded kids from next door were running up and down the street wearing nothing on their feet. Pigeons had pebble-dashed the windscreen of his disused Micra. Arthur began to feel calmer. Everything was back to normal. Routine was good.

He read the leaflet then placed it carefully with the others that Bernadette had posted for him—'Friends Indeed', 'Thornapple Residents Association', 'Men in Caves' and 'Diesel Gala Day at North Yorkshire Moors Railway'—then forced himself to go and make a cup of tea.

Bernadette had compromised his morning, thrown him off balance. Flustered, he didn't allow his tea bag enough time in the pot. Sniffing the milk from the fridge, he winced at the smell and poured it down the sink. He would have to take his tea black. It tasted like iron filings. He gave a deep sigh.

Today, he wasn't going to mop the kitchen floor or vacuum the stairs carpet so hard that the threadbare bits grew balder. He wasn't going to polish the bathroom taps and fold the towels into neat squares.

Reaching out, he touched the fat black telescope of bin liners that he'd placed on the kitchen table and reluctantly picked them up. They were heavy. Good for the job.

To make things easier he read through the cat charity leaflet one more time: 'Cat Saviours. All items donated are sold to raise funds for badly treated cats and kittens.'

He wasn't a cat lover himself, especially as they had decimated his rockery, but Miriam liked them even though they made her sneeze. She had saved the leaflet under the telephone and Arthur took this as a sign that this was the charity he should give her belongings to.

Purposefully delaying the task that lay ahead, he climbed the stairs slowly and paused on the first landing. By sorting out her wardrobe it felt as if he was saying goodbye to her all over again. He was clearing her out of his life.

With a tear in his eye, he looked out of the window onto the back garden. If he stood on tiptoe he could just see the tip of York Minster, its stone fingers seeming to prop up the sky. Thornapple village, in which he lived, was just on the outskirts of the city. Cherry blossom had already started to fall from the trees, swirling like pink confetti. The garden was surrounded on three sides by a tall wooden fence that gave privacy; too tall for neighbours to pop their heads over for a chat. He and Miriam liked their own company. They did everything together and that was how they liked it, thank you very much.

There were four raised beds, which he had made out of railway sleepers and which housed rows of beetroots, carrots, onions and potatoes. This year he might even attempt pumpkins. Miriam used to make a grand chicken and vegetable stew with the produce, and home-made soups. But he wasn't a cook. The beautiful red onions he picked last summer had stayed on the kitchen worktop until their skins were as wrinkly as his own and he had thrown them in the recycling bin.

He finally ascended the remainder of the stairs and arrived panting outside the bathroom. He used to be able to speed from top to bottom, running after Lucy and Dan, without any problem. But now, everything was slowing down. His knees creaked and he was sure he was shrivelling. His once-black hair was now dove white (though still so thick it was difficult to keep flat) and the rounded tip of his nose seemed to be growing redder by the day. It was difficult to remember when he stopped being young and became an old man.

He recalled his daughter Lucy's words when they last spoke, a few weeks ago. 'You could do with a clear out, Dad. You'll feel better when Mum's stuff is gone. You'll be able to move on.' Dan occasionally phoned from Australia, where he now lived with his wife and two children. He was less tactful. 'Just chuck it all out. Don't turn the house into a museum.'

Move on? Like to bloody where? He was sixty-nine, not a teenager who could go to university or on a gap year. *Move on.* He sighed as he shuffled into the bedroom.

Slowly he pulled open the mirrored doors on the wardrobe.

Brown, black and grey. He was confronted by a row of clothes the colour of soil. Funny, he didn't remember Miriam dressing so dully. He had a sudden image of her in his head. She was young and swinging Dan around by an arm and leg—an aeroplane. She was wearing a blue polka dot sundress and white scarf. Her head was tipped back and she was laughing, her mouth inviting him to join in. But the picture vanished as quickly as it came. His last memories of her were the same colour as the clothes in the wardrobe. Grey. She had aluminium-hued hair in the shape of a swimming cap. She had withered away like the onions.

She'd been ill for a few weeks. First it was a chest infection, an annual affliction which saw her laid up in bed for a fortnight on a dose of antibiotics. But this time the infection turned into pneumonia. The doctor prescribed more bed rest and his wife, never one to cause a fuss, had complied.

Arthur had discovered her in bed, staring, lifeless. At first he thought she was watching the birds in the trees, but when he shook her arm she didn't wake up.

Half her wardrobe was devoted to cardigans. They hung shapeless, their arms dangling as if they'd been worn by gorillas, then hung back up again. Then there were Miriam's skirts; navy, grey, beige, mid-calf length. He could smell her perfume, something with roses and lily of the valley, and it made him want to nestle his nose into the nape of her neck, *just one more time please, God*. He often wished this was all a bad dream and that she was sat downstairs doing the *Woman's Weekly* crossword, or writing a letter to one of the friends they had met on their holidays.

He allowed himself to sit on the bed and wallow in self-pity for a few minutes and then swiftly unrolled two bags and shook them open. He *had* to do this. There was a bag for charity and one for stuff to throw out. He took out armfuls of clothes and bundled them in the charity bag. Miriam's slippers—worn and with a hole in the toe—went in the rubbish bag. He worked quickly and silently, not stopping to let emotion get in the way. Halfway through the task and a pair of old grey lace-ups went in the charity bag, followed by an almost identical pair. He pulled out a large shoe box and lifted out a pair of sensible fur-lined brown suede boots.

Remembering one of Bernadette's stories about a pair of boots she'd bought from a flea market and found a lottery ticket (non-winning) inside, he automatically slid his hand inside one boot (empty) and then the other. He was surprised when his fingertips hit something hard. Strange. Wriggling his fingers around the thing, he tugged it out.

He found himself holding a heart-shaped box. It was covered in textured scarlet leather and fastened with a tiny gold padlock. There was something about the colour that made him feel on edge. It looked expensive, frivolous. A present from Lucy, perhaps? No, surely he would have remembered it. And he would never have bought something like this for his wife. She liked simple or useful things, like plain round silver stud earrings or pretty oven gloves. They had struggled with money all their married life, scrimping and squirrelling funds away for a rainy day. When they had eventually splashed out on the kitchen and bathroom, she had only enjoyed them for a short while. No, she wouldn't have bought this box.

He examined the keyhole in the tiny padlock. Then he rummaged around in the bottom of the wardrobe pushing the rest of Miriam's shoes around, mixing up the pairs. But he couldn't find the key. He picked up a pair of nail scissors and jiggled them around in the keyhole, but the lock remained defiantly closed. Curiosity pricked inside him. Not wanting to admit defeat, he went back downstairs. Nearly fifty years as a locksmith and he couldn't bloody get into a heart-shaped box. From the kitchen bottom drawer he took out the two-litre plastic ice cream carton that he used as a tool box; his box of tricks.

Back upstairs, he sat on the bed and took out a hoop full of lock picks. Inserting the smallest one into the keyhole, he gave it a small wriggle. This time there was a click and the box opened by a tantalising few millimetres, like a mouth about to whisper a secret. He unhooked the padlock and lifted the lid.

The box was lined with black crushed velvet. It sang of decadence and wealth. But it was the charm bracelet that lay inside that caused him to catch his breath. It was opulent and gold with chunky round links and a heart-shaped fastener. Another heart.

What was more peculiar was the array of charms, spread out from the bracelet like sun rays in a children's book illustration. There were eight in total: an elephant, a flower, a book, a paint palette, a tiger, a thimble, a heart and a ring.

He took the bracelet out of the box. It was heavy and jangled when he moved it around in his hand. It looked antique, or had age to it, and was finely crafted. The detail on each charm was sharp. But as hard as he tried he couldn't remember Miriam wearing the bracelet or showing any of the charms to him. Perhaps she had bought it as a present for someone else. But for whom? It looked expensive. When Lucy wore jewellery it was new-fangled stuff with curls of silver wire and bits of glass and shell.

He thought for a moment about phoning his children to see if they knew anything about a charm bracelet hidden in their mother's wardrobe. It seemed a valid reason to make contact. But then he told himself to reconsider as they'd be too busy to bother with him. It had been a while since he had phoned Lucy with the excuse of asking how the cooker worked. With Dan, it had been two months since his son had last been in touch. He couldn't believe that Dan was now forty and Lucy was thirty-six. Where had time gone?

They had their own lives now. Where once Miriam

was their sun and he their moon, Dan and Lucy were now distant stars in their own galaxies.

The bracelet wouldn't be from Dan anyway. Definitely not. Each year before Miriam's birthday, Arthur phoned his son to remind him of the date. Dan would insist that he hadn't forgotten, that he was about to go to the post box that day and post a little something. And it usually was a *little* something: a fridge magnet in the shape of the Sydney Opera House, a photo of the grandkids, Kyle and Marina, in a cardboard frame, a small koala bear with huggy arms that Miriam clipped to the curtain in Dan's old bedroom.

If she was disappointed with the gifts from her son then Miriam never showed it. 'How lovely,' she would exclaim, as if it was the best present she had ever received. Arthur wished that she could be honest, just once, and say that their son should make more effort. But then, even as a boy, he had never been aware of other people and their feelings. He was never happier than when he was dismantling car engines and covered in oil. Arthur was proud that his son owned three car body repair workshops in Sydney, but wished that he could treat people with as much attention as he paid his carburettors.

Lucy was more thoughtful. She sent thank you cards and never, ever forgot a birthday. She had been a quiet child to the point where Arthur and Miriam wondered if she had speech difficulties. But no, a doctor explained that she was just sensitive. She felt things more deeply than other people did. She liked to think a lot and explore her emotions. Arthur told himself that's why she hadn't attended her own mother's funeral. Dan's reason was that he was thousands of miles away. But although Arthur found excuses for them both, it hurt him more than they could ever imagine that his children hadn't been there to say goodbye to Miriam properly. And that's why, when he spoke to them sporadically on the phone, it felt like there was a dam between them. Not only had he lost his wife, but he was losing his children, too.

He squeezed his fingers into a triangle but the bracelet wouldn't slip over his knuckles. He liked the elephant best. It had an upturned trunk and small ears; an Indian elephant. He gave a wry smile at its exoticness. He and Miriam had discussed going abroad for a holiday but then always settled upon Bridlington, at the same bed-and-breakfast on the seafront. If they ever bought a souvenir, it was a packet of tear-off postcards or a new tea towel, not a gold charm.

On the elephant's back was a howdah with a canopy, and inside that nestled a dark green faceted stone. It turned as he fingered it. An emerald? No, of course not, just glass or a pretend precious stone. He ran his finger along the trunk, then felt the elephant's rounded hind before settling on its tiny tail. In places the metal was smooth, in others it felt indented. The closer he looked though, the more blurred the charm became. He needed glasses for reading but could never find the things. He must have five pairs stashed in safe places around the house. He picked up his box of tricks and took out his eyeglass: every year or so it came in handy. After scrunching it into his eye socket, he peered at the elephant. As he moved his head closer then further away to get the right focus, he saw that the indentations were in fact tiny engraved letters and numbers. He read and then read again.

Ayah. 0091 832 221 897

His heart began to beat faster. Ayah. What could that mean? And the numbers too. Were they a map reference, a code? He took a small pencil and pad from his box and wrote them down. His eyeglass dropped onto the bed. He'd watched a quiz programme on TV just last night. The wild-haired presenter had asked the dialling code for making calls from the UK to India—0091 was the answer.

Arthur fastened the lid back onto the ice cream box and carried the charm bracelet downstairs. There, he looked in his *Oxford English Pocket Dictionary*; the definition of the word 'ayah' didn't make any sense to him—*a nursemaid or maid in East Asia or India*.

He didn't usually phone anyone on a whim; he preferred not to use the phone at all. Calls to Dan and Lucy only brought disappointment. But, even so, he picked up the receiver.

He sat on the one chair he always used at the kitchen table and carefully dialled the number, just to see. This was just silly, but there was something about the curious little elephant that made him want to know more.

It took a long time for the dialling tone to kick in and even longer for someone to answer the call.

'Mehra residence. How may I help you?'

The polite lady had an Indian accent. She sounded very young. Arthur's voice wavered when he spoke. Wasn't this preposterous? 'I'm phoning about my wife,' he said. 'Her name was Miriam Pepper, well it was Miriam Kempster before we married. I've found an elephant charm with this number on it. It was in her wardrobe. I was clearing it out…' He trailed off, wondering what on earth he was doing, what he was saying.

The lady was quiet for a moment. He was sure she was about to hang up or tell him off for making a crank call. But then she spoke. 'Yes. I have heard stories of Miss Miriam Kempster. I'll just find Mr Mehra for you now, sir. He will almost certainly be able to assist you.'

Arthur's mouth fell open.